Ink

Dreams

Stories by members of Authors' Tale

AUTHORS'·TALE

Ink Dreams

Cover by Joel Torres
Edited by Cayce Berryman, Crystal MM Burton, and Michelle King
https://kingsmanediting.com

ISBN: 978-0-9964432-0-3
First Edition April 2019

https://authorstale.wordpress.com

Copyright page continues on the next page in acknowledgments listing additional contributors and writers to the anthology.

Acknowledgments

Authors' Tale would like to acknowledge, as a continuation of the copyright page, additional contributors to the anthology. Those who either took part in formatting or even those who helped with the selection of stories in the judging process, we thank you for all your hard work, willingness to learn, and eagerness to create. This anthology would be nothing without you, and we're excited to be able to present unique, unpublished work to the world.

To our editors and formatters, Cayce Berryman, Michelle King, and Crystal MM Burton, it's not a book without your help and dedication. This anthology's edits and design are the result of all your hard work and effort as it makes its way to readers both digitally and in print. Your contributions are forever appreciated, and working with you is always a great pleasure and gift.

To our cover designer, Joel Torres, who volunteered time and talent in creating our beautiful cover. Your gifts are greatly appreciated, and your friendship even more so.

To our anthology submission judges: Cayce Berryman, Jeanne Felfe, Michelle King, Ekta R. Garg, Colin David Palmer, Tori Gollihugh, Penny J Johnson, Jas Newman, and Kerry A Waight. Your hard work allowed the stories within this anthology to make authors shine. Their work is immortalized by this book, and your decisions helped them receive that spotlight. Thank you for your contributions and dedication to Authors' Tale.

To our authors in this anthology, most of whom eagerly took part in a monthlong workshop to further your talents as writers and to create an environment in which others can share, teach, serve, and fulfill the mission of Authors' Tale simply by being part of its events. Cayce Berryman, Broken Wings; Crystal MM Burton, The Messenger; A. M. Deese, Finding Happy; Jeanne Felfe, Mother Earth, Ekta R. Garg, Talk to Me and Worlds Away; Richard Happerger, The Sum of All Souls; Cari Jehlik, Eve Discovered; Penny J. Johnson, My Life in the End; Vickie J Litten, Button Eyes; G Dean Manuel, When the Ink Dries; i.a.n., Return to Sérénité; J. C. O'Neil, Varsity Dreams; Colin D Palmer, Gotta Have Rhythm; Tyronica Smith, Bethany's Story and Tempus Fugit; E. R. Smo, What Dwells in REM; Matthew Stevens, Reintegration; and Kerry A Waight, Follow the Light and Where Dreams Die. All stories are appearing for the first time. Thank you for sharing.

Those interested in contributing or writing for future anthologies can join the Authors' Tale community, where we write to surprise others but keep learning to surprise ourselves.

Table of Contents

Foreword

Being a writer is hard work. I don't think most people really know what all goes into the making of a story, but there's a lot to it. Not that it isn't fun; it's an incredible experience. Coming up with an idea is like opening a door. Figuring out the best way to tell it — that's an adventure. Sharing it with the world? That's the dream.

When I joined Authors' Tale a few years ago, my dream was to one day write novels. More than that, I wanted the world to acknowledge that I had done something with my life. I never imagined there would be so much to it or that I had so much to learn. Despite my love for reading, I was laughably inexperienced. This amazing community of writers didn't laugh, though, and they didn't make me feel like any less of a writer. In fact, they encouraged me to keep at it, supported me in my struggles, and offered all the advice they had gleaned from chasing their own dreams.

Writing is a skill that takes an insane amount of practice. Writers will spend years constantly learning and applying new knowledge in an effort to improve. If there is one thing I can say for sure, it is that growing as a writer has nothing to do with being better than someone else but has everything to do with being better than I was yesterday. Authors' Tale focuses on this fact with our motto: "Write and surprise others, but keep learning and surprise yourself." We encourage our members to compare their skill level only to their own past endeavors. The overwhelming positivity and support this community shares are humbling to say the least, and I am so proud to be a part of it. I would not be the writer I am today without Authors' Tale.

It's an exhausting journey, being a writer, but it's also an extremely rewarding experience. Every story takes a little piece of the writer with it out into the world, and every writer keeps a little piece of each story with them for the rest of their life. Putting one word after another, marking where we are in our personal growth by weaving ourselves into the page, is how the Authors' Tale anthologies are made.

This is our third anthology. Each year, I've tackled the challenge of weaving both a theme and a prompt together into a short story. But, despite being familiar with the routine of coming up with an idea and getting it onto paper, I struggled with the theme of *Ink Dreams*. A lot of us did. Just the words "ink dreams" bring to mind everything the life of a writer encompasses: our hopes and fears, the immeasurable time and effort we put into a story, how we connect with the world around us through our words. I agonized over this theme for months.

Ink Dreams called for something more than just a story. It called for me to accept that I hadn't reached my dream yet. It showed me that, in actuality, my dream had changed with my personal growth. I no longer required the world to acknowledge me, but for me to acknowledge myself.

More so, it reminded me once again that it isn't about where I'm headed, it's about the difference between where I was and where I am now. The stories herein were crafted by writers who have come a long way from where they first started, and today I am pleased to show you the results of their hard work in the form of *Ink Dreams*.

— *Crystal MM Burton*
Crystal MM Burton is an editor for Ink Dreams and an officer of Authors' Tale.

Introduction

Every year, new challenges arise, new lessons are learned, and new goals are made and met (or not). When Authors' Tale began in 2014, I didn't expect to come across so many authors who shared a similar hunger for growth. In this community, we have the privilege of trying, failing, and succeeding together. Growing. Learning.

With the publication of the third anthology in a row, our annual series has turned into a grand lesson for authors, be it through the workshop, the editor feedback, or the comments after the publication of the book. As a community, the hope is to continue offering services to incredible people and keep their curiosity strong. To be part of their lives in a way few get to. Because of this desire, we dedicated this third anthology to the community. It takes more than hope and ambition to reach a dream. It takes time, money, and perseverance. Authors' Tale's mission should never become a materialistic endeavor, but the small goals through which we can reach our primary ones will require a bit of a push, and with the help of our members, we'll get there. So through this anthology, we will voice our mission to the world: write and surprise others, but keep learning and surprise yourself. Whether you're a writer or a reader, you have a goal, a dream, and this year we get to share ours with you.

Dreams can be tangible or profound, and they come in many forms after that. These stories will take you through the dreams of many characters, some realizing their own faults, others grasping for the hopes found only in another's eyes, and a few whose dreams will never be reached, but their reality guides us through a story only found in other worlds. Whether you want to read a story with a happy ending or simply want to read through the eyes of another creature, there's a story for you here, and one that will take you on a journey through parchment and ink, across fields and down stairways into the depths of a nightmare. Find a new dream in a story with us, and discover something unique.

These stories are our gifts to you, our characters' dreams made reality, or not. As the Authors' Tale community becomes closer, we're not just a group of writers; we're a family, and every week, a few people teach us new lessons or share new stories with us. It's an experience that we get to share, and coming together each year for a workshop and an anthology just makes the time together stronger. Our relationships become deeper and more meaningful, making us more of a family of people with a common interest.

This anthology includes stories about dreams, and it's our dream to see this through. To continue to help these authors reach their dreams by offering what we have and what we know, and by allowing others to find the same fulfillment in sharing what can be found in the gift of giving.

You see, it's not just about writing or reaching a goal but about being part of something bigger than yourself. In life, we can only try, and in trying, we will eventually do. But that's only if we take a step toward a goal and reach for those dreams until we finally make them a reality.

— Cayce Berryman
Cayce Berryman is an editor and the founder/administrator of Authors' Tale.

Featured Stories

These stories were chosen by judges and are given a place in front of the anthology. They are in no particular order, unlike the remaining stories, which are listed alphabetically. The prompts used are provided with each story.

The Messenger

Supernatural

Crystal MM Burton

Prompt: As quietly as possible, she lifted the sleeping infant from the crib and crept down the staircase.

I HATE MY JOB.

Standing at the top of the staircase, I struggle to take that first step. I know why I'm here; I know why it has to be done. But it doesn't make it any easier. My eyes are red and sore from the mob of tears fighting for freedom. The funny thing is that I'm just the messenger. No postal worker cries this much when they deliver a letter.

Then again, the delivery isn't what gets me, either. It's the collection of that which must be delivered. Had I known what this career path entailed, I would have . . .

Would have what? It's not like I had a choice. If my life were a book, this job would be the inevitable journey the hero is forced to make. Except I must be the villain, because each step leads me further into darkness.

With a reluctant sigh, I trudge downward. The first few steps are a brilliant white, so bright I have to feel for the edges so I don't trip. The farther down I go, the shine fades. They are still white, but nothing altogether special. I briefly wonder where they'll lead this time, then quickly shove the thought away. I never know until I get there. I never want to know. Soon enough, each step is a dull, colorless platform.

As always, I count the steps. Counting helps keep my mind off my task, but eventually I lose myself and a new count begins, this one counting back through time to each job I've done. With each collection, I wish I could forget.

Farther down I go. The edges are scuffed; the paint is peeling. I'm nearly there now. Before long, the steps are no longer painted at all but are simple, practical wooden boards. The landing comes into view below, and my heart sinks. I just want to turn back.

Thankfully, I reach the bottom of the staircase before I can start counting my tears as well. Wiping my eyes, I give my surroundings a cursory glance. I'm in a home. Well-kept, from the looks of things. Anxiety creeps across my skin, and with a shudder, my emotions get tucked away into their dark corner where I reprimand them and tell them to stay — stay put! Stay, or else I'll . . . I'll . . .

It's an empty threat. My shoulders slump and I shake my head. Stay or I'll break, I tell them. Please, just stay. Let me get through one more job.

I delay the inevitable by looking anywhere but forward. To my left, I squint down a short, dark hallway that extends to what I assume is a bedroom. The door is cracked open just a hair, allowing the soft, dulcet notes of a piano to drift through the house. To my right, I can make out a dim living room with moonlight streaming in through an open window. A chilling breeze sends sheer curtains billowing out into the room like ghostly dancers in a romantic tragedy.

I'm just stalling now. Best to get this over with.

With a shiver that reaches my bones, I drag my eyes to the doorway before me. It holds a simple door made of cheap, processed wood. I can smell the fresh coat of pink paint that must have dried just this week. Though I've never been through this particular door before, it resembles so many others whose thresholds I've crossed.

Some were also fresh and new, while others were worn and aged. A few were made of bars, more of cardboard, and others of guilt.

I take a deep breath and straighten my spine, lengthening my torso and lifting my chin. For a few minutes I simply hold that pose and focus on my breathing. I heard somewhere once that if you stand tall and feign courage, you will in fact feel courageous. I can't say for sure whether it works, but I think I feel a little bit braver. Not enough, though. Never enough.

This would be the part of the story where the villain makes their move. The hero thinks they are ready but they can't win, not against this. This is the part where the darkness rises.

Placing my hand on the cold brass doorknob, I twist it gently and push the door open. The wood whispers as it brushes across the top of the carpet, but it's too faint to wake any of the sleeping tenants.

I slip inside, easing the door closed behind me. The plush gray shag mutes my footfalls, but the subflooring creaks softly with each step. My lips betray my heart with a small smile as I see hundreds of tiny stars light the walls and ceiling, projected from a lamp sitting on a dresser. The dark lampshade, covered in tiny pinholes, spins slowly in place over the lightbulb. As my eyes adjust to the room, I'm drawn to a clutter of various picture frames taking up the rest of the space on the dresser. Not all of them have real pictures in them yet—a few still show off the example family from the store—but my wandering gaze stops at a framed set of footprints. They can't be any longer than my thumb. My smile is gone in an instant. These are the details that break me.

The rest of the room seems just as cluttered as the dresser: a changing table topped with packages of diapers and wipes; baskets of lotions and creams, all wrapped with colorful bows; a swing here, a walker there, still in their boxes; a fluffy rocking chair with a matching ottoman. My heart aches knowing that none of it will get used.

Hearts. I just had to bring that up. As if on cue, the tender beat of an infant's heart echoes in my head, reminding me why I'm here.

I follow the sound to a wooden crib on my left, and my legs grow weak at the sight of it.

Let me get through one more job.

The wooden rails are a light, natural shade that matches that of the dresser. On the wall just behind the crib, a detailed mural offsets the simplicity of the furniture. Smooth pastel strokes paint out the name Tabitha in a perfect arch, surrounded by fluttering butterflies and freshly bloomed flowers. It's impressive even in the darkness, so I'm sure in the daylight it's almost magical.

When I step up to the railing, I close my eyes. The scent of fresh linen hovers in the air — with a hint of lavender, I think — and it's almost calming. I try to imagine I'm here for a letter, a happy invitation to a better place. For some jobs, it really is. I tighten my grip on the top rail until my knuckles hurt. I've done this millions of times; what's one more? It's not like this is the end or anything. Just the quickest route to the next beginning. So why is it so heart-wrenching?

I take a deep breath. It's just another delivery.

In many books, the villain cries to the hero, "You forced me to do this!" when really they had a choice. I think I will write myself a choice in my book. Otherwise, what sort of villain am I, really?

I open my eyes to see the most beautiful infant in the world lying on her side. I think I say that about every one of them. Each child is so delicate, so precious. Her skin looks as soft as fresh down, and her fingers are so small I can't help but place my pinky in her outstretched hand. Even in sleep, she curls her little fingers around mine and holds my heart.

I'm not sure how long I stand here, marveling at this tiny miracle, before I finally register the rest of the scene in front of me. Her crib is decorated fashionably, and although it's a picture-perfect setup, it's just not practical. Lacy white bumpers line the inside of the slats with embroidered animals dancing across the fabric. A crowd of stuffed animals circles the head of the crib — a pink giraffe, a white knit elephant, and a fuzzy tan bear with a giant purple bow all stare down at the baby girl with wide, threaded smiles and cold, black eyes. A curved pillow cradles her head and shoulders, propping her up on her side, and a white quilted comforter is tucked beneath her arms.

Her heart beats faster now; I can hear it struggling. A second, smaller, decorative pillow is pressed up against her teeny nose and mouth, barely visible beneath the curve of the larger one. How it made its way to her face is anyone's guess, but there's no question what this means for her.

The beautiful, soft skin on her face and hands gradually takes on a purple hue. I want so badly to move her, to help her, to save her in this life. But, that's not my job.

I let out a whimper as hot tears stream down my cheeks. My breath catches in my throat, and I spin to look at a baby monitor sitting on a nearby shelf. This is where the hope sits on the page. Hope for a hero to come to the rescue only just in time. Clasping my hands together, I pray the parents heard me. Pray they woke and wondered if they had truly heard anything at all. Pray they decide to check on their newborn baby girl just for a second, just to be sure. My gaze drifts to the door as I hold my breath. Seconds tick by, and so does my fleeting hope.

My tears never stop. I blink until I can at least see my surroundings, then I return my attention to the now unconscious child. Where she isn't a deep purple, she's taken on a sickly gray.

As carefully as possible, I slip my hands beneath her and wait. Like a song coming to a close, the puttering of her failing heart fades into nothingness. What little heat is left of her life begins cooling almost instantly.

I lift the infant to my chest and wrap my arms around her. These first few moments are the most important, and I tighten my embrace to reassure her that she is safe. With a sniffle, I tilt my head to either side and wipe my tears on my shoulders. The hardest part is over.

I peer down at her face and smile. She looks so peaceful. I

suppose she is now. I don't feel much like smiling, but I know she can feel my aura, so I put on my best visage of love and comfort. It's not hard to show those things in the presence of such innocence. I guess a real villain would show hostility. Malignance, perhaps. I might not be the hero, but I may not be the villain I thought, either. Smoothing back the soft wisps of hair on her head, I turn and carry her to the door.

Just before I leave the room, I look once more around her nursery. Lighted stars still glow across the ceiling, and as my eyes follow their path, I notice a narrow side table all but hidden by the rocking chair, with a mug forgotten on the wooden tabletop. I reach out to touch it, but as I expected, it's cold. Just like my heart ought to be after all this time.

In retrospect, I wouldn't be fit to do this job if I had a cold heart. Souls, regardless of their mortal age, need empathy, compassion. They need a friend. Even if it's just long enough to get them up the stairs, I can be that friend. That's why I'm here. I spent a lifetime believing my heightened emotions were a curse, but when I was given this job . . . Well. I can't say they aren't still a curse, but to a certain degree, I learned they have a purpose. Just not always a happy one.

My eyes follow the lighted stars a moment longer before I turn my back to the lovingly decorated room. With a silent, wistful sigh for days that will never come, I slip out the bedroom door as quietly as I entered.

I pause at the base of the staircase and stare down the hall. Soft music still drifts through the barely open doorway at the end. They'll never understand. They'll never forgive themselves. My eyes well with the last of my unshed tears. I wish I could console them when they find out. Tell them it wasn't their fault.

Tell them she'll be okay.

But, that's not my job.

The least I can do is give them one last night of peaceful sleep, as I know they won't rest well again for a long time. And so, without a sound, I creep up the long staircase with the baby girl against my chest. For a while, I just hold her, allowing the steady rhythm of my steps to rock her back and forth. Once I'm high enough, when the stairs are white again, I whisper soothing words and hum age-old melodies.

I never count the steps on the way back up.

I look down into her eyes as we near the top of the stairs. In the smallest and most selfish of ways, I'm grateful she's too young to ask why. I hate looking into someone's eyes and seeing the sea of unanswered questions brimming beneath the surface. For the nth time, I wish I could deliver something else for a change. Anything else. Why can't I deliver happy news or long-lost greetings? Why not Christmas cards or get-well wishes? I'd even carry junk mail if it made a difference.

A warm breeze floats down from above and brings a smile to the baby girl's face, disturbing my introspection. For all the sadness of collecting her, of taking her away, her dimpled cheeks and simple joy remind me that she's going somewhere good. And she will still be loved; that will never change. With a quick exhale of amusement, I wonder if she was here for me more than I was here for her.

If my life were a book, and if this job were the journey, maybe . . . maybe I'm not the villain. It's been a peaceful journey, all things considered. And she wasn't alone for it. She had me beside her, to keep her safe, despite the sorrow I allowed into my heart. What I should have done was open my eyes, as she has, and feel the warmth that surrounds me, as she has.

I return her smile and lift my gaze, focused on moving forward. After all, I am not delivering death; I'm collecting life. I am bringing peace. And it is good.

To learn more about this author, please visit:
https://crystalmmburton.com

Mother Earth

Women's Fiction

Jeanne Felfe

Prompt: Your adoptive mother tells you, while on her deathbed, that you were born on a different planet. You have always suspected you were different because of the one thing that separates you from the rest of humankind.

I *AM RUNNING OUT OF* time.

    I sit by Mom's bedside, where I've held vigil for the past week, listening to her raspy breath. The air is punctuated by the rhythmic thrum of her oxygen tank. Star nuzzles and purrs under my hand, and I stroke her silky fur. Mom's calico has barely left her side in days, except to eat. It's like she senses something.

    I've always known I would lose her long before my friends lost their own mothers. After all, she'd already seemed old by the time I came into her life. I just didn't know it would be this soon. I want—no, I need—more time.

    She still has not followed through on her promise.

    Although Mom is the only mother I've ever truly known, there was another—I just don't remember her. I first became obsessed with learning about my birth mother when I was twelve and met this odd little boy who showed up at church one Sunday. He told me he had dreamed about her. Violet—that's what he said her name was. I didn't believe him. How could he know my mother's name when I didn't? Why would he get the dream instead of me? I have dreams, too. Lots of dreams. So different from those of my friends, I quit sharing them. Their strange looks became unbearable.

There was something about him, and what he said haunts me still.

Every year since, on my birthday, I've asked my adoptive mother to tell me about the woman who gave me life. Every year, she says, "When you're older, Marta." But each year, I never seem quite "older" enough for her to tell me. I'm twenty-one and apparently still not "older" enough.

Grief squeezes my throat as I open the gulf-facing window and inhale salty sea air. A slight iodine scent of seaweed wafts in with the breeze and saturates Mom's room. Turbid surf pounds the shore a hundred yards away, down the hill from the house. Offshore lightning flashes in the dampness, sending tingles across my scalp and down my arms to my fingertips. Litter from the previous day's beachgoers twirls in the wind, but it will have to wait.

Mom stirs. "Thank you, Marta. I have . . . always loved . . . the smell of the gulf." The wet, sucking breaths rattle her chest, punctuating each word. She pats the bed next to her. "Come. Sit with me awhile," she says, smiling even though every word is a struggle.

Inhaling another lungful of the pungent balm that has always grounded me, I move to her side and lower myself onto her bed, taking her hand in mine. I search her eyes, wondering if today I'll hear the truth.

So many questions. So little time.

Mom's eyes sparkle and dance the way they did when I was a child. We used to build castles in the sand, spending hours on turrets and moats. The gray pallor of her skin pinkens as if nearing the end of life gives her body an extra boost. It's almost like my touch added the color. But that's not possible.

"My sweet Marta," she begins, her breathing now effortless for the first time in over a week. "You have been such a blessing to me. When your father came to this coast with you twenty-two years ago,

it was an answer to my prayers."

This part of the story I know. She's told it many times, but I cherish the telling on every occasion. I trace the greenish-blue lines of knotty veins on her hand and then smile at her, waiting for each tidbit, as if hearing it for the first time. It is my only connection to my father, Martin, after whom I am named. Much as I struggle to find one, I have no true memory of him. My only memories are fabricated from the photos Mom has scattered around this sparse beach house where I grew up.

"When he arrived, you were a wee motherless babe, wrapped in a rainbow-colored blanket. I remember that first knock on my door like it was yesterday. He looked as if he'd lost his best friend, and I suppose he had. He rented the upper-level apartment and you both moved into it, and into my heart."

Mom removes the cannula from her nose and leans her head against her pillow. Her lids close as she inhales the humid air and exhales a long sigh.

"It was obvious from the start that your father knew nothing of babies, so what could I do but help? Caring for you began to heal my own broken heart."

When she pauses, I speak. "Mom, you promised to tell me of my birth mother. Please?" *Before it's too late.* But this is for my thought alone.

She stares at me with gray-blue eyes. The color has faded but still reminds me of the sky in Port Aransas after a storm. Taking a long breath, she nods. "In the closet." She points to the tiny room I am never allowed to enter. "Go on," she instructs.

I slip around to the other side of the bed and place a tentative hand on the knob. *This is it.* I glance back at her before opening it, feeling like I might be tempting Pandora by doing so.

"On the top shelf all the way in the back," she calls.

I tilt my head up toward a shelf about a foot below the ceiling, amazed Mom had been able to access it. At five-six, I tower over her and still can't see what's on top.

As I puzzle this, she says, "There's a step stool behind those dresses."

I push flowered, floor-length frocks aside to reveal a small, white, collapsible stool, perfectly hidden. I pull the lightweight device out and open it under the shelf. On shaky legs, I climb up until the wooden ledge is even with my chin.

"What am I looking for?" I say over my shoulder.

"The green box labeled Martin."

At first I don't see it, so I sweep aside several cardboard boxes. Behind them hides a shiny green box about one-foot square or so. I drag it to the edge, surprised by how incredibly heavy it seems. I again wonder how Mom could possibly have gotten it up here. Maybe my father did it before he died. I struggle to balance it against my chest, so I can lower it enough to wrap my arms around it, and step down.

Mom gestures for me to bring the box. When I do, I see something written on the top and side—DO NOT OPEN UNTIL 22.

"Your father left this box for you."

I think of the man I only know from pictures. As soon as I was old enough to comprehend, Mom told me about the cancer that ravaged him, claiming him quickly.

My heart aches for the love of two parents I know little of.

I tell myself not to overreact. She must have a reason for keeping this from me. But I am tired of waiting.

"Why didn't you give this to me sooner? Didn't I have a right to it?" Anger churns deep within. Anger that, until this instant, I'd mistaken for longing and curiosity. Now, I see it for what it is—pure, burning grief.

"My child. Your father made me promise." She pauses and places a hand on the lid, hesitating. "I've never even looked inside myself."

"Promise him what? That you'd keep my real mother a secret from me?"

Control yourself. Give her a chance.

"Promised to only show you this when you were old enough."

"I know that, Mom," I snap. Trying but failing to control my attitude, I instantly regret it and soften my tone. "I'm sorry," I say, squeezing her hand. "You've reminded me of that every time I've asked. How is it possible I've not been old enough for all these years?"

"Because your father said twenty-two and not a day earlier." She points to the lettering on the box and holds my frozen glare, which thaws to a bewildered gaze after a moment.

Twenty-two?

I glance at my fitness tracker. How have I forgotten my own birthday? My twenty-second birthday, even the day of the week, has slipped by, repressed since Mom's been so ill.

Lightning explodes in storm clouds on the horizon, casting an eerie glow across the room. Electricity crackles in the air, and I consider closing the window but don't.

"Feels like a storm is coming in." Mom reaches over and clicks on the weather radio beside her bed. Its Klaxon warning shrieks and a mechanical voice warns, "Tropical Storm Violet threatens the Texas coast from Galveston to Corpus Christi. Take shelter immediately. Risks of high wind, flooding, lightning, and hail until 3 p.m. tomorrow. Residents in low-lying areas should seek higher ground."

"Violet. Hmm . . . a storm for your birthday." Mom glances over with a twinkle in her eyes.

"We should probably head to the mainland."

"No. I won't die away from this beach. It's my home and I love it. If it gets bad, we'll move up a level."

The upper level contains the apartment I've lived in since turning eighteen while attending college in Corpus Christi. It has everything I need, affords me some privacy, and is free, which balances the long drive. After early graduation, Mom took ill, so I stayed, putting the continuation of my environmental sciences education on hold. Saving the earth will have to wait.

The wind kicks up, howling around and over the house,

causing the yellow curtains to flap wildly against the frame. I rush to the window, searching the horizon. My fiery red curls whip around, slapping me in the face. When rain pelts me and drenches the curtains, I close the window.

"Should we go up?"

"Not yet. Sit." She pats the bed again and smiles up at me. "Happy twenty-second, my angel. I'm so sorry there's no carrot cake this year, but . . . " She sweeps a hand through the air over her bed. "I've been a bit busy dying."

"Mom! You are not dying. Don't say things like that."

Her sweetness melts me and I fight back tears.

"It's okay, Marta. I've had a good life. You gave me a second chance to be a mother."

I pull her into a hug and when I lean back, she says, "Are you ready, sweetie?" Her smile grows mysterious and she nods at me to open the lid.

Inside, a silver pocket watch lies nestled in a bed of white tissue paper. My hand trembles as I reach for it and flip it over — To Marta, my life, my world. I press the side button and it pops open, revealing a tiny version of my favorite picture — one of my father and mother entwined in a hug. Pressing it to my lips, I try to sense their presence.

Closing the watch, I pull the tissue aside and find a folded sheet of purple paper. My dearest Marta is scrawled on the outside. The blue ink is tea-stained and smeared. Was the weight of his cup too heavy even for a sip, but he wrote me this note anyway? The letters are disjointed and appear to have been written with much effort, in some places digging into the paper, leaving tiny tears.

My heart flutters with anticipation as I unfold it, and I read my father's words aloud.

"Happy twenty-second birthday, my child. Oh, how I'll miss holding you. Singing Itsy Bitsy — you always giggled when the spider tickled under your arms. I so wish I could have been here to see you all grown up. Perhaps married? But alas, life has other plans for me.

25

"I'm at a loss for what to tell you about your mother so I'll start with the easiest detail. Her name was Violet."

His revelation stuns me. The boy's dream was true. Mom lied to me. As if to punctuate the moment, a streak of lightning brightens the room, and the rumble of thunder shakes the house.

A small whimper escapes my lips and I lower the paper. "You knew her name."

She nods but doesn't explain.

"I told you about that boy's dream when I was twelve. You knew and yet you lied to me."

"Sweetie, I didn't lie. I just didn't tell you. That's all."

"That's all? How —"

"I promised," she interrupts, her eyes glistening. "Go on. What else does the letter say?"

I bite back tears and continue. *"What can I tell you about the woman who melted my heart and gave me you? Violet was but a whisper in the wind. We shared one year and only moments. One morning she was simply gone. Vanished, leaving behind a letter explaining everything. Explaining nothing. I believed none of it. Oh, Marta, how I wish you could have known her. I imagine you are just like her."*

My hand trembles as I wipe tears and look at Mom. "Did you know this?"

She simply shakes her head and tilts her head toward the letter, urging me to keep reading.

"Your mother returned one year later with the most beautiful baby I've ever seen and I fell in love all over again. Only she couldn't stay. She was running from something and minutes after she laid you in my arms, she disappeared again, this time right in front of me. And I mean that quite literally. I didn't understand what she told me, but I know what I saw, and I saw her become translucent, and then she was simply gone. You probably think I'm a crazy person or that I'm making this up so you don't feel bad about having a mother who abandoned you. But I swear to you on my grave — which is coming

soon, I'm sure — this is the truth. I miss having her letter — my only comfort without her. I read it so often in the year she was gone, it was thin as tissue. But when she returned with you — oh blessed day — she insisted on burning it before she vanished, wanting to leave no trace, and leaving me alone with you to raise."

I drop the paper onto my lap and heave a raspy sigh. "Why didn't you just tell me my father was a stark raving lunatic?"

"Because he wasn't. He was lucid and clear right up to the moment he last closed his eyes. I admit his words sure sound crazy, but keep reading. Maybe he explains more."

I am seriously tired of parents not telling me things, but I pick up the letter anyway.

"I remember how your wild red curls whipped in the wind at the beach. They were just like hers. Do you have her mystical eyes? Have you noticed yet?"

"Noticed what?" I opened my eyes wide at Mom. "Do you see anything?" Not waiting for her answer, I race to the mirror, hoping that might explain something. All I see are plain blue eyes staring back. Nothing mystical. Nothing special. I slump back onto the bed.

"Are you going to finish?" Mom asks.

"Why?" I huff out a heavy sigh. "It's just crazy talk."

"Because you need to know."

She's right. I know that. So I continue reading.

"Maybe not, but perhaps soon if today is your birthday? But I'm getting ahead of myself. When Violet told me she was from far away, I thought she meant Canada. I never learned where she was really from, but she explained it took her three months of travel on what she called 'crude non-effulgent vessels,' whatever that means. Something about not being able to travel using light. I know this is all confusing. At least it is to me."

I lower the paper and roll my eyes. "Confusing? Damned right it's confusing." I jump up in frustration and step to the window, peering out through shattered raindrops. Or perhaps they are tears. The weather sock now stands straight out — not too unusual for the beach, but the way it is flipping and spinning, the wind speed must be over forty miles per hour already. Still safe enough for this hurricane-proof house, but something to keep an eye on.

The name of the storm roils through my mind and rattles me to my core. How had that boy known?

"Come on back and finish the letter," Mom urges and then falls into a coughing fit.

Her color is once again ashen. Sunken, purple circles engulf her eyes, giving her a skeletal appearance. "Mom?" I rush to her side, but she waves me away.

"Fin—" She covers her mouth with one hand as coughs rack her, not giving her time to catch her breath between. Over and over she hacks until she settles back, exhausted, on the pillow, small red droplets staining her gown.

At the sight of blood, I blanch.

No.

It's too soon.

"We need to get you to the hospital before the storm grows any worse." I begin racing around the room, grabbing various items I think she'll need.

"Marta, stop."

I turn pleading eyes toward her as she continues.

"I am not going to the hospital. I don't want to die hooked up to any more machines than just this stupid air thing. I want to die at my beloved beach. Now finish the letter before I run out of time." This last part is a command I dare not ignore.

Reluctantly, I return to the side of her bed and sit, taking the letter into my hands. I pick up where I left off.

"All the answers you seek are inside this box. Your mother left it, adamant it should only be opened when you turn twenty-two. Not a day before. If you're not yet twenty-two, please wait. She made it sound critically important. I love you with all my heart, your dad, Martin."

Tears burn my eyes and my throat tightens as I clutch the

watch to my chest. My daddy—I still know almost nothing about him, and yet I miss him so much. But how can that be when I have no memory of him? Still, the hollow place in my chest, the one I've been unable to fill, bites as if embedded with thorns.

I reach into the green box and lift out an ornate, wooden rectangular block covered with what look like ancient carvings. My fingers trace the outline of what could be writing, as if they can understand it by touch.

It's heavier than it seems, so I place it on the bed before running my hand along one edge, seeking a way to open it. There doesn't appear to be a lid—instead, it looks like it's a solid, eight-inch-long carved slab of wood. The two short sides contain matching indentions, so I place my thumbs into each and press. Wooden clicks emanate from the box as it vibrates. An intricate pattern emerges as the box begins to shift and transform, with some pieces poking out and others pulling in, like a Jenga puzzle game.

My breath catches in anticipation. Mom looks mesmerized, also.

The box splays like the blooming of a flower and emits an ethereal sound—part whale song, part wolf howl, part something I couldn't identify—unlike any I've ever heard. The music continues as a shaft of light beams from the inside and seemingly right through the ceiling. At the same time a blast of lightning sizzles on the beach at the base of our hill, not twenty feet away. The thunder that follows rocks the house. I scream and jump to my feet. Star hisses and bolts under the bed.

In an instant, the light disappears. All sound ceases, except that of the tumbling surf. The rain also stops, plunging us into near silence. I race to the window, fearing the storm intensified when we weren't paying attention, and that perhaps we are in the eye. This is the most dangerous time for a storm surge and we must move upstairs quickly.

Instead of seeing the low tide I expect, a woman with fiery red curls that cascade to her waist hovers over the sand less than ten feet away. Sparks snap from her fingers as she peers through the window toward me. Seeing her is like looking in a mirror. I know her immediately. It is Violet — my mother is the storm.

My heart stops as she walks toward the house. But walking isn't quite accurate for what she is doing — she seems to float and is at the window before I can take a breath.

I stumble away and fall backward onto the bed. I expect her to stop outside, but she seems to melt through the wall and is standing beside me before I can right myself.

"My daughter."

I feel rather than hear her words and respond the same way, having no idea how this is even possible. "Mother."

I swivel my head toward Mom and freeze for a split second before rolling over and crawling to her. Her head slumps to one side and her mouth hangs slack. As I feel for a pulse, I sense Violet speaking in my head.

"There is no need, child. Her earthly body is no more."

"What? No!" I scream using my voice this time. "Mom!"

I shake Mom and she flops over. I dissolve into tears, my legs buckling as I crumple to the floor into a fetal position. I knew she was dying — I just didn't know it would be today. This is all too much.

Too many losses for my twenty-two years.

I lie like this, alone in my grief, until my tears dry and I am an exhausted mess. When I look up, Violet is sitting on the floor next to me, only a foot away. Her gaze penetrates my soul and she places a hand on my shoulder.

"Be still, my child. This is as planned."

I shake my head. "As planned? I don't understand."

"Celeste knew."

"How do you know my Mom's name?"

"Because I came here twenty-two years ago and made a deal with her. She was broken with grief over losing both her husband and son to the sea. She was preparing to walk into the water and drown herself when I arrived only a day before your father. Dear,

sweet Martin. Oh, how I've missed him."

I frown and shake my head. "I don't understand."

"I told her I could take her pain away and give her a child."

"Me," I say in a whisper.

"You. But it's not as you think. I didn't want to leave you. I never wanted to leave you. But they were coming. If I stayed, they would have taken you. Done experiments on you. I couldn't allow that."

"Who are they? And why were they after me?"

"Marta . . . I'm not like you or Celeste or anyone else. You know that, right?" she asks, shrugging and tilting her head.

"Yeah, I can't imagine what gave you away. Oh, I know. Maybe it was you walking through a wall. Or maybe talking without words." My sarcasm might sting but I don't care. From what I can see, this woman has killed my mom.

"No, child. I did not kill her. I—"

"Stay out of my head," I scream and begin pacing.

"I kept her alive. Her earthly body would have given out twenty-two years ago if not for me—my energy and light."

Right now, I want to hate this woman. I don't want to hear this, so I say nothing and she continues.

"When I came here, Celeste's pain was overwhelming. Perhaps if she had a child to love, she wouldn't want to walk into the sea and die. So we made a deal. She would carry my essence and be your mother until I returned, and I would keep her alive. I left an untraceable, vital piece of my being in her, and then returned home, knowing you would be safe."

Confusion swirls in my head. Pictures begin to form of another world—like the ones from my dreams—light-years away but I can't give in. "I don't believe you."

"Come. I want to show you something." She stands and gestures to the mirror and I shuffle to face her. "Look into my eyes."

I peer into them and notice that they are a deep emerald green. Weren't they blue just a moment ago? A line of fiery red appears around her pupil. I lean in and see that the line is spinning. Something foreign, like symbols, whirls within the green. And her pupils feel bottomless, like they reach to the other side of forever.

"Now, look at yours." She points her head toward the mirror and I lean closer.

My normally blue eyes are now a shocking green, like hers, and they have the same red swirling line. I jump back, only now remembering what was so strange about that boy. His eyes were just like mine have become. I demand, "Who are you? Who was that little boy?"

"I am your mother. Violet. I am also Princess Dianthus. The boy is my son, Sibelius, your brother."

"I . . . I have a brother." It is all too much, and I collapse on the floor, afraid I will pass out. "A brother?"

"Half. He is not part human like you."

"What happened to him?" He'd been so small and now I worry for him.

"I brought him home when he'd done what he was sent for — to check on your progress. Do you wish to know the rest?"

I nod and she continues. "I came to your world twenty-four years ago on a mission to study humans. In doing so I met, and fell in love with, your father. It was not planned, nor was it allowed. When my commander learned of this, she recalled me. I did not know I was pregnant with you at the time. Did not know that was even possible. As soon as you were born, I fled my world before they could experiment on you."

"Why would they have done that?" I ask, hoping to catch her in a lie. But how would I know a lie from the truth?

"Because you are the only one like you." She pauses and tilts her head, looking puzzled. "The only child born from mating with a human."

"So . . . I'm not human?"

"Well, yes. And no. You are certainly half human." She pauses and releases a heavy sigh. "My planet is dying. I came here to determine if Earth could support my kind."

"You're probably lizard people disguised in human skin planning to take over our planet." I push away from her, filling with disgust. I will not allow myself to fall for this nonsense.

Her laugh peals off the walls like one of Mom's giant wind chimes. "We are not lizard people—in fact, we look mostly the same as humans. And we are not trying to take over your planet. Earth's people have interesting imaginations. If they only knew what existed beyond their sky." Her attention drifts to a place past the window.

I don't trust what she's telling me. This is how it all starts. Some human trusts one of these things and then it all gets out of hand.

"We are much like humans, but far advanced in many ways. A peaceful people; however, through no fault of our own, our planet will soon be gone, when the sun that supports life implodes, as do all stars at the end of their lives. We can't save it, but we can save yours. This thing you call, what, climate change, has an easy solution. We developed the technology and wish to share it."

"Why did you wait twenty-two years to come back?" My heart aches with questions.

"Two reasons. First, I knew you wouldn't come into your power until you were fully mature—which I calculated it to be roughly equivalent to our own—twenty-two years for a female. The second is far more complicated. When I returned home, I was arrested for treason even though I am a princess. My family was dethroned in a struggle over how best to approach the humans. Some wanted to simply take it. My family wanted to bond. The House of Dianthus rose to power again several years ago, but I chose to wait until I could show you the change in yourself. The change that would only materialize at the right age. Otherwise, you might not believe me. Now it is safe for me to bring you home."

"Home? I am home." I speed up my pacing, ideas racing through my mind. I'm not sure what to do and now have no one to ask. What if I agree and am wrong?

"I meant to my home. So you can see for yourself who we are.

Then you can be the bridge between our cultures so that we can help each other. Let me show you." She places a hand on my shoulder. "Close your eyes."

I hesitate, still not trusting her. In an instant, a familiar vision fills my senses — it's the one from my dreams. It isn't just in my mind, however, it is everywhere. More accurately, it feels as if I've been transported to a different world. The sky is a brilliant blue with streaks of purple and white. The plant life is beyond green — it seems to snap with hues that shimmer. The people move about in harmony, and I sense a happiness that is missing on Earth.

Suddenly, I am back in Mom's room, but I feel lighter than air. I look at my hand, marveling at the translucent image that was once solid. As I twist it palm up and then down, it gradually takes on more substance until it is solid once again.

I meet Violet's piercing gaze.

"Now do you believe me?" she asks.

"What just happened?"

"I took you to my home," she says, but then pauses and frowns. "No, that's not exactly true. I only showed you the spirit of it. It takes a bit longer to actually go there." She pauses and eyes me. "Now will you come with me?"

My eyes fill with tears. Finding my mother is what I've wanted my entire life. And now I have a brother. "I can't. I need to plan a funeral for Mom." Although it breaks my heart to see her that way, I turn toward the bed.

It is empty.

"Where's my mom?" My voice fills with panic as I run to where her body had been just a few minutes before. "What did you do with her?"

"She has gone to where humans go at death."

"That's insane. Our bodies don't just disappear when we die."

Violet smiles. "I know this is hard for you to understand, but Celeste's body was held together by the fabric of my essence. Once removed, her earthly body simply vibrated out of existence. It's part of the plan my people have for earthlings."

"So you are going to snatch our bodies. I knew it!"

"You're quite the imaginative one, aren't you? We aren't going to steal your bodies. We will just fill them with a magnificent luminance that will improve so much. There will be no more suffering."

This feels like Nirvana. No more suffering. But then I think about all the wonderful inventions created because of the struggles people endure. Without the struggle, what would life hold? Would we all just sit around and become lazy?

"Violet," I say, finding I'm not comfortable calling her mother. "There's something you don't understand about humans. Suffering is part of what makes us who we are."

Violet simply smiles. "So it would seem. But does it have to be that way?"

The reality of what she is offering sinks in and I know the truth. Humans aren't quite ready for this. It will take the younger ones to bring us to that point. I try to explain this to Violet and after a while, she nods.

"There is much I do not yet understand about humans. This is why we need you. Come and help us learn so that we can save your planet. Ours is dying—it might have ten of your Earth years left. Your planet, on the other hand, is still young by comparison and has eons left unless humans destroy it first. We can stop that from happening in exchange for a new place to settle our families."

I almost laugh out loud at the absurdity of this. I explain to her about how some countries, including my own, treat immigrants. How they aren't welcome. "How do you think they will react to someone who really is an alien?" I ask her.

"I think you will see that the technology we can offer to help your planet and to grow food more efficiently will more than make up for the scant resources my people will consume."

I stand by the window bathed in the salty breeze. "Will I get to meet my brother?"

"Of course. Prince Sibelius is waiting, anxious to meet you once again."

The roar of the waves pulls my attention and I stare out at my beloved gulf, still churning from the storm. My home. The only one I know.

"My time here is growing short. I must return and advise my council." Reading my thoughts, she adds, "You will only need to be away from your beloved sea for a brief time. And when you return, you will be able to save it."

Save the Gulf. The oceans. The air. Everything. This is what Violet is offering. It overwhelms me that the future of planet Earth may be up to me.

I've always known I am different. Those childhood dreams weren't dreams at all. They were visions sent by Violet so I would recognize her when she arrived. They were to prepare me for my destiny. When I reach my decision, I am filled with a lightness I haven't felt since before Mom became ill.

I bend over and reach under the bed to where Star has been hiding since the thunder. Pulling her out I lift her toward Violet. "Do you have cats in your world?"

To learn more about this author, please visit:
http://jeannefelfe.com/

Where Dreams Die

Historical Fiction

Kerry A Waight

Prompt: It's unfortunate to be good at something that's not good at all.

*T*HERE WAS A SPACE in my heart that always ached. I often wondered what life would have been like with a mother — my mother. She lost her life while giving birth to me in 1868. Would I have been expected to conform to societal norms had she lived? Would I have been a different person with a female role model in my home who was not an employee? Would my father have had more time for me had I not been responsible for my mother's death? I expect the answer to these questions would be yes. How much so, however, would never be known. There was no point dwelling on it: nothing could be changed.

"Tradition killed your mother, Isabelle. I do not expect you to follow tradition; in fact, I would prefer you not to," my physician father would say on the rare occasions I saw him. In those precious times, he was always encouraging me, particularly when I displayed interest in reading his medical books. Thankfully, I found the material fascinating and devoured as much detail as I could. And this pleased Papa. I suspected that my intelligence and ambition gave him comfort.

But my dreams were elsewhere. The written word was my drug. Not only did I read my father's books but anything else I could get my hands on. There was Dickens and Crane, of course. And the *Cornhill Magazine*, with the works of numerous authors, was one of my favorite publications. Then there was the Bell family of writers: Currer, Ellis, and Acton—rumor was circulating that they were, in fact, three very talented sisters with the surname of Bronte, forced to write under pseudonyms so they could be published. I saw them as inspirational, but I was determined to be a woman published as a woman. Not, however, as a writer of fiction. My dream was to be an investigative journalist, with my name as widely known and respected as my hero, W. T. Stead.

Pioneered by Stead, investigative journalism was the latest trend in newspaper journalism. His articles investigating the misuse of children by their often-drunken parents who sold them into prostitution as young as ten years old convinced me that the women who were involved in this trade were the lowest of the low, given that they knowingly allowed this abuse of childhood to happen.

* * *

MY FATHER WAS MURDERED in Whitechapel on the sixteenth of February, 1888. I was never told why he was in the East End in the first place, but I was old enough to guess. He was, after all, a man. He used to tell me that he could never love another woman the way he loved my mother, and it was not fair to ask a woman to play second fiddle to a memory. But his love for my mother and passion for human flesh cost him his life. So while I recognize that many people will see it as unreasonable, where and why he was knifed made me despise the ladies of the night even more than my peers did. After all, if they had some pride, they would not be selling their bodies to any man with a few pennies or pounds to spare. And my father would still be alive.

It wasn't just that he was murdered chasing carnal pleasures with low life. His apparent love of fornication robbed me of the attention I needed when I was growing up. When he wasn't working, he was out entertaining, leaving me with a succession of nannies and housekeepers. Had harlots not been available, Papa probably would have remarried, negating his need to wander into dangerous territory.

By the end of July, I was ready to put in motion the steps necessary to make my dream of writing and publishing an exposé on homewrecking whores a reality. Although still awaiting probate on my father's will, I had enough money at my disposal to rent lodgings in Whitechapel. My room was small and cramped, but clean. My plan was simple, really. All I needed to do was infiltrate the ranks of the lowest harlots and write the articles that would expose them to the world for the filthy whores that they were.

After spending twenty-four hours residing in Whitechapel and observing from my first-floor window, I knew that my clothing would attract attention, certain to raise suspicion. It was vitally important that I blend in with the squalor, so I took some of the opulent dresses I had tired of and, traveling to the streets of Spitalfields, I offered them to the girls who were starting their trade for the evening, asking only for their clothing in return. I was careful to approach only those wearing clothes that, while not the quality of mine, were clearly purchased to make the best of one's appearance — in the hopes of attracting a better class of clientele, I imagined. I surmised that these were the girls who, while having jobs in factories and the like, still felt that they needed to do a few men a favor or two in order to make ends meet. My reasons were not altruistic: if I had to dress like a whore, I at least wanted to be one of the better-dressed harlots.

Not one of them asked me why I was prepared to swap my clothes for theirs. I suspect more than one of them thought they were the ones taking advantage of me. They could think what they liked. I knew I was about to expose them and their kind. Our clothing swaps happened in the filthy backstreets behind public houses. The joy they got from what I considered to be simply a well-made item of clothing was pitiful.

* * *

I WILL NEVER FORGET the date: the sixth of August, 1888. Bank Holiday Monday. It was drizzling, which seemed appropriate. I donned one of my newly acquired dresses. It felt rough against my skin, so I understood why my discarded garments caused such excitement. For a fleeting moment, I felt some sympathy for girls who worked hard all day and all night. Then I remembered that, if not for the likes of them, I would still have my father.

I waited until around midnight, a time when I thought it more likely that I would find what I was looking for, whatever that was. The gas lamps vaguely illuminated the street below, giving the impression that a mystery lay beneath them, waiting to be exposed. I was giddy with anticipation: the dream started as soon as I stepped outside. I realize now that, as well as my journalistic ambitions, I was harboring an opportunity to avenge my father. Regardless, I was about to embark on the adventure of a lifetime, and I indulged myself with a few moments to relish the sensations that flooded my body.

My consciousness was assaulted by the agitation that was Whitechapel. The streets were crawling with the unwashed masses, and I could not bear the noise and the stench. My observations from the safety of my tiny retreat above could not have prepared me for it and, I am a little ashamed to say, I was genuinely frightened. It was not enough, however, to stop me in my quest for the necessary information.

I was drawn to the light coming through the window of the Two Brewers public house, crowded as it was inside. Without hesitation, I pushed the heavy oak door open and entered. I was expecting some respite for my senses, but the noise inside was just as overwhelming, and the reek of stale smoke and urine churned in my stomach. Normal conversation was not in evidence. Everyone was yelling, be it at a barman, friend, acquaintance, or enemy. I was beginning to wonder if I had made a mistake entering what was an area far more crowded than the cobblestone street outside; I seriously doubted that I would be any safer than I was on Brick Lane.

I was about to take my chances back on the street when I felt a gust behind me as the door to the public house swung open. I turned and saw a dirty, plump, middle-aged woman, obviously the worse for drink. She looked me up and down, and the disdain on her face told me that, for some reason, my presence was not appreciated. Her raspy voice assailed my ears.

"Slummin', are ya darlin'?"

I took a breath and steeled myself. How could she know that I was from a better class and area? However, while I found her repulsive, she could be just the person I wanted to talk to.

"I'm sure I don't know what you mean." In that very moment, I could hear the surrounding tones and colloquialisms bouncing against the walls of the bar, and I knew that mine did not fit in.

Her eyes looked me up and down again. "Well — don't that just answer me question. Bit toffy for 'round 'ere, ain't ya?"

Before I had a chance to think of a response, she grabbed me by the arm, pulling me closer to her and talking into my ear like she was telling me a secret. "Ya won't survive in 'ere, lovie. Tell ya what. Buy us a Beefeater, an' I'll show ya the ropes."

While I had no idea what "the ropes" were that she was going to show me, her invitation was too good to refuse. I was sure I had discovered a filthy harlot who would speak with me. She motioned to the barman, who gave her a nod. With that, she guided me to a corner of the room that seemed to be a little quieter.

Again, I must confess, I did have a moment of panic. Was I being set up? I reminded myself, however, that I had a small knife in my purse if I needed to use it. If the cost of my information was spending time with this hag, I could do it.

The barman brought two drinks to our rickety wooden table, the surface of which was worn smooth except for the engravings of unspeakable acts carved into the wood. He looked expectantly at me so I handed him the largest note I had in my purse, not knowing the going rate for gin. A smirk crossed his face, and after shooting an appreciative glance at the wretch, he made his way back to the bar. I knew I would not be seeing any change, so I simply considered that to be the price I had to pay to keep her talking. I resolved on the spot that I would not drink the gin placed in front of me.

Following a hacking cough, which brought up phlegm that she promptly spat on the floor, the as-yet-nameless horror addressed me.

"First thing ya gotta decide, lovie, is whether ya wanna be at an 'ouse with a bawd lookin' out for ya but takin' a big chunk of ya money, or a walker what's gotta keep her eye out but whatever ya earn ya keeps for yerself."

Oh, good Lord! She thinks I want to be a whore! I struggled not to look shocked as my mind accepted that this deception was my purpose. While I had no intention of following through, the thought of my successful deception thrilled me.

"Oh. I see. Yes, I think I would like to keep all the money I make." *Getting out of a brothel with my dignity intact would be far too difficult. At least this way, I could run my own life.* "What is your name, by the way?" *I wanted to be able to refer to her by name. Make it more personal. I might get more information that way.*

"Call me Martha, lovie. An' ya made the right choice. Them bawds make ya go to doctors an' they check ya bits to make sure ya ain't poxy, like. Buggar that! I got it somewheres. Don't mind sharin'."

With that, Martha burst into laughter that brought on yet another coughing fit. But it meant that I had hit the jackpot. That night, she was the poxy whore I was looking for. My story on the depravity of prostitutes, with revolting detail, was right in front of me. I fought to ensure that I hid my contempt, but I need not have bothered. She was too drunk to notice.

I spun her a yarn about having to leave home because my parents died and my brother's wife kicked me out. After that, she told me everything she thought I needed or wanted to know. I made copious mental notes while battling not to let my disgust in her vileness show.

It was then I had a genius thought. In all the newspaper reports on trollops, I had never seen one where the journalist was shown exactly where the filthy deeds were performed. It might be the edge I needed.

"Martha, do you think you could show me where you take 'em? To—you know." I was learning quickly to take on the appropriate language so as not to draw too much attention to myself. Fitting in was vital to my success. I silently thanked my father for encouraging independent thinking. Maybe leaving me to my own devices as much as he did would work in my favor.

Martha looked at me with suspicion, and I wanted to slap her. Who was she to judge me? But I held my tongue and hand. Finally, she spoke.

"You gonna drink that, lovie?"

I saw my moment. "No. You 'ave it. Then we can look at your special place, yeah?"

"Deal," she replied as she stretched out her grubby paw for the gin.

After finishing my drink, Martha sat in her seat, blankly looking at nothing in particular. I knew that if I didn't take some action, my night's torment would have been in vain.

"C'mon, Martha. Ya promised." When she didn't move, I had no choice but to grab her by the arm and heave her up. I could feel the grime and wondered how any man could bear to touch her. She smelled, and she was vile, with her filthy clothes and filthier habits.

"What's in it for me?" Martha slurred.

Never had I felt so much contempt for a living being.

"I'll buy you another gin." My response was terse. I was well beyond any form of cajoling.

"Done!" Martha staggered forward, pushing aside anyone in her way.

As we left the pub, Martha lamented, "I wasn't always like this, ya know. I got kiddies. Wasn't meant to be this way." I didn't know if she was talking to me or herself, and frankly, I didn't care.

She led me to an area known as George Yard, with the George Yard Buildings to the left at the end. Although a residential area, it was dark, with enough nooks and crannies for a whore to perform the "four-penny knee-knocker" abomination with enough cover to satisfy her clients.

"What's up there?" I indicated a first-floor landing and wondered if she lived in a room in the dilapidated building. Without saying a word, Martha grabbed my arm, more for stability than as guidance, and led me up the uneven stone steps. From the landing, I could just make out how easy it would be to disappear into the shadows to earn a few pennies. I could feel the bile rising from my gut and swallowed hard.

Without warning, Martha turned her swollen face to me and spat on the ground.

"Don't you be gettin' no ideas, lovie. This is my area, ya understand? I'll run ya through if I sees ya workin' 'ere."

With that, Martha pulled out a dagger from a crack in the stonework and waved it at me. "Keep this 'ere to protects meself an' me area."

The audacity of her comments hit a nerve in my psyche. Before I knew what I was doing, the knife was out of my purse and in her stomach. She slid noiselessly to the ground, and her skirts ended up around her waist. Something primitive overtook me as I pulled the blade from the initial wound and thrust it with venom and at random into her abhorrent body. Martha did not utter a sound, possibly a trait learned from years of servicing men in public areas.

Then I remembered her dagger that she threatened to use on me. Poetic justice. I felt the area where I knew her heart would be. The wetness on my hand told me that she would not live long, although there was a faint beat. I had to make sure I finished her off so she could not identify me. Positioning the blade over her sternum, I leaned on it with my full body weight. After the initial resistance, I felt the weapon plunge through.

Removing the dagger, I looked at the mess I had created. I had one more thing to do to take any suspicion from myself. Holding my breath, I leaned down and spread her legs. It was all I could manage without vomiting.

I quickly left the scene and headed back to the sanctuary of my lodgings, avoiding street lighting where possible. Hurriedly, I locked the door, ensuring that, at least for now, my actions were known only by me.

I did not, and do not, consider what I did to be a crime. After all, dear Martha had freely told me that she was spreading her pox without a care. As far as I am concerned, I did the world a favor. But I did not want to be discovered. I just wanted a story.

Carefully, I cleaned my knife and my newly-acquired blade. I secreted them at the back of the only closet I had in the room. Once I had dealt with the weapons, I peeled the blood-splattered clothing off my body and disposed of them in the fireplace. As I poked the guilty material into the embers and flames to ensure they burned thoroughly, it occurred to me how simple it had been. It was alarming just how easy it was. And how exhilarating it felt.

I washed the blood from myself in the basin of water that I always kept at the ready in my room. Even after a daytime excursion into the East End, I always felt dirty and needed to wash Whitechapel away. So, thankfully, I pre-filled a basin before I had left that night.

The morning newspapers were full of the news of the dreadful and brutal murder of Martha Tabram. Every reference to her over the following days talked about the savagery of the man who had killed her. I did, indeed, get away with murder.

I started my piece for the newspapers, with plans to submit to all the prominent publications, including the East London Advertiser and the East London Observer, with the report on my conversation with Martha and an insight into her depravity. Surely, they would publish this. But I started to have second thoughts. Would they get suspicious, given I was talking to her only hours before she was murdered? Maybe I would need a longer piece, bringing the details from a few whores together and keeping them nameless. That would get me published. And as myself, not a man. My course of action became clear. I needed another subject.

Suddenly, I could see my entry into journalism via retribution for my father—a dream fulfilled and a nightmare revenged at the same time.

* * *

I MADE A QUICK return to my home in the West End. I wanted a particular book of my father's on female anatomy. If I was going to sully myself with filth and depravity, I was going to send the whores a clear message of what I thought of them. It would also provide a reporting direction: devilish crimes targeted at devilish body parts. Every good exposé needed a hook, and I found mine.

Before I left, I also grabbed his bag of surgical instruments.

* * *

THE STREETS OF SPITALFIELDS and Whitechapel blurred into commonality, particularly in the drizzle of the post-midnight hours of the thirty-first of August. I thought it best to seek my next subject in a different pub rather than draw attention to myself by performing in the same place again. The Frying Pan on the corner of Brick Lane and Thrawl Street seemed as good a place as any to start. I pushed the door open and scanned the room for a suitable candidate. Leaning against a wall so that she would not fall, a woman of about thirty-five years looked to be considerably cleaner than Martha.

"Ya want a gin, love?" I asked.

I knew what the response would be.

"That would be grand, it would."

The response was overstated. Had it not been, it would have been impossible to understand through the slur. When the barman came over, I handed him sixpence. I had discovered since the Two Brewers that the going price of a large gin was threepence.

Soon enough, she told me, "Just call me Polly. That's what people call me."

Other than the fact that she was missing teeth, I noticed the pride she took in her appearance. She was clean, and her clothes, although aged, were in good repair. With her high cheekbones and wistful, gray eyes, I could see that in different circumstances she could have been somewhat attractive.

"D'ya know," she stated with pride after her third gin from me, "I'm nearly forty-four years old. D'ya think I look it? No one does, ya know."

"No. I wouldna guessed you was that old," I answered her truthfully.

Polly sighed. "Wanted somethin' better than this, for sure. Dunno what 'appened. But, 'appen it did." She took a swig from her now empty glass.

I motioned to the bartender to refill it. I knew he would.

Quickly, I diverted the conversation to her trade. I could not afford to like her. Thankfully, she could tell that I was new to the trade, and like Martha, she was happy to share her information. My detestation did not take long to return. The matter-of-fact manner in which Polly recounted sordid details sickened me. When she stood to leave, I knew what to do.

As Polly staggered down the street, I followed, ensuring that I wasn't seen. She turned onto Bucks Row, and about halfway down the street I saw my opportunity. The street was dark but inhabited. The possibility of discovery pushed adrenaline through my veins. I guaranteed her silence, however, with a swift incision from one ear to the other, severing the source of her life. But I wasn't finished. As soon as she hit the ground, I flung her skirts up to her waist and plunged the knife as close to her womanly organs as I could guess in the dark, sinking the knife several times to ensure that I did sufficient damage to make a statement before hurrying home in the darkness.

I followed the same procedure at home as I had following my successful dispatch of Martha, including the burning of my clothing. I was too charged to sleep, so I added to my piece, this time on the sordidness of even the nicest-looking harlots. I contemplated mentioning that it was not her preferred choice of lifestyle but quickly dismissed it.

As with Martha, the newspapers were full of the news of the violent murder. Apparently, the wounds I inflicted in the lower abdomen were severe enough for her bowels to be protruding. I would need to study my father's books again to reposition my target area. It had to be right. No — it had to be perfect.

It took a few days to identify Polly. Her real name was Mary Nichols. My exposé on the depraved was growing. It would not be long before I could write the perfect piece. I had to ensure there were enough subjects that they could remain unidentified in my work, thus ensuring my anonymity as the murderer — and saving my neck.

* * *

I WAS LOSING PATIENCE with taking so long to write my story, so I decided to try something different. Meeting scrubbers in public houses had only given me a limited perspective. And it made me more visible.

I had heard that the rear yard of 29 Hanbury Street was often used by prostitutes. How the tenants of the three-story residence put up with that, I did not understand, but put up with it they did. While I did not know exactly what I was going to do, I decided that it would be a different place to start.

I was getting anxious to expedite the process. Since my confidence was growing, I didn't want to wait as long as before for my next subject. During the early hours of the eighth of September, I made my way to the location and hid in the shadows, clutching my father's bag and waiting for an opportunity. The difficulty was that every whore who entered the yard with a man left with him, leaving me no prospect for action. I was about to give up when I heard a muffled exchange on the other side of the fence. The female voice sounded weary. I decided to wait.

The speed of the sexual act, coupled with the swift disappearance of the customer, created the perfect situation for me. In my darkness-adjusted eyes, I could see a plump woman leaning up against the fence.

"Can I help ya, love?" Another thing I had learned was that many of the prostitutes looked out for each other. I thought I would try that angle with this pitiful soul.

My question was met with a racking cough followed by a breathless, "Na, I'm right, lovie. Just need t' catch me breath's all."

So, I chatted with Annie—she told me her name was Annie without me even asking—while she got her breath. She told me she had only been selling herself for a bed for the last few years since her ex-husband had died and the money he was giving her died also. While I felt sorry for her momentarily, I quickly decided that I would rather sleep on the street or jump into the Thames than sell my body. And I could tell the sun was not far off making an appearance, so I could not waste much time.

She saw me remove my knife from my bag and shook her head in disbelief.

"No," was all she could manage in her fear.

As she turned to go, I grabbed her, dragging my knife swiftly across her neck. There was no remorse. I was doing her a favor anyway. She told me herself how sick she was and how she didn't think she was long for this world.

She had fallen in a position that I thought appropriate for someone in her trade: on her back with her legs spread apart. I planted her feet on the ground, spreading her knees further. Before I realized exactly what I had done, her intestinal organs were sitting on her shoulder and her reproductive organs were in my hand. Carefully, I placed my tools in my bag and left the yard just in time to see the sun making an appearance. Thankfully, I knew the routes home that provided less chance of raising suspicion. As I went, the stray dogs were given a feast of which they had never partaken and probably would not again.

Annie Chapman was identified quickly by her friends. They seemed to like her. Maybe that was an angle I could take. I sat down to write about Annie. But I didn't write anything. I was still too charged up to concentrate on brilliant prose. I decided that I could do it later and poured myself a gin instead.

* * *

I SPENT WEEKS CONTEMPLATING what my next move should be. I knew I would kill again and that excited me, perhaps more than the prospect of the story. It had to be right. It had to be perfect. On the morning of the first of October, however, the headlines shocked me. Every single newspaper was announcing the two horrific murders by the Whitechapel Murderer. I hadn't done a thing, and yet I was being credited with more murders.

The realization that I was not worried about being blamed but was hoping that whoever did it had not tainted my reputation stopped me in my tracks. At this point in time, I acknowledged to myself that the dream of publishing my work had all but gone. My exposé lay dormant in the cupboard. Annie had still not been written in. I had decided I could do that when the next whore was added. The nightmare of revenge and hate was more important.

And someone wanted to take credit for my handiwork. The same newspaper released a letter addressed "Dear Boss," purporting to be from the murderer, bragging about what he had done and what he was going to do. And he gave "us" a name: Jack the Ripper.

To be truthful, I wasn't sure how I felt about that. Clearly, I was no Jack. But it also kept any suspicion far from my door, freeing me up somewhat.

Over the coming days, the newspapers had more and more information. The two victims were Elizabeth Stride and Catherine Eddowes, neither of whom were prostitutes. This annoyed me. I would never murder — let alone cut up — a woman who was simply down on her luck but in the wrong place at the wrong time. As details emerged, I became enraged. Stride's murder bore no similarity to my method except for the slashing of her throat. And Eddowes — well, Eddowes was just messy. I had never disfigured a face, and the abdominal work, while done with precision by the sounds of it, gave no indication as to why she was whacked. If they were victims of the same murderer, they were clearly interrupted during the Stride killing. I was never that careless. The East End was enthralled with the growing legend of the individual that was now Jack the Ripper.

* * *

LIZZIE, MARIA, AND JULIA introduced me to Mary Kelly on the evening of the eighth of November. I had integrated myself into the East End to the extent that these women considered me their new friend. I met with them regularly, and they told me more than I wanted to know. Their lack of wariness of strangers had kept them safe — from me at any rate. I had been seen with them once too often to do them any harm.

Mary Kelly, however, signed her death warrant the day I met her. She waltzed up to the table where I was drinking with the other three harlots, her pretty hair and fair complexion highlighting her green eyes, making her more attractive than many of the prostitutes. It struck me that she was also a good deal younger than many of them as well. Her accent, while enhancing her allure, was hard to identify.

Curiosity got the better of me. "So, where ya from, Mary?"

"Born in Ireland but grown up in Wales. Yeah—I talk a bit funny," she said with a gentle laugh.

"She's a clever one, our Mary is," Maria proudly announced, as if being friends with Mary endowed her with some of Mary's learning.

It didn't take me long to work out that Maria was, indeed, correct. Mary was obviously educated, with a knowledge of the arts. I was relieved when Lizzie, Maria, and Julia left the pub for a while to earn more drinking money. I was keen to discover how Mary Kelly found herself whoring in the East End.

The more Mary drank, the louder she got and the freer she was with her information. I used this to my advantage, quizzing Mary while buying her gin. As it turned out, she had married at sixteen years of age and was widowed a few years later. It was upon her move to Cardiff that a cousin got her into prostitution.

"I decided," Mary said, choosing her words, "to travel to London rather than have my family shun me for the way I had to earn my income."

I spun Mary my story about being turned out by my sister-in-law, giving us a common background. It must have made her feel that I could be trusted with more of her story. This was where she made her fatal mistake.

"So, when I went to London, I worked in a high-class brothel in the West End. Even went to Paris with one of my regulars."

My heart stopped, and my blood ran cold as I recalled the trips my father took to Paris. I had begged him to take me, but he would not. I pulled myself together. I had to keep going.

"Lucky girl! Didn't his missus mind—or was he single?" I forced myself to punctuate this with a laugh.

"Widower. Had a daughter, I think. About five years younger than me. That felt weird. But he was nice to me. And very generous."

Thankfully, the other three returned, giving me a chance to disappear. I needed to steady myself and decide what I was going to do. I was starting to suspect that I may have met the very reason my father was in the East End on the night of his murder.

* * *

I WANDERED THE STREETS near the Ten Bells public house where the woman who would be my next target was still drinking. I wanted to get more information out of her before I did what I do best, and I knew how I was going to do it. Maria had told me that Mary Kelly was generous to her fellow prostitutes, often allowing them to sleep at her place when they found themselves with nowhere to sleep. I intended on being homeless that night.

I slipped into the shadows as Mary came out of the Ten Bells. I didn't want to be seen with her, so I followed her at just enough distance to avoid suspicion. Once on Dorset Street, Mary stumbled onto Millers Court, stopping outside number thirteen and pushing on the door. I knew it was time for me to act.

"Mary. Mary, it's Sally. Do you remember me? I met you at the pub tonight."

Mary turned, looked at me, and smiled. "Of course I remember you. We are kindred spirits, you and I."

"I need somewhere to stay tonight, Mary. Can't afford a bed. Spent my last penny on this gin." I shrugged, showing her the bottle that I knew she would welcome.

"I got room. Always got room for a friend that needs somewhere to rest their head."

As I entered her room, I started to hope that my assumptions about her connection to my father were wrong. In another time and place, we could have been friends.

Mary showed me to a seat, handed me two glasses to fill, and burst into song.

"Scenes of my childhood arise . . . " She stopped and looked at me. "Do you know this one? 'Violets From My Mother's Grave' I think it's called. Sing it with me."

I didn't know the song, but Mary took it back up. She had a lovely voice, and I was becoming mesmerized. Unfortunately, at a pivotal moment in the song, Mary flung her arms out, connecting with the gin bottle, knocking it from my hands and sending it crashing to the ground.

Abruptly, Mary stopped singing. "Oh no! I'll have to go and get some more."

I tried to convince her not to bother, but she was insistent. She was also insistent that I stay right where I was, which I agreed to do. Leaving now would undo all the work I did getting to her place without being seen.

I couldn't say how long Mary took to return home. I spent the time looking at the humble lodgings, noticing how clean and tidy it was. I wasn't surprised. Mary was neat and tidy too. I also formulated just how I was going to find out what I needed to know. For the first time, I wondered if I could get through my slaying.

Mary returned in the early hours of the morning. Although it was now the ninth of November, it was still the dark of night. The time for truths to come out. As Mary poured us both a gin, I knew I needed to act now or never.

"Tell me more about your sweetie that took you to Paris, Mary."

She laughed, not maliciously but almost whimsically. "He wasn't my sweetie. He thought he was. He wanted to be."

I had to remain focused. "Tell me about him anyway. What was he like?"

"He was generous, that's for certain. And smart." Mary absently looked out of the window as she talked. "We used to have some wonderful conversations about all sorts of things. And he knew I was smart. He treated me well."

"So, what was the problem? Sounds like a good deal to me."

"I don't want to spend my life doing this. I want to save some money and live a normal life. But there was no way a physician who knew what I did was going to make an honest woman out of me. But

he was obsessed, all the same. He was the reason I left the West End brothel and came to this cesspit. But he followed me here." She shook her head in mock disbelief and took a swig of her gin, draining the glass.

I could feel the logic draining out of my brain. My father, it would appear, had replaced my mother with a prostitute who was not much older than I was. And she had rejected him. This realization was insulting, not just to my father but to my poor mother. *Please let me be wrong this time.* I had one more question to ask.

"Does he have a name, this generous man?" I hoped she could not detect the contemptuous tone in my voice.

"Um . . . Let me think . . . Oh, that's right. Gordon Henley."

My blood ran cold. I was in the presence of the reason my father was in the East End. The reason why he had left me in the care of others. The reason why he was dead and I was all alone in the world.

I reverted to my own true self. She needed to know that she was not dealing with street filth.

"There's something I need to confess to you, Mary. You see — my name isn't Sally. It's Isabelle. Does that ring any bells for you?" I hoped that it didn't. The idea that my father would refer to me by name with a slut made me sick to my stomach.

Mary's eyes opened wide and her jaw dropped open in disbelief. "Are you kiddin' me? You ain't Sally? Why would you say you was? And why should Isabelle 'ring bells'? 'Ave ya gone daft?" A mixture of concern and indignation crossed her face.

"Oh, I see. Mr. Gordon Henley didn't mention his daughter's name, did he? I suppose that is a good thing. Clearly, he didn't want to soil her name with the mud of depravity." I was enjoying watching her confusion. I wondered if my father was confused when this harlot took his generosity and threw it in his face. I remained silent, eyeing off my trusty bag of tricks.

Mary started to fidget with her sleeve, a clear indication that she was nervous. "Ya scaring me, Sally. Or Isabelle. Whateva ya name is."

I looked her in the eye, taking great pleasure in her rising discomfort. "My name, Mary, is Isabelle Henley. My father is dead because he was in Whitechapel—to visit with you, as it would appear. I didn't come looking for you. I didn't know you existed. But—here you are."

I held my sanity long enough to watch the color drain from her face. She seemed to sober up in that instant.

"Oh Sal—I mean, Isabelle . . . your father was a lovely man. But I couldn't let myself get involved, don't ya see? What good was that t'anyone? Including ya father. I didn't kill 'im. Didn't know 'e was dead. 'E was lovely, your father."

Her ashen face and the terror reflecting in her eyes when she saw my blade revealed that she knew she was about to die. Did my father have that same look of horror on his face? Or was he spared the flash of silver before his life was extinguished? It may not have been Mary who wielded the knife, but the result was the same.

Mary managed to squeak something about murder, but that was the last thing she ever said.

I don't remember doing any of it. After her pitiful attempt to draw attention to her fate, the next thing I remembered was being dressed in one of her better gowns and thrusting my blood-soaked dress into the fire with the poker. There was no way I could have worn that dress out into the street, even using the excuse that I was a midwife that I planned to use if ever questioned on my way home.

As I looked at the destruction I had inflicted on her body on the bed, I could understand the condition of my clothing. I felt no remorse. Just a sense of satisfaction. Quickly replaced by a sense of loss. I knew I would never write again. The thrill I got from putting pen to paper and my dream of sharing my words with the world could not match my obsession with the adrenaline rush of murder.

Would I murder again? At that moment, I honestly didn't know. But my father had encouraged my ego—and I was good at murder.

To learn more about this author, please visit:
https://storiesofthen.blog/

Stories from the Ink Well

These stories vary in genre but delve into tangible and intangible ideas of love, loss, and the hope of reaching our dreams.

FINDING HAPPY

Finding Happy

Fantasy

A. M. Deese

Prompt: The day I lost my wings.

SHE DOESN'T FALL FROM the sky. Rather, she appears on the ground, staring at the grass between her toes and blinking in confusion. The woman has long hair; if there is a color blacker than ebony or richer than a moonless midnight, then that is its color. It hangs in long braids over her shoulders and down her back, a stark compliment to the rich copper tone of her skin. Maybe she is normally pretty, but now her face is twisted and worried.

She doesn't notice me leaning against the massive trunk of the tree, curling up in its roots. I'd been napping, or rather, trying to nap, before the woman had appeared.

I want to ask if she is an angel, but before the words can form, I catch the woman's attention. She walks toward me. Glides, actually, her long dress rustling in a breeze only she can feel.

"Hello." Her voice is soft and melodious, melted sunshine and ice cream on a hot day. "I need your help."

And I want to help her. I will do anything she wants, really, just to get her to continue talking to me.

She smells wonderful, like strawberries soaked in a summer rain.

"Oh. This must be one of those realms where your kind doesn't speak." She sighs, and I can tell that I have disappointed her, although I don't quite know why. I hurry forward, throwing myself at her feet and begging for her to give me another chance. I will do whatever it takes to make her smile at me again because surely this woman — this magnificent creature — is the thing dreams are made of.

She squats down to my level and pushes at the shaggy fur above my eyes. *"Hey now, don't be sad. We can still be friends. I'll just probably need to find a human . . ."* I stop listening once she starts scratching behind my ears. The sensation is glorious!

After too short a time, the woman stops and stands up. I rise up on all fours beside her, tail wagging.

"What should I call you, boy? Huh? What's your name?"

I think of how much I like to run and how most of my friends know me as the smell you get after you run through the woods and roll in the dirt. But, I'm not sure how to tell her that so I just wag my tail harder. This seems to work.

"My name is Aroha. If you could talk, I would tell you to call me Aro." The corners of her lips turn up in a smile. *"Also, if you could talk, I would ask you to tell me about a certain place. You'd know it if you've been there, and your species is always so susceptible . . ."* She sighs again. *"Basically, I'm looking for a specific place where if you've been there you may have felt . . . well, different. Almost as if there is a charge inside of you or maybe one that makes your fur stand the wrong way."*

Yes, yes! I know this place! I begin to bark, turning in a circle and catching a glimpse of my furry arch nemesis, the bit of fluff growing out of the end of me. I chase it in a few dizzying circles until I remember Aro needs my help. I stop short in front of her, my giant tongue lolling to the side as I pant.

"Truly? You know the place?"

I have made her happy, and this makes me happy, and this is the best day ever and I just want to be with Aro all the time and — ooh, a chipmunk! I love chipmunks. They're so cute and squeaky.

I've never had one, but I bet they're delicious and . . . A sharp whistle snaps my attention, and I look back at Aro. She doesn't seem happy anymore, and I tuck my tail between my legs in apology.

"We don't have time for this. I . . . I haven't even learned my lesson." *When she looks at me, her eyes glisten with water, and I just want to lick her face until she feels better. But, she doesn't seem to want me much closer, so I settle for leaning my weight against her legs. I guess that makes her happy because then she scratches my ears again.*

"You know, they only sent me here because I was selfish. I can hear Malia's voice even now: 'You're too concerned with yourself, Aroha. If you don't learn to love someone else—'" *She cuts herself off with a growl that could rival any of my own. She is silent for several moments before murmuring,* "It was an accident, you know? It wasn't fair for them to banish me here, wherever here is. And to say I can't return until I learn to love someone aside from myself . . . well, that's just ridiculous. I've never heard of such a curse! Loving yourself or getting someone to love you, those are easy. But . . . oh dear. I've bored you with all this talk about me, and now you won't want to take me to the Doorway."

I lick her hand so she knows that would be impossible. She smiles.

"You're such a happy little dog. I think I'll call you Happy."

This makes me wag my tail. Happy is a fine name because happy is how Aro makes me feel. I haven't known her for that long, but already I will do anything for her. Of course I will take her to what she called the Doorway; I'll take her to the ends of the earth if she asks. Aro is my dream come true.

She's waiting for me to lead the way, but I don't bound off like I normally would because I want to remain close to her. We take a shortcut I know, which means we have to cross the street. Aro doesn't bother to wait on the sidewalk like some humans do. She doesn't seem to care about humans at all. Then again, she smells better than any human I've ever known.

People turn to stare at her, some even calling out in an effort to get her attention. They must all find her as beautiful and intoxicating as I do. But, Aro doesn't seem to notice. She seemed happier when we were back on the grass. I don't blame her. I much prefer the soft earth instead of the hard pavement beneath my paws. The park is up ahead, and it used to be my second favorite place in the world, right after that tree I had been napping at earlier. Now it's my third favorite, and the tree is my second, because my favorite place is at Aro's side.

We travel for a bit more in silence, and I don't mind the slow and steady pace Aro sets or the gentle weight of her palm riding on my back. The sun is setting, and the crickets have begun to sing. I love this time of day, but it makes Aro look sad.

She turns to me with a worried smile. "I don't suppose we'll be there soon?"

Because I don't have good news for her, I dip my head in disappointment and let out a soft whine.

"Don't fret, my friend. This human body grows tired and is in need of rest anyway. If I'm to have any chance of accessing my magic and getting back home, I'll need to be at my best before I reach the Doorway. Do you know of a safe place to sleep?"

I think of my tree and the morning nap that had been interrupted by my beauty and I shake my head. No, that is too far, and we are already almost halfway to the special place. Instead, I lead her to an overrun courtyard. It smells like cat urine and rotten oak — safe smells — and my Aro smiles in gratitude when I guide her to a weathered stump.

"Thank you, Happy." She sighs. "Malia, if you're watching this, I hope you're amused." Aro sounds upset despite her words. Although I'm confused, I don't dwell on it. I'm just happy to be spending the night huddling against Aro's warmth. It's better than my lonely tree trunk any day.

"I don't think I'm so selfish, really." Her voice is a soft whisper in the moonlight. "Most of us don't like the humans. I only did what we all . . . no. Who am I kidding? It was wrong. I was wrong."

I wonder about the wrongs she speaks of because my lady is flawless. She doesn't say more, and I am content to simply be with her. I snuggle as close as I can. Aro sighs softly, her breath warm against my fur.

WHEN I AWAKE, THERE is a bad smell in the air. My fur stands on end and a low growl escapes between my clenched fangs. Someone is out there.

I see nothing in the darkness, no movement except for the steady rise and fall of Aro's chest. But I know I haven't imagined the sensation. I stand up, sniffing at the air.

There.

A frightening, feral thing. His eyes glow yellow in the darkness. I lunge forward, snarling and defending what's mine.

Aro awakens with a scream, and I bark at her wildly, warning her to stay back as I once again attack the other, larger dog's legs. His is an ancient breed, unchanged throughout all these generations. He towers over me, howling for his brothers to join him.

I let out another frustrated growl of my own. He will not win tonight. He sprints forward, trying to get past me, to get to Aro, but I don't allow him. I tackle him from the side. The beast grunts in pain then turns back with an agility I can't fathom. His vicious teeth sink with ease into the soft skin of my neck. I want to cry out for Aro to stay away but then she is just there. She wields a large stick as a warrior with a blade and just as quickly the beast departs, frightened by the fierce attack from my lady.

She mends my wounds quickly, and the only sounds are the crickets and the gentle tsk that escapes her lips.

Her fingers are cool and tender on my skin. I rest.

IN THE MORNING, *I catch her watching me with a serious expression. She smiles when she notices I am awake. I bounce to my feet, a bit too eagerly perhaps. Oh, I ache. But, I don't want my lady to think less of me, so I greet her and the day with a wagging tail.*

We don't have long on our journey. To please my lady, I hurry us along. It is important to my Aro, and so it is important to me. A part of me knows that reaching our destination will mean that my lady plans to leave me, to go back to whatever mythical land she comes from. Yet that same part of me hopes that, if she can't be persuaded to stay, then perhaps she can be persuaded to take me with her.

We continue at our brisk pace for nearly an hour. Already I can feel the strange pull that comes from that magical place in the park. My fur stands on end and there is a delicious spark to the air. I wonder if she feels it, too. Cats can feel it, but I'm not surprised she didn't go to one of their kind. Shifty little creatures.

"I used to have wings," she says suddenly, and I stop at the sound of her beautiful voice. She seems to be far away as she continues, eyes half-closed. "Just yesterday. Things are so different here, you know? The air, the way everything feels." She gestures around her. "I feel different here." She snorts. "I suppose that's why Malia sent me here to find someone to love besides myself. Well, won't she be surprised when I come back home on my own. You see, she doesn't know that I know where the Doorways are . . . or rather, the fact that I know your kind knows how to find them." She looks down at me with another one of her beautiful smiles and pats my head. "Of course, she didn't think I would luck out and find the smartest of your species on my first try, now did she?"

I pant in appreciation, and she laughs. "Thanks, Happy. I hope it's not much farther."

It isn't, but her comment still urges me to hurry down across the street to get to the park. I want so badly to get her back home that I don't even stop and chase the chipmunk, even though it runs right in front of me. There will be time for chipmunks later. Now is the time to hurry and make my Aro proud. I push myself harder. Aro runs after me now. We are almost there, and she will be so proud of me. I ignore her calling for me to slow down. Slow down? I love running almost as much as I love Aro, and we are almost there.

I run, faster and faster. I run straight into one of the giant steel boxes the humans chase each other in.

There is a terrible squealing and the delightful smell of burning rubber.

Such pain. Everything hurts, I can barely open my eyes, and worse, so much worse, I have made my lady unhappy.

"No, no, Happy, no!"

Aro wails beside me, her hand feather-light as it cups my face. I want so badly to lick the tears off her face, to make her happy again, but it is too hard to move. I can't even wag my tail.

"Happy, don't go. I—"

I blink against the blinding light.

"Wasn't there a lady with that lab?" The new voice—a man's— seems to come from far away. His footsteps echo strangely on the pavement as he comes toward me.

"Yeah, just a second ago. Where did she go?" Another voice. My body feels heavy.

I close my eyes.

Aro? I can smell her.

"Falling in love with someone else broke the curse and sent me back home. Happy . . . I love you. Come home to me."

It is her! My Aro, she is all around me and I can tell she is happy again. I wag my tail.

To learn more about this author, please visit:
https://amdeese.com/

Talk to Me

Women's Fiction

Ekta R. Garg

Prompt: In your rush to get off one flight and catch the next one, you grab the wrong carry-on. You don't discover this until later, and one item in there changes your life.

CONFESSION: I'M THE REASON Jenna almost missed her flight that day.

I wanted to shake her up. It didn't matter whether she missed the flight or caught it. I wanted Jenna to take the opportunity to step back and breathe. She hasn't drawn a deep breath since the funeral.

Even though I'm new here, I made several special requests. I asked You-Know-Who to let a hiccup interrupt Jenna's plans. Maybe it would make her stop and think — really think — about what she needed to do.

She did, finally, after that flight. But even I couldn't have predicted what happened next. To understand it, though, you have to know what Jenna was like before.

* * *

Six months earlier
Carnegie Hall, New York City

In August on a Sunday night

JENNA LISTENED AS APPLAUSE roared around her.

Through the years she'd heard audiences express their appreciation, but now she understood why people spoke in awe about Carnegie Hall. Its history gave concertgoers the luxury of assumptions. The performers almost always delivered. Then came the applause.

She stood and clapped with everyone else and watched as her older sister, Madeline, took her bows then kissed her fingers and spread her arms wide. Just behind her sister stood a grand piano, its elongated dark body gleaming with pride after participating in the last three-and-a-half hours of another page in the Hall's history.

The thunderous standing ovation continued along with calls of "Encore!" Jenna knew Madeline wouldn't oblige. She'd already indulged the audience with two short pieces; she never engaged in a third.

Not good for the arm muscles, Jenna remembered Madeline saying years ago. *My body is as much the instrument as the piano is, and I don't want to over-tire it. It would affect my next performance.*

No one heard the sigh that escaped Jenna's lips now.

If people gave me this much attention, I'd play until my arms fell off.

Her other sister, Elizabeth, came back to the empty seat on Jenna's right and rolled her eyes.

"I told the hospital no calls about anything non-urgent. Why do I have to be carrying my pager on the day when half the nurses don't understand what 'non-urgent' means?"

Jenna shook her head, more out of habit than sympathy, and turned her attention forward again. A man in a suit crossed the stage with a bouquet of roses, which Madeline accepted with a hand on her heart and a bow in his direction. He returned her bow and clapped, which made the audience clap harder.

Elizabeth leaned toward Jenna. "She finally made it to Carnegie. Can you believe it, Jen?"

This time Jenna added a half smile to the head shake and kept clapping. Then she listened, hard, like always. Audiences across the world had felicitated her sister, appreciating the talent and nuance Madeline brought to the music by the masters, but they couldn't applaud forever. The sound would start to decrease, first in intensity, then in volume. A few concertgoers would turn around to retrieve programs and fallen purses and scarves. The diehard enthusiasts would keep clapping, but even they would stop.

She liked that time the best—when the applause ended. Jenna had never told anyone this, because, of course, the younger sister of two accomplished older sisters always supported them, and she would never want anyone to assume she resented her siblings. Jenna had clapped as loud as anyone else at concerts and graduations and awards functions. But she liked the quiet that came after the applause the best.

That silence meant that, for a little while, they were all the same.

* * *

THE CELEBRATORY DINNER WENT late, as usual. Jenna sat at the end of a long table full of people who had rearranged their lives to attend Madeline's debut at Carnegie. Her mother and father sat at the far end with Madeline who blushed and dipped her head in appreciation for those who praised her. Jenna listened to the compliments and observed, once again, Madeline's humility. Her sister had none of the diva-like attitude so many other concert musicians displayed; instead, all the adulation got funneled back into Madeline's music.

Elizabeth left the table four times that night to answer calls to her pager. Each time she returned, the conversation stopped swirling around Madeline and curled around Elizabeth's work as the head of the department of medicine at the Ivy League school she had bestowed with her presence. Jenna remembered how Elizabeth agonized over the decision of where to work; if she chose one university, would her potential to change patients' lives be diminished by declining the others?

Jenna got up twice, once to use the bathroom and the second time when she dropped her fork. She tried flagging down the waiter about the fork, but none of the waitstaff saw her raised hand. She went to the host station, where she startled the man on duty when she requested clean silverware. Her presence surprised him.

She didn't mind, though. Jenna had long ago accepted her position as the afterthought. Often, during her childhood, her mother would introduce Madeline and Elizabeth with a verbal resume.

"This is my oldest daughter, Madeline. She won the prestigious Campbell award when she was ten years old, although we've never forced her in her music. If that's what makes her happy, that's what her father and I support her in. And this is my daughter, Elizabeth. She's known since she was six that she wanted to be a doctor. She actually skipped a year of college because of all the summer school she did. What's the rush, we'd ask her, and she'd always say, 'The faster I finish school, the faster I can start taking care of people.'

"Oh, and this is our youngest, Jenna."

And the introduction would end. Jenna never felt neglected or unloved. She just wanted to be remembered.

* * *

JENNA OVERSLEPT THE NEXT morning. Her humble finances meant she couldn't stay in the swanky hotel in the city with the family, and she didn't want to embarrass them with her lack of funds. She stayed near the airport instead.

No, you don't need to see me off, she told them. I'll manage.

She almost missed the flight altogether and raced through the terminal, only to discover the plane had been delayed due to a technical issue. When she'd checked on her phone, it hadn't bothered to inform her of the delay. Maybe it, too, had forgotten its duty to her.

Jenna paced in front of the gate. She had to make it back to Illinois on time; she couldn't miss her shift at work that evening. Only people who worked the shifts got paid for them, and Jenna needed the money.

The full flight from New York left an hour late, and when it landed in Chicago, Jenna, in the window seat, asked her seatmate if she could exit first. The bus to Champaign would leave in twenty minutes, and she had to catch it. The understanding older woman waved her on, and Jenna scrambled into the aisle. She popped open the overhead bin four seats down from her own, grabbed her carry-on and yanked it out, then scurried off the plane to the bus terminal.

The engine of the vehicle rumbled as she shoved her carry-on into the luggage compartment inside its belly. She ignored the acrid odor of the exhaust fumes as she trotted to the door of the bus, which hissed closed right behind her. Only then did Jenna allow herself to sigh in relief.

* * *

FOR ONCE THE UBER came on time, and Jenna asked him to drive as fast as he could. She tossed a quick thank you over her shoulder when they arrived at her apartment, pulled her suitcase out of the trunk, and trotted into the building. Leaving the carry-on in her small living room, she went to her bedroom to change for work: tennis shoes, khaki pants, and a plain black-collared T-shirt. A simple watch, small hoop earrings, and her hair pulled into a low ponytail.

She didn't bother with makeup; Jenna never did.

Taking huge bites out of a granola bar she'd snagged from her tiny pantry, she arrived at the grocery store just in time for her shift. Jenna power walked to the staff break room, empty for now, and chose a locker on the far wall for her purse and keys. After securing the lock, she went to the table in the opposite corner, signed in for the day, and picked up the clipboard with the day's assignments.

Register six. Okay. At least it's not the self-checkout lanes. Honestly, people can work their smartphones but they can't use a scanner.

Jenna went to the register on six, punched in the code that signed her into the store's system, and balanced her drawer. She made a note in the computer of the amount of cash at the start of her shift then flipped on her light and waited. Within minutes, a customer brought a cart laden with items from the garden section: two green hoses rolled into serpentine coils, a trowel, a small shovel, two thick pads to protect the knees while kneeling, and several packets of seeds. With schools reopening that week, summer merchandise sat ripe for the picking.

That transaction ended and the next one began, then the next one and the next. For six hours, Jenna punched in coupon codes, reminded people to insert their chip cards instead of swiping them, and bagged groceries. She didn't pay attention to her aching feet or her scratchy eyes; ignoring both had become as much a part of the routine as the tasks she performed. They didn't require a brain surgeon; she would know. When Elizabeth answered her pager, it sounded much more complicated than convincing a computer to accept the correct code for a double-discounted bottle of nail polish.

After work Jenna drove home. She'd bought vegetables from the store and made herself a simple salad for dinner. With the salad bowl in hand, she went to the living room and settled in front of the TV. After several bites and the start of a commercial, her attention went to the carry-on.

Ugh, now I have to empty it out. I wonder how long I can put it off . . . but I do need my toothbrush at some point. And those black pants. I could wear them on Thursday. And I should take out the dress.

The dress. The black one she'd worn to the funeral fifteen months earlier. The same dress she'd worn to Madeline's concert. When her mother texted her the details about the performance, Jenna considered buying a new dress. Then she reconsidered. Why bother?

Jenna's gaze remained on the carry-on. Now that she had a few minutes to focus on it, the color seemed wrong. The height, too. She put her bowl on the coffee table and went to the little suitcase. Unzipping the outer pocket, she put her hand inside and swiped it back and forth, searching for the large oversized luggage tag in the shape of a comical-looking owl. Nothing.

Ben had given her that tag. He used to say he loved how she looked first thing in the morning when she'd put on her glasses to help her navigate a world that looked fuzzy without them. She wore contacts now, but she couldn't bring herself to get rid of the tag. He'd given it to her. He. Ben. Had given it to her.

She laid the carry-on flat on its back. Her hands shook as she unzipped the suitcase and saw items she didn't recognize. A designer toiletries case, two pairs of pinstripe pants, and four smart blouses in various pastel shades. A large manila envelope containing sketches of a building. A jewelry case holding a high-end brand-name watch, a string of rice pearls, and a ring with an oversized blue stone. The color reminded Jenna of the domed churches in Santorini.

Where's my stuff? I need my pants for work. And my luggage tag. And my toothbrush!

Her heart started to race, and her lower lip trembled. She couldn't believe she wanted to cry over a suitcase. She could replace everything in it with an hour-long trip to Target. She could even replace the luggage tag.

She couldn't replace the way it identified her as belonging to Ben, though.

Before she became hysterical, Jenna whirled around and headed to the bathroom. It was Monday anyway, her thinking day. The TV called to her, but she ignored it while she filled the large tub with water as hot as it could get. Under the gush of the tap, she dropped Epsom salts and a bath bomb. When the tub filled, she left her clothes on the floor and eased herself inch by downward inch into the steaming water. A sigh escaped her lips, of relief and release.

After ten minutes, Jenna made herself think about the suitcase again.

The hot water had done its job. She no longer wanted to bawl at the thought of losing Ben's tag. What could she do to get it back?

Maybe the airline would know.

She grinned in embarrassment. Of course the airline would know. They would have suggestions, too, on what to do with the carry-on that had arrived with her.

As long as they don't think I stole it. Maybe I can just contact the owner directly. Those sketches had a letterhead. Was there a phone number? I'll have to check. I wonder if that person lives in New York.

New York. In her mind she sifted through memories of the city. End-of-term concerts for Madeline at the conservatory. Visiting Elizabeth as she spent summers doing medical research. Jenna had traveled with her family to the Big Apple almost every summer throughout her teen years.

Ben talked about moving to New York. Jenna would have more prospects to pursue a serious interior design career there, he said. Maybe he'd switch careers, leave science behind to join Wall Street, and they would become NYC's next power couple. She could still hear the way he laughed at that.

Ben.

Jenna squeezed her eyes shut and plunged. She didn't care how the water splashed out of the tub or that she'd have to mop up the puddles. She just wanted to hold her breath until the tightness in her chest eased. On most Mondays, it didn't.

She heard her own heart beating and thought about what it might be like to listen until it slowed down. How long would it take someone to find her? Would Elizabeth assess her condition post-mortem? Would Madeline play a concert in her honor? Would she get to see Ben again?

There it was, that lack of oxygen and her body's instinct to fight against the ultimate threat. She pushed herself above the surface of the water and coughed hard. This was why she only allowed herself to think once a week.

She got out of the tub and dried herself off, then cleaned the floor. The TV still called for her attention like a puppy eager to please its master. Jenna put on her pajamas, pulled up her electronic boarding pass on her phone, and called the airline. Within minutes, a pleasant young woman confirmed that due to security reasons, any bags left on the plane would have been offloaded at the arrival airport. She couldn't help Jenna with anything more than the direct phone number of the lost-and-found department at Chicago's O'Hare International Airport.

"You'll have to wait until the morning," the representative said. "They close at 5 p.m."

Jenna glanced at the oversized clock on the wall above the TV that told her it was now just past ten; her heart sank as she ended the call.

What if my roll-on isn't there? What if someone else grabbed mine like I grabbed . . . What's the person's name?

She went back to the suitcase and took out the sketches.

Amelia Montgomery, CEO, Founder, Juliet's Balcony, Architecture and Design. Juliet's Balcony? Really?

She dropped the manila envelope next to her on the sofa, grabbed her phone again, tapped the screen, and found the website for the company. Images appeared of grand buildings with dramatic arched windows and austere columns. Jenna didn't care for the color palettes used inside some of the buildings, and she cringed at a hideous statue that she would never have chosen. Still, one thing made sense: Juliet's Balcony, as frivolous as the name sounded, had done some impressive projects around New York and in other cities around the world. Amelia Montgomery was an important person, it seemed.

And I just swiped her suitcase from the plane. Oh, crap!

Jenna navigated to the keypad and began jabbing at it as fast as her pruny fingers would allow, her eyes darting from the letterhead to the screen as she dialed. She jiggled her leg through the ringing and then the robotic voice mail assistant. Stumbling through her name and the fact that she'd picked up the roll-on by mistake, she asked for Amelia to call back. Before she made it to the kitchen with her dinner dishes, her phone rang and she came back to it.

"Jenna Carpenter? This is Richard. I'm Ms. Montgomery's executive assistant."

His voice, as smooth as a newly shaven face, slid right past her half-spoken response.

"Ms. Montgomery is currently in Chicago, but if you'll hold I'll get her on the line."

Classical music played through the phone, and Jenna picked up the TV remote to mute the sound. A few more minutes went by, and she took her dishes to the kitchen, then came back to the living room. Her fingers had begun drumming a random rhythm on her leg when the classical music stopped playing.

"This is Amelia Montgomery," a voice said in a crisp British accent. Jenna sat up straight on the sofa even though no one could see her. The woman's tone demanded people's attention.

Jenna introduced herself, but before she could get any further than that, Amelia interrupted.

"My god, love, you gave us a fright."

Jenna frowned. Us?

"When I discovered that my carry-all had gone missing, I gave the flight crew a good telling off. Of course, it did me no good. They told me I would have to wait for the person who took it to contact them or me or something. I called Michigan Avenue today and ordered new clothes, but they can't very well replace my sketches, now, can they?"

Jenna murmured she didn't think Michigan Avenue—As if the entire street works for her!—could.

"What's that?"

She repeated herself.

"Now, come on, love, if you're going to make yourself heard, then speak up!"

She tried a third time, and Amelia clucked her tongue.

"Are you ill? Doesn't matter. Where are you?"

Jenna informed Amelia of Champaign's two-hour proximity to the city.

"Well, bring the sketches to me, and this will all be sorted then," Amelia said. "I need them for a client meeting at lunch tomorrow."

Jenna's mouth dropped open. What the . . . Is she serious! I took off the entire weekend to go to New York. And I still have no idea where my own suitcase is!

She tried to voice an objection, but Amelia kept talking.

"Richard will send you the details of where to come. My meeting's at half past noon, mind, so I need the sketches by then."

Before Jenna could protest, complain, or even breathe, the classical music returned.

But — but — did she — I can't —

Jenna gulped a few times, trying to get her pounding heart to slow down. Had she wanted, she could have kept Amelia's carry-on and no one would have ever known. Maybe she should have.

That would have taught her a lesson. Going on and on about her sketches. What about my owl?

When she tried to gulp again, a burning sensation in her throat stopped her. The owl. Ben. Oh, how she missed him.

Several minutes later, Richard's smooth voice filled her ear.

"Ms. Montgomery is staying on Michigan Avenue," he said. "Will you require transportation to get there?"

Tears ran down Jenna's face, and she swiped the screen to end the call.

She leaned into the sofa, letting her head rest back. Her phone rang, but she didn't answer. It stopped after several rings, and a little chirp told her she had a voice mail. Jenna ignored it. Right now, she didn't want to talk to anyone.

* * *

THE NEXT DAY JENNA'S shift started at 9 a.m., but she woke before seven.

Ben's gone.

Every morning the same phrase wrung her heart and dripped the acid of the memory into her chest. She spent the next ten minutes, as she did every morning, rubbing small circles on her skin just below her left collarbone. Ben used to wake her up like that every day, and she'd kept doing it to convince herself to get out of bed.

She brushed her teeth with the temporary toothbrush she'd found under the sink, padded into the kitchen for coffee, and took the steaming mug back to the living room. Her eye caught the sketches again, and she pulled them toward her. Instead of reading the pages, however, she just held them in her lap. After several minutes, Jenna came to an important conclusion. Amelia Montgomery was crazy.

She's a control freak! And Richard. Mr. Executive Assistant. Who in their right mind would work for someone like her? I wonder if they're related. Like, she could have married into the business and he could be some slacker stepson totally screwing with her life and her clients. Or he could be a serial killer.

Not that Jenna had vast experience with either serial killers or slacker stepsons, so she couldn't draw a fair comparison. Plus, something about the settled reassurance in Richard's voice told her so much more than his words did. Still. Amelia's deadline made her nervous. And, on a more practical level, she did need to return Amelia's suitcase and get her own back.

Seeing Ben's tag would more than make up for all the craziness this woman exhibited.

Guess I better call lost and found. And I should probably check the voice mail from last night.

Her heart twinged again, this time with guilt. Amelia Montgomery may have been a dragon lady, but even she didn't deserve to lose her personal belongings. Especially that ring.

I wonder if someone gave it to her as a gift.

She heaved a huge sigh and dialed the airport.

"I need a few minutes to look for it," the airport agent said. "I just got here, and the lost and found isn't a little box in a closet. And you said you didn't put a luggage tag on it?"

Jenna confirmed that she hadn't attached one onto the bag itself. After a moment, and with great reluctance, she told the agent about the owl. Sharing the information somehow made Ben feel that much more gone.

"Do you want to wait while I look or call back?" the agent asked.

Reassuring the agent she had time to wait, Jenna curled her feet under her and took a sip of the coffee that had now become lukewarm.

Please let it be there, she entreated whatever superior power might deign to listen. Let Ben be there. That's all I have left of him.

The agent came back on the line. "Well, son of a gun, I found it."

Jenna's heart soared.

"Now, all you need to do is come to the airport with your photo ID, provide us a detailed list of the items in the carry-on, and give us your contact information, and you can take it home."

After working her mouth a few times to try to speak, Jenna finally managed to eke out a humble request for the airport to ship the suitcase to her. She would pay for it, she added. As the agent began speaking, Jenna could practically see her shaking her head.

"Sorry, hun, but airport security won't allow it. If you want your carry-on back, you're going to have to claim it in person in the next forty-eight hours, otherwise TSA has to confiscate the item."

Her heart crash landed. She explained that she lived in Champaign. It would take her a day or two to sort out her schedule, she said. The woman reminded her about the forty-eight-hour deadline and told her to have a nice day.

Have a nice day, sure, Jenna thought as she navigated on the phone to her voice mail app. *Ben's owl is in Chicago, and I have to tell the dragon lady's assistant that her meeting today's going to be ruined. Oh, and I still have to talk to Matt about taking a day off even though I just took two days off. Yeah, sounds like a fantastic day to me.*

She listened to Richard's polite request to call her back so they could work out the details of the return of Amelia's suitcase, and she grimaced. Guilt made her finger hover over the keypad, but instead she dialed her boss's number.

"Hi, this is Matt. I'm either on the phone or in the store. Leave — "

Jenna hung up. No sense in leaving a message when she would see him in a little while. She took her coffee cup to the sink and dumped out what was left.

Might as well go in. Maybe Matt will give me the day off after all . . . ?

She doubted it, but the optimism — a welcome friend after so many months of feeling its polar opposite — energized her just a little bit.

* * *

JENNA ARRIVED AT THE store almost a full hour before her shift and went straight to Matt's office.

"Can I help you?" he asked, looking up from his desk.

She took a moment to look around the windowless space just large enough for a beige filing cabinet and the desk. She wondered today, as she did every time she went to see him, whether he used the cabinet. Maybe Matt's predecessor had left it. Either way, it added nothing to the room. She wished she could suggest a few changes. Even a coat of paint would make a difference.

"Janelle? No, Jennifer. Jenna. Sorry," Matt said, brushing his shaggy hair out of his face. "What can I do for you? Did we have a meeting?"

He gestured to the creaky chair with faded faux leather in an unnatural green color on the seat. Jenna sat, folded her hands in her lap, and explained her dilemma with the carry-on suitcases and the crazy woman who expected her to dash up to Chicago as if she were crossing the street. Matt dropped his pen on top of a paper with old coffee rings on it.

"Look, Jenna, I get it, really, but I can't let you out today. It wouldn't be fair to everyone else who let me know in advance about the days off they need. And you did just get the weekend."

She looked down at her hands and examined her nails.

"Okay," Matt said through a sigh, "um, how about if you head out to the city tomorrow, get your stuff back, and then you make up for it by working through this coming weekend?"

She reaffirmed in a soft voice her commitment to the store and her gratitude for Matt's understanding.

"It's fine," he said, waving a hand in the air. "Happy to help where I can. You're a good worker. If I could just clone you, it would make my life so much easier."

He laughed, and Jenna smiled to make him think she agreed.

She thought of Ben then. Of how he would urge her to think beyond the borders of their small town. They'd fought about moving, and the more they fought the more determined Ben became. He didn't buy her argument—excuses, he would call them—that ordinary women like Jenna didn't belong in a large city, that she and those women were all the same. Madeline and Elizabeth and others suited those places more than she ever would, she would say.

"You've got talent, Jen, and you're just afraid of it! You're letting your sisters keep you down because if you went out and did something, maybe for once you'd be more important than them and then maybe your whole family would have to pay attention to you and you'd have to live up to that attention!"

She didn't need to do it, she wanted to say every time. He made her special. He made her stand out.

He fought on her behalf with the family, and, sometimes, with her. On that last night, he'd come home just as she put the finishing touches on their new living room. She still remembered how he gaped for a full five minutes at the transformation. When he started talking, the conversation began as an enthusiastic exhortation of her talents; it ended, again, in a fight.

"We need to do this, Jenna. I'm sick and tired of you being afraid all the time. We need to move. For yourself and for us."

She never got to find out what or why or how or even where they would go. That night, after stating in a flat voice that he needed to work on some experiments on campus, he slammed the door to the house. Then the lab exploded and set Jenna's world on fire. She'd tried to breathe normally since then and couldn't.

"Jenna? Jenna?"

She thanked Matt again for giving her the next day off and left his office.

* * *

WITH ABOUT FORTY-FIVE MINUTES left before the start of her shift, Jenna went out to the car to call Richard. He answered on the second ring. This morning, however, he didn't sound quite as genial as the previous night.

"Ms. Carpenter, you've put Ms. Montgomery in a terrible position," he said. "Those sketches were the focal piece of her client luncheon today."

Jenna apologized while trying to hide her irritation.

She's not the only one with a life!

". . . called last night and didn't hear from you, I had to call her back and then listen to her tear into me. Do you understand what that's like at the end of a long day? And on a Monday! I know this is just a big mistake, but Ms. Montgomery needs her suitcase today.

Without exception. I'll have a courier come pick it up. What's your address?"

Jenna gave him the address then waited as she heard the clacking of computer keys through the phone.

"Someone will be there within ten minutes," Richard said.

She glanced at her watch. If she raced home now, she could be back in time to start work and no one would be the wiser. She agreed and ended the call then slammed shut the driver's side door and started the car.

Despite her best intentions, two red lights delayed Jenna's progress. When she reached her apartment complex, she managed to take up two spaces in the lot and ran to her building. There she saw a vehicle idling in the parking spot nearest the entrance. A large magnet on the side of the car advertised speedy courier deliveries. With a wave at the driver, she knocked on his window and told him she'd be right back out with the roll-on.

Jenna doubled her efforts at running into her building and thanked her lucky stars for a first-floor apartment. She fumbled with the keys and dropped them then snatched them from the ground and unlocked her front door. Her breath came in spurts and a stitch had begun in her side as she dashed down the short hallway and grabbed the suitcase. Retracing her steps, she yanked the door shut behind her and gave the doorknob a solid twist to make sure she had locked it.

She raced back to the courier driver and apologized three times as he yawned and handed her a clipboard to sign. Jenna scribbled something on the line he indicated, threw the suitcase into the trunk, and slammed it shut. The driver gave her a dirty look, but Jenna didn't respond as she ran back to her own car, hopped in, and drove back to work. This time the lights favored her, and she pulled into the store's parking lot with five minutes to spare.

She allowed herself a few gasping breaths before grabbing her purse and heading inside.

* * *

THREE HOURS LATER, IN the middle of navigating the computer system for the correct code for taro root, Jenna's phone vibrated in her pocket.

She ignored it the first time. Matt wasn't a slave driver, but he didn't like his employees spending work time on personal calls. The caller probably just wanted to try to convince her to contribute to the life-saving treatment for a crown prince in exchange for nine million dollars in personal wealth.

The phone kept vibrating, however, and after several minutes Jenna flipped off her light and pulled the device out of her pocket. Five missed calls from a New York number. Richard.

She dialed the number, and this time the first ring didn't get a chance to finish before he answered.

"Where the hell are Ms. Montgomery's sketches?"

The sketches. They were in Amelia's suitcase . . . weren't they?

In her mind she relived the memory of the previous night. She remembered pulling the sheaf of papers out of the manila envelope, glancing at the letterhead, and doing a search on Amelia. Next came the memory of calling Amelia's office and the revelation that she would have to return to Chicago for her owl. The tears, getting into bed, getting out of bed this morning, the race back to the apartment—

Jenna clapped a hand to her mouth. She'd dropped the sketches on the sofa. Her voice trembled as she explained to Richard that she'd used them to find out the identity of the owner of the suitcase and must have forgotten to put them back.

"How the hell is Ms. Montgomery supposed to do her presentation now?" he demanded.

She gulped but didn't answer. She couldn't. She stammered her way through an apology, but Richard didn't let her finish.

"This throws off Ms. Montgomery's whole itinerary! She left New York yesterday for a weeklong trip that was supposed to include four cities, all of them for new business clients. Do you understand what you've done?"

Jenna's mind tripped over the sequence of events. How could she make this better? She'd caused Amelia to lose her bag in the first place.

In a flash of inspiration, she explained the one-day allowance Matt had given her to retrieve her own bag from the airport. Maybe, she said, she could deliver Amelia's sketches herself. Amelia would have to wait a day, but at least she would get them back.

"That's the least you can do!" Richard thundered. "How early can you make it to Chicago tomorrow morning?"

Jenna pleaded for a few moments of his patience. She pulled the phone from her ear and navigated to Amtrak's website. After a few swipes, she confirmed for Richard that she would be on the first train out of Champaign the next morning at 6 a.m.

"I'm going to hold you to it, Ms. Carpenter," he said. With that he hung up.

Jenna squeezed her eyes shut to keep all her emotions inside of them and stood that way for several moments, then swallowed hard, opened her eyes, and flipped on the light for her register.

* * *

IN THE EARLY MORNING hours, Jenna boarded a train with the few other passengers brave enough to wake up before dawn. She put the manila envelope with Amelia's sketches on the empty seat next to her and smoothed an invisible wrinkle from her black dress pants. After she'd gotten home the previous night, Jenna had done more digging online. Her respect had grown, albeit begrudgingly, for Amelia and all she'd accomplished during her fifteen-year career in the States.

I guess, when you've done all that, you can stand to show people your fangs, she thought now. *She probably won't even say thank you, just grab the sketches and be on her way.*

The thought of the notorious sketches made Jenna curious. She took them out of the envelope. They'd caused so much trouble for her that it probably wouldn't hurt to take a peek before she had to relinquish them to Amelia.

Okay, dragon lady, let's see what you've got in store for this "important client."

Jenna studied the preliminary plans for what looked like a twelve-story office building. Amelia had included enough details to pique her client's interest. She saw a few of Amelia's signature touches: quoins at the corners of the four exterior walls, jack arches in contrasting color bricks, and a pediment that topped off the building in a classical style.

I'm so glad she didn't want to put a Juliet balcony in there, Jenna thought with a chuckle. That would have been so stupid. I wonder if she's put any thought into what she wants to do inside . . .

The notes, however, made no mention of the interior. As Jenna stared at the pages, her mind began to whir with ideas. She recalled sitting in her first design class in the Milwaukee Institute of Art and Design where she'd found her passion.

She took out a pen and pulled out one of the blank sheets of paper from the envelope. After scrutinizing the sketches once more, she began making notes: color palettes, furniture placement, window treatments. The more she wrote, the more her years at MIAD became fresh in her mind—how her best friend, Heather, introduced her to Ben, visiting from Madison for the weekend. His persistent, patient courting, not voicing a single complaint as he followed her to office buildings and old theaters so she could stand in their lobbies and study their design choices without saying a word to him. He would listen as she babbled on and on about the work in her classes and celebrated every assignment, big or small, that came back with glowing remarks.

The thrill of it all returned now along with that distinct feeling that every recommendation she made would elevate the building, even in concept. The more she wrote, the more she realized Ben had been right all along. She needed to find a way to use her zeal and talent for more than loading printer tape into the cash register.

"Attention, passengers. We'll be arriving at Union Station in Chicago in a few minutes. Please make sure to take your belongings . . ."

Jenna looked up and blinked a few times, her brain readjusting to the high-rises and asphalt that had replaced the acres and acres of corn and soy fields. She tucked Amelia's sketches into the envelope just as the train pulled into Union Station, and she secured her purse strap on her shoulder. Within minutes she exited the train and joined the throngs of morning commuters and tourists scurrying to their destinations.

As soon as she left the station and reached the street level, Jenna spotted a taxi waiting at its requisite stand at the corner. She hurried to it and asked the driver to take her to the Sofitel Hotel on Michigan Avenue. As the driver navigated the traffic, Jenna gazed at the tall buildings around her. Their names sparked more memories, some from her years at MIAD and learning about the design significances they represented. Some from visits with Ben and the way they'd laughed together and loved one another through these same streets.

Just then the driver guided the taxi into the driveway of the Sofitel. Jenna paid him in exact change, gripped the manila envelope hard, and trotted inside the magnificent lobby with its warm cherry tones and black marble floors set in a diamond pattern. Some of the diamonds showed smaller diamonds in the center that lit up, which echoed a theme of little points of starlight placed throughout the space with thought and care.

Jenna didn't know where to look first, but she understood why Amelia chose this hotel. It showed class and tradition while offering little pops of whimsy like sprays of flowers bursting out of extra-tall vases. For the first time in more than a year, Jenna had the urge to sit and observe like she used to do when Ben would accompany her.

Jenna's breath caught then. She thought of Ben, always, without fail, even in her dreams, but this week she'd also thought about herself. Her heart swelled but not with grief.

Movement caught her attention, and she turned toward a tall figure coming her way.

Is that her?

The ruffled blouse gave it away. This time Amelia had paired it with a navy pencil skirt and stiletto heels with straps that snaked around her ankles. The shoes didn't deter Amelia's progress as she approached Jenna at a fast clip.

When she got closer, Jenna could see the tension easing in Amelia's blue eyes. Face to face, she didn't look quite so much like a dragon. More like a high-powered executive used to making things happen.

"Bloody hell, you know how to make a mess of things, don't you, love?" Amelia said as she held out a hand. "Amelia Montgomery. Have you got it there then?"

Jenna shook Amelia's hand and dropped the manila envelope. She and Amelia both bent to retrieve it. Amelia reached it first.

"I nearly sacked Richard for making me postpone the meeting," Amelia said, pulling out the sketches, "but he knows how to reason with me, I suppose. Hang on, what's this?"

She'd reached the pages with Jenna's notes and skimmed the paper then looked at Jenna again, her eyes narrowing.

"You do understand this is proprietary material. You weren't even supposed to open the envelope."

Jenna shook her head hard and fast, reassuring Amelia with a barrage of words that she would never dream of stealing anything. She started to explain about her own design background, but Amelia rolled her eyes. Then she glanced at her watch.

"Sorry, love, I can't make time for your doodles. Doesn't matter, really—"

"Yes, it does," Jenna said. Her own eyes widened. When was the last time she'd heard her own voice at that volume?

"What's that?" Amelia asked.

"I said, it *does* matter," Jenna repeated. Her heart started to pound. "I matter."

Amelia held out a hand, a clear dismissal. "Thank you for bringing the sketches. Have a lovely day."

Jenna took the hand and shook it. Before she could say another word, Amelia left. She took a long minute to stare in the direction Amelia had gone then went to a bench in the lobby and sat down.

Am I going to be standing at a cash register for the rest of my life? What about everything else? What about Ben?

She looked around the lobby again, considering the furniture, its lines and the colors. Would she have chosen these same sofas and club chairs for this space? She wavered in the decision, allowing herself to enjoy it for the first time in months.

"All right, Ben," she said aloud. "You win."

She hurried out and hailed another taxi.

"To the airport," she told the driver. "It's time to get moving."

* * *

OF COURSE, JENNA DIDN'T just do a total 180 when she got home. She spent a long time thinking about what she wanted. For weeks, she considered the pros and cons of a major move and changing every aspect of her life. I know, because she started talking to me. She couldn't see me, and she didn't know I could hear her, but she talked and I listened. In all the time we were married, I don't think I ever heard her talk so much.

She applied to the Pratt Institute in New York and got in without a hitch, which didn't surprise me. I wanted to throw my arms around her and tell her how much I loved her, how proud I was of her, and how I knew she'd do well. Before she left Champaign, she went to the cemetery.

"So, here I go," she said to my headstone.

Atta girl. You've got this.

"I'm scared, Ben. I'm scared of failing. And I'm scared about what might happen if I actually succeed."

I know. I believe in you anyway.

"All right, well, I don't want to be late for my flight. I love you. And don't worry, you'll keep hearing from me."

I saw the little owl hanging from the strap of her purse, and I couldn't wait for her to talk to me again.

To learn more about this author, please visit:
https://thewriteedge.wordpress.com/

Worlds Away

Women's Fiction

Ekta R. Garg

Prompt: You are lost.

*A*GUST OF WIND SHOVED *Aarti off-balance, and she stumbled sideways three steps. On instinct, she clutched the strap of her purse. Just as she found her footing again, the taxi driver dropped her suitcase next to her on the sidewalk.*

"That'll be thirty-five dollars," he said.

Thirty-five dollars, Aarti repeated to herself in consternation as she dug into her wallet. For that much back home, I can hire an auto to drive me from our flat to the market for a week! And people say India is expensive.

She stared at the requisite bills for a moment then handed them to the man. He waited, but Aarti turned her attention to her suitcase. She pulled the handle and wheeled her luggage over the uneven sidewalk to the front door of the apartment building. America may have been a new place for her, but anyone in any country could recognize a person expecting a tip.

Not a single word from the airport to here, didn't take my suitcase to the door. He just acted like I was some sort of commodity. No, no tip for him.

Her resolve in handling the situation weakened when she entered the building and found herself in a small receiving area.

Another door blocked her from going into the main part of the building; its speckled glass, with a flower design that must have come from decades ago, clouded the view. The clear windows on either side of it allowed her to see a set of stairs.

Dizziness made her stop. The exhaustion from thirty hours of nonstop travel made her rethink the need to go inside. Maybe she could curl up right there in the small enclosed entryway until a resident took pity on her.

Why aren't you here, Hari?

The thought came, unbidden and without warning. If Hari had been here, Aarti wouldn't have come. She wouldn't have needed to trek halfway across the world to do all this.

If Hari had been here, that would have meant he hadn't died.

Small things, Aarti reminded herself. *Di-Di said to focus on small things so I could do the big ones. I have to focus on how to get inside the building.*

She thought of when she said goodbye to her older sister, Prerna, at the airport in India. They'd both fought tears, but even then Prerna had found a way to stay composed long enough to offer Aarti the advice about staying on task.

Thinking of Prerna filled Aarti with homesickness. She didn't want to stand here looking like a fool. She didn't want to go inside and upstairs.

She didn't have a choice, however.

Small things.

Aarti gulped back the burning in her throat and examined the door. She tugged on its heavy handle, but it didn't budge. Next to the door, she saw a speaker-type system. Below it, a square button jutted from the wall in perky alertness. She pressed the button, and a buzzing noise made her jump back.

"Welcome to the Sherman Street Apartments," a voice announced from the speaker. "How can I help you?"

"I am looking for Mrs. Perkins," Aarti said, hating how unsure she sounded, questioning the very nature of her own presence. She had every right to be in this building. Hari lived here. Or had, anyway.

"I'm Mrs. Perkins. What can I do for you?"

"I think my husband's friend called you. Ajeet?"

The speaker went silent. Aarti wondered whether Ajeet had, in fact, called. Maybe he forgot. He and his wife lived next door to Hari in this old but well-kept building. The friends had moved in within days of one another before meeting during orientation week at the university the previous year. Aarti had never met Ajeet in person, but Hari talked about him constantly.

Ajeet had been the one to contact Aarti with the news of Hari's death. Her mind had distilled the memory until it stood apart from all other thoughts and ideas in her head. A portion of her would hate Ajeet for the rest of her life because of that phone call.

Just then, a woman appeared on the other side of the window and opened the door for her.

"Hello, dear," she said, pulling her cardigan closed at the neck. "I'm Mrs. Perkins. Come on in."

Aarti tried to smile, glad to leave the bone-crushing temperatures of a Chicago winter outside. Mrs. Perkins waved her in as if that would make Aarti move faster. She didn't help Aarti with the luggage, but this transgression Aarti could forgive. The gray topknot and the way Mrs. Perkins peered at Aarti over her glasses spoke to the woman's age, and Aarti would never expect her elders to do what she could do for herself. Her culture taught unquestionable respect to those older and wiser.

Sometimes even that respect isn't enough for them. Sometimes by disrespecting them, we're able to show a little respect to ourselves.

Her conscience chided her.

"You can leave that in the foyer there," Mrs. Perkins said with a nod to Aarti's suitcase. She entered the small office to the right of the glass door and trotted around the desk with a computer on one side and papers in a neat pile on the other. Opening a drawer, she

94

retrieved a set of keys on a giant ring and kneed the drawer shut as she began flipping through the keys.

"I'll take you right up," she said as they exited the office and went back into the foyer. "Hari was a wonderful tenant. I'm so sorry about . . ."

For the first time in the few minutes since they'd met, Aarti saw the woman's confidence morph into pity. Aarti stopped right there as a wild thought possessed her: maybe Hari had orchestrated this elaborate ruse to coax her to leave India. Ever since the wedding, he'd urged her to come with him. Could it be that he hadn't been killed after all? That their dream to spend the rest of their lives with one another would come true at last?

"It's only going to get harder the longer you wait," Mrs. Perkins said in a kind voice. She stepped forward and took one of Aarti's hands in her own. "Oh, look at these bracelets! They're lovely."

She didn't bother to explain that she had no right to these red bangles anymore. Only new brides wore them. Before Ajeet had called, Aarti was a new bride. Married all of three months. Now, she was a widow.

The realization made her knees buckle, and Mrs. Perkins caught her as she started to collapse. The old woman supported her with a strong hand under her arm. They waited there, the two of them, with Aarti standing like a criminal convicted of a weak spirit. Mrs. Perkins started rubbing little circles across her back, and the gesture, while foreign, soothed her.

"No sense in putting it off, dearie," Mrs. Perkins said in a soft voice.

The illusion dissipated then. Hari hadn't played some terrible joke on her. He wouldn't open the door upstairs with his trademark grin. Her trip to the US didn't signal the inauguration of their dreams come true; instead it represented the culmination of her worst nightmare.

Aarti nodded, the marriage bracelets clattering as she wiped away the few tears that had slipped out, and she readjusted the hold on her suitcase. Mrs. Perkins held Aarti's arm for another moment then let go and started up the stairs. As they climbed, Aarti tried to imagine Hari and Ajeet going up these steps a dozen times a day.

The picture wouldn't resolve in her mind. She'd only known, and loved, Hari in India. And she couldn't picture Ajeet at all. In the last year, she'd only spoken to him twice. The first time she talked to him had been when he, Hari, and some other friends had returned from a movie in celebration of Ajeet's engagement. Hari had called her to introduce her to the gang of young men who stood as his temporary family.

The boys called her *bhabi*, addressing her as sister-in-law out of respect. They teased her about what a good-for-nothing she'd married, about how they wanted her to come to the US to cook so they could eat real homemade meals for a change. Their voices mingled on the phone, competing for her attention and air space on the speaker, crisscrossing one another and the miles between the US and India.

Their exuberance had drawn her into their world for a little while. She'd laughed with them, softly, demurely, as a new bride should. It pleased her to hear the title they used for her. It gave her a sense of belonging, of permanence in Hari's life, which was so hard to come by when they lived so far apart. Her in Punjab, all the way in the north of India; him in this city that throbbed and swelled and killed husbands because people didn't understand what a turban really meant, that it had nothing to do with political or ideological allegiances.

They stopped at the top of the third flight of stairs where Mrs. Perkins unlocked the first door to the right of the landing.

"This was Hari's home?" Aarti asked.

Mrs. Perkins nodded. "Mm-hmm. Like I said, Hari was a kind, respectful young man. He didn't deserve what he got, and I want you to know I support you and all of your people. Not everyone in this country hates you."

Aarti scoffed at her naivete but didn't respond with words. Mrs. Perkins looked away in embarrassment for a moment. Then she turned back to Aarti.

"You can stop by the office later, and I'll give you another set of keys. Now, if you need anything — anything at all — you come right down, all right?"

She patted Aarti on the arm and went back downstairs. Aarti sucked in a long breath and pushed the door open. A small wall greeted her with an old contraption consisting of a few buttons and a small speaker. To her left she saw a large room; in it, next to the far wall, sat a metal frame supporting a mattress covered in rumpled sheets. Across from the bed against the wall sat a TV on a large table. Under the table, a crate held several DVD cases.

She stepped deeper into the apartment, and the scent of a space not lived in enveloped her. Hari had died only five days earlier, yet the apartment smelled lonely. Empty. Deceased.

On the far side of the TV she discovered a doorframe leading to a small kitchen that wrapped behind the wall. A small kernel of amusement settled inside her heart at the thought of her tall brawny husband moving around this space. No doubt he would have crossed the entire kitchen in less than two strides.

It took her four to get to the fridge where she found a small container of milk and a carton with three eggs. A loaf of bread sat on the top shelf, and she found two tomatoes, four small onions, and two potatoes in the drawer. A bottle of ketchup and a glass jar of a strange green chutney rattled in the bin on the door when she pushed it shut.

Where is the real food? she wondered. No sabji, no daal, nothing. Did Hari really survive on bread and eggs?

She turned to the cabinets, as if she could find the cooked vegetables and lentils in there. Instead she found a few boxes of cereal and a cylindrical tub with a man in a funny hat on it. It

declared the contents as "steel-cut oatmeal," and Aarti remembered
Hari telling her during one of their many video chats that this food
item came the closest to the *daliaa* they ate in the winters in Punjab.

*What did Hari eat during the day? Why didn't he tell me he struggled
so much? How am I supposed to make sense of all this?*

She returned to the main room of the apartment, the emptiness
creeping up on her again.

*Maybe . . . maybe if I . . . oh, my mind isn't working. Maybe if I take
a shower, freshen up, that would help.*

Aarti brought her suitcase to the center of the room and laid it
flat on the floor. When she ran the zipper around its sides and
pushed back the lid, the aroma of India sprang from it: spices from
the kitchen and dust from the roads, exhaust from the cars and sweat
of the people fighting every day to get ahead and stay alive. All these
impressions and more nearly made her rock back on her heels.

She had seen none of those things since landing in the US hours
ago. It frightened and exhilarated her all at the same time. In India
Aarti knew the rhythm of the day, of the population, and how to
handle challenges. In this kitchen she couldn't find decent food to
eat; she didn't even know where to look for it.

She sat on the floor. She could unpack, yes, but where should
she put her clothes? Aarti had no idea where Hari kept his clothes or
his shoes. The cloth pieces he folded into his turbans. A comb to
make his beard look neat. A towel to dry off after he bathed. And
socks. What about the thick socks she'd bought for him just before he
left? Where did he put them? Did he still have them, or had he given
them to one of these friends?

She ignored her hunger pangs and fought the demons of jet lag
and time difference to crawl to the mattress on the metal frame. A
shower sounded beyond the scope of her abilities at the moment.
Pulling herself onto it, she dropped in a heap on top of the sheets.

Here at last she found the essence of Hari. She recognized it
from those first heady days after the wedding before he had to rush
back to the States for the start of the term at the university. She stared

at the ceiling, not bothering to turn on a light as day turned to dusk, then twilight, then night. Instead she considered the task before her.

Ajeet and his wife had called her three days before their own flight to India for the winter break. He couldn't change his plane tickets—nonrefundable, he said in an apologetic tone—but he encouraged Aarti to use his home if staying in Hari's flat proved too hard. He'd already spoken to Mrs. Perkins and told her to allow Aarti access to anything she needed.

"It's not a large home, Bhabi, but whatever we have is yours," he said. "Kiran says you can use her winter jackets. *Bahut thand hoti hai*; it's very cold in Chicago, different from our cold in India. Don't feel shy; it's your home, too."

She remembered how his voice had broken under the weight of responsibility. He'd failed, he said through tears on the phone, to take care of Hari. He'd failed Hari, and he'd failed Aarti.

You didn't fail, Ajeet, she thought. *My love for Hari wasn't enough to keep him safe either.*

Now Aarti had two weeks to make sense of a country she didn't know. Two weeks to learn to navigate a city unfamiliar to her. Two weeks to find a lawyer and ask him to help her formulate a list of questions she would need to ask to work through the mire of the justice system when a woman's husband had died as the victim of a hate crime.

Hate crime. Those used to be things we heard on the news when America seemed so far away. Now . . . now it's right here. Here where I don't want to be.

Had it not been for Prerna, in fact, Aarti would have stayed in Punjab keening in a corner of the flat she and Hari had rented just before he came back here.

"Go there and find out what happened," Prerna had said in a firm tone. "Make sure you take care of Hari's things. You . . . you need to bring . . . Hari . . . We need to perform . . ."

At that, Prerna's voice cracked. Aarti's own voice had long since fractured from all the hours she'd spent crying, which was just as well. She didn't want to finish Prerna's thought: that Aarti had to bring Hari's body home for a proper cremation. She didn't know how Westerners took care of their dead, but she would certainly take care of her own.

Tears slipped from her eyes and fell onto the pillow beneath her head. Aarti heard them drop next to her ears like little puffs of breath hitting the fabric. Those puffs sounded like her own ragged breathing.

* * *

HOURS LATER, A RUMBLING sound from outside made Aarti bolt upright. For a few minutes she couldn't recognize the room. Had she visited Prerna at some time yesterday and fallen asleep? But this didn't look like Prerna's house.

Memories of her sister brought back the crushing realization of where she lay and why she'd come. The skin around her eyes had stretched taut where her tears had dried. She rubbed them with her fingers then stood and stared in the direction of the window. Her eyes adjusted to the semi-darkness, and she could make out a streetlight.

Light from out there, but I have no idea where the lights are in here. I was so stupid. I should have left the kitchen light on at least. Hari showed me the whole city on FaceTime, but he couldn't show me the light switches in his flat.

She wanted to yell at him. She wanted to cry and scream and beat his chest with her fists. She'd left him at the airport months earlier with whispers of love and good wishes for his studies. She'd forgotten to order him not to die.

Holding her hands out in front of her, Aarti made her way across the room with small steps until her fingers bounced against the doorframe into the kitchen. She let her fingers crawl across the wall on the kitchen side until they touched a plastic rectangle and found a switch. She flipped it, and light flooded the space.

Her stomach growled, reminding her that she'd had nothing to eat since the flight the day before, but she couldn't stand the thought of touching the items in the fridge. Hari had stood in this kitchen less than a week ago. Maybe he would come back to claim everything if she left it alone.

Within minutes she'd found other lights in the apartment and turned on all of them.

What time is it? Six forty-five – hai ma! I slept all night. Chalo, koi nahi. Doesn't matter. I can get ready and do my prayers and then go . . . go find something. A lawyer. Someone to help.

She explored the bathroom, turning on the taps in the shower several times to remind herself what tap controlled what temperature, and went back to her suitcase. After an hour she'd showered, dressed, and had begun researching lawyers on her phone. They all sounded the same to her—names and listings of qualifications, all of them smiling in their photos as if immigration law only meant joyful reunions of families in Bollywood-style endings to dramatic stories. Her heart clenched as she copied down the information for one who sounded Indian enough and stuck the paper in her purse.

Her stomach rumbled again, and with a great deal of reluctance, Aarti went to the kitchen for a glass of milk.

It's not bad, she conceded after the first few sips. *At least it doesn't taste like the doodh wala poured water into his can before delivering to all the flats.*

The memory of the milkman stretching his wares for an entire building caused a laugh to escape her lips, but Aarti cut it off by clapping her free hand to her mouth.

Natural light filled the room, and she looked toward the window. The weather app on her phone said no snow today, although the temperatures forecasted made her wince. Regardless of the climate, she had to find answers.

She invoked the name of Guru Nanak for strength, shrugged on three sweaters and wool leggings under her jeans, and left the apartment.

* * *

THE WIND STOPPED FOR a moment, and Aarti blinked its iciness from her eyes. She held up the paper and stared at it again, even though she could have recited the address by heart. That didn't mean it made any more sense. The street names all sounded the same, words in English that may have held significance for her husband but meant nothing to her.

She trudged down the street between the tall buildings with the odor of car engines wafting toward her from the road to her left. What had the sign at the corner said? Canal Street? Was she going in the right direction? Even the helpful suggestions from the maps feature on her phone didn't help.

Hari had sent dozens of pictures, hundreds of them, from the Windy City and had often FaceTimed with her while he wandered the streets. Through the magic of technology, he'd shown her most of his favorite haunts. She thought, sitting thousands of miles away in India, that she knew Chicago as well as she knew their small hometown.

A screen couldn't translate the loneliness Aarti felt now, though; it couldn't convey how the frigid weather must have pressed on Hari's body as it did her own. When she inhaled, she drew the winter into her lungs. The hurt reminded her of the pain deeper in her heart from when she'd gotten the call.

A blaring horn redirected her attention. She looked at the street and saw cars edging forward for an advantage, although none of them tried to create an extra lane of traffic as was so common on India's roads. There, if the paint on the asphalt designated three rows of cars, the sheer force of the population guaranteed to turn those three into six or seven.

She missed the messiness of streets teeming with people and animals and vehicles. In the distance a steady beeping suggested a truck of some sort, and even the beeping sounded patient. In India no one waited for permission.

Here, pedestrians hurried to their destinations with heads ducked against the weather that snarled and snapped instead of merely biting at them. To her right, someone in a jacket that looked thicker than her own exited the building. She watched as the person strode down the sidewalk with confidence.

How many mufflers was that person wearing? I have two around my neck, and I still feel cold. If Di-Di hadn't given me this cap, I would be walking around with ice for my hair.

She pushed a stray strand behind her ear and into the wool beanie on her head. Prerna had stuffed the hat into her bag just before she'd entered the airport to come to the US. A surge of affection for her sister burst through Aarti's heart, and it cracked open. Tears stung her eyes.

No, I can't. I have to be strong. There's no one else here to help me.

The door that the confident city dweller had used swung open again, and this time Aarti caught the whiff of fresh bread. Sweetness mingled with the aroma of baked goods. She gulped back her loneliness, stuffed both the phone and the paper in her pocket, and entered the shop.

Customers filled the bakery, pressing shoulders against one another in the booths and at the tables, while employees stood behind the counter making beverages and serving pastries. The hum of conversation mingled with the tanginess of coffee and the hiss of machinery. People talked and ate and drank and contributed to the busyness of it all, yet Aarti marveled again—for what seemed like the hundredth time—how orderly everyone behaved. Hari had mentioned this many times during their video calls. Everything and everyone in America followed a system, a set of rules.

The culture worked in direct contrast to the culture back home where everyone scrabbled and fought their way to the head of the line, by hook, crook, bribe, or bluff. Now that she'd seen it in action for herself since landing in the country, Aarti didn't know quite how to behave. The ground under her own two feet didn't feel solid.

"Ma'am? Can I help you?"

Aarti blinked once or twice, turned around to look, then realized the woman behind the counter had directed the question at her. She stepped forward. Everyone else in line had taken a minute to examine the tall menus on the wall behind the counter, so Aarti did the same.

The woman smiled at her. "How are you doing today?"

Aarti offered a small smile back. "I'm fine, thank you."

"Do you know what you want yet?"

She shook her head. So many choices. Too many. Hari had mentioned this, too, that the US seemed to revel in options. Too many types of coffee drinks. Too many types of cereals. Too many types of people.

Why then, Aarti wondered, if there were so many different types of people here, had anyone had a problem with Hari? All these options meant they should have understood diversity. Didn't the American TV programs talk about it, this diversity, this commitment to appreciating differences?

"Would you like some suggestions?"

Aarti looked back at the woman. She seemed nice enough. Middle-aged with hair that had been colored to look blonde, although dark roots anchored those blonde locks.

"Yes, thank you," Aarti said.

The woman smiled again. "Well, do you like more coffee flavor or chocolate?"

"I think chocolate."

She nodded. "Got it. I'll make you a nice mocha and bring it out. Anything else?"

Aarti looked at the bakery case to her left with cookies and pastries she couldn't name lined up in neat rows. All of them looked too large to be shared by two people, never mind be consumed by one. Despite her hunger, she shook her head.

"Okay, great, that'll be three dollars and twenty-five cents, please."

Great? Aarti thought as she pulled out her wallet. Why is it so great if I refused to eat?

She took out some bills and examined their corners, looking for the numbers.

All American money looks the same. Why can't they have different sizes of bills like in India? So much easier to tell them apart.

The coins didn't prove nearly as tricky, and after two tries she retrieved a twenty-five-cent piece from the center zipper pocket. She handed the money to the woman and turned to face the crowded bakery to look for an empty seat.

If Hari had been here, he would have taken care of the money, she thought as she navigated her way around jackets puddling on the floor at the bottoms of chairs. Where did Di-Di get so many dollars at the last minute? What would I have done without her?

Time and again, Prerna stood by Aarti in the biggest moments of her life. When Aarti and Hari decided to get married, against the express wishes of both their parents, Prerna accompanied them to the registrar's office as well as the *mandir*. She handed money to the priest in the temple and followed his dictums during the ceremony, performing the various rituals for both the groom's side as well as the bride's family. Now Prerna was the only one to comfort Aarti in her widowhood.

The dull ache of reality pressed on her chest, and she grasped the edge of an empty table.

"Ma'am? Are you okay?"

Aarti turned and saw the woman holding a steaming oversized mug of coffee. Its smell made Aarti's stomach clench. How could she sit down to a cup of coffee when her husband was dead?

"I . . . I'm . . ."

The woman put the mug on the table and took Aarti by the elbow. "Why don't you sit down for a minute? It might help if you unbutton the top couple of buttons on your jacket."

Aarti followed her advice and also unwound both mufflers from her neck. It surprised her how much air that small gap below her neck allowed. She hung the mufflers on the back of her chair, and both of them slipped right to the floor.

"Here," the woman said, picking them up from the floor, "if you put them between the slats of the chair, they don't tend to fall as much."

Swallowing hard, Aarti tried to talk around the burning ball in her throat. She redirected her attention to taking off her gloves and dropping them into her purse. The woman pulled out the chair across from her and sat down. Aarti raised an eyebrow in question.

"I'm on break," the woman answered with a shrug. "My name's Monica." She held out a hand, which Aarti shook.

"I'm Aarti."

Monica tried and fumbled Aarti's name then apologized, but Aarti just shook her head.

"It's all right. Some of the American names are hard for me to say also."

"So you're new to the country," Monica said with a kind smile.

"Not to live," Aarti said, lowering her gaze to the coffee on the table. "I'm only here for a short time."

"For the holidays?" Monica said, her face lighting up. "Chicago's beautiful at this time of year. I know we've got harsh winters, but you should go check out the Mag Mile. It's amazing!"

"No," Aarti said, shaking her head, "I'm not here to celebrate anything. I . . . I'm supposed to meet someone, but I'm having trouble finding the correct office."

"Do you know the address?" Monica asked. "I could try to help."

Aarti fished in the pocket of her jacket and pulled out the paper. She had also e-mailed the information to herself so she could retrieve it on her phone. No sense in taking a risk with a matter as important as this.

"Immigration Lawyers of Chicago," Monica murmured. She glanced at Aarti, and Aarti sensed the shift in Monica's attitude. Curiosity and a little bit of skepticism edged the open friendliness Monica projected.

"Yes," Aarti said, "it says Way-bash . . . ? I don't know how to pronounce it. I think I'm on this Way-bash, correct?"

"Wabash," Monica said in a gentle tone, making the first syllable sound like someone had asked her to open wide. "Do you have an appointment with someone?"

Aarti shook her head. "I landed in the US yesterday only. My husband . . ." She swallowed hard. "It's about my husband. I don't know anything about the laws and the way the system works here. I've been walking all morning, and I feel so tired . . ."

Her vision blurred, and she gave in to the tears. Mama always used to say Aarti should keep smiling, that she should never show any negative emotions, but her mother had also said she would never speak to Aarti again if she married Hari. Prerna would have taken charge here, but Aarti couldn't just call her big sister at all odd hours of the night every single time she ran into a challenge. Had Hari been here . . . But then, if Hari had been here, Aarti wouldn't have gotten lost.

"Wow, just yesterday, huh?" Monica said. "That's gotta be tough. Do you have a place to stay?"

Her sympathy made Aarti fight more tears. She nodded and used the napkin on the saucer beneath her coffee mug to wipe her eyes.

"Okay, well, at least you don't have to worry about that. Let me see if I can help you figure out where the office is. I'm just going to go grab my phone and be right back."

Monica smiled at her again and got up from the table. Aarti watched her go behind the counter, grateful and dismayed all at the same time that someone had volunteered to help her. She didn't even *know how to get to the lawyer's office. How would she manage to go back to Hari's flat from here?*

And I forgot to get the key from Mrs. Perkins. At least she liked Hari. I think.

She thought of the flat and wondered whether Hari had considered it home. When he first came to the US, he promised to come back to India for good when he finished his studies. Back when they thought their parents would bless their marriage, they talked about making their own little home either in the same town or in a metro not far away. Aarti found it easy to dream about a blissful life together.

She scrutinized the lawyer's address. The pen she'd used to jot down the information had run out of ink. She'd had to press hard on the paper until the last few letters became punctured by holes. It made her think of her marriage.

Hari had presented the idea to approach their own families first about getting married and then visiting one another's parents. Surely, he reasoned, when they saw the mature method both of them took to what they proposed, everyone would agree. In Aarti's house the discussion made the walls echo, the thunderous objections reverberating in her heart for hours afterward. Hari persisted with the idea of the visits; neither went well.

They talked about breaking up, about running away, about staying friends. Every time they tried to separate, an unseen force brought them back together. In the end, Aarti said, if they loved one another and both utilized their education well, that should have been enough for their parents. It shouldn't have mattered that Hari was a Sikh and she a Hindu. They lived in 2018, not 1918.

It shouldn't have mattered, but it did. Now Aarti found herself in a coffee shop in downtown Chicago during one of the coldest months of the year relying on a stranger for help. Prerna had pleaded with her to delay her trip to the US to give her a chance to approach their parents, but Aarti had refused at the time.

"Mama-Papa should be happy now, na?" she said as they rode to the airport in the taxi. "They were always against me having a love marriage, right?"

Prerna took Aarti's hand but turned to look out the window. "Mama-Papa never wanted him to die, Aarti. This much you should know, too."

"All I know is that Hari is gone, and I have no one. His parents didn't want us to get married; Mama-Papa didn't want us to get married. Now everyone got what they wanted, and I'm all by myself."

"Aarti?"

She attempted a smile as Monica settled herself back in the opposite chair.

"So I looked it up on my phone, and you're actually pretty close. We're on Wabash right here . . ." She turned her phone around and pointed at the screen so Aarti could see. "The office is close to the corner of Wabash and Forty-Seventh. That's East Forty-Seventh, so don't go in the wrong direction. We're on the corner of Wabash and Fifty-Third right now, so only about six more blocks."

Aarti stared at the phone and nodded. A heart-deep yearning for her family threatened to split her in half right where she sat. She pushed the phone back in Monica's direction to distract herself.

"Thank you so much. It looks so easy. I don't know why I was having so much trouble."

Monica shook her head and smiled as she stood up again. "It's okay, I'm happy to help. If you're new to a place, it can be pretty overwhelming when you're trying to find your way around." She gestured to the table. "Can I take that for you?"

Aarti looked down at her large mug, now empty. When had she finished her coffee?

"Thank you," she said. She stood also. "I must go and find this office."

"You're welcome." Monica glanced over her shoulder and then looked back at Aarti. "I have to get back. My break's over. But if you need any help with anything, just come back. Wait a second . . ."

She trotted to the counter and back again then handed Aarti a business card.

"That has the café's address."

"Around the Corner Bakery and Café," Aarti read aloud. Her eyes met Monica's again. "Thank you. I . . . I will most definitely come back. Chicago is such a big city, and it's nice to know someone here otherwise . . ."

The burning in her throat threatened to burst. She swallowed hard to force it down. Aarti still had so many challenges in front of her. She couldn't lose her composure every time she faced one.

Monica patted her arm. "Good luck, Aarti. I hope things work out for you and your husband."

Aarti nodded and rewound the mufflers, then buttoned her jacket and tugged on her gloves. She managed to get the wool cap back on her head after struggling with it for a few moments. Looping her purse across her body, she made her way to the entrance. Just before leaving, she turned and exchanged another wave with Monica.

She stepped back onto the street, still unsure of how she would navigate the rest of her time in the US, but a little less frightened of the prospect of making her way to the lawyer's office. The wind sliced through her layers of clothing, but Aarti managed to ignore it. The kindness she received from a stranger made her loneliness abate just enough to convince her that maybe—just maybe—she would find herself once again.

To learn more about this author, please visit:
https://thewriteedge.wordpress.com/

Button Eyes

Speculative Fiction

Vickie J. Litten

Prompt: Take me through your typical day in colors.

W HEN I WAS A *young child, my nonna would tell me bedtime stories about our ancestors long gone. My favorite story was the one about my distant grandmother, Tala Castiglione, a young mother living on her family's large prosperous farm in the heart of Tuscany, Italy.*

It was late summer, on the eve of San Lorenzo, the night of the falling stars. The evening air was crisp; it had not rained for several weeks. Inside the farmhouse, Tala paused at the door of each child's bedroom and listened for their slow, measured breathing. In her own bedroom, she draped a gray woolen shawl over her shoulders and retrieved a little cloth doll with black button eyes from the bottom drawer of her chestnut chest. Leaving behind her husband's deep rumbling and cradling the doll in her arm, she quietly slipped through the large oaken front door and went outside to sit on the chilly marble bench under the vine-covered veranda. With her children and husband safe in bed and sleeping peacefully, she turned her attention to the doll, first smoothing the faded blue skirt, then nestling the cloth doll in her arms as if it were a living, breathing bambino. She leaned back against the rough blocks of stone that made up the wall of the aged farmhouse and closed her eyes.

Holding the doll tight, she let the tears flow, immersing herself in the gray blanket of sadness smothering her heart. But on this night, a clacking sound interrupted her ritual of misery. It was the sound of hooves on the stones packed into the dirt of the road leading to the farmhouse. She saw the shadow of a man and mule walking toward her, bathed in the dim light of the moon. Startled, she jumped up and rushed to open the door, intending to wake her husband.

"Salve, Signora!" the stranger called out. "Please, wait."

Tala paused, her hand on the latch.

"I did not mean to frighten you, Signora. Please. I am looking for the road to Florence. Please, if you will just direct me, I will be on my way."

Tala turned and saw an elderly man with a scraggly gray beard, wearing worn clothes and covered in road dust.

He removed his black, brimmed hat. "Please, Signora."

She pulled the shawl tight around herself and turned toward him. "Signore, you should not have taken the fork to the left. The main road would have taken you to Florence. If you follow our road back and turn left, you will be on the correct road once again."

The man's shoulders drooped, and he hung his head. "Thank you, Signora." He turned around and attempted to lead the mule away, but the mule would not budge.

Tala pointed to a bucket sitting next to the well. "Perhaps he is thirsty?"

"Thank you, Signora, thank you." He bowed to her several times and crossed over to the well. After both he and the mule had sated their thirst, he returned to the edge of the veranda, leading the mule.

"We will not bother you anymore this evening, Signora. I thank you again for your kindness."

Tala, worried that tragedy could befall the old man and his mule if they traveled in the dark, said, "It is many miles to Florence,

Signore. You do not need to walk all night. You can bed down here, either in the barn with the goats or over there in the clearing next to the well."

"You are kind, Signora." He took a step forward and pointed to the doll, held tight in Tala's arms. "May I see your doll?"

Tala looked startled and pulled her shawl down to cover the doll.

He took a step back. "I am sorry, Signora. I did not mean to upset you."

Tala sighed and shook her head. "You did not. This is a special doll. I cannot allow anyone else to hold her."

"It is your daughter's doll, Signora?"

Tala's chest heaved, and tears welled in her eyes. "It is . . . I mean, it was."

"What was your daughter's name, if I may ask, kind Signora?"

"Giana. Her name was Giana." Tala wiped at her tears. "It's been so long since I said her name. Giana."

"When did you lose her?" he asked gently.

"I haven't lost her," explained Tala, shaking her head violently. "She is always with me. I love her the same today as I did the first day I laid eyes on her, and I miss her as much today as I did five years ago when God tore her from me."

"You have other children, Signora?"

She looked at the old man with anger. "I have six, and I love them dearly. Do you think I miss her less because of them? You do not understand. How could you know a mother's grief? I relive the pain of her loss every day." She pounded her chest with her fist. "Every day I feel the pain here."

"No, you are correct, Signora, I cannot understand. I never had a child to call my own. But I would like to know about Giana. Can you tell me of her?"

Tala moved back to the bench and sat down. "I did not mean to get so upset." She looked at the doll in her arms. "Giana was love. She loved everyone and everything. She was never cross, always happy, laughing, and so delighted with everything around her. I did not understand her, but I adored her. We all adored her." She dropped her face into her hands. "Why did God take her from us? She was so good! Why her?"

"I do not know, Signora." The man looked pensive and rubbed his beard. "Perhaps I could help you."

"Many have tried to help me, Signore. Do not waste your time."

"I would like to repay you for your kind offer of water and shelter. Please, Signora."

"If you wish it, but I warn you, it will do no good." She shook her head. "I am destined to live my remaining days broken."

"Nevertheless, I wish to help you." The old man went to the worn leather pack on the mule's back and fished around, then pulled out a brown wine bottle.

"Are we to have a drink?" called out Tala.

"No, Signora, the bottle is empty." He held the bottle upside down to show her. "We will now fill it." He went to the well and poured some water into the bottle. "Water is the essence of life, Signora." He came back to the veranda, stooped over with much groaning, and collected a handful of dirt. Letting it sift through his fist into the bottle, he said, "Because your roots are deep into the soil of this place."

He stepped onto the veranda, held his hand over her head, and said, "May I?"

She nodded, perplexed.

He plucked a dark hair from her head and slipped it into the bottle. "Because you love her." On the side table, next to the bench, was a stale crust of bread. He broke off a tiny piece and pushed it into the bottle. "All things need nourishment to grow."

Then he reached for the doll in Tala's arms. "May I?" he asked.

She hesitated, her grip tightened then relaxed, and she passed the doll to him.

"This doll went everywhere with Giana," he said.

"How do you know that?" asked Tala.

He smiled. "This doll saw all that Giana saw."

He set the wine bottle on the table, held the doll over it, and squeezed the black metal button eyes. A steady stream of black liquid poured into the bottle.

"How . . ." Tala couldn't believe what she was seeing. She had sewn those buttons on herself. They had once adorned her husband's old suit.

"Now it is finished." The old man covered the mouth of the bottle with his palm and shook it fiercely. "You must take only one small sip a day. No more." He handed the bottle to Tala.

She took it with reluctance. She did not want to hurt his feelings, but she knew she would never drink the foul muddy water sloshing around in the bottle.

"Thank you, Signore, and now I must retire and bid you good night."

Once inside with the door shut, she peeked out the window and saw the old man laying out a blanket on the ground near the well.

The next morning at the breakfast table, she broke off a chunk of bread and handed it to her eldest son, asking him to take it to the old Signore sleeping next to the well. In a few minutes her son came back.

"Mamma, there is no man at the well."

She ran out to check and found no old man. The ground was not even disturbed where she had seen him lay his blanket. Confused, she ran to her bedroom and checked the bottle of foul water. It was still there. She picked it up, and as she lifted the bottle, the aroma of cooked cherries and plums tantalized her. She put her nose to the opening. There was a strong scent of sweet red wine, but it could not be. She had watched the old man put the dirt and hair in the bottle. She knew there was only filthy water in it.

She shouted for her daughter to bring her a glass and poured a small amount into it. It was black as ink, but there was no hint of dirt or anything else in the liquid and it smelled delicious. She crossed herself for protection and took a sip. It tasted like a fruity, aged Chianti. Tala was confused and thought perhaps she had mixed up the bottle with the dirt in it and an actual bottle of wine. But that wouldn't explain the color. It was as black as the baby doll's button eyes.

Tala was still mulling over the mystery when she went out to gather the eggs from the chickens. She started putting the eggs in her basket and then paused and held one in her hand. She must have collected hundreds of eggs, but she had never before noticed what a beautiful golden brown they were. This egg had little dark-brown freckles on it. She smiled. Why had she never noticed how pretty the eggs were?

She moved on to the goat pen to check on her eldest daughter, who was doing the milking. The goat turned around and looked at her. Its eyes were so funny looking. A slash of black on an amber background. Tala felt herself giggling. Every time she looked at those eyes, they were funnier and funnier.

Her daughter sat in shock. This was the first time in a long time she had heard her mother laugh.

Tala felt her emotions blossoming with intensity at the pig pen. When she looked into the pig's eyes, they looked almost human. The white pig had blue eyes with a round black center and luxurious white lashes. Tears welled in her eyes and she finally understood why Giana had always cried when it was time to butcher a pig.

On the way back to the farmhouse Tala noticed their small vineyard. It was lined with long neat rows of verdant green vines, speckled with gold and heavy with indigo bunches of grapes. She felt an overwhelming urge to run along the path between the vines. Unable to resist, she laid the eggs down, kicked off her shoes, and ran. She felt almost pulled by the straight lines of the paths, racing up one and down the other. She ran until her chest hurt every time she sucked in air. She felt the golden warmth of the sun on the top of her head, the sweat trickling down her back, the stinging blush of pink on her cheeks, and the sandy grit of the dirt on her feet. It felt so good to feel.

When she went inside to make lunch for the children, she sat entranced by a tomato. It was engorged with juice, its vermilion skin stretched taut. She had never before noticed how colorful the food was: the earthy brown of the sausage, the light green of the lettuce, and the mossy-green olives. The smell of the food cooking was so intoxicating she felt dizzy with excitement.

Once lunch was prepared, she and the younger children carried it out to the field where her husband and his workers were bringing in the last hay cut of the season. She kicked her shoes off again and danced across the ochre stalks, though they bit and poked at her feet. As though she were a magnet of joy, her children and husband joined her in dancing.

When evening came, she discovered even the dark was a beautiful azure bathed in cream. She looked up to the sky filled with a multitude of glittering stars and, for the first time in five years, felt peace.

Tala never found out who the old man was and after the first day never mentioned him again. For several months she drank from the bottle every morning, but she needed less and less of the sweet black wine as time passed.

My nonna told me that Tala did not drink all of the wine, and before she left this world she buried the remainder somewhere on her farm. It has never been found and is still there, waiting, an old brown bottle with an aged cork containing an inky black wine that will allow you to feel the joy, and to see the world through the eyes of a child.

To learn more about this author, please visit:
https://www.facebook.com/VickieJLittenAuthor/

When the Ink Dries

Contemporary Fantasy

G Dean Manuel

Prompt: It's unfortunate to be good at something that's not good at all.

"*I*T IS EXACTLY AS *we discussed, Mr. Reilly. We will come into possession of ten years of your life and you will be given one million dollars a month and this hotel room for the duration of your remaining time," Manheim said.*

His face was a stone mask, body language portraying only cool confidence. He was . . . crisp. Everything was strategic about his person from the way his hair was cut, to the manicure of his nails, to the lines of his Armani suit. He sat there, playing with his cufflink — it was his one tell that betrayed any sort of annoyance.

Manheim turned the freshly scribed contract toward Mr. Reilly. It was specially treated lambskin vellum inscribed with flawless penmanship. The script was tight and small but readable.

"How much time I gonna have left after that?" Mr. Reilly said, his breath a combination of stale whiskey and rotting teeth. The locals knew him as Shopping Cart Pete, and he was chaos-given-flesh. His hair was a tangled nightmare that even a day of soaking hadn't managed to unravel, and his skin held grime that had probably been around for two presidents' terms of office.

Manheim favored him with a tight smile. "That, I cannot say. I won't lie to you, you may have two days or twenty years." He knew, of course. He'd chosen Mr. Reilly specifically because he would only have a month after the ten years. He had a liaison from the Grim Reaper's office who owed him favors.

Shopping Cart Pete stared at the contract with wild eyes. He regarded it like a viper waiting to bite him. "Yer bosses, they gonna take my soul, too?"

"The disposition of your soul will be solely based upon the life you have lived, Mr. Reilly. I merely deal in time." He made a motion to retrieve the contract. "If you aren't interested in the deal, I won't be wasting any more of your time. Please, enjoy the hotel room for the rest of the night; it is paid until morning."

"Wait! Wait! Wait!" Mr. Reilly screeched, his voice pitching up an octave.

Manheim stopped his hand and sat back into his chair. He searched Shopping Cart Pete's face and smiled inwardly. His own face betrayed no emotion. He'd found what he was looking for. Greed. It was the other reason he had chosen Mr. Reilly. He saw fear, too, but it was overridden by Mr. Reilly's baser lecherous nature. Even unlucky people thought fate would one day deal them a perfect hand.

"Yes, Mr. Reilly?" His tone was calm, controlled, and cultured.

"That's it? I ask a question and yer just gonna get up and leave?"

Manheim saw through Mr. Reilly's anger. It was a novice tactic in such negotiations, a strategy born of this world's "the customer is always right" culture. It wouldn't work at his table. He was too old and had brokered too many deals for such a maneuver to work.

"Time is valuable, Mr. Reilly. Considering my business and my employer, I am in a unique position to understand just how valuable."

Shopping Cart Pete harrumphed.

"I'm sorry, Mr. Reilly. If what you want is assurances, those I cannot give. What I have told you, I've told you honestly. The contract prohibits any action taken against you to cause your untimely death before your natural demise. It also prohibits you from unnaturally prolonging your life. You are, of course, free to pursue any manner of undeath, as such a transition will lead to your true death and the contract only stipulates until such an event. So, should you become a vampire, the Company would no longer be beholden to provide you with your stipend or the use of this hotel room." Manheim's lips turned up in a good-natured smile. It was robotic and didn't reach his eyes.

"And you ain't takin' my soul?"

"As I've stated before, that isn't my department." Manheim pushed the contract closer to him and pointed at a specific section. "Subsection C-28 details that we do not have any claims on your soul and that the allocation of your soul after death will purely be a function of how you lived your life."

Pete barely glanced at the referenced section. "Where do I sign?"

Manheim's face shifted imperceptibly to annoyance for a moment. He didn't like when fools thought they were being smart. Such people were invariably making deals beyond their ken and asked all the wrong questions. The stony mask was back before Pete could notice the expression. "Right here at the bottom."

Manheim stood up, withdrawing a fat pen from the inside pocket of his suit. It was an antique fountain pen, a lever on its side to draw in ink and a large bulbous glass vial for a reservoir. "This is what you will sign it with." He showed the pen to Mr. Reilly.

"Okay." He glanced askance at the pen.

Manheim stood up and moved around the table until he was directly behind Shopping Cart Pete. "Stay seated," he said when Pete attempted to stand up. Pete grumbled but remained in his seat. "The contract cannot be signed in normal ink. I apologize for any pain."

Manheim jabbed the pen into Pete's neck and pulled the lever on the side. The pen quickly filled with blood. He grabbed a handkerchief out of his pocket and pressed it to the wound as he withdrew the pen. The wound was shallow and superficial.

"Son of a bitch!" Pete exclaimed, his face a caricature of pain. "You coulda warned me!" He took hold of the handkerchief pressed to the wound.

Manheim sat back down across from Mr. Reilly. He knew that the man was being overly dramatic. He shrugged. "I have years of experience doing this. It wouldn't have made much difference; no one is ever prepared to be stabbed."

Mr. Reilly subsided to grumbling. "I woulda been prepared . . ."

Manheim continued as if Pete hadn't said anything. "Are you ready to sign?"

"What if I'm not?"

"I will walk out that door." He gestured with the pen. He eyed Pete impassively. "You don't have anything that I can't find in a hundred other people around the next block. And once I leave this room, there will be no deal."

Shopping Cart Pete glared at Manheim. "You could be a bit nicer. You are taking ten years of my life."

"I am taking nothing, Mr. Reilly. I am trading you one commodity for another. Don't confuse this with anything personal; I am merely doing my job."

Pete snorted derisively. "Whatever helps you sleep at night."

"I assure you, whether you sign or not, I will sleep just fine." Manheim held out the pen. Pete didn't notice, but Manheim's body was tense. No matter how many contracts he made, he couldn't help but feel the tiniest bit of guilt for his part in the exchange. He knew, logically, that if it wasn't him it would just be someone else, but that didn't stop him from feeling this way. Plus, even if it wasn't the greatest deal, Mr. Reilly would walk away with more in the next month than he'd ever had in the last twenty years of his life.

Shopping Cart Pete snatched the pen and angrily scribbled his name on the bottom of the contract. Once he was done signing, Manheim quickly turned the contract and pulled a pouch out of his pocket. He took a small pinch of fine sand from the pouch and spread it over the contract. He set a timer for twenty-four hours on his phone, then retrieved his pen from Pete.

"Mr. Reilly, the ink will take twenty-four hours to dry. That is all the time you have to reconsider. Once dry, the contract becomes unbreachable." Manheim stood up and handed a business card to Mr. Reilly. "If you should change your mind within that time, call that number and we can move forward with breaking the contract. Otherwise, enjoy your new home. The money" — Manheim paused to check his phone, then handed him another card — "will be in this account now."

Without further ado, he walked out of the hotel room.

AFTER AN HOUR'S TRIP *through dense city traffic via Uber, Manheim stood in front of an unremarkable office building on Main Street. It looked like a hundred others lining the roads of Main streets all over America. He steeled himself before entering.*

A bored security guard behind a long counter snapped to a semblance of attention and said, "Good afternoon, Mr. Manheim."

Manheim said nothing. The guards were normal men, hired for their low aptitude and aggressive natures. They weren't part of the Company and often disappeared — Manheim assumed they were killed — so there was no point in pleasantries. Plus, he knew it added to his reputation.

Manheim passed his hand over a sensor next to the door, and there was a loud beep as it sensed the RFID chip implanted in his wrist. He opened the door and walked into a hallway that was dark from the outside. Once the door shut, everything changed.

The walls, which had appeared plain gray with the door open, transformed into a mural from the mind of a madman painted in all gray and black. Figures writhed in many forms of unimaginable torture. Manheim had heard they were actually the souls of those time merchants who had failed to live up to their end of their contract. It was exactly the form of intimidation the Company liked to use.

He made his way to a door down the corridor. He ignored the walls, knowing better than to let them trap his gaze. When he reached the other end of the hallway, he hastened through the door.

Inside was a simple, unadorned room. The far wall was dominated by a mirror bisected by a table with a chair beneath it. The mirror frame was completely black except for arcane sigils etched into its surface. Manheim set his briefcase on the table and sat down. He opened his briefcase, folded his hands into his lap, and waited patiently for his liaison to arrive.

Manheim knew they watched him, so he remained perfectly impassive, staring at the mirror. The mirror was a strange thing; it held an image of the room, but Manheim wasn't reflected in it. Thirty minutes passed before anyone came.

The other person was dressed much the same as Manheim, but his appearance was slick. Almost oily. His skin had a reddish cast and his eyes were so dark they appeared pupil-less. Before he closed the door on the other side, Manheim caught an impression of a hellish red light and leaping shadows. "You're late," the man stated. He opened his briefcase and shuffled papers.

"No, I'm not." Manheim was the picture of coolness, meeting the other man's statement with a stare.

The liaison gave him a little shrug. "You could have been. I wouldn't have known." He paused and read a sheet of paper. "Ah, yes, you were brokering a deal with Subway Pete?"

"Shopping Cart Pete."

"My mistake." The man glanced up at Manheim, checking to see if he was annoyed. "So many Petes, I get confused." He shuffled the papers once more and clicked his tongue against the roof of his mouth.

Manheim knew the game. The liaisons tried to annoy the time merchants. It was merely a power play, a way for petty people to assert dominance on those they felt were beneath them. It had been that way for a very long time and Manheim had determined the best course of action was not to react. Soon, the other man would become bored and they would get down to business.

The liaison tried a few more half-hearted attempts to get under Manheim's skin then gave up. He pushed a button on the table in front of him and a small recess, covered in arcane runes, opened in front of Manheim. "Put the contract through," the liaison said, his tone now brusque.

Manheim took the contract from his briefcase and put it in the recess, sliding it closed. A corresponding recess opened up on the liaison's side. He pulled the contract out and looked it over with a critical eye. He sighed deeply and put it down on the table.

"Looks perfect ... as always." He looked downright disappointed. "How much time does he have?"

Manheim glanced at his phone. "Twenty-one hours and fifteen minutes."

The liaison merely nodded. "You know I can't give you payment until the contract is set?"

"Of course."

"Well, it isn't like you'll be running out of years anytime soon."

Manheim shrugged. It was true. Time merchants were given an allotment of years depending on the contracts they signed. Every five contracts a time merchant brokered, they were rewarded with an additional six-month allotment. Some time merchants lived allotment to allotment. Some fell through. Manheim was good at his job. Even if he were to quit brokering deals, he still had enough years to live another millennium.

"Unless there was anything else?" Manheim asked.

The liaison didn't even look up from the contract in his hands. "Duke Sartagard requests that you agree to a transfer to Soul Services."

Manheim smiled inwardly. He had anticipated such a request. "Politely tell the duke that I am very happy with my current position with the Company."

"You do realize that time merchants are the lowest of the low? You've basically been stuck in the mailroom for almost two thousand years."

"I'm an old dog that doesn't want to learn new tricks." Manheim stood up from the table. "Unless there was anything else?"

The liaison waved him off with a disgusted shooing of his hand.

* * *

MANHEIM SAT IN THE back seat of the Uber traveling down a palm-tree-lined boulevard near the beach. He had been doing this for almost a year now, aimlessly wandering the city in the back of an Uber. Some might call him paranoid; Manheim believed himself cautious. He figured after a year, anyone who was suspicious would have become bored. He glanced at his phone. It was half past three. Manheim stuck his head out the window and could see the moon's shadow beginning to creep over the sun. The eclipse had begun.

"Take me to this address now."

The driver looked at him in the rearview mirror with his dark eyes and nodded. He was some sort of either Middle Eastern or African. He and Manheim had been driving around the city randomly for about an hour and a half.

Manheim wasn't foolish enough to believe the Company was above monitoring the activities of their agents. The eclipse would provide him mystical cover to do his business. It was like a jammer for the magical frequency, making it impossible to remotely view Manheim for the duration. He needed the cover because he couldn't let them catch him; he was far from finished.

The driver was good to his word and had Manheim in front of the home in less than ten minutes. It was a simple house, an A-frame design with a yard that could be better tended and a fence that had seen better days. Manheim handed the driver two crisp hundred-dollar bills. The driver eagerly grabbed the bills and sped away.

Manheim wasted no time; he went straight to the front door and knocked. The door was made of some flimsy material that didn't have a good tone when he struck it. He was afraid no one would hear and began looking for another spot to knock.

He caught movement to his right and saw the curtain draw back from the window enough for an eye to peek through. The woman slammed the curtain shut when she realized Manheim had seen her. Manheim waited patiently.

Almost a full twenty seconds passed before he heard the turning of locks. There was a series of clicks as locks were disengaged and deadbolts released. He counted at least seven. A tiny Mexican woman pulled the door open and Manheim opened the screen door.

"Ms. Lopez—" he started.

"We don't want any!" the tiny woman screeched through the barely open door then attempted to slam it, but Manheim had inserted his foot in the way.

"I'm not here to sell you anything, Ms. Lopez," Manheim started again. "I'm here to speak to Kevin."

"You some doctor?"

"No, ma'am."

"Reporter?"

Manheim merely shook his head.

"Then what?" Ms. Lopez was glaring at Manheim's offending foot.

"Ms. Lopez, this is a somewhat delicate matter and it would be best if we discussed this in private." Manheim sighed when she wasn't willing to relent her position at the door. "This has to do with a deal that you made some time ago."

Ms. Lopez's eyes became round like saucers. "No more deals! What else can you take from us?" Spittle flew from her mouth.

"I'm not here to take anything; I'm here to help, but time is of the essence. I must speak to Kevin. There won't be another opportunity for me to help him before he dies."

Ms. Lopez took a moment to consider his words. Manheim used this time to look over the lady before him, at least what he could see. She was young, probably in her mid-thirties. She didn't have the perfect body, but he wouldn't call her fat. She had "mom curves." He saw a few gray hairs creeping into her otherwise black hair. The one glaring eye he could see was a beautiful shade of green that reminded him of moss growing in a forest. She wore an artist smock covered in paint.

Manheim heard the rattle of a chain being retracted. Ms. Lopez opened the door to the point where Manheim could squeeze through. She stopped and looked at him expectantly.

He took the cue and did his best to slip in through the space provided. He felt the buttons of his shirt scrape against the wood of the door. Once he was inside, he turned and said, "Ms. Lop—"

Manheim was interrupted by the cocking of a shotgun. He looked down at the small Latina woman holding a gun that would probably throw her through a wall if she fired it.

"Ms. Lopez." Manheim took the development in stride, adopting a calm voice and adjusting his cufflinks. "I understand what you must be feeling. I assure you, even though I work for the Company, I have no ill intentions for either you or Kevin."

Ms. Lopez nudged the barrel of the gun forward, obviously trying to be threatening, and said, "What are your intentions?"

"I plan to give Kevin twenty years of my life."

"And what do we have to do for it?" Ms. Lopez asked, the tip of the gun lowering an inch.

"Only befriend a boy, one who will need guidance in the future," Manheim said, gently pushing the gun barrel away. He sighed inwardly when she didn't resist. "But this contract must be made with Kevin, so I need to speak with him."

"Whatever you want to say to Kevin, you'll have to say it in front of me."

"Certainly."

"This way."

Manheim followed her through the small house. The front room was covered in cloth and had many different canvases in different stages of completion. The pervading symbolism was dark. Ms. Lopez was a woman tortured by past decisions. There weren't many pictures of her or Kevin. Manheim chalked this up to guilt. They stopped in front of a door with a sign that sported a skull and crossbones and the words "KEEP OUT."

Ms. Lopez seemed to be reconsidering her decision to let him speak to Kevin. Manheim quickly said, "Ma'am, with all due respect, the eclipse won't last long and what I must say to you and Kevin can't be said outside of the eclipse, otherwise prying eyes will be watching. I promise, if you don't like what I tell you or offer you, you merely say no and I am on my way."

She rolled the thought around in her head and nodded. She opened the door. "Kevin, someone is here to see you."

Kevin sat in a giant hospital bed that dominated the room. He looked up weakly from his barely seated position. He was rail thin and his body was festooned with tubes. Kevin had stage four leukemia and had been brought home to die at the tender age of fourteen. Emaciated as he was, the resemblance between him and Ms. Lopez was undeniable.

"Hello, Kevin. My name is Manheim." He stuck his hand out.

Kevin put his hand in Manheim's, his small hand engulfed by the much larger hand. "Nice to meet you," he wheezed. "Are you another doctor? They all seem to want to see the dying boy."

"No, I'm not a doctor."

Kevin looked at Manheim. "Lawyer?"

"No," Manheim said, giving Kevin a gentle smile. "I assure you that you would never guess what I'm doing here in a hundred years."

Kevin made a burbling noise. It took Manheim a moment to realize that he was laughing. "Well, you're in luck. I don't got a hundred years."

Manheim's face didn't betray any emotion, but he cringed inwardly. Gallows humor. That wasn't a good sign. "What if I said I could fix that?"

Kevin's eyes narrowed into small, hard, glittering emeralds. "You said you weren't a doctor."

"I'm not. Have they ever been any help?"

Kevin's eyes unfocused as he thought about the question. After a few moments, he looked over at Manheim and said, "No."

"That's because your sickness isn't natural."

Kevin looked incredulously at his mom. She glanced away. Looking back up at Manheim, he said, "What do you mean? Like it is a weird strain or something?"

"No, I mean the cause of your leukemia isn't natural. The doctors never had a chance to cure it."

"But you can? How much is it gonna cost? A million?"

Manheim's mouth crooked in a half smile. "It won't cost money."

"Oh, so you are just giving this miracle cure away for free?" Kevin blew a raspberry in Manheim's direction.

"I didn't say that. I said it wouldn't cost money. Listen, you are sick because your mother made a deal with some bad people."

Ms. Lopez, who had been watching her son intently, turned away to pace against the corner of the room. Kevin watched her. "Mom, what's he talking about?"

The expression on Ms. Lopez's face could only be described as beyond distressed. "Kevin . . ."

When she made no move to continue, Manheim said, "Kevin, your mother made a deal for her artistic ability. The price was your health."

"Mom, what's he talking about?" Kevin's voice rose an octave. "Mom, say something!"

"What do you want me to say, Kevin?" She whirled around, tears streaming from her eyes. *"He's telling the truth . . . I . . ."* Ms. Lopez fell to her knees.

Manheim looked out the window. The sun was almost fully covered. *"I am telling the truth, Kevin. You can either accept that and move on to how I can help you, or waste time, which will mean that we lose this opportunity."*

"What do you mean?" Kevin struggled to sit up fully.

Manheim stepped to Kevin's side and helped him to a seated position, stuffing pillows behind his back. *"I mean that I only have before the eclipse ends to broker this deal. Once the eclipse ends, bad people will see where I am and the opportunity is lost. Are you willing to listen?"*

Kevin's eyes burned holes in the back of his mother's head from where she sat on the floor. He looked up to Manheim and asked, *"How can you help?"*

Manheim admired how quickly Kevin was dealing with the situation. *"I work for the same people that your mom made a deal with."*

"Then why should I ever trust you?" Kevin asked dryly.

"Fair question. Because I am trying to bring down the Company from the inside. To do so, I have to work in secret when the chance presents itself." Manheim straightened his lapel. The sight of Kevin was bringing up unpleasant memories and he needed to remain focused.

"How are you going to help?"

"I want to offer you a contract for twenty years of my life." Manheim was able to push the memories fully down, falling into the familiar pace of negotiation.

"Twenty years of living like this?"

"No, once the contract is made, your cancer will go into remission. It will come back when your time is up; I can't change that. But the years I give you will be cancer free." He cleared a table and pulled out a long piece of vellum paper.

Ms. Lopez started babbling. "When I made the deal, I knew I wasn't going to have children. I knew. I was nineteen and I was sure of everything. Really I was sure of nothing, except that I wanted to be an artist. So I made the deal. Then everything changed in one night. I went out drinking with friends and I met a man. One night, one man, and I was pregnant with you." Her face was an ugly mask of tears and mucus. "Kevin, can you ever forgive me?"

"You made me sick," he said in a barely controlled, even tone. Storms were raging behind his eyes.

"I didn't know you! Back then, you weren't even a possibility. A year later, I was pregnant."

"Kevin, don't lose focus. You have to lock your emotions down. Remember, we're on a ticking clock." Manheim checked outside. The sun was almost completely blocked by the moon.

"But she ruined my life! For what? So she could draw pictures?" Kevin tried to flail his arms but didn't have the strength.

Ms. Lopez babbled from the floor. "After that, even when I painted and drew, I could never sell it. No amount of money would ever be enough because I knew how much it cost just to draw the picture." She finally looked up to Kevin, her eyes bloodshot and tearstained.

Manheim looked down at Ms. Lopez and adjusted his cufflinks. "I understand, but you can't lose focus. Both of you need to be focused. I'm offering twenty years of my life."

"Fine." Kevin crossed his arms. "Why me?"

"The Company doesn't make deals that do not benefit them explicitly. The very fact your mother was given a deal that didn't have her soul as the price meant you are special." Manheim took a few steps to Ms. Lopez and held out his hand, helping her to her feet.

"But how am I special?" Kevin asked.

"I've consulted oracles and diviners of all types, and from what I can tell the signs point to you befriending a boy and helping him realize his destiny."

"From what you can tell?" Ms. Lopez's voice bordered on hysterical. "How do you not know for sure?"

"There are gaps in my memory. I've had to remove certain events and only have notes regarding them. I cannot allow the chance that the Company will scan my mind and find anything. It is safer this way."

"So, what's special about this boy?"

"He's one of the key components in bringing down the Company. I've waited a very long time for him."

"So, I'm not really special. He's the special one." Kevin deflated.

"Kevin, we don't get to choose the role we play," Manheim said softly. "We just play the hand that we are given and hope the world is a better place."

Kevin looked up at Manheim with a thoughtful expression. "What role do you get to play?"

"That would be a long story."

"Well, explain it quickly."

Manheim blew out a rough sigh. No avoiding the memories now. "I made a bad deal. The sad thing" — Manheim looked down at his wrists, fidgeting with his cufflinks — "is that it took me too long to realize it. My son was sick, and a plague ravaged the city we lived in. A city time has forgotten. My son and I are the only survivors. I made a deal to save us. My service for our lives.

"The problem is that contracts are unbreachable." A confused look crossed Kevin's face. "Unable to be broken. As long as I serve, my son lives. I thought it was the perfect deal. I was wrong. I was seeing it through a father's eyes. So, I never saw the toll the years would have on my son. When you live as long as we have, the years have a way of making you a monster."

When Manheim didn't continue, Kevin prodded, "Your son is a monster? Why aren't you?"

"Honestly . . ." Manheim spread out his hands and shrugged. "I don't know. Maybe it is because I work with evil every day. I see *it, I breathe it. I guard against it. In comparison, my son lived a life of indolence. Eventually, I looked up and he had become something I didn't recognize. Corrupted by the long years. People start looking like ants when you have eternal life. You don't remember that they are people and start treating them like playthings." Manheim shook his head. "He's been known by many names through the years. He was an adviser in Genghis Khan's horde. The Russians called him Rasputin. He was a scientist and loyalist in the Third Reich. By the time I realized what he had become, it was too late." Manheim pulled a chair and sat down heavily.*

"Why didn't you quit?" Ms. Lopez asked. Manheim had forgotten she was still there.

"I couldn't. Quitting wouldn't have solved anything. Without me the Company would have continued. My son would still be a monster and even dead, he could serve the Company in another capacity. If I leave, I want the Company no longer there."

Kevin reached out and took Manheim's hand. A simple gesture, but it lifted an unfathomable weight off his shoulders. "What do we need to do?"

Manheim smiled at Kevin. "I'll make the contract and all you need to do is sign. It will stipulate that you befriend a boy named Trey."

Kevin nodded.

Manheim pulled an athame from his briefcase. He quickly sliced his palm with it, dripping blood on the vellum paper. He muttered a few words in Middle Enochian and the blood formed words. In a matter of seconds, a contract was completed.

"Normally you have twenty-four hours to rescind a contract. It is the time it takes the ink on the contract to dry. This one stipulates that you will forget the contract after the eclipse." Manheim gathered Kevin's eyes with his gaze as he wrapped the wound on his hand with a rag. "I need you to be sure that this is what you want to do because you won't remember there is a contract to break."

"But how will I remember to befriend . . . Trey, was his name right?" Kevin said, trembling as he tried to sit up straight.

Manheim gently put his hand on Kevin's shoulder. "Right, Trey. Don't worry. As long as you are alive, the two of you will be drawn to one another."

Kevin digested the piece of information like everything else that had been said. After a moment he looked up and said, "We gotta play the cards we're dealt, right? So, I'm not going to remember any of this, right? I won't remember the deal my mom made, will I?"

"Kevin, I have to be honest, tampering with someone's memory isn't precise. While you won't remember the specifics of this event, you will retain . . . echoes. Faint traces. They will pop up from time to time. Feelings of déjà vu or just weird feelings in general. If something resonates with you strong enough, you'll remember it without having any reference to why you remember it. But as to the specific events, no, you won't remember those." Manheim started to fiddle with his cufflinks again, stopped himself, and instead favored the sick young man with a reassuring smile.

Kevin nodded, sidelong glancing at his mother, who was staring at him. Guilt was written clearly on her features, tears standing ready to fall at a moment's notice. "Good. I wouldn't want to live the rest of my life hating her."

Ms. Lopez recoiled as if slapped.

Manheim drew out his pen and told Kevin, "I'm going to have to take some blood. Just a little. Enough for you to sign."

Kevin nodded bravely. "Stage four leukemia, man. I'm used to getting blood taken."

"Fair enough." Manheim carefully pricked Kevin on his arm and drew back the lever. The young boy winced but forced a smile. Manheim handed the pen to Kevin and turned the contract toward him.

Kevin took a deep breath and signed.

* * *

A FEW HOURS LATER, Manheim exited the Uber in front of the nondescript office building. He gave the driver a fifty as he hurried inside. There were two men standing at the security desk with the guard. They were all in an intense conversation.

Manheim tried to walk past the trio but one of the men waved him over. Manheim recognized him as one of the older time merchants, named Chester. The man was not as keenly dressed as Manheim but was by no means a slouch. He had talked infrequently with Chester through the years and maintained a lukewarm relationship.

"Have you heard?" Chester asked.

Manheim readjusted the cuff of his suit. He looked down at his hand. It felt stiff, as if the flesh had not properly stretched. "Heard what?" he asked, distractedly massaging the palm of his hand.

"Oh, something has got the department heads in a tizzy!" said Chester's companion excitedly.

"What do you know, Manheim? What's going on? I know you know something."

Manheim felt the gap in his memory keenly but didn't focus on it. Outwardly, he simply shrugged. "Honestly? I don't know a thing. It's safer that way."

* * *

Twenty years later . . .

THE ONLY THING KEEPING Kevin upright was the back of the hospital bed. He tried to speak but his throat was raw and all that came out was a raspy wheeze. He weakly signaled for some water. A young black man jumped forward and held a cup up to Kevin's mouth. He took a couple small sips, the effort torture.

"Trey." Kevin's hand scrabbled around blindly on the bed. Trey set down the cup and took Kevin's hand in his. "Trey, don't be angry. Angry isn't the way; I wasted a lot of time being angry." Kevin shook his head weakly. "Leukemia. I was angry at life, angry at God. Be better than me, Trey. Be bet—"

"How can you tell me not to be angry, man? You're all I got in this world." Fresh tears streaked the young man's face. He honestly hadn't known that he had any more left to cry, never had much in life to cry about until this day. "You been like a father to me. You know that. You gotta know that, man. I ain't know my dad. My mama, she just some junkie. You're it, man. You ain't some reason to get angry, you the only reason in my life to get angry." Trey felt the tears start burning his cheeks as he pressed Kevin's hand against his forehead.

Trey lifted his head and continued. "You remember how we met? Do you know how many people had given up on me?" Trey shook his head, the hint of a bittersweet smile playing on his lips. "I can't even remember how many there were."

Kevin simply smiled and nodded his head. "I remember," he wheezed. "You looked so young, sitting there by yourself. And you were angry. So angry."

"I was . . ." Trey shook his head slowly from side to side, eyes staring back in the past. "The world was a lonely place for me. Couldn't trust nobody. Then you came over and said, 'I think you're the one I'm here to help.' I just looked you up and down like you were crazy."

"And you said, 'What are you, the tooth fairy?' That's when I was sure you were the one I came to help. Someone once told me that we don't get to choose the roles we play, we just have to play the hand we're dealt and hope we leave the world a better place. I don't remember who told me that, but I know the world is a better place because it's got you in it." Kevin motioned to the side table where Trey found an envelope. "So, Trey, these have been the best ten years of my life. In there, you will find your inheritance." Kevin put up his hand to forestall any argument. "It's money from paintings that I sold when my mom passed. I don't know why she kept ahold of them, and I could never bear to look at them. They left me uneasy." Kevin lurched forward, a coughing fit wracking his frail form, but he waved off Trey's assistance. "Knowing you, watching you grow up into the young man sitting beside me. I couldn't be more proud of you, son." Kevin choked over the last word because of the raw emotion entwined in it. He tried to take a full breath to calm himself but had to settle for half a breath because his lungs wouldn't cooperate. Kevin knew his time was short. "Trey, promise me, don't get stuck in this moment. You have so much to offer this wor—"

Kevin's voice trailed off as the level tone of the heart monitor flatlining filled the room. Trey's hands became numb, Kevin's hand slipping listlessly out of his as doctors and nurses rushed into the room. Trey stood up and gently pushed away from the bedside. His mouth worked silently, trying to form words, too overwhelmed with grief. Finally, the words forced their way out, no louder than a whisper.

"I promise."

Trey slipped out of the room. He felt his eyes burning in anger but didn't realize that they were ablaze in blue light. He was so wrapped up in his grief he almost slammed into an impeccably dressed man. It startled him and he looked up, the blue fire around his eyes winking out.

"Trey, my condolences for your loss. Kevin was a good man," Manheim said, adjusting his cufflinks. "I know this is a difficult time, but I thought it was also time for us to meet. My name is Manheim."

"Yeah, so. What's that gotta do with me?" Trey, even in the throes of his grief, instantly became distrustful.

Manheim's eyes softened. He gently put a hand on Trey's shoulder. "A long time ago, some very bad people tried to steal Kevin from your life before you could get a chance to meet him." Manheim paused as he looked past Trey to the hospital room where Kevin's body rested. "I'm the man that made sure that didn't happen."

"You here for a thank you? Or what, you want money?"

"No." Manheim played with his cufflink, this conversation not going as planned. "I'm here to help you. There are bad men out there that tried to hurt you and tried to hurt Kevin. And they are still trying to hurt you and other young men and women like you." Manheim let out a heavy sigh. "I've been waging this war a very long time, Trey. I've been waiting on you to take this war out of the shadows and into the light."

"You say they tried to steal Kevin from me?" Trey chewed on those words, repeating them to himself, his face scrunching up as he found them distasteful. Slowly, his eyes began to glow once more, glinting a clear, brilliant blue. He looked back over his shoulder to the room where the doctors were pronouncing Kevin dead. Looking up at Manheim, he said, "Where do we start?"

To learn more about this author, please visit:
https://www.gdeanmanuel.com/

Return to Sérénité

Literary

i.a.n.

Prompt: There are two kinds of people in the world.

*"You can't go . . . back home to romantic love, back home
to a young man's dreams . . . and some foreign land . . .
back home to someone who can help you, save you, ease
the burden for you, back home to the old forms and
systems of things which once seemed everlasting but
which are changing all the time—back home to the
escapes of Time and Memory."*

—Thomas Wolfe

*I*T'S BEEN TWENTY-FOUR YEARS *since my last visit, and that brief
return to Sérénité now seems to have been a hazy dream, or a
nightmare. But the lessons I learned live on in vivid reality. How
did I end up on the far side of the earth decades after my first sojourn
there—back on the tropical island where I had once spent the most
marvelous months of my youth?*

*Until a fateful day in 1994, I'd long since resigned myself to
never seeing Sérénité again. But life deals us unexpected hands. Mine
was dealt early one evening twenty-four years ago. I'd done pretty
well since returning home from Vietnam in 1969. A quarter century*

later, I enjoyed a happy family life, a nice house, a garage of fine cars, and our last kid was off to university. I was immensely content and self-satisfied. At that point, I could have felt at peace with the prospect of riding off into my affluent-but-less-than-fully-satisfying sunset. At least that's how I viewed my life until that evening I came home from work, totally oblivious to the drastic change about to befall me.

When I entered our family room that evening in 1994, Pam was sitting on her beige, floral-patterned, upholstered sofa—a bottle of Chardonnay and an empty glass on the low table between us, another glass in her hand. The glass she held was half-empty, as was the bottle. While I crossed the room to deliver a perfunctory cheek-peck, she filled both glasses, rose from the sofa, and fended me off by holding one glass out to me across the table.

Pam announced, "We need to talk, darling."

Uh oh! What now? "Sure, sweetheart. What is it?" My stomach churned.

She settled back onto the sofa. "You know, with the house empty now, I've been thinking . . ."

"Yes, so have I. But you first. What've you been thinking about?"

"Remember, you said we should make a New Year's resolution to change our lives?"

"Yes, of course. I've been thinking about—"

"I think we should consider a separation." Her cool blue eyes fixed on mine. She blinked away a tear and used the back of her index finger to wipe her cheek. I noticed a tissue box sitting on the sofa next to her. On the floor beside the sofa, a veneer of discarded tissues shrouded the bottom of a trash basket.

Stunned, I sank into my leather recliner without my expected hug. "A separation! You mean us? You and me? Why?" My mouth went dry. I gulped from the wine glass she'd thrust into my hand. "I thought we were happy. I'm happy. Aren't you happy?"

"I've been happy, but there must be something more, something more for each of us." She paused. Words failed me. "Your turn now. What were you thinking about?" She crossed a leg away from me and jiggled her foot.

I cleared my throat. "Well not this, for sure."

"Come on, Andrew. What're your thoughts?"

"I doubt that my thoughts are all that important now."

"Sure they are. Take your time and tell me." She glanced at her watch.

"Actually, I've been thinking we could get an RV and tour the national parks."

Pam sighed. "You see, that's why we should each do our own thing. For you, life on the road in an RV sounds exciting. You get to escape from your day-to-day routine." She looked away and took a sip of her wine. Refocusing her eyes on mine, she went on. "To me, that sounds like more of the same—cooking, cleaning, laundry—but in a smaller, less convenient space and without knowing the neighbors. Escape for me is different. If I hit the road, I want to be somewhere somebody else does the grocery shopping and cooking, the laundry and the housecleaning—the chores that make my life humdrum."

There was more—lots more. But she remained adamant, and I eventually saw the futility of fighting a losing battle. The bottom line was that one long chapter of my life was closing, and—although I failed to see it at the time—another chapter was opening.

* * *

IN MY YOUTH I had spent the better part of 1968 on my magic isle of Sérénité. After several carefree months of life as a beach bum, I had returned to "The World," soon met a girl, soon gotten married, soon begun a family, and settled into a mundane suburban life, supported by a lucrative albeit unexciting career.

Over the years, I'd escape the tedium with moments of reverie, when I'd muse on my secret dream of a return to Sérénité. Of course, that was just an idle dream. Well into middle age, I assumed I was far past such adventures. But after the kids grew and left home, followed soon after by my wife's split, I suddenly realized I was free to pursue my dreams. But life was seeping away, and I needed to take action if I ever wanted to see my dormant dream come to fruition.

From under a dusty pile in the attic, I dug up an old trunk. I broke out a cache of letters with ink fading after more than two dozen years in hiding. Maybe this was meant to be. I need to visit, even if just to see what might have been. I need to see Shaylah again.

A little research revealed that over the years, Sérénité had gained independence, built an airport, and become — please forgive the oxymoron — a well-known "secret" destination for Aussie holiday-makers. As I'd done back in '68, once again I mustered my savings — well, what was left after the community property split, alimony, and college expenses — packed a few belongings, and booked Qantas to Sydney.

* * *

As I settled into my transfer flight out of Sydney to Papeete and the plane headed northeast, high above the sun-sparkled Coral Sea, I dug into my carry-on bag and began rereading Shaylah's letters. Would she still be there? Can I find her? The return address, neatly inked into the upper left-hand corner of each envelope, bore a return address of only "Poste Restante, Sérénité" — the equivalent of an American general delivery address. My best lead would be her father's restaurant — The Black Parrot.

It hit me that this would be my first return to the South Pacific in twenty-six years. Much would have changed. I might be chasing a pipe dream. In 1968, I'd been an aimless young man recently discharged from the marines in Hawaii after two tours in Vietnam, and I felt eager to travel around the Pacific in search of adventure before heading back to the mainland.

Old South Sea sailors told me wild tales of a paradise at the far edge of Polynesia. Historically, as a far-flung outlier of French Oceania, Sérénité had enjoyed a fair measure of autonomy from Papeete. The island had long upheld a proud tradition of maintaining independence by shifting allegiances. The European population had descended from mutineers and ship jumpers from British or French vessels put into the harbor to replenish provisions. The islanders, both native and European, saw their best outcome laid in quickly satisfying any visiting sailors' needs and sending them on their way. The ensign that flew from the stern of the ship in the lagoon was matched by a similar flag run up the shore pole, and a "governor" of the appropriate descent trotted out to welcome the ship's landing party and offer the island's hospitality.

Early in World War II, Sérénité carried on under laid-back French rule, changing flags back and forth from Vichy to Free French according to whether the warships sailing past were Axis or Allied. Then in 1942, the island was "liberated" without a shot by a small combined force of American and Aussie troops. The locals merely retired both their French flags — the plain tricolor of the Gaullist Free French and the tricolor with seven stars and battle-ax of the Nazi-affiliated Régime de Vichy — and hoisted the Australian colors displaying the Southern Cross. After the war and a few years of benign neglect under Aussie supervision, the locals opted out of returning to French rule and voted in favor of continuing under Aussie protection. In this situation, Sérénité remained largely forgotten and isolated from the winds of change blowing throughout the outside world.

While I'd been knocking about Hawaii in '68, old-timers boasted to me that on Sérénité a man could trade one fish for ten bananas, one banana for ten coconuts, and one coconut for ten women. And the bay, one of the world's most beautiful natural lagoons, was teeming with fish.

Charged up with youthful dreams, I'd taken my accumulated combat pay, packed my seabag with swimwear and dive gear — including a speargun — and headed to Papeete, whence, back in the '60s, one could book deck passage on the monthly copra schooner that served as the only commercial transportation between civilization and the outlying islands.

* * *

IN '94, FLYING OUT *of Sydney and lulled by the drone of jet engines, my mind once again drifted to long-submerged thoughts of Shaylah, wondering if I could find her. I closed my eyes and saw her, still barely twenty. In retrospect, I couldn't even make sense of the reasons I'd left. Moving on had just seemed to be the thing for a young man to do, especially when his recently widowed mother wanted to see her only son after he'd survived two combat tours in Nam. My thoughts and fantasies morphed to pondering the relentless flow of time, day after day, month after month, decade after decade — sands slipping through the waist of an hourglass.*

To calm my burgeoning excitement, I let my mind drift back twenty-six years to my first journey to Sérénité in '68. During that trip, on the schooner Ta'aroa — a genuine two-masted, gaff-rigged relic of a bygone era — there had been another young world traveler. He was the authentic article, rather than a newbie civilian with a military buzz-cut and a duffle bag. Ken had tramped along the Hippie Trail, as did many youths of the sixties in search for nirvana, but — as had been the case with the young St. Augustine — he was not yet ready to renounce earthly pleasures encountered in the course of his wanderings.

Ken had backpacked across three continents — hitchhiking across Europe via the Balkans; through the Middle East via Afghanistan and the Khyber; across the hump of South Asia; through Burma, down the Malay Peninsula; and then taken passage on a Royal Mail Ship from Singapore to Darwin, whence he had hitched across the Outback to Melbourne, then up through the Snowy Mountains to Sydney. Eventually he made his way to the same copra schooner carrying us both to Sérénité.

Despite our resembling *The Odd Couple* — he, with a grizzled beard and long dreadlocks, a stash of hash, and always wearing Afghan-style *paijama* with *kurta*; I, clean-shaven with buzz-cut hair, straitlaced, and wearing Bermuda shorts with Hawaiian shirts — our mutual interests bonded us during that passage. Apparently he had heard similar accounts of our destination, because he also had a dive mask and speargun in his kit. His odyssey had lasted thirty-three months to that point, and — like Scheherazade — Ken seemed to have a tale for every night of that time.

Ken should be the one relating this; he'd have volumes of fascinating tales, and he'd spin you a few fair-dinkum accounts. I have only this one.

* * *

IN 1994, GIVEN THE absence of copra schooners, from Papeete, a regional airline flew the final leg to the Sérénité International Airport. As the little plane began its descent, a green dot rose into view on the horizon — an emerald set among pavé sapphires. Upon closer approach, the single blob of green separated into myriad faceted hues of lush verdancy.

When I'd arrived in 1968, immigration formalities had consisted of wading ashore and wandering the beach to find a hut to accommodate us — us, because on the schooner Ken and I had decided to team up and pool our resources. By 1994 the large, modern terminal had queues for immigration, customs, currency exchange, and taxis. Other than on wall posters, I saw no sign of a beach.

Finally, after official formalities, a taxi took me on the road from the airport toward Grand Anse Resort, a huge hotel complex occupying what had once been our sweeping crescent of palms, sandy beach, and sea where Ken and I had rented a thatched hut in exchange for a string of fresh fish each morning. Now the old coconut groves adjacent to the beach had been replaced by patios, pools, swim-up bars, and tiki huts in the courtyard, which was enclosed by four-floor glass-and-block buildings where rich tourists paid more per night for a room than we used to spend each month on everything our hearts desired. In '94, the only coconuts in sight sat on the bar to advertise piña coladas.

En route to the resort, I had been unable to avoid the sight of countless billboards touting the glories of life in the workers' paradise under the leadership of President-for-Life Ricard. Trees, rocks, walls, and lampposts were festooned with cartoon-style posters showing the president in various lionhearted poses — Ricard helming the ship of state through capitalist shoals, Ricard fighting off imperialist sharks, Ricard receiving garlands from adoring little girls, Ricard pinning medals to the chest of his heroic police chief — who, according to the taxi driver, was also Ricard's brother-in-law.

Other broadsheets announced the universal opportunity for all Sérénité teens to join the Youth Brigade, with its camp on *Ile Ronde* — Round Island — where all teens would enjoy special training uninterrupted by outside influences — such as family or church busybodies.

The taxi took me along a stretch of road I remembered as the old coastal trail between the mountains and the lagoon, but now — across from the mountain, facing the road — endless chains of corrugated-sheet-metal warehouses blocked any glimpse of the shore.

I asked the driver, "Didn't this used to be beach and ocean — right here where these buildings are?"

"Yes, when I was a child this was a wasteland, just sand and trees, and sometimes the sea came right up near the road. President Ricard has performed wonderful miracles for us. Would you like to see? It will take us only a few minutes off our way."

"Can we?"

"Of course. I have a friend."

"Sure, I'm here to see the changes. Might as well start now."

The driver came to an open gate in the chain-link fence and turned right, onto a road running between two of the warehouses. He stopped at a barrier and spoke briefly to a guard toting an AK-47. After a moment of bantering in a patois I couldn't catch and the handoff of a cigarette to the gendarme, that gentleman slung his rifle over his shoulder, raised the barrier, and waved us through.

I had thought the warehouses were merely blocking the view of the lagoon, but when we passed the first row of buildings there was another row, then another row after that, and more beyond those. There was no sign of a shoreline. Finally, past the buildings, I was confronted by not water but a vast field of gravel. In this field, concrete foundations awaited the erection of yet more rows of warehouses. Far beyond the rocks, I glimpsed the turquoise blue of the lagoon.

As we drove along the edge of the rocky field, we passed a large cluster of women, hundreds I guessed, squatting on their haunches and lethargically wielding hand sledgehammers to pound bowling-ball-sized boulders into smaller rocks. A conveyor line of men passed woven raffia baskets full of these smaller stones, man to man, to the end of the queue in the field where the last man dumped the load and a parallel queue of women — presumably on break from their sledge duties — passed the empty baskets back to be refilled.

I reminisced about torch-lit full-moon nights of a quarter century earlier, when the men would paddle out into the lagoon in pirogues and beat the rippling surface with palm fronds, driving schools of fish toward the shore. The women waited in playful lines, having waded waist-deep into the lagoon, holding a long net to trap the fish being driven toward them. All the while, both the men in their pirogues and the women in the shallow warm waters were singing and laughing. Now I didn't see any of these men or women singing, or even smiling.

I asked, "Why are they doing this? A single machine could crunch all those stones to gravel in a fraction of the time it takes a hundred women to break them with hammers, and then another machine could move the gravel into the field and distribute it evenly."

"But then all these people would not have jobs. They would be idle and not have money to buy food or clothing."

"Their parents fished and gathered fruit from the trees. They wore simple sarongs—not T-shirts, jeans, and flip-flops. Do you really think this is an improvement?"

"Of course it is. This is the twentieth century. We live in a modern world now. People need a regular income. The president provides us with free education for the jobs we need to earn that income." The driver made eye contact in his rearview mirror as if to ensure I was listening. "President Ricard started the Youth Brigade so even the poorest children can get away from their family conditions and be trained in the youth camp for a productive life." He seemed wound up with zeal. "All citizens have the opportunity to be tested for their positions and get training in that field for a government job."

"Ah, yes. I saw the posters about Round Island. Isn't that the big island on the far side of the lagoon, the one without a water source, or a bay, or even a landing beach?"

"Yes, but the government built a cistern to collect rainwater."

"I remember Round Island. The French used it to house exiled troublemakers who'd been deported from French colonies. When I was here in the sixties the British used it in a similar way. It was off-limits for visitors. Can I visit there now?"

"Oh no, only the youth and the Youth Brigade staff are permitted there. It is best you don't ever ask about Ile Ronde." The driver became less communicative and headed back to the main road to continue in silence to the resort.

* * *

AT THE RESORT THAT *night, I pondered how to go about finding Shaylah. My only address for her was the useless Poste Restante fading on the old letters. The next day I learned that 1994's Sérénité had a telephone system, and the resort concierge had a phone book. First, I checked for Le Perroquet Noir Restaurant. There was no listing. With low expectations, I searched the listings for Shaylah. In the faded ink of her return address, I rechecked the spelling of her full name—Shaylah Liat Nuyen—but I assumed she might have a different last name now. Her grandparents had been from Tonkin. Her grandfather had been majordomo for a prominent French businessman in Hanoi who had brought the family to Sérénité to work in his South Sea household. Her father had married a half-French, half-island girl and started the only Vietnamese restaurant—indeed, one of the few restaurants—on Sérénité. I'd met Shaylah while she was serving as a waitress in her father's restaurant, Le Perroquet Noir, three months into my stay—about the time the impersonal bartering of fish for bananas and coconuts every day was growing monotonous. She had saved me from a soulless existence by imprinting an indelible face on my happiness—a face that had never faded from my memories.*

To my surprise, the phone book listed her by the name I'd known. There was a four-digit phone number and an address on Cascade Road. I remembered Cascade Church as a bit of a local landmark; in fact, an image of the church graced a few of the colorful stamps on her letters. I assumed Cascade Road might be the short road that wended uphill from the church to the waterfalls. I asked the concierge to get me a taxi to the church.

* * *

WHEN I ARRIVED, THE *church bells were chiming euphoric tintinnabulations, as if in celebration of my life's relaunch. Sure enough, the road meandering uphill from the church was Cascade*

Road. I paid off the taxi and ambled up the road until I found the address.

From the road, it seemed a nice property, with a lush garden behind a low wall. The home itself lay largely camouflaged behind the garden, flourishing with trees and bushes splashing with color — delicate white jasmine, bright yellow hibiscus, waxy pink frangipani, and vivid scarlet helicon resembling large crab claws strung on vines sprawling over the walls. Standing outside the gate, I closed my eyes and drew a deep breath. Will she remember me? If she does, will she hate me for not answering her letters? For not returning . . . sooner?

I exhaled a slow, controlled, "Ommm," opened my eyes, and wiped my palms down the thighs of my shorts. Then I strode through the open gate. A subtle aroma of jasmine engulfed me. As I passed, I plucked a single jasmine blossom to take to the door as a lucky talisman.

Like a teen about to ask a girl to the prom, butterflies hovered in my stomach, but I had come too far to chicken out now. The phone's listed in her name, so it seems she's single. But that used to be standard for Sérénité — formal marriage was the exception rather than the rule, at least back in '68. Sequential liaisons were more common — Ken called it serial shagging. She might have a partner here. The house seemed nice, like a double-income home, but she probably inherited her father's restaurant and that could explain the apparent cornucopia of comfort.

I took another deep breath, let it out, and walked up to the door. Noticing what appeared to be an electric doorbell, I pondered on how much the milieu of Sérénité had changed since '68. I pushed the button — just a short jab — and heard a jingle within the house. A fleeting thought of rapid retreat crossed my mind, but before I could give flight serious consideration, the door opened.

There she was, more than twice as old — a woman rather than the girl I remembered — but still trim and attractive. She stared into my eyes for a moment. Then her eyebrows rose as her mouth gaped open without any sound coming out. Her hand rose to cover her lips, which had given a hint of a quiver. She recovered and lowered her hand. "No, it can't be."

"Shaylah, I . . ." My mind went blank. Whatever words I'd rehearsed escaped me and never returned.

A smile spread across her face and the corners of her eyes crinkled. "Oh, my Lord! Andy, I can't believe it."

I raised my hands in a blend of shrug and abject surrender. "I shoulda called . . ."

"You should have written."

Not knowing what to do, I held out the jasmine blossom.

She took the blossom and tucked it behind her ear. "You promised you'd come back, but I never dreamed you'd take this long."

"Shaylah, you look great. There's so much I've been thinking I want to tell you, but now, I don't know what to say . . . where to begin . . . Do you have time to talk? Would you like to go get some tea?"

"Of course. I want to hear what you've been up to the past twenty-five years."

"Twenty-six. But who's counting?"

She glanced over my shoulder toward the road. "How did you get here? Are you alone?"

"Taxi. I walked up from the church."

"You don't have, um . . . anyone waiting?"

"No, I sent him away."

Her forehead furrowed as if she were puzzled.

"I guess it was like burning my bridge behind me, ditching the taxi so my fear wouldn't tempt me to retreat."

"Oh, okay. Let's take my car and go into town." She gestured to a fairly late-model four-door sedan parked at the side of the house.

A Mercedes, looks like a 300E — the restaurant must be doing okay. I went to wait beside her car while she went into the house to fetch her keys. Waiting, I began to wonder if her offer to drive me into town might be her way of putting our reunion in a public venue, keeping me out of the privacy of her home.

After a few minutes, her voice floated from a side window. "Andy, please be patient a few more minutes. I have an idea, but I need to do something."

Soon she appeared, carrying a basket. "I made us a small picnic—just a few things. Would you like to go to our old spot overlooking Grand Anse? If we can find it . . . I haven't been up there for years, but I've seen a dirt track off the main road that seems to go up toward it."

"Sure, that sounds great." My heart danced. I had many fond memories of that spot. But back in the day we had to hike up to enjoy sunsets in privacy.

When we got into her car, I realized we'd never been in a car together before. I'd never even been in a car the entire time I'd lived in 1968's Sérénité, and I'd never seen her in one. And now she's driving. The times, they are a-changing.

As she drove, she said, "I still have your letters. What happened . . . when you stopped writing?"

I slouched in the passenger seat and stared down at her car dash. "The letters took so long to complete a full cycle . . . Things just happened. Life . . . you know. I met somebody, but I . . . well, to be frank, I was too much of a coward to tell you when I got engaged. It seemed easier just to keep putting it off, until it became easier to just not write at all. I'm sorry." Swallowing hard, I forced myself to look at her. "That was unforgivable of me."

Shaylah stared ahead. "I got over it. I didn't really think you'd come back anyway, not when I was realistic about it. It was just a dream—a pleasant, youthful dream." She kept her eyes fixed on the winding road over the mountain—a good excuse to avoid eye contact. "In those days, before the airport, or cruise ships, Sérénité was about as remote from America as you could get. It wasn't easy even for Aussies to get here. And a few of them also promised to come back."

She turned her car up a narrow dirt track and ascended to our small clearing overlooking Grand Anse far below, and the sea beyond. There was a slight drizzle, so she opened the basket in the car and took out a paper sack of fried bananas and a bottle of rum.

"Shaylah, you remembered my favorites. You're amazing. How did you prepare this so fast?"

"I'd already made them for my breakfast this morning. Well, not the rum—the bananas. These were leftover."

"Well, thank you. Leftovers or not, this looks delicious. And I'm glad you remembered how much I love your fritters. I've never found anything quite like yours since . . . since I left." I helped myself to her banana fritters while she poured rum for us.

"I've never forgotten." She passed a glass to me, took a slow sip of her rum, and then asked, "Do you remember the first time we came up here?"

"As I remember, we had our first kiss here. I've thought about you . . . about us . . . a lot over the years." My heart swelled with warm reminiscence. I sensed an invisible aura about her; a trace of the scent of coconut oil ushered old memories rushing back to me. My fingers tingled with an urge to reach across the console to touch her.

"Yes, I have too . . . thought of us a lot."

I finished her last fritter.

She handed me a fortune cookie. "For luck."

Cracking it open, the print was tiny—the ink blurry to my eyes—and what I could make out was in French. "My lingo's gone rusty over the years." I passed the little slip to her. "Could you, please?"

"Let's see." She pulled a pair of reading glasses from the console. "It says, 'Ce sera votre jour de chance.'" Her eyes twinkled at me above the rim of her glasses. "Sounds like this may be your lucky day."

She stopped talking, but her lips remained parted and close to mine as she leaned over the console to top off my rum glass.

That was all the invitation I needed to pick up where we'd left off over two-and-a-half decades earlier. She welcomed the resurgence of our youthful yearnings.

* * *

IN THE AFTERGLOW, WITH rain plashing a gentle rhythm on the roof of the car and droplets trickling down the windows, I reflected on how lucky I felt to have rediscovered my paradise, to have reconnected with the island girl of my dreams, and to have done so without all the drama I'd feared might greet my belated return.

As if nature chose this moment to celebrate with a melodramatic display, the low-hanging clouds parted, the sun shone through to sparkle in the surf rolling onto the barrier reef, and a rainbow arched over the calm waters of the lagoon.

Shaylah besieged me with a slew of questions. I filled her in about Pam and the kids.

When she grew quiet to take aboard all I'd told her, I asked, "So, Shaylah, you know my story. How is it you've evaded all the guys who musta been chasing after you?"

"Oh, I haven't. For twenty-five years now, I've been living with Patrick—a great Aussie bloke. I met him soon after I realized you'd stopped writing me."

Nature intervened with its pathetic fallacy as dark thunderheads closed in again, and the rainbow faded to a gray pall over the seascape.

I shifted in the seat, now aware of the muggy air and feeling cramped, as if the space were closing in on me. "Oh? Uh . . . what does Patrick think we're doing now?"

"He's in Sydney. He spends a week there each month. Sometimes I go with him, but usually he goes alone. My work keeps me here most of the time."

Desperate to change the direction of our conversation, I asked, "Your work? Are you still at the restaurant?"

"Oh no, not for years now. I'm an MP—"

"A military policewoman?"

"No, silly. I'm a member of parliament—l'Assemblée Nationale. I represent the Cascade District for President Ricard's Workers' Party."

This news jarred my reverie. Again, I tried to recover by changing the subject. "I don't know anything about that. I just know this is wonderful, being here in the rain, just you and me in nature." I tried forcing a smile, but I felt an inkling that all was not well in paradise.

"Andy, you're so poetic the way you talk about us and being alone in nature. I love the way you relate to the natural world. I wish I could entertain such idyllic thoughts. I have to be more practical. I've been thinking about how terrible the weather is."

"Really? Is that all?"

Her eyes gleamed. "No. Of course not . . ."

My slumping sentiments began a rebound. I smiled and squeezed her hand to encourage her to go on. "Uh-huh?"

"I've also been thinking I'll introduce a bill to widen the road up here and macadamize it, bulldoze the jungle over there" —she gestured toward the uphill side of the clearing—"and pave a car park—big enough to handle tour buses from the cruise ships. Then we'll pour concrete in the clearing to make a viewing platform. We should erect guardrails around it so the people won't wander off when they come up here for a bird's-eye view of the government projects around the port. We must keep them organized so they won't get lost." Her voice resonated with excited fervor. "We could install those big pedestal-binoculars—you know, the kind that takes coins. And we'll put up large signs identifying this as Comrade Ricard Park, and that" —she pointed out toward the sea—"will be Ricard's Overlook."

"I hate to think about construction here in our special spot." I felt as if a plug had been jerked from my heart, draining all the warm feelings.

"Andy, you're far too sentimental. That's nice, but the people would really want a Ricard project to open this view for them."

"Shaylah, I saw all the construction along the lagoon road. It's awful how they've turned a beautiful lagoon into an ugly industrial park."

"That was absolutely necessary. I chaired the sub-committee for the project. We couldn't have the airport without filling in a lot of the lagoon. We've created hundreds of hectares of land where there was only sea and coral before. You know, it turns out coral makes good building material. What was useless lagoon is now the international airport and the RIZ."

"The RIZ? What's that?"

"The Ricard Industrial Zone. The airport has created a tourism boom that boosts our economy. That allows us to import all the things modern civilization needs. It provides employment for the people and tariffs to fund government." Her eyes glittered with enthusiasm. "With their new jobs, the people can buy TVs, motorbikes, imported clothing, and so much more. This is progress. Besides, there's still enough lagoon to accommodate cruise ships. We get three a week, and that brings in a tidy sum of revenue in port fees and tourist spending in the casinos and the government shops in the Duty-Free Zone."

"Don't you remember how nice it was before you had so much government, before you had organized tourism, before the people needed to work for money to buy imports they didn't need then?"

"Andy, don't be so naïve. All these changes are for the good of the people. We have to bring them into the twentieth century."

* * *

PERHAPS THE BEST WAY to describe my disappointment would be Pam's trite "We had grown apart." It really was true; we had become different people. In my memory, Shaylah had remained in her naïve state — naïve in its primary sense, natural, not artificial. While I had *spent years dreaming of returning to nature, it turned out she had spent years aspiring to escape to civilization. We had passed each other in the darkness and continued our journeys in opposite directions—in my case, toward romantic idealism; for her, toward amassing the accoutrements of modernity.*

We returned to her house, where she invited me in for a nightcap. On her side table, I saw a frame holding a five-by-eight-inch black-and-white photo. I recognized myself—a young, muscular me with a deep tan—peering out from the frame.

"I don't remember that picture. When was it taken?"

"Of course you don't remember it. This is the first time you've been in here. That's my son, Andrew." Her eyes studied mine. "He's twenty-five and a PhD student at the London School of Economics. When he finishes there, he'll come home and take up a senior post in the Sérénité government. President Ricard has his future all planned."

"Andrew? . . . Uh—"

She picked up the picture and laid it face down on her table. "Andy, we can't be together after tonight."

"What do you mean?"

"Tonight must be our final farewell."

"But, Shaylah—"

"Patrick's due back from Sydney tomorrow, then he and I plan to fly to London to visit Andrew—our son. You must know how it is. And it's best that Patrick never meets you. I'm sure you understand." Her intent scrutiny told me I'd best understand without any further questions.

"Sure. But, I hope someday—"

"No. Never. You really haven't changed all that much over the years."

So much was rushing at me so fast, for a moment I mistook her words as a compliment. My heart tried to rally. "Thank—"

"Patrick must never see you. Nor should Andrew. You do understand, don't you?"

"I guess . . ."

"Good. Now let's make the most of our hour of splendor."

"Of course." I felt my heart contracting as if it were destined to become the black hole of my universe—the heaviest, most dense core, sucking in all matter in its orbit.

Too soon, or maybe not soon enough, Shaylah called a taxi to meet me opposite the church. I bid Shaylah farewell, and then I descended to the bottom of the road. As I waited outside the church, the bells knelled an excruciating finale—a dirge for dying dreams.

* * *

THE EXPERIENCE WAS A disappointment due to the nature of the unexpected changes I'd found waiting for me. These were not merely physical, but rather changes of outlook and attitude toward life. I had spent decades remembering a dream life in the lap of nature's bounties, awaiting my plucking in an unspoiled tropical island paradise. That's how I remembered Sérénité from the sixties. In those times, my island had been one of the most isolated and naturally beautiful spots on earth. In my unsophisticated dreams of those days, Shaylah and I were blessed with eternal youth, living in perpetual springtime.

On my return in the nineties, the world had discovered my paradise. It had been developed to cater to high-end tourists rather than backpacking young wanderers. My native girl had become a force within the local government—a government which had been nonexistent and unnecessary in my youth, when the islanders lived happily in a protectorate under the benign neglect of a distant laissez-faire guardian. To make matters even worse, the new government seemed a nasty mix of Marxism and mercenary rapaciousness, with a touch of corruption and nepotism tossed into the mélange.

Teens, at least those without political connections, were forced into youth camps for indoctrination. My dream girl had become a champion for the very governmental development projects that were ruining the idyllic setting, and she was a wholehearted apologist for economic policies that made nearly everything too expensive for either new backpackers or most of the locals to afford. It was all "for the people," but the people had become slaves of the government elite and servants for rich tourists.

Bitterly disappointed by the shattering of a lifetime of dreams, I finally realized that time does not stand still for anyone, as much as we may will it to. I pondered how much my own actions, and my inactions, may have contributed to the despoliation of my dream paradise. If I'd stayed, or if I'd even written when Shaylah needed me, how might those dreams have turned out? But whatever might have been, she's made it apparent she no longer needs me, and I no longer fit into this brave new paradise. My best play now would be a graceful exit.

Now, at long last understanding life's dynamism imposed by nature's ever-changing course, my hard-earned knowledge allowed me to finally grow up and move on with real life.

The next evening, I hiked up to the clearing overlooking Grand Anse. At sunset, I burned my old letters, watching the flickering flames render the crumbly paper and faded ink to gray curls of ash and smoke, which wafted away on the sea breeze. Then I returned to Grand Anse, where I packed away my youthful dreams and booked an early departure.

I never found Ken, but it occurred to me how he might turn my disappointment into an interesting story—maybe something about the disillusionment of youthful dreams, maybe something to illustrate Thomas Wolfe's observation, "You can't go home again."

Bethany's Story
Literary

Tyronica Smith

Prompt: The light was hauntingly surreal.

ETHANY HAD KNOWN MANY joys and pains in her life. Her greatest joys were her two children, Tiffy and Hayden. Both put a smile on her face and at least three gray hairs in her head each day with their shenanigans. Tiffy, a rambunctious thirteen-year-old, was the main character of many a humorous tale to family and friends. Hayden on the other hand, feeling out his eight-year-old senses, was a precocious lad much too big for his britches, as Bethany's dad had put it. They kept her in stitches. She saw them as the most effective pain management she'd ever had, with laughter being a close second.

Night fell like a great stage curtain over the earth, bringing a fantastic end to the day. Bethany was tired and ready to get on with it. She stretched the sore spots of her body and winced at a phantom pain rummaging through her joints. The day's activities and the children had worn her out, and now she was just looking forward to relaxing at home with the kiddos—if possible without moving a single toe from the sofa. She hoped to wrangle them into watching

Spirited Away or *Howl's Moving Castle*, but they insisted on hearing one of her own grand creations, otherwise known as story time.

"Are you guys ready yet?" she said from the hallway, eyeing the couch from where she stood.

"No! We have to get our hot chocolates and our cookies and our blankies and our wubbies!" Hayden said, nearly out of breath.

"Mustn't forget the wubbies." Mocking Hayden, Bethany looked down the hall at her son as he bolted from one end of the house to the other.

"Nope! Wubbies are important, in case the story gets scary — but I never get scared . . . ever!" Hayden preached.

"Oh yeah?" his sister chimed in.

"Shut up, Tif!"

"I will not. What about the time Mom told us that ghost story about the house down the street? You couldn't even look out the window toward the house without seeing one!"

"Yeah, so?" In a defensive stance, Hayden faced his sister.

"It was just a stupid curtain."

"The curtain moved by itself! Besides, Tif, aren't you too old for story time?" he smarted back.

"Nope. As long as Mom tells the stories, I'm gonna listen. I'll be thirty-five asking Mom to tell me a story and you know what — I bet she does."

"Yeah right. Every kid knows grown-ups don't like story time."

"Hayden. Isn't Mom a grown-up?"

"Well . . ." Hayden said, scratching his head. "Sure, she drives the car and makes the food and pays for lunch at school and gives us a house to live in . . . but she's different. Mom is like . . . cool. Better than cool. Awesome!"

"Okay, Hay, whatever."

"You know it, too — Mom is different! She listens to kids and she plays games and she's fun and she tells great jokes . . ."

"Nah, I beg to differ on that one, bud. Mom's jokes are horrible." Tossing her piggy in the air, she circled Hayden.

"But they aren't worse than Dad's and Missy's jokes."

"You got me there. And I do agree, Mom is pretty awesome." Tiffy threw her stuffed animal in the air a final time, letting it fall onto Hayden's head.

"No wonder you quit softball. You suck at catching."

"I'll catch you! You brat!" Tiffy dove after Hayden then tackled him to the floor and began an aggressive tickling of her brother.

Bethany peeked her head around the corner to see the two roughhousing on the floor. She giggled a bit at what the children said of their dad and his new wife. Silently, Bethany pumped her fist in celebration of her own awesomeness, then whispered, "Points for me!" while excitedly bouncing from foot to foot as much as her body would let her. A little winded, she calmed and came to a halt when a small tinge of pain echoed in her joints, putting an end to her hushed revelry.

She limped to retrieve her hot chamomile tea and walked slowly past the kids' rooms, stretching her ear as far as it could go without separating from her head. She had been compared to her ex-husband's new wife, Missy, before but never let it bother her. She was, after all — in super caps in her mind — MOM! Complete with a starburst.

"Missy is nuts. Mom is way cooler an' way saner."

"Hahaha! Remember that time Missy tried to get us to call her Mom?" Tiffy said, barely able to control herself.

"Yeah. I told her I already had one. But I made her feel better by telling her she was like a big sister to me," Hayden said, doubling over with laughter.

"Hahaha! Dad was not happy."

From the hallway Bethany chuckled quietly, shielding her laughter with a hand over her mouth. This news definitely improved her mood and her night.

162

"Hey, I gotta be true to me," Hayden said, knocking his little fist to his heart.

"Oh my God, who taught you that? And do you think Dad told Mom?"

"Why yes he did, kiddos. And you weren't in the wrong for saying how you feel." Bethany broke in, leaning against the doorjamb in the hall.

"Mom, you been listening the whole time?" Tiffy said, swinging her stuffed Minecraft pig in the air.

"Like a hawk! Are you guys ready yet? Momma is tired and ready to call the hogs."

"What's that mean?" Hayden asked with his face scrunched.

"It means she's ready to sleep and make snoring noises like piggies do."

"Oh. Yeah, Mom, you do snore loudly."

"I know, and it's going to be doubly loud because I am so tired. Let's go to the couch. What do you guys want tonight? I'm taking orders."

"Well . . . can you tell us a story about the Northern Lights?" Hayden managed to speak with only a little whistle from his missing tooth.

"Umm . . . hmm . . ." Bethany thought for a moment before answering the kids. "My only frame of reference for the Northern Lights is this video I saw on the tubes. I've never actually seen it with my own eyes," she said, easing down onto the couch.

"So do they even exist?" Hayden said, leaning in on his elbows.

"Oh yes, they do. Your dad's seen them, but I have never. He tried to take pictures of it while he was on a business trip in Anchorage. You should ask him to show you sometime."

"Maybe next time when we visit I'll ask to see them, but for now, Mom, the spotlight's on you." Tiffy thrust her arms forward to frame her mother's face with her fingers.

"I'm ready for my close-up, Mr. DeMille," Bethany said in her Hollywood starlet voice.

"Who?" they asked in unison.

"Cecil—never mind. Google him later."

"But what did he do?" Tiffy said, giving her full attention to her mother.

"He produced the Ten Commandments."

"But I thought Moses did that." Hayden looked at his mother, confused, as her sails deflated.

"Yes, Moses did—" Bethany said abruptly.

"But why did you say it was that Cecil guy?"

"Dude, let Mom talk!" Tiffy warned.

"The movie was produced by Cecil B. DeMille."

"The Bible has a movie?" Hayden asked with a confused look on his face.

"Several."

"Where you been, kid, sleeping under a rock?" Tiffy said, ruffling Hayden's hair.

"I'm eight years old!"

"Dude, you Google everything else. Google that."

"All right, kids, you two can have at it. Mom's tired and needs to rest."

"No, Mom!" they said in unison.

"Come on . . . give me a break. It's been a hard day. I just want to sleep," Bethany whined in a childlike manner.

"Sleep when you're dead, woman!" Hayden said with his chest puffed out, not sensing the danger of his mother's glare until it was much too late.

Mom flipped him over and planted a hand on his backside then righted him up again. Hayden giggled through it.

"Dude, you are one brave little man with a good pain tolerance. Must be from being dropped—"

"Tiffy!" Bethany chided.

"I'm kidding, Mom."

"Look, kids . . . I'm beat. Four stores, a post office, two grocery trips, a vet's visit, an argument with your dad and the cable company for movies we would never watch, and a haircut later, I'm here willing myself to stay awake." She situated her headscarf and let out a loud yawn.

"Mom, just say something. Once you start you'll keep going."

"Fine!" Bethany said, staring out of the window with both kids leaning on her legs.

"Yay!"

"No 'yay!' It's going to be short and sweet," Bethany said, exhausted and ready to get on with it.

"Aww . . ." The children spoke in unison again with very sad faces.

"Kids, are you ready?" Mom began, thinking of the topic beforehand and spinning her tale.

"Yeah!" they resounded.

"Aurora stretched out her pen across the night sky and let the ink trail behind the nib. In one broad stroke, the colors merged and swam together, mixing in a rainbow of neon hues on her broad canvas. When she removed the nib from the canvas, the colors of ink transformed into lights and began to wave as if they were an ocean. She allowed her imagination to spill from her fingertips and roar forth in a passion that the world would experience. She did this almost every night, and almost every night, the people would stand outside and watch in awe and contemplate what it all meant or how it came to be.

"Right there in the Land of the Midnight Sun, or Alaska as we know her, the inhabitants treated this phenomenon as something of a normal occurrence. But to a few, the lights were something mystical to pore over in their studies and observations. Aurora saw this and loved the way the people treated her creations. She had plans to show them more of her creations as the winter went on. Aurora, otherwise known as 'the dawn,' decided to put off the dawn approximately sixty-seven days during the winter so the lights could be seen clearly. The next eighty or so days would be filled with sunlight day in, day out. The sunlight would cause the ink she used to glow vibrantly through its life-giving, irradiated rays and show the inhabitants of Earth that while the sun gives them the warmth they needed, the night would give them the beauty they wanted. In the warm months the Northern Lights would hardly be visible in the sky due to the 'midnight sun' shining those eighty days. Winter would hold the glory of her best work."

"Good job, Mom!" Tiffy said.

"Thank you, now hush."

"Why is it called the midnight sun, Mom?" Hayden inquired.

"Because in the summer months the sun is visible at midnight, thus it is called the midnight sun."

"Does it happen here?" Hayden asked perched on the couch.

"Afraid not, hon."

"Aww man!" he said, shoulders slumping, dispirited.

"Can we get back to it?"

"Yes!" they both chimed.

"Now, she paced the broad expanse of the cloudsphere above and thought about how she would like to proceed with her next work of art. Seeing the lights in the sky was all fine and well, but to win over the hearts of the humans on Earth, she wanted to do something more. Aurora said to herself, 'The heartstrings of humans hold the music of the soul. One need only strum those strings to hear the perfect melody of love.'"

"Wow. That sounds beautiful," Hayden said with his mouth slightly ajar.

"What do you know about beautiful?" Tiffy said.

"Thanks, and leave your brother alone. So Aurora did something amazing for the spectators of her art show. She called on the Four Winds — North, South, West, and East — to whistle and hum as she drew her masterpieces across the sky. Something so wonderful that the people would take notice almost immediately. She sat at her canvas and crafted with pure precision her next piece while the Four Winds sang their soft melodies over her.

"When she finished, she watched as the lights danced in the sky. She watched how the people looked curiously on her creation then went about their business. But there were a few, only a handful, who saw and heard the symphony of colors and music in the way that Aurora meant for it to be discovered. Those people not only paused in disbelief of what they were hearing and seeing but began to dance along to the music that they were present enough to hear. Aurora was so pleased by all of this that she sang with the Four Winds in a beautiful harmony in honor of Earth."

Bethany shifted on the sofa, vying for a more agreeable position for her body, but didn't want to disrupt the comfort of her children. She loved the closeness of the kids, but she ached from the day's activities and stress on her frame. When she found a more suitable angle to rest on the sofa, she lifted her body from the back of the couch to rub at a phantom pain rising in her lower back. When she was done, she reclined back into position among the pillows, blankets, and children.

"That's kind of beautiful, Mom." Tiffy hugged her mother close, careful not to cause her any more pain.

"So only a few people could hear the music?" Hayden said with his face scrunched in disbelief.

"Yep!" Bethany tapped him lightly on the leg then reached over and hugged him closer to her.

"Well that doesn't seem fair," Hayden grouched with his arms over his chest. "I demand another story! One that makes sense."

"This one does make sense, and you are proving my story right. Would you hear the music? Could you block out all the noise of your life and enjoy what's around you? Could you, and would you, find entertainment and joy in the simplest things in life even though you've seen it a million times?"

"I don't know, Mom. I guess so? I mean, I'm a kid."

"Doesn't mean you shouldn't be thinking about enjoying the things around you. Sometimes, people get so caught up in what they are doing that they never take the time to fully appreciate all that surrounds them, sweetheart. We have to stop and smell the roses as well as water them so that there is a season to enjoy the fruits of our labor." She looked to Tiffy and received a knowing nod from her daughter.

"Hayden, what is something that you always see, every day all the time?" Tiffy asked, leading her brother.

Hayden scrunched up his little face in deep thought. He scratched his head as to get his brain started and rubbed at the little spot of eczema on his elbow. His eyes grew wide as he turned to his mother.

"Mom. I see you every day, all the time."

"No, goofball, I mean—"

Bethany hushed Tiffy and looked Hayden in the eye. "Honey, do you appreciate the fact that I am here and am your mom?"

"I think I do. I mean, who else would wash my clothes, clean my room, make me food, and give me money to buy ice cream and candy?"

"In a kid-logic way . . ." Bethany nodded while looking her son in the eye. "That works. Now what if I weren't here anymore? What would you do?" she asked, rubbing his knee.

"What do you mean, like if you disappeared?" Hayden asked fearfully.

"No, not quite. What if I had to go away and never come back? Would you appreciate me then? Could you appreciate the memory of me?"

"I don't know, Mom. I don't like to think of you going away and never coming back."

"I know, honey. I just want you to appreciate what you have, who you have, while you have it. Like your sister, your dad, the things we take care of for you day to day. Okay?"

"Okay, Mom. I think I'm ready to go to bed now." Hayden gave a visible shake at the unpleasant things running through his mind. Goosebumps rose over his skin as his breath hitched in his throat. *Hayden slid off the couch, stood in front of his mother, and posed a question. "Mom, will you be here when I wake up?"*

"Of course I will, honey."

"I ask 'cause Dad wasn't here when I woke up that day. Are you sure?"

"I'll be here."

"Okay, Mom." Hayden gave a half-hearted smile as he hugged her then yawned his way down the hall toward his bedroom, nearly bumping into the wall.

Bethany and Tiffy sat on the couch and waited to hear Hayden's door close. They looked each other over and pulled each other close. Tiffy spoke quietly to her mother.

"Mom . . . when are you going to tell him?"

"When the time is right, Tif. He's not ready just yet, but I'm hoping that he grasps what I'm trying to say through these stories I tell him. So I don't want you telling him. That's for me to do. Got it?"

"Yes, ma'am."

"All right." Bethany planted a kiss at the top of Tiffy's head and rubbed her shoulders.

"Chemo tomorrow?"

"Yes, chemo tomorrow. You'll be with your father and Missy until Monday."

"Grreeaat. So much fun to be had. Can't wait." Tiffy's sarcasm was palpable.

"Try to get along with her. Who knows how long she'll be with your father. Just try."

"Okay."

"Help me up." Bethany stood to forty-year-old aches and pains. The scarf covering her newly cut hair slipped off her head and landed on the sofa.

"I like your haircut, Mom."

"Thank you, puddin'."

Tiffy picked it up and tied it back on her mom's head. Lovingly, she wrapped her arms around her mother's waist to hug her, taking in the scent of her. She thought back to her mom's story and what she'd told Hayden as she rested an ear on her mother's chest.

"I can hear it, Mom. I can hear the music."

To learn more about this author, please visit:
https://bloggishone.wordpress.com/

Reintegration

Science Fiction

Matthew Stevens

Prompt: You hear a knock at the window and find a bird, a metal bird, waiting there. It has a message for you.

SHELLEY DIDN'T HEAR THE first tap on the window over the sound of her fingers on the keyboard. From another room came the clatter of what could only be broken glass, causing her to halt her typing. Living on the fourth floor, it was more than an unexpected sound, and her stomach dropped like the first hill on a roller-coaster.

She scanned the room for a weapon. Writing utensils. Books. Her computer. Shelley wished she had a softball glove or a hockey stick lying around that she could use as armor or for defense. Nothing. Aside from the occasional run in the park, she didn't play sports. Never had. And her smelly running shoes were out of reach in the front hall closet, not that the stench would be any help against someone intent enough to get into her upstairs apartment.

The only items on her desk were charts and notes from today's rounds at the hospital, a cup of pens, and a thin three-ring binder. All offered zero real protection, but the binder was her best option. Shelley emptied it of its contents, snapped the rings closed, and wrapped her finger through the middle ring. She crept forward with the pathetic makeshift shield raised. Halfway there, she stopped, scurried back to her desk, and grabbed an uncapped pen. Better than nothing.

Tiptoeing down the short hallway, she approached the bedroom. At the edge of the doorway she listened, trying to picture what was happening around the corner.

A dull plodding sound alternated with a metallic clicking. Shelley's mind spun in wild and dark directions. Before she could fall too far into the depths, there was a scrape across the floor, like someone dragging a knife along the top of an old wooden table. A short, high-pitched croaking followed.

Sweat left Shelley's grip on the pen tenuous. One side of the plastic binder had fallen against her arm and stuck there, creating a useless panel of armor. Quick, shallow breathing made her throat scratchy as her pulse thrummed in her neck.

The noises ceased. She took a deep breath and swung around the corner, holding the pen and binder-shield at the ready.

In the middle of the bed hopped a giant crow. Its black, almond-shaped head jerked toward her as it spread its ink-black beak and croaked. The sound was piercing. Shelley dropped her weapon and armor, pinching her eyes shut and covering her ears.

The sound faded. She cautiously opened her eyes for a closer look at the creature that had begun nesting on her bed, and she gasped. The bird dancing among the covers was a monstrosity, unlike anything she had ever seen before. Crows were a common sight in the city, but this one was larger and decidedly . . . abnormal.

The crow stopped strutting around and focused on her. For a brief moment, the bird kept completely still, and in that instant Shelley's attention was drawn from the haphazard pile of blankets to one eye. Instead of a beady shifting black pupil surrounded by a brown iris, she found herself staring into an iris she knew well, one she had looked into while contemplating the great wonders of magic and medicine, a bright green eye circled in amber. She'd only ever met one person with eyes like that: her best and closest friend.

There was a connection between them in that second of contact that sent a stillness coursing throughout the room. They both felt it. Before Shelley could move, the crow deliberately got down off the bed and hobbled the few feet between the bed and the doorway where Shelley stood frozen. It stopped directly in front of her and bent over, placing its beak to a talon. There was a metallic click and a hiss, almost as if a soda can had been opened.

The bird dropped a tiny rolled-up scrap of paper from its beak at Shelley's feet. Then, with a quick, almost elegant hop, the crow returned to the bed, continuing to shuffle the blankets around. She retrieved the note from the floor.

Shelley unrolled the scrap of paper and instantly recognized the angular and compact handwriting. She had copied his notes on numerous occasions and deciphered his ramblings on countless lab reports throughout medical school. Her friendship with Bruce McClane began on the first day. She moved to sit next to him in their introductory lecture when he spouted a line from Roman Holiday. She answered seamlessly with Hepburn's response. They broke out in a fit of laughter.

Even after Bruce failed out and resigned himself to science rather than medicine, they stayed in touch. But, during the last few months, Shelley had been forced to limit their contact. He had begun publishing papers openly condemning the internationally imposed barriers for Healers, those gifted enough to be conferred a PhMa, or Doctor of Magic degree. His criticism, questionable research methods, and outspoken attitudes had heightened his public profile. And as a healer—a highly regulated vocation—her only option was to create space between them.

Her attention shifted back to the present as she studied the words written there.

If you're reading this, then I fear the worst. I dreamt of success but fear I have learned of failure.

—McClane

The message was cryptic, yet he had signed his name. And it had been given to her by a strange bird with an eye eerily similar to Bruce's. The pieces didn't add up.

Watching the crow as it pecked around on the bed, she noticed for the first time its different, mismatched parts. Half of the creature's head was covered in a metal cap that continued forward and down, completely covering one eye, which had been replaced with an optical sensor of some kind. The optic flickered eerily. One moment, the deep black of a crow's eye, then for a split second the unmistakable amber-rimmed green that matched Bruce's eye, before finally settling on a haunting blood red.

The bird stretched its neck and flexed its wings, pulling Shelley's attention there. One wing, which appeared as if pieced together entirely of polished knives, made the disturbing sound of gardening shears being opened and closed repeatedly. A dark red substance all along the edge caused her brow to wrinkle unconsciously. From her time as a Healer, there was no mistaking that color as anything but blood. The prospective deadly nature of that wing gave Shelley pause, while the creature's other wing appeared normal apart from a small metallic brace that ran from its nape across the top edge of the wing.

Taking in the rest of the bird, she understood what had made the alternating hard and soft sounds she noticed on her way to the bedroom to investigate. The bird's foot below the robotic wing was also completely fabricated from nonorganic parts, and like the wing, it appeared to be stained with blood.

Mired in trepidation, Shelley took a slow step back, away from her bed and this strange creature.

What kind of disaster had befallen this poor bird? What prompted someone to attempt such a chaotic reconstruction? And why had it reminded her so intently of Bruce? The crow squawked, seeming to sense Shelley's uneasiness, then abandoned its nesting and shifted to the edge of the bed.

Birds were not Shelley's area of expertise. Scant amounts of her medical training focused on any one type of animal; most provided merely a brief overview to acclimate each student with the concept of LEQ, or Life Essence Quotient. Each animal had a different LEQ, or the limit of how much life essence a Healer could safely extract from an animal—for the purpose of human healing—before presumably doing irreparable harm. Her finite knowledge aside, the bird's posture indicated severe agitation.

Apart from the bird's strange composition, her mind couldn't fit the pieces together. Surely she hadn't imagined the crow's bizarre eye color. She had witnessed that before seeing Bruce's handwriting on the note. And the blood on the bird's dangerous, if not lethal, extremities made her mind spin.

The crow was now closer to her improvised protection than she liked, and Shelley feared that any sudden movement might spook the bird into attacking. Without moving her head, she searched for another weapon or armor. She had no better luck here than at her desk.

Her focus returned to the bird balanced on the edge of her bed. It stared at her, cocking its head to one side, that eye transforming again as she watched. Shifting from green to black and white, studying her. It was as if they were contemplating the same question: friend or foe? Was the other a threat? Weathering such a studious gaze from a creature that shouldn't have that degree of sentience unsettled her, sending a chill down her spine. Hairs all over her body stood on end as she shuddered involuntarily.

In an instant, the crow chose survival over observation. It sprang into the air with talons drawn and wings—both natural and perverse—spread. Shelley tripped backward over her own feet, tumbling to the floor in a panic to avoid the weaponized appendages.

The crow hung inexplicably, mismatched wings slicing through the air. Seizing the second of indecision, Shelley rolled, yanking a thick blanket off her bed and cocooning in it for whatever protection it could offer. She lay still, praying the creature might not comprehend where she disappeared. It landed on the floor.

Lifting the corner of the blanket, she dared a peek, only to find the crow eyeballing her. Unfazed by her petty trick, it left gouges in the floor as it leaped up before landing on her back. With claws and beak, the beast tried to uncover her, slicing through the blanket, propelling stuffing into the air in large tufts. In desperation, she unrolled herself, casting off the bird. Her hands still grasping the corners of the blanket like a caped superhero, she swung hoping to dispatch the creature.

Surprised, the bird lost its grip and tumbled away in a mess of metal and feathers. It quickly righted itself and, taking to the air, positioned for the most aggressive dive manageable in the small space.

Shelley swung the blanket. A corner eclipsed the flapping bird. She grabbed it, enveloping the crow. With it trapped, Shelley swung the blanket like an Olympic hammer throw, smashing the bundle against the wall with as much force as possible.

The impact shook the room. Pictures tumbled over, knickknacks fell off shelves, and the door rattled on its hinges. White-knuckled and gasping for breath, Shelley held the edges of the blanket. The cybernetic crow she had just pummeled out of existence twitched and jerked on the floor, producing a cacophony of outlandish noises as the organic muscles spasmed after death.

After what seemed like hours of waiting and watching for the bundle to remain still, Shelley finally felt confident enough to unwrap and inspect the creature. Based on the number of sharp edges protruding from the jumbled mess, she had expected more gore. Her gaze, drawn to the crow's head, settled back on its natural eye, which morphed one last time, moving from the animalistic black to the familiar amber and green before dimming with the emptiness of death.

Seeing that change yanked Shelley back to the end of her first semester of medical school. She and Bruce had spent every spare moment studying, rereading, quizzing, and cramming for finals. They continually reminded each other they hadn't gotten that far only to fail. Then she thought about the disappointment, the uncertainty, draped across Bruce's face the day he'd been told he was out of the PhMa program.

Fear and uncertainty enveloped her brain with dark speculation. It had been a while since they'd spoken, but Shelley knew that only seeing Bruce face-to-face would assure her that all was well. She was going to have to risk a visit to her old friend. And she could ask him to explain the meaning behind the note.

Shelley jumped in her car. She sped through stop signs and even a couple red lights. The scribbled note was tucked in her back pocket. Her mind automatically carried her to the worst possible scenario—a thought that brought her to tears.

The tires squealed as she yanked the wheel hard, steering into Bruce's driveway. She didn't pull quite hard enough, and the driver's side tire thumping over the curb rocked her, almost cracking her head on the window. She threw the car in park and shoved the door open, landing one foot on the driveway.

Shelley leaped up the front steps two at a time. Her fist slammed repeatedly on the door. She inched back, bouncing on her toes. There was no familiar thud and clunk as McClane unlocked the deadbolt. Only silence answered. She pounded again. Still no response. Shelley jogged around to the side of the house. There, she tugged on the side entrance, hoping—praying—that it was unlocked. No luck. Shelley knocked, but again, no response.

Any remaining uncertainty of whether McClane might answer the door vanished. Shelley was a tightly wound ball of panic, frantically checking the usual hiding places for an extra key. She scouted under the rugs, atop the doorjambs, and she turned over landscaping rocks only to come up empty. For being a successful scientist, McClane had a black thumb, so there were no potted plants in which to hide keys.

Smashing a window and letting herself in was the easiest solution, but her position as a Healer—and the legal intricacies it brought—stopped her. The cursory knowledge she held and her presumptions about the sensitive nature of some of McClane's experiments made calling the authorities a last resort. Her last hope was to search the garage for a key. Unlike most crazy scientists, McClane never kept any of his work in the garage. She guessed that it wouldn't be locked and discovered she was right.

She found the spare key taped to the bottom of a dust-caked toolbox that hadn't been opened in forever and ran back to the front door to let herself in. She rushed through the house, stopping in each room only long enough to confirm whether McClane was there. Bedroom, bathroom, kitchen, all empty. Shelley found no sign of him.

A few years earlier, McClane had added on to the back of his house. The only entrance to the addition was through a door at the back of his kitchen that was always locked. As much as McClane wanted his privacy for experiments, Shelley also knew he liked things simple. As she suspected, the key that opened the front door also unlocked the lab.

Shelley opened the door to McClane's lab, where a stiff, weighted black panel met her. It didn't budge when poked with a finger, even staying in place when she placed a whole palm against it and gently pushed. With two hands and a little weight, she finally got the panel to move far enough to allow her to slip sideways into the room.

Inside, the air was warm and stagnant. The only light emanated from the computer monitors in the farthest corner. As dark as the space was, the little bit of light revealed that the same type of panel that blocked the door covered every other inch of wall. Shelley rapped a fist against one of the panels. They were rigid but coated in a type of padding. Apart from blocking the light, she wondered about their purpose.

She shuffled as she moved further, not wanting to step on something unexpected. At the far end of the room, she turned sideways to scoot between two tables covered in piles of miscellany. Unsure of what any of it did or could do, Shelley avoided touching anything. If McClane could see her dancing in the pale blue light through his lab, he'd double over with laughter. Extricating herself from between the tables, her foot knocked against something that felt firm but still gave way slightly.

"Where are the damn lights, McClane?" Shelley grumbled, pawing the wall for a switch.

Finally finding a small cutout in a panel, she flicked a switch, illuminating the room. Four banks of overhead fluorescent lights hummed to life, drowning the blue glow from the computer in a warm white light.

Shelley turned around to find what tripped her and had to grab hold of the nearest table to avoid collapsing into a heap. The tears she stifled when she entered the house came flooding back. On her knees, sobs wracked her body, hands covering her face to hide the horrific scene of

McClane's supine body from her sight. She knew instantly that he was dead.

When the tears slowed and her vision cleared, she pulled her hands back, gathering enough strength to crawl the few feet to his lifeless body. As a Healer, a close friend, and, presumably, the first to see him in this state, Shelley had to exercise the utmost caution examining McClane's corpse.

The scratches and gashes splayed across his face and neck were numerous and varied. Some were long and had sliced to the tendon or bone, while others were shorter and shallow, as if he'd been attacked with multiple weapons. Many of the less serious cuts were clustered in groups of three. On closer inspection, Shelley found a couple spots where it appeared that divots of flesh had been removed.

Studying his chest and abdomen, she recognized the same wound types and patterns that spotted his face and neck. Moving the body was out of the question. Shelley knew that. Without removing his shirt her investigation could only be cursory. She turned her attention to his arms, which took the brunt of the damage and suggested Bruce had been in a massive knife fight. But even as brutal as the attack seemed to have been, Shelley did not believe that any of these wounds alone, or even cumulatively, would have been immediately fatal.

One of a Healer's first lessons was how to free their mind from emotions and dampen physical senses, allowing the Healer to focus on their own life essence. If a Healer could do that and then connect with their patient's life essence, the Healer could identify the source of the pain, and the healing could begin. Shelley fought her instinct to reach out, searching for whatever remained of McClane's life essence to ascertain answers. She knew that it would change nothing, and doing so would leave an impression.

The consequence for interfering with or manipulating magic in an unregistered setting was Disillusionment, a risk Shelley wasn't willing to take no matter how much she wanted quick answers to what happened here. Once the authorities arrived, they'd bring an auran who would read the energies and know what magic had been touched. They could come in and uncover the answers she desperately needed. But even as Shelley strained to avoid contaminating the scene with her own energy, another energy, one she couldn't place, hung around her. It urged her toward an unknown obligation to find her own answers before the room was tainted by "official" energies.

With the lights on and her tears completely dried, she noticed that tiny pockmarks dotted the surface of the black panel she pushed past to gain entry. McClane had secured the pieces to the walls. Aside from the panel covering the doorway to the kitchen, only one other piece wasn't bolted down tight enough to avoid being carried off in a tornado. It was blocking the fireplace opening.

Shelley explored for other evidence of what might have left her friend lifeless. How did the crow that had broken into her apartment connect to McClane and his work? The door had been locked, so if the crow had been in here when McClane died, how did it escape?

The tabletops gave no concrete indication as to his most recent project. The piles of metal, wires, and connectors led her to believe it was primarily cybernetics. McClane's fascination with cybernetics was no secret, but Shelley could only posit that a creature rebuilt solely with machinery had constraints.

Against the far wall, she noticed a few empty cages for mice or other small mammals and a few terrariums that might have been home to lizards or snakes. Making her way around the largest table in the center of the room, Shelley stumbled, hand planted against a table, as she caught her feet on a length of chain secured to the table leg. The chain rattled as she reached down, checking its length. It terminated in a small bolt snap, for what she could only assume would be restraining a medium-sized animal.

There was a tiny faction, mostly anonymous, inside the healing community that suggested that, by using the proper amount of life essence with the utmost care and exactitude, a Healer could, in fact, bring a person back to life. It remained a forbidden area of study in the magical healing community based on the fact that the theories assumed it could only be done as a full exchange, life for life, and that went against the moral and ethical code each Healer swore to uphold when receiving their degree and placement assignment.

McClane had a fair degree of skill when it came to the manipulation of life essence, but his lack of precision, the inability to transfer necessary but accurate amounts, is what cost him his chance at being a Healer. Shelley couldn't fathom him bridging the gap between science and magic on his own. Then again, the panels on the walls led her to believe that he must have been working on something so secretive or controversial that his only option was to seclude himself and hide his work.

If he had been blurring the lines between science and magic, she no longer wanted to be here when the authorities arrived. As a certified Healer, if she was suspected of having association with underground, unsanctioned experiments . . . Shelley tensed. Disillusionment would be the least of her troubles.

Unable to determine anything else from the work tables, she moved to the computer desk. For all else McClane had done to protect his work, what with the wall panels and nothing conclusive on the tables, finding his notebooks was shockingly simple. They lay open to the left of his computer monitors.

The top of the first page bore the bold headline "Reintegration." Flipping through the pages, Shelley determined that McClane had made actual, if limited, attempts at this new theory for a few months. If she was reading his notes correctly, it appeared that this whole phase of experimentation started about the time she had been forced to decrease their interactions. She paused, looking at the wall of cages. How many of those had held what the notes referred to as "donors," and which had been homes to the "reintegration subjects"?

A few of the pages even had calculations, which appeared to be predictions of how much life essence a "donor" could give before expiring and falling into the "R.S." category. Shelley shook her head. McClane had always had some ideas that were considered "out there," but she was having a hard time believing he had really strayed so far into the fringes of healing science.

A red marker tumbled out from the back of the notebook. Shelley recognized it as the same type used to write the note tucked inside the crow's metallic leg. It landed on the keyboard, waking the computer.

The middle of the screen showed McClane frozen, half bent over, face directly in front of the computer, squinting. Without hesitation, Shelley clicked the triangular button to play the video and slid into his chair.

At first, all Shelley saw was the lab from the perspective of the computer monitor. Then, McClane's brown mop of hair came into view in the corner of the frame. He was inches from the camera.

"Hello?" His eyes, those same eyes she'd seen a couple times today, checked the four corners of the video. "Is this thing on? Is it recording? Because I'm not sure I can do this twice."

McClane paused and his eyebrows rose. "Okay, good. So, time stamp." He shuffled some papers and read the date and noted the time.

Shelley paused the video, checking the time on her phone against the time in the corner of the video. She could tell from the condition of McClane's body that he'd died fairly recently, but, based on his video, that had to be less than six hours ago. Her mouth fell open, and she restarted the recording.

McClane backed to the far side of the room where he pushed a metal cart into the frame. Shelley gasped when she saw the same crow from her apartment lying on the table. It was dead, or it certainly looked that way—unmoving on the bare metal. Shelley moved closer to the screen to scrutinize the image, to determine if the bird was breathing. As best as she could tell, it wasn't. She shivered in anticipation of what was surely coming next.

McClane moved the table closer to the camera so the crow could be seen in better light and began his explanation of what was about to occur.

"I'm well aware of the legal repercussions of what I am about to attempt. In fact, if you can see the walls and the panels that are covering, well, everything, then you know that those are because the government forbids this practice or even attempting it. But I cannot go on living without making a full-scale pursuit of reintegration. This is an experiment I've wanted to try since I understood how life essence works." McClane turned away from the camera briefly, focusing on the small cages against the wall.

He gestured to the cages. "In these enclosures, I kept my first trials. Started small. Less life essence required, mistakes were less costly. But, with promising only minor successes, I needed to try something bigger. While the odds of failure increased, the triumph would be that much greater. Hence, my current reintegration subject."

McClane suddenly bent down. When he stood, he held a rat in his hands — one with an optical sensor like the one in the crow's head. He smiled.

"I thought I'd lost you!" He held the rat up for the camera to see more clearly. "One of my first achievements."

The rat scurried out of his hands and up his arm, dancing across his shoulders and down to the other hand where it stopped, fidgeting like a typical curious rat. Then it froze as if the video paused. Its appendages locked before it tumbled over in his hand. Dead. He shook his head and gently set the corpse on the table.

"You did good, buddy," he said with a pat and returned his attention to the inert crow.

"I found this poor creature on the side of the highway three days ago. Half of his skull was crushed, one wing nearly ripped clean off, and his leg was shattered. I set to work fixing him up, knowing he would be perfect for this next experiment."

McClane shifted around, positioning the crow directly in front of the camera. "Let me put aside all speculation about what is going to occur here. These experiments are unsanctioned. They are illegal. They are forbidden by all of those who seek to control the usage and application of magic, in particular restricting the extent of how beneficial extensive life essence transfer can be. Here today, I intend to prove that reintegration is viable. Life essence can be reintegrated into a currently dead being. And, most importantly, it can be done without the sacrifice of other living creatures. I know you can't see any other living creatures currently. That is because they aren't here, here. The goats from which I will pull life essence are secured in an adjoining room. Close enough to sense and extract the necessary life essence, but far enough away to keep the incessant baying and general ruckus from distracting me as has happened during past *experiments. Oh, and just in case anything were to go wrong, inside a small compartment I fitted into the crow's leg is a note. Hopefully, it will direct the right people in the right direction. Now, enough talk."*

Closing his eyes, he opened his palms, holding them a few inches above the dead crow. From his nearly motionless lips, Shelley heard the mumbling of the words McClane used to initiate the transfer of life essence.

Each Healing student chose something different. For some it was a lullaby in their native tongue, others used words to a favorite poem or a recitation they'd learned rote in school. The words themselves were inconsequential. It was simply the practitioner's way of clearing their mind and connecting with the life essences they were about to modify. She hadn't heard Bruce's words since medical school, but they were instantly recognizable.

Green motes began to float through the wall, undeterred by the paneling. Shelley could see the life essence from the other animals being pulled toward its new home. The motes began to congregate in a circular shape above McClane's hands. Noise erupted, presumably from the goats in the adjoining room. Shelley leaned closer to the monitor. The noise was enough, just for a moment, to distract McClane. His eyes opened, and he tilted his head ever so slightly. As McClane refocused on his task, Shelley noticed a crease in his brow.

The motes continued to swirl but were joined by more motes of a deeper green. They came from an additional source, but Shelley couldn't determine the origin. The grimace on McClane's face grew. The motes funneled past his open hands to the crow's chest as if they were being sucked down a drain.

Half of the life essence had disappeared into the bird when its wings started twitching and its talons clawed against the metal table. As the last specks of green disappeared into the crow's body, McClane hunched over, exhausted. When he lifted his face to the camera over the stirring bird, Shelley saw pain in his eyes and they lacked their typical shine.

The crow got to its feet and hopped upright on the table. Beak open, it let out a caw that would have rattled the windows if they weren't covered. Mechanically, as if relearning how to move, the crow turned its head, its non-cybernetic eye locked on the computer screen.

Shelley's knees buckled as the bird's lone natural eye met hers. An eye she'd seen not long before, in her own apartment; bright green ringed in amber, the same that had stared at her across lab desks and over operating tables. Even through the computer screen, the look she shared with the crow was the same she'd seen in her apartment. Recognition.

McClane bumped the table, causing the crow to wobble and flex its wings to maintain balance. The metallic wing swung out and sliced through the flesh on McClane's forearm.

Shelley clamped her hand over her mouth, stifling a cry of shock.

The severity of the injury escaped McClane. He was in a daze. The glaze in his eyes remained, as if a part of him were missing. But she noticed a sense of understanding, of fear. The experiment went wrong and the bird in front of him wasn't what he'd intended. It was more. It was unnatural. It shouldn't exist.

It knew.

Somehow, during the transference, Bruce had contributed some of his own life essence to the bird's reintegration, unintentionally imbuing a part of himself into his creation.

The remainder of the video was too awful to watch, but the sounds were enough. The injuries on McClane's body. The eerie feeling with the crow in her own apartment. The wounds that while ugly, would normally be survived—unless one's life essence was nearly depleted or transferred. That realization, along with the certainty of what came next, was too much. Shelley could no longer hold herself together and collapsed. Bawling, she curled up with her knees tucked against her chest as her entire body shook.

She knew that eliminating the crow was the right thing to have done. It had taken her friend's life. But, in turn, she had ended both lives.

The gruesome sounds of the deadly interaction had ceased, and Shelley dared a look at the video. She watched as the crow hobbled away from the computer, wedged its beak under the panel covering the fireplace, and slipped away. Escaping. Heading to her apartment.

Shelley knew what she had to do. The bird was gone, and there was no way she could bring back her friend. Or could she? For years, she had viewed those—including McClane—who in secret had pushed the boundaries encircling the science and magic used for healing as crazy. What they were trying to do was impossible. Wasn't it? And yet, she had just watched her friend bring a dead creature back to life. If it worked with a rat and a crow, surely with the right preparation it could work on a person. No! It's nuts!

Shelley shook her head. She was a Healer, a job she'd dreamed of since she was a child. If she started down this road and was discovered, her career would be over in the blink of an eye. But, the eyes. They were Bruce's. He died here, in this room, but a part of him had remained alive in that bird, at least for a little while. Before she extinguished it.

As Shelley stood, deciding, she could hear Bruce reassuring her at the end of that first semester. "We haven't come this far to fail."

To learn more about this author, please visit:
https://www.facebook.com/matthewstevensauthor

Stories from the Dream Cloud

Whether from the imagination or real-life circumstances, all people seek happiness, some through awareness and others through the simple passing of time and acceptance of life as it is. Read these stories to experience a temporary reality or a realized dream.

Broken Wings

Literary

Cayce Berryman

Prompt: The day I lost my wings.

I ASKED A MAN IF *he'd seen my wings, and boy did he look confused. It shouldn't have shocked me. I mean, think about it. Some ragged woman in a dirty white dress races down the road in the oncoming rain and nearly face-plants when she sees you before asking if you saw a pair of wings anywhere. I obviously wasn't thinking about social cues. He had every right to look at me like I was crazy. Give me a break, though. I was freaking out.*

Those wings held more meaning than the wedding dress. They were symbolic. A memory, or at least a representation of it. I needed my wedding to be everything it could be, and without those wings, the history my husband-to-be and I had couldn't share our spotlight. I was trying to be cute and unique. Something that made him think about the way we met. He made me think about it every time I looked at him, and it was always a moment of magic. That's what I wanted to give him for our wedding. That moment of magic. From me.

Despite my rude and probably disturbing appearance, I stared at the man like he'd have an answer while he stared at me like I was a ghost. My chest would not stop heaving, and my eyes felt dry. I didn't even consider pulling back the hair stuck to my chin and cheeks. Rain was darkening the white dress and chilling my already pale skin, so I should have considered the possibility of looking like a ghost to him. Poor guy. He wasn't that put together himself, though. His baseball cap wore grease stains that had been there since 1947 when the Yankees finally started using that logo. And I bet he was proud of that hat. Probably his dad's or something, and maybe his dad was even a baseball player. Point is, I wasn't thinking when I yelled at him.

I started to wonder whether they were even important anymore — the wings — because now the dress might as well have been made for a zombie walk. The wings would just add to the ensemble. I'd be an undead angel. Glorious. The man only shook his head; he hadn't seen anything. When I trudged away, I imagined him preparing a sacrifice to offer the dead bride on her way back down the street later.

It wasn't always about the wings. Mark probably didn't even know how important they were. I mean, how symbolic they were. I did, though. I was the broken one, and he liked me despite it. He made me feel like I was worth so much more than the broken mess I've always been. I'd spent years trying to make sure he knew what our relationship meant to me, but as abrasive as I was, I didn't think I ever did a good job. Sometimes I felt like I took him for granted, and when I rolled my eyes at his silly gestures of affection or realized I was angry about something stupid, I thought about the day we met. Because it was a small gesture that made me want to know him and made me want to be part of everything he did. Those wings were my chance, my gesture, and I knew it would be something only we would understand.

It's weird how "I love you" doesn't seem to be enough when actions show it better than your words could express. Even Mark's imperfections, his lack of patience for my long lectures or even his annoying lack of timeliness, made him too perfect for me. He was the weight on the other side of the scale, balancing me out, and I always felt like I had so much more to give that I failed to give him. This wedding, these wings, would have been the perfect thing that told him I would spend the rest of my life making sure he knew that I would do everything in my power to be his balance, his constant, because that's what we were promising tomorrow. The wings were my final grand gesture of love. A symbol of how we became us. And it had carried away any ridiculous fear of him leaving me, so when those wings flew away, I had to admit that bad luck superstition was settling in. My insecurities were at an all-time nonsensical high.

I met Mark when I was, what, eleven, when our buses dropped us off sometime after school. Well, my bus. He was just walking down his street. We lived in the same neighborhood but went to different schools. Fancy Pants went to some private school on the other side of town, and I went to the one with a dolphin for a mascot. Intimidating. Beats the shamrocks mascot in preschool, though. You wouldn't see that on a baseball team.

Anyway, I fell trying not to step on a pigeon. Young me broke my stupid wrist because I didn't know how to land. The pain from sliding on the pavement was nothing, though my arm was stiff and blood lit up the base of my palm. I cried. It was because of the bird, though, not the fall. I thought I broke the bird. Its wing was crooked, and tufts of feathers were sticking up and out where something had bit it or whatever. Didn't matter. The wing was totally broken. I hadn't noticed Mark, but when he bent over the bird first before even giving me the courtesy of an "Are you okay?" I knew we'd be friends. Not that I wouldn't have wanted a hand, but in that moment I thought the bird's situation was because of me, and the bird needed someone's care. And because animals are more important than people. Period. People are stupid. Just ask the 1947 Yankees guy who saw a crazy lady in a white dress.

Mark had moved the bird to a small bit of grass, and man did it hate him for it. Despite being injured and in pain, it tried to bite him. I'd be mad, too, I guess. When Mark finally decided I existed, he basically jerked me to my feet and told me to move away from the bird.

"Its wing is broken," he said.

My eyes were still on the pigeon. "I'm so sorry, bird," I'd whined, wondering if any of its insides were sticking out under the splayed feathers. White feathers peeked out from under the large gray ones, and I had to make sure that wasn't bone before I let another tear fall. "I didn't mean to crush you."

"You didn't."

I looked up, almost insulted. "How would you know?"

"I saw it on my way home from school. I went home to get a box." He gestured toward the small shoe box behind him before pulling out a rag from his pocket, setting it in the box, then gently laying the bird into it.

"Are you taking him to the doctor?"

He nodded his head like it was a maraca. "My dad's a vet." He started to walk away, but I pursued him, nosy weirdo that I was, and lucky for me, he didn't mind.

"Are you learning to be a vet?" I asked, eyeing how gently he carried the box, gazing at the bird like every breath might be its last.

He didn't answer at first, so I assumed he was. You know those kids who hang on to their parents' every word so they can be just like them. We were kids after all, but some kids were prodigies. I assumed that's what he was. I'll spoil this now: he wasn't.

When we got to his house, his dad noticed my wrist, which I'd forgotten about, and I guess it was swelling or something because he asked me what my home number was so he could call my parents. You know, back when home phones were a thing and cell phones didn't exist.

"You might have a broken wing, too," he'd said, offering me an ice pack and a seat.

His dad had come back with the phone, its line uncurling as he stretched it across the room. "What's your name, honey?"

"Paige."

He nodded and returned to the phone dock. I heard the dial tone and my mom's voice on the other line. When I looked back at Mark, his eyes shone with awe. That's when I think I really noticed him. Bright green eyes enchanted with me. Or with my broken wrist. Either way, my stomach fluttered and I realized that I liked him. I realized my arm hurt, too, but when you're a little girl under your new crush's stare, what's a broken arm? A part of me had regretted following him home, as quickly as all his attention had turned to me, but in the same instant, I imagined holding hands and freeing birds and flying around above the clouds. I guess I was in between the stages of life when I was happy not to be noticed, yet having someone's attention still gave me flutters.

"How'd you fall?" he asked. Blond hair fell in front of his eyes like he was some dreamy Backstreet Boy. At the time, that was dreamy.

I shrugged, my imagination fluttering away. "I didn't want to crush the bird."

"And you thought you did," he said, our earlier conversation seeming to make sense to him now.

"I thought I broke its wing."

"Nope." He smiled. "You just broke yours. You're like the pigeon." His grin widened like he'd come up with the cleverest joke. "Paige the Pigeon."

I giggled, thrilled to have a nickname and hopeful that it didn't mean anything bad. "Yep. What are you?"

"Mark." He said his name with less vigor, but I smiled and tried to help him out.

"Mark the Pigeon Hero." Not as clever.

We were inseparable after that. He never talked much, but that was fine because I talked for him. I told him what he needed to know about the "real world" and public school, and he told me about Jesus and school uniforms. Actually, I'd already heard something about Jesus when we went to Mass with my grandma once, but he talked about him differently. It was more interesting. Everything he said was interesting. His mom started inviting me to church, and that was the first time he'd ever begged me to do anything.

"Please, Pigeon," he always said.

He always called me that. Paige the Pigeon was the beginning of it, but after a while, it was just Pigeon. His lack of forcefulness and undeniable compassion also made me realize he was too good for me. I would have dragged him wherever I wanted him to go, but he never forced me into anything and never made me feel bad for it. At first, I thought it was because he didn't care one way or the other, but as time went on, I realized it was respect. Something I didn't afford him much or at least not in that way. I still don't, no matter how many times he says I do. Sometimes I wished I could show him what he did to me so he'd understand how subpar my attempts were. But that was impossible. The least I could do was show him how much every little thing meant to me. Hence the lace wings on my dress.

When we were teenagers, not much had changed, and my feelings didn't go away. I started dreaming about our wedding. We weren't dating. He'd never kissed me. But I never got over my childhood crush, and our friendship had been mostly me making decisions and telling him what's what, so I'd always fantasized about a relationship and us getting married. The problem was that I thought it was one-sided. I was abrasive and I knew it, so it made sense that he didn't like me more than a friendship allowed.

It wasn't until we were in high school and relationships were something people cared about that anyone wondered about us. His hair had darkened to a reddish-brown, his voice had deepened, and his smile had widened. He wasn't anyone's first pick, but I was definitely anyone's last. I knew it, too, but I didn't try to fight it. My pin-straight brown hair never saw dye, I never wore makeup, and I embraced every freckle on my face. Still, I was insecure, especially around Mark. I just didn't try to hide who I was. I brought up whatever I wanted, so I never could figure out why I couldn't just talk to him about us dating. Thankfully, his mom had a bigger mouth than I did.

Mark was telling his mom about a trip he wanted to take with my family. It was a long-shot question that we both knew the answer to, but he asked anyway.

"What is she to you, Mark?" she'd asked. "You two have been stuck like glue and glitter since you were kids, and it's sweet. But a trip with her? I'm not sure. It's not really appropriate at your age. What exactly are your intentions with her?"

I could not have been happier that his room was connected to the living room when I heard that. She probably wouldn't have been eager to know the answer if she knew I'd snuck into his room a few times and had been there that very moment. Girls weren't allowed in his room, myself included, but he had better video games and I wasn't too chicken to climb through a window. Looking back on it, I should have considered the thought of him liking me since he asked me to sneak out to hang out with him, but hey, a long friendship blinds people to things. Fact.

"What is she to you, Mark?" his mom had repeated, and man that's when I totally blew it. I hated myself for it, but my stomach hurt so bad from not laughing, I had to let it out. I think I lost a few points with his mom that day. I know I did, actually, but I'll get to that. She never got a direct answer from Mark, but he did get grounded for several days.

We started dating that next week.

His mom spent our first couple of months together telling Mark that I wasn't what he needed. I don't know what she thought he needed, but I have to say I agreed with her for a while. I had to prove myself to her, and while that sounds awful, it really opened up a lot to me. I was always great at being harder on the outside than on the inside, and Mark and I had gone from friends to partners so quickly, I think I needed the challenge. Now she likes me more than she likes Mark, but we won't tell him that. Well, you won't. I've told him. He agrees.

But even after I earned his mom's respect, I fought with the thought of not being good enough. That time spent figuring out his mom, I also spent seeing how much his mom loved him. How much she showed it just by being there for him and talking to him. It tugged at me a lot; I wasn't like that. Not really. If Mark wanted me to know something, I knew he'd tell me, but something about how she treated him made me feel, yet again, subpar.

But it sure didn't stop me from falling in love.

Our first kiss was on the sidewalk where we'd found the bird. I don't think he planned that, but I was so filled with girly emotions when he pointed it out that I kissed him without thinking. Looking back on it now, I regret nothing. I'd do it again, and I bet he would, too.

Our first dance was on his back porch after he'd snuck out to see me. Another time he was grounded, but that time it wasn't my fault. Our first anniversary was spent on a mission trip to New York, where we spent one afternoon feeding pigeons and reveling in the symbolism of that event. Okay, I reveled in it. I soaked that day up like a sponge. It was freaking adorable. He just did it for the birds. Okay, no, he did it for me. That one was for me.

I still laugh at that memory though, because I almost threw the engagement ring he'd put in my bag of seeds. On accident of course.

That was how we met, how we became us. It was how I ended up screaming at a man about a pair of wings that a windy, randomly stormy day took from me, dragging it around the neighborhood until it looked like a shredded bat wing.

I won't pretend it wasn't my fault. I live in an apartment with the prettiest courtyard, and I wanted to feel like a princess and walk around it in my wedding dress. The courtyard was why I lived there, really. The fresh spring grass, the calla lilies spilling color from their stems, and the magnolia trees giving off the most amazing perfume smell while the dogwood trees hid me from the rest of the world. It was perfect despite the wind, and it was a strong wind, too. That's what happens when you don't check the weather before you take clothes outside that are more expensive than your car.

I was a bit insecure sometimes about our relationship despite being the one making most of the moves, but I did know he loved me. I knew it before he told me, and he showed it when he brushed the words across my lips after he proposed. Just a few years after graduation, and he'd shown me in one kiss everything I needed to know about his love for me. He showed it in how he spoke. He showed it in how sincere his green eyes were every time they bore into mine, aching to know every thought lurking behind the windows to my clichéd soul. Everything he did for me was beautiful. But me? All I had to call beautiful, all I had to show him how much he meant to me in some grand gesture were these wings. I'd searched the entire neighborhood, freaked out a guy, and now I didn't know where to go. They could have been in someone's backyard in the next neighborhood over at this point. Either way, they were gone, and my dress was officially a mess.

I started to head back home, remembering that Mark was going to pick me up for one last date before we couldn't see each other, and I passed that scruffy man again. I hadn't noticed the first time where he lived, and now that I did, I felt kind of envious. His white brick house had two stories, a harbor-blue shingle roof, and dark-blue shutters. Just like I wanted one day. And Yankees Jr. had it. I found myself glaring at him as I walked by, and he just waved absently, probably staring at me as I trudged down the road. Probably thankful I hadn't been there to kill him.

I was in tears by the time I climbed the last set of stairs and walked through my front door. I crumbled to the ground and didn't care that my mascara was losing its volume to the beige shag. Those wings were our story. He first noticed me when my wing was broken, when we had something that pulled us together, and I wanted to bring that spark of magic to our wedding tomorrow. It was such a small thing, and only we'd understand it, but that was all that mattered. It was all the magic I'd had.

I bawled until I realized my nose was not being fair to the carpet, which probably took all of three seconds, and I sat up only to fall backward when I noticed Mark. His eyes were wide, and his mouth hung open. He leaned into the bathroom and came out with a towel, which he draped over me before encasing me in his arms, warming my skin like the perfect furnace he was.

"What happened?" he asked, holding me closer.

His question made me cry again, and he turned me in his arms so I was against his chest. He knew I wouldn't speak, not while I was crying, so he didn't ask again until my sloppy sobs died down to dribbling and drooling and laughing at my own idiocy.

He wore a sad smile, his dark hair falling over his eyes. I sighed. "You're not supposed to see me in the dress."

"We're way past that." He pulled hair away from my face. "I think it's safe to say you'll look even better in whatever you wear tomorrow anyway."

I nodded, my eyes squinting as I tried to stop more tears. He was right. I wasn't wearing this tomorrow. I let the towel fall around me and noticed the dark stains that touched the bottom folds of the dress, the clumps of mud that probably got on there when I had fallen the first time. Yeah, I fell more than once. Shut up.

Mark squeezed my shoulders for reassurance, which allowed me to stop crying altogether, and I sucked in a deep breath and held back a curse word that I knew he'd get on me for saying.

"What happened, Pigeon?" he tried again, this time with a slightly playful smile. "Dancing in the rain?"

I laughed, but it sounded forced and pathetic. "No, Mark . . ." I groaned. "I had a surprise thing for tomorrow, and it came in today, and . . ." I sighed. "Jeez, I'm so stupid. I had wings."

His brows rose. "Wings?"

I nodded. "The rain came in out of nowhere and the wind took them like they were a freaking kite. Stupid cheap Velcro wings."

He chuckled, turning away from me. Despite the smile that tugged on my lips, I punched him in the shoulder.

"It's not funny."

"Oh, Pigeon, yes it is." He pulled me into him and kissed my forehead, his body shaking with laughter. "You know it's funny."

"And now my dress is messed up, too."

He moved backward, glancing down at my dress. Then his eyes lingered, and I followed his gaze to my arm. He sighed, the sound thoughtful and reminiscent. "So you have a broken wing."

I smiled, barely stopping myself from rolling my eyes. "I have a broken wing."

And there it was. The spark of green and the eyes full of wonder I'd hoped to see when I walked down the aisle. The glowing smile that showed exactly what I always felt. It confirmed what I already knew, but I needed to see it. The feeling he gave me every moment. The love that swelled my heart because he put it there. It was there in his eyes, but now it was filled with all we added in between.

To learn more about this author, please visit:
https://cayceberryman.com/

The Sum of All Souls

Literary

Richard Happerger

Prompt: A mysterious stranger hands you a business card.

GABRIELA CLENCHED THE DEFIBRILLATOR paddles until the knuckles of her blood-deprived fingers turned white beneath her blue surgical gloves. The ascending whine of the electrical charge reaching its peak complemented the steady tone of the heart monitor. Several minutes had passed since the last pulse registered. Each new jolt that fired through the small body was answered with the same cold response. Beads of sweat on her forehead remained unchallenged.

"Doctor . . ." said Nurse Irene.

After a minute, Gabriela lowered her head and shook it slowly. She placed the paddles back in their holster. The other members of the pediatric emergency triage team remained silent. They all knew what Gabriela refused to accept. That it was another night that the good guys didn't win. Another night in which all they gave wasn't enough. Gabriela signaled the nurse to turn off the machines. The faint hum of the defibrillator stopped and the flatline on the heart rate monitor faded away. For a moment, the only sound she heard was the faint pulsing of her own heartbeat, until the room was punctured by her voice. "Official time of death is 1:32 a.m."

"Are you okay, Dr. Lang?" asked the nurse while carefully removing various hoses and wires from the motionless body. The calm words comforted Gabriela and she took a deep breath before straightening herself. She exhaled slowly.

"I'm fine, Irene," she replied, barely able to squeeze the words through her dry voice. She cleared her throat and wiped her forehead with the back of her hand before turning to the rest of the emergency triage room. "Thank you everyone. We tried. Please finish up here for me."

The brief calm in her voice was quickly overpowered by the tightness in her chest. The revolving carousel of Gabriela's thoughts spun faster with every heartbeat. Why would a ten-year-old boy be in the back seat of a car at two o'clock in the morning? Why wasn't he in bed sleeping? Perhaps he was returning home with his parents after a trip. He never felt the jolt of the truck slamming into the back of the family car. In her mind she rehearsed the words she would say to the parents who waited for news from their own hospital rooms. She learned to relay this kind of news with grace, with calm professionalism, and without flinching at every incision her own words made, separating the fibers of her own heart. She learned to be a good liar.

Gabriela left the room, tossed her surgical gloves into the waste bin, and removed her surgical gown. Her pace quickened as she slammed her body through the door to the washroom. It was empty as she burst into the empty stall and bent over the edge of the porcelain basin. The retching sounds echoed off the tiled walls, but only a few drops of anguished bile dropped into the water. The sound was accompanied by the faint squeak of shoes with rubber soles entering the washroom. Gabriela steadied herself against the wall of the cubicle stall and closed her eyes. A warm teardrop ran down the side of her cheek, leaving a cold trail.

"Are you all right in there?" asked a soft voice from the other side of the stall.

"Yes . . . I'm fine, Jane. I'm fine. It must have been something I ate earlier. My stomach has been bothering me all day."

"Oh no. Maybe you should lay down and rest for a bit."

Gabriela wiped the dampness off her cheek with her sleeve and pushed the cubicle door open. She walked to the basin and struggled through the tightness of the faucet to turn on the water. She washed her hands and threw some water on her face. Her blurry reflection in the mirror highlighted her dry and anemic-looking skin and her blonde hair, disheveled by the cap she wore during surgery. It contrasted the dark rings around her eyes. The white fluorescent light brought out every sleep-deprived crevice in her face. The story about the mild bout of food poisoning seemed plausible, she thought.

"I just need to get a bit of water. My shift will be over soon. I can go home, have a nice relaxing hot bath, and go to bed. I think that's what I need right now," said Gabriela. She dried her hands with a paper towel but clasped them after she tossed the towel into the wastebasket. Her fingers always gave away the trembling in her hands.

* * *

THE SHIFT ENDED. DAYLIGHT had arrived an hour before, but she squinted, adjusting to the bright sunlight. The streetcar stop was a short walk from the hospital, and she got on the 501 tram that just arrived. It a was ten-stop ride straight back to St. George station and from there a fifteen-minute walk to her apartment. She was reluctant to drive a car. She abhorred the results of their misuse, having seen many of the victims. Instead Gabriela preferred the calming rattle and creaks of the train, kept restrained within its steel tracks. It allowed her mind a chance to wander and escape the things she encountered every day of her calling, but it didn't always help. She slid her middle finger over the inside of her wrist and slowly counted to ten, which she sometimes did to quickly check the pulse of a patient. Too fast. Slowing her breathing only helped briefly. The surrounding voices of passengers blended with the sounds of the streetcar to resemble a machine that struggled with lack of oil. Gabriela turned to gaze through the window beside her, looking at nothing.

* * *

SHE ARRIVED AT HER apartment building and opened the third-floor unit. She tossed her keys into a glass dish beside the door, but the force caused them to slide out and drop onto the floor. The noise startled her cat, Misty, who scurried behind the nearby sofa. Mail had collected on the floor after being dropped through the slot. She pushed it aside with her feet.

Gabriela pulled a random bottle of wine from a metal rack on the kitchen counter, opened it, and filled a tall water glass to the rim. She carried it and the half-empty bottle over to the coffee table in front of the sofa. The table was cluttered with papers, books, and an opened laptop. She sat next to a plaid flannel blanket that lay crumbled. This is where she would stay when she couldn't sleep, watching recorded TV shows. She always knew when it would be another bedtime where dreams came back. Often, they were the kind of dreams that jolted her awake, leaving her heart racing and her nightgown drenched in sweat. Sometimes the dream would end with the same monotone sound and a heart rate monitor showing only a solid flat line, or herself, surrounded by people whose gazes descended on her with disappointment etched into them. Parents looking for answers. But, she would be unable to utter a single word, her jaw frozen.

Gabriela emptied the glass and refilled it with the remaining wine from the bottle. She powered up the slim silver laptop sitting on the coffee table. The screen lit up to reveal a partially written letter addressed to the hospital administration. She took another sip and stared at the blurring words before typing the final text "I hereby resign." She positioned the cursor over the send button and clenched her blurry eyes. A tear left a trail down her cheek as her finger pressed down on the mouse to make a single click.

Gabriela reached for the small white bottle of pale-blue pills sitting on the table. She opened it to retrieve one, but the entire contents poured out into the palm of her hand. She stared at the smooth round shapes before letting them roll back into the bottle. All except for two that she swallowed and chased with the last bit of the wine. She hoped they would help her sleep through the dreams.

* * *

THE NEXT DAY THE streetcar was filled with business people coming from work, identified by the various shades of gray and navy, contrasting the scuffed cream-colored interior of the train. There were students who had finished their classes. Their blurred shapes were more colorful and animated in her peripheral vision. Other people clutched shopping bags. Her workday started when everyone else's ended.

She found a window seat just as someone got up to leave at the next stop. The window was smudged with a pink substance and someone's initials were carved into the glass. The tram continued to crawl through the heavy rush-hour traffic. The background hum of human voices and the creaking of the aging hull of the tram were peppered with the intermittent chiming of a bell. Every time the exit doors opened, a new wave of outside fumes refreshed the inside air. The scents of exhaust mixed with the exhaled breaths that gave away the wearer's lunch choices. Gabriela rubbed her temples in a futile attempt to reduce the throbbing headache.

She felt the train shudder and stop again, but she did not break her gaze from the window to see who got on. She noticed a shadow move closer in the corner of her eye.

"Is this seat taken?"

Gabriela turned away from the window to look up at a woman who pointed toward the empty seat in front of her. The woman had long gray hair that reached just past the shoulder, tied together into a simple ponytail with a clip. The stranger carried a brown leather briefcase with a gold buckle. It looked new without marks, matching the navy-blue business suit. From all the trips Gabriela took on this streetcar line, she had never seen her before.

"No. It's all yours," replied Gabriela.

The woman smiled. She took her seat and placed the briefcase on her lap. Gabriela turned her gaze back toward the passing cars outside. The streetcar continued to inch forward through a sea of cars and made frequent jarring stops to avoid hitting the cars that cut in front. With the rocking motion of the train, her eyelids became heavy, but she perked up when the woman in front of her spoke.

"Rough day?"

Gabriela rubbed her eyes and looked at the woman. She got a closer look at her. The lines in her face were smooth and her skin clear. Her eyes were a pale blue. She looked younger than her gray hair indicated. The new rider could have dyed it, like she did. Gabriela was only thirty years old but had started to cover up the increasing number of gray strands in recent months. More alarming were the ones that had fallen out.

"I'm sorry?" asked Gabriela, but she had understood. She had intended to reply with vexation, not for the question, but for the moment of anonymous solitude that was stolen from her. The woman's persistent smile robbed her even of the will for that.

"I apologize. I didn't mean to interrupt your thoughts, but I couldn't help noticing," said the woman.

Gabriela tried to talk but couldn't bring herself to. She noticed on the other side of the aisle was a mother with her two children. The older one appeared in age and mannerism to be a teenager, while the other was seven or eight. Between them was a pink backpack. The younger child was sitting up with her knees on the seat to give her *more height as she peeked over the shoulder of her sister, who was scrolling through images on her phone.*

"Stop it, and stop chewing in my ear," said the older sister, pushing the younger back into her seat. The younger lost her balance slightly and reached out to hold on to something. Unfortunately for the older sister, it was a few strands of her shoulder-length hair. She let out a loud groan. Their mother told them both to settle down. The younger girl dropped back into her seat and continued to bite into a large cookie with white glaze. Gabriela noticed it now. It was the faint aroma of sugar, cinnamon, and nutmeg. She felt her mind wander, scrolling through images of her past, but remembered the question the woman in front of her had asked. She was still smiling.

"Yes. It was. I guess you can tell. I probably look like a mess." Gabriela ran her fingers through some tangles in her hair.

"No, you don't. I just read people. It's a little skill I acquired over the years. It helps in my line of work. I'm sorry. I don't mean to be so forward and nosy, but I noticed your ID tag from Hope Valley Pediatric Hospital. You are a doctor."

"I am."

"That's a wonderful profession. You help those who are suffering. I should introduce myself. Call me Angela. Nice to meet you."

The woman reached forward with her right hand and waited for Gabriela to meet her halfway between. After a moment of hesitation, Gabriela reached forward and noticed the firmness in Angela's hand.

"I'm afraid I'm not helping," replied Gabriela in a low tone, returning her glance toward the sanctity and escape of the window. She closed her eyes momentarily before closing her jacket and folding her arms tightly in front of her. Gabriela relaxed her eyes and aimlessly scanned the blurred images sweeping past her window. She sensed that Angela had not turned her head and was still looking in her direction as if unsatisfied with the conclusion of the conversation.

"I know you are."

"Helping?" asked Gabriela while facing the traffic through the window.

"That you are afraid."

Gabriela's head turned slowly toward Angela. Her mouth opened briefly as if to reply, but she took a deep breath instead. In the seats behind them a group of students were chatting, and she hesitated until she was sure no one else was listening.

"I am? What am I afraid of?"

"Of failure. I think we're all afraid of that at some point," said Angela. She smiled at the little girl with the cookie. "I just love the smell of freshly baked gingerbread. Doesn't it remind you of your childhood?"

"A little."

Among the students, Gabriela noticed a young woman about the same age as she was when she started university. She didn't talk to the others around her but kept her backpack on her lap with her arms around it. The contents made a sharp outline in the stretched fabric of the bag. Books. Gabriela remembered the sore shoulders she often had from carrying a heavy bag.

"So, are you a psychiatrist? You seem to know a lot about me, but we've only just met."

"Yes and no. Yes, I often have to get into people's minds, but I'm not a trained psychiatrist. No, I'm more what you would call a life coach or even a personal troubleshooter. A consultant maybe. I go wherever I'm needed to bring the world back into balance for someone."

"Are you on your way to a case now? To look into someone's mind I mean."

"Yes I am. It's another worthy cause. They all are," said Angela as a smile came over her. "It's the first time I had to come down this way, but I'm glad I did."

Gabriela wondered how many times she had ridden the streetcar, but not once did anyone start up a conversation, especially someone who seemed to be able to read her mind. Gabriela was equally alarmed and skeptical. Her fingers fidgeted with her hospital identification tag while she tried to avoid direct eye contact with Angela. She looked at the traffic on the other side of the window, but she felt the unwavering gaze from Angela.

"So, what kind of troubleshooter are you? Do you fix things . . . or people?" asked Gabriela.

"Kind of. I do fix people, as you say, but not like you do. No. I don't physically fix them. I try to figure out what people are thinking and how they feel about the world around them. I try to get to the root cause of the issue and find a way to steer a person out of a bad situation."

"I see . . . So, how does someone know if they need your help?"

The woman took a long pause and looked straight into Gabriela's eyes. After a while Gabriela was tempted to break the contact, but she couldn't. She felt a layer being removed from her outer shell, like a sheep that had the warmth of the thick fur shaved off, only leaving it shivering with a few stubbles of hair. A faint breeze of cool air overcame her, but soon the warmth returned, as did the nervous smile.

"They have the wrong kind of dreams," said Angela.

"Interesting."

For Gabriela the tram went silent. She no longer heard the background chatter of voices, the creaking of the train as the wheels bumped along the iron rails. She felt another layer being removed, but this one came off more slowly. It seemed thicker and more attached. As much as Gabriela tried to hold on to it, she felt powerless to stop it. She continued to smile politely at Angela and crossed her arms, clutching her ID tag. A cool breeze briefly came over her again, which surprised her since it was warm in the streetcar. She could sense her perspiration whenever the slightest movement caused the faint turbulence in the air to touch her skin. The train jerked to a stop again and opened its doors. A few people stood up to head to the exit, and Gabriela jumped out of her seat. As she reached for the metal pole to balance herself, she noticed her hand was shaking.

"My stop. Nice to meet you," said Gabriela, clutching her purse and dangling ID tag.

"Wait. Let me give you something." Angela reached into her briefcase and pulled out a small rectangular piece of paper. She pulled the cap off a black pen, exposing a gold nib with a tiny drop of emerald-colored ink. Faint metallic swirls embedded in the pen appeared and disappeared as she wrote on the back of the paper. She blew on it to let the ink dry.

"Here . . . take my business card. I hope to chat with you soon. Take care, Gabriela."

Gabriela nodded with a brief smile and slid the business card through a gap in her purse.

* * *

THE HUMMING OF THE floor polishing machine echoed throughout the empty hallways of the emergency ward. Gabriela thought it felt like a fine dentist's drill probing for cavities in her forehead above her right eye. The pain had shifted and had become more focused. Her eyes followed a spinning symbol on the computer monitor inside a small office near the nurse's station. Stacks of paper surrounded her, and an inspirational message adorned the month of September on the calendar pinned to the corkboard in front of her. Only two cases had arrived since her return to work three hours before. One case of elevated fever in a boy diagnosed with a painful ear infection, and a girl with a stomachache. Only walk-ins. No ambulance had arrived so far during her shift. Gabriela hoped for a quiet night. She tapped at the computer keyboard in front of her, repeating the same sequence, but the spinning symbol on the screen did not respond.

"What's wrong with the e-mail today?" Gabriela called out aimlessly to anyone in the nurses' station.

"Oh . . . e-mail has been down all day. Apparently, the server crashed or something, and they had to restore it from yesterday's backup," called Nurse Joan from behind the reception desk.

"What about all the e-mails from today?"

"Gone, they say. That's okay, I didn't really need another invitation to take a course today."

"All of them?" asked Gabriela, rubbing her eyes with the palms of her hands.

"I guess."

Soft footsteps with a faint squeak came closer until they stopped in the doorway of the small office. Nurse Jane held a tiny paper cup containing two orange tablets. She placed them on an empty spot on the desk in front of Gabriela.

"Here. For your headache. I've known you long enough to know when you need some. How are you feeling today? You were in pretty rough shape yesterday."

"Fine. Just a bit of a headache. Thank you."

"No problem. We are lucky we have an unusually slow night. Maybe we have time for a nap."

Jane laughed and returned to her desk at the station while Gabriela swallowed the pills and took a sip from a coffee cup to drown them. She reached into the outside of her purse to pull out a pack of gum but caught a business card instead. It was the one given to her by Angela on the streetcar. Gabriela let out a chuckle. The printed information on the business card only revealed a simple "Angela. Guardian of Lost Souls" and no address or phone number. She let out a sigh and dropped the card into the waste bin. She rubbed her eyes again and pushed the keyboard toward the monitor with the spinning symbol that had now stopped spinning. Hidden from view in the tiny office, her head dropped onto her crossed arms on the desk, used as a pillow for a few minutes of rest. The humming sound of the polishing machine faded until it was gone. Darkness descended over her eyes.

At first Gabriela heard a single faint pop that resembled a child clapping its small hands together. Another pop came a moment later, but it was louder. Her curiosity started with a glimmer of light, but it increased in intensity as Gabriela strained to open the lids of her eyes. The blurred bright lines turned into a sharp contrast and revealed the source of the sound. It was a small girl with blonde pigtails, round cheeks dotted with pale freckles, and a sharp grin that was directed at Gabriela. The girl's face stared into Gabriela's, close enough for her to catch the scent of gingerbread cookies on her breath.

"She is awake. She just opened her eyes," shouted the girl to a group of people behind her. The loud voice helped push some of the cloudiness out of her mind, but she felt the weight of her limbs and face. Her eyes opened wide enough to fill in the details of the human silhouettes in front of her. It was a small group of all females. They were of different ages. The youngest of them stood right in front of her. The girl tilted her head to the side to line up with Gabriela's, who was still resting on a pillow. Gabriela sat up and scanned the room. It was a cream-colored patient room, and she was in the center of it, resting on a bed while attached to tubes and wires leading to machines set up beside her. She traced a set of green and red wires to an ECG machine turned to monitor her heart rate. The flickering numbers on the screen displayed zero above a solid green line. A red exclamation mark flashed in the corner of the monitor. She felt the tightness forming in her chest and neck. It took all her strength to slide her right middle finger over her left wrist, but she could feel no pulse. Her finger dug deeper into her wrist, leaving a red-and-white mark in her skin. Her eyes widened to scan the figures around her.

"It's about time," said a young woman who was sitting on a reclining chair with her legs pulled up. She never looked up while her fingers jabbed at the shiny glimmering screen of a phone that rested against her knee. The sleeves of her blue hooded sweater were pulled over her hands, leaving only the fingers exposed. She looked familiar and younger than Gabriela thought at first. She was a teenager. As Gabriela looked around the room, she realized that everyone looked familiar. Faces attached to a moment of time that was brief but lingering. One stood out more than the others as she recognized the random stranger from the streetcar, Angela, standing in the middle of the group. Gabriela tried to speak, but only air escaped her lips. She made another attempt.

"Who are you? What . . . what happened to me?" asked Gabriela, but her voice trailed off as an older lady stepped forward. She had a warm smile and long, straight gray hair tied together with a single clip. Gabriela tried to speak again, but again she had to repeat the words. "I know you. I know you from the streetcar yesterday. Are you visiting a patient?"

"Yes. We are visiting a patient. We are visiting you."

"I don't understand. I'm not a patient . . . Why is everyone here from the streetcar? Wait a moment. This must be a dream. This can't be real. This. You . . . can't be real."

Gabriela tried to pinch herself and rub her eyes. Anything to wake herself, but every attempt failed. She looked around and every detail seemed clear. Everything else in the room was exactly as it should be. It all seemed real. Alarmed by the flashing red exclamation mark on the monitor and the flat green, she traced the wires to small patches attached to her chest. They were firmly attached. *Perhaps the machine is defective,* she thought.

"Yes, you are having a dream, but it's a bit more complicated. This is no ordinary dream."

"If I'm having a dream, why does it feel so real? Why are all of you here? Where are the rest of my colleagues? This doesn't make any sense. I'm not sick. Why doesn't this machine show my heartbeat?"

"I told you she's not going to get it," said the teenager, but now the hood from the sweater was down and Gabriela could see long strands of unkempt blonde hair covering up most of her face.

"Be quiet, Princess. You're so mean," said the little girl in a loud voice. She squinted her eyes and her lower lip was pushed over her upper one. She walked over to the teenager and grabbed a few strands of her hair, pulling them, causing the teenager's head to jerk to the side.

"Stop it! I'm so going to kill you," yelled the teenager, swatting at the little girl's hand but missing.

"She won't," whispered the young girl to Gabriela with a wide smile. "She is mean on the outside, but she is nice on the inside. You'll see." The teenager did not reply and pulled the hood back over her head. Her attention returned to random images on her phone.

"You kids need to be nice," said the older woman with a stern voice.

"Princess?" asked Gabriela, and she turned toward the chair with the teenager. "My mom always called me that, usually when she was mad at me for something."

Gabriela could see the teenager's head rise a little from her phone and it looked like her hand was about to part the curtain of her hair, but the glimpse of her delicate pale facial features soon disappeared.

"Whatever," replied the teenager, but she was no longer looking at her phone. She had clasped it between her hands, which were half-covered by her sweater's sleeves. Gabriela's gaze turned back toward Angela with a quizzical expression. Angela nodded slowly and stepped forward.

"I can explain. This will seem very confusing to you, but you needn't worry."

"Why is everyone here from the train we were on?"

The little girl reached under the footboard of the bed and pressed a button with an arrow pointing up. A whirring sound emanated from below the bed, and Gabriela felt the back of her bed rise until she was almost upright.

"You see, all these faces here. They are here to help you remember something. They are images of how you saw yourself at different points in your life."

Gabriela realized that despite the fact that she was surrounded by complete strangers, she could feel a sense of familiarity. She had met the people only once before, but it seemed to her that it was more than a casual reunion. She wanted to know why she felt like she needed to be with them.

"Remember what? I don't understand."

"I knew she wouldn't get it," mumbled Princess.

Angela turned toward her but didn't reply. Gabriela thought for a moment that Angela would scold her, but a slight smile broke out in the corner of her lips. Instead of a frown, Angela only reflected a look of compassion.

"You sure were a handful at that age, Gabriela. Your mom had a lot to deal with, but you know you didn't mean to do the things you did — to say the things that hurt your mom. Deep down you were still mourning your father, but we are not here to remind you of that. We are here to help you remember the journey that made you become who you are today."

"Who am . . . I mean, why are you doing this? Why do I need to remember?" asked Gabriela.

She wondered why no one else was around in her dream. Aside from the people in the room, she heard no one else. No squeaking shoes or beeping machines. No whirring of the floor polishing machine. The quick and steady heartbeat in her ear became the background noise.

"Why you became a doctor. People depend on you, but you are about to make a big mistake. It will be the biggest mistake of your life. I will try to make you see we are all here for a reason, and that includes you. Bear with me. Let's take Princess, here, as an example. When you were her age, you were still mourning your father's death from a year earlier."

"Yes. I had just turned fourteen. He went to work on a Friday morning. When he came home, we were going to go on a road trip to Florida. It was going to be our family vacation that summer. He never came home. I remember the packed bags in the hallway. They sat there for a long time. For years, every time I saw a pile of bags, I would . . . You don't need to remind me of that. It's very clear to me."

Gabriela pulled a strand of hair from her face and wiped her eyes with the back of her right hand, while her left hand twisted the corner of her blanket into a spiral.

"I'm not trying to remind you of that incident, and I'm sorry you had to go through all that. It's what happened next."

"What?"

"You saved your first life."

"Michael," Gabriela mumbled, but everyone heard it. The deafening silence in the room would make a simple drop of a medical cotton ball strain the strongest eardrums. Even a faint whisper of a thought would not escape the ears in this room. She tried to search for words to explain how they knew his name but found only questions. "How do you . . . ?"

"Know? This is your dream. We know everything about you, but first let me continue. You were in the same grade and went to the same school, but you didn't talk much. He lived two houses down from your home. It was close enough for you to hear his cry for help."

"I was in the back yard planting flowers. My mom thought it would be good for me. I heard yelling, and I recognized the voice. It was a neighbor's kid, Michael. He had fallen into the pool. I knew he couldn't swim. His family had this big pool, but Michael never learned how to swim."

Gabriela remembered dropping everything at the time and running toward the scream. The little shovel with the shiny chrome blade, the gardening gloves of which she only found one afterward. She had been planting a red Gerbera. It was her favorite type of flower. She had returned later to plant it into the ground and named it Michael after the boy she rescued.

"It was good for Michael that you were there. The screaming stopped after a few seconds, but you climbed over two fences, ran over into his back yard, and jumped in with everything you were wearing. You didn't think twice. You grabbed him and pulled him out. By the time you got there, he had already been under the water and he wasn't breathing."

"No, he wasn't. I was so scared. I started to perform CPR. I took a course because my mom thought it would be good if I wanted to be a babysitter. I never thought I would remember how to do it. I tried to breathe air into his lungs; I didn't know if I was doing it right. I was shaking so much."

"You did do it right, and he still tells everyone that it was his first kiss. As you saw his eyes open up after coughing up all this water, it was at that moment you realized that when one day you became a doctor, you would work in a place like this here. A place where you can see someone come back to life. You found a purpose. You wanted to be there to help someone when they need it most."

Gabriela opened the palms of her hands and spread her fingers. She didn't recognize the hands she saw trembling years ago. They were dry and steady. She clenched them into fists until the whites of her knuckles showed. On the monitor, a tiny jagged blip interrupted the solid line. She let her arms drop to her side.

"I can't always help."

"Yes. That is very true. I have something to say to that, but first I want to introduce you to someone else you will remember."

Angela walked over to the young woman Gabriela had seen on the streetcar clutching the same backpack filled with books. She placed her hand on her shoulder to bring her closer.

"What's your name?" asked Gabriela, watching her step forward. The entire time, she hadn't spoken a word, but her face lit up as she gave a nervous smile. Her cheeks became red.

"My nickname is Professor," said the young woman.

"You too? That was me back then, too—Professor Gabriela. That's what my friends called me, because I was always studying or something. I didn't have much time for them."

Gabriela's thoughts turned back to Michael, who for a few years attended the same university until she started medical school. They dated whenever she had time for him, until his studies in filmmaking landed him a position as a screenwriter for a local production company. He told her recently he was working on a story about two long-lost lovers reuniting after many years but was having trouble with the ending. He was still bugging her for help with that perfect ending.

"They gave you that name because you were studying so hard. You had one goal. You made many sacrifices, and probably more than you needed to."

"Yes, Michael always complained that he didn't see me enough. He still does. He deserves better," said Gabriela with an aborted laugh that dissipated with the quick exhalation of her breath. She closed her eyes and shook her head slowly. "I remember all that now, but it doesn't matter. I don't even know why I did all that."

The youngest member in the group stepped forward to stand between Gabriela and Angela. Her hands were hidden behind her back as if she held something. She made sure Gabriela could not see what it was, even as she tried to look around her back. The young girl shifted to keep it out of sight, eliciting a grin with a wrinkled top of her nose as she outwitted Gabriela's curiosity.

"What do you have behind your back, little girl? What's your name?" asked Gabriela, but the girl continued to wrinkle her nose in defiance.

"You have to guess my name. If you get it right, I will show you what's behind my back. You already know what it is, but you just need to remember."

"Can you give me a clue?"

"Okay, but just one."

"Tell me," pleaded Gabriela.

"Did you smell the gingerbread cookies?"

"Gingerbread cookies. Yes . . . yes, I remember smelling them on the train . . . but . . ." Gabriela cupped her hand over her mouth and closed her eyes. A small tear formed in the corner of her eye. "Grandma made gingerbread cookies after I said I wanted to become a doctor. I was seven."

"You made a promise," said the girl, but the smile was gone and so was Gabriela's.

"You're right. I did promise Grandma. She told me the story of her twin sister who was very sick when they were young. She was only seven years old when she died. I promised that I would become a doctor when I was big and cure every child in the whole world. Grandma always called me Dr. Gabriela after that."

The little girl moved her hands from behind her back and held out a small bowl with gingerbread cookies decorated with icing and multi-colored sprinkles. There were red, blue, and green ones. Gabriela remembered thinking that they had different flavors, and had been sure the red ones tasted like strawberry. She pulled a small one shaped like a mitten out of the bowl. She took a small bite, but it was enough to unleash a torrent of memories. She pictured her grandmother passing her the big wooden spoon to mix the ingredients in a large metal bowl, slightly dented after years of service, and her arms becoming tired but refusing to give up. She wiped the dampness from her eyes with the back of her hand.

"Gabriela, I hope you understand, because now we have to go. There is work to do," said Angela as she pointed to a set of sliding doors at the end of the room. Gabriela hadn't noticed them before, and she could see flashing lights and shapes of people moving rapidly past the opaque glass. Everyone in the room stood up and proceeded toward the automatic sliding doors.

"Where are you all going?" asked Gabriela.

"You are so funny, Gabriela. You mean we," chimed in the little Dr. Gabriela who started to giggle before saying, "Remember, we are all you. Now hurry, they are coming."

Gabriela looked around the assembled group and through them recognized herself at different points in her life. She realized that sometimes people have to remember where they came from in order to rediscover why they need to be where they are.

"You are here for a reason. You are in the right place. You can mourn the ones you cannot save, but please do open your eyes and

heart to see the many lives that you help," said Angela as she placed her hand on Gabriela's shoulder and gave it a gentle shake.

"If you are all me, then who are you, Angela? I haven't been like you."

"You will, one day. One day you will stand in front of another young woman and ask her not to give up."

"Wait, I want to go with you, but I . . . I can't. I can't move. Why can't I move?"

"We need to wake you," said Angela in a calm voice.

Gabriela could feel Angela's hand grip tighter on her shoulder. She felt it move back and forth. It became more vigorous each time. Gabriela's eyes widened with bewilderment as she heard the high pitch of a charging defibrillator. She tried to grab Angela's arm but couldn't move. The sound of the pitch peaked.

"You just need a little jolt."

"Wait . . . no. Don't," pleaded Gabriela, but it was too late.

She felt her chest compress and explode at the same time. Every muscle seemed to tense simultaneously. One by one, all the faces and memories faded until Angela was gone as well. The wires attached to her disappeared. The scent of gingerbread cookies was replaced with the clinical aroma of sterilizer and medical equipment. When she woke she took a deep breath, but it was the kind of gasp one took after emerging from a pool of water after having nearly drowned.

"Oh my God, Gabriela. Are you okay?" asked Jane as she noticed Gabriela starting to move. Gabriela rubbed her eyes and gazed toward the large sliding doors. "You must have been in a really deep sleep. Sorry, I had to wake you up. One just pulled in."

"Yes. I'm fine. I'm all right, Jane. I smelled it. I really did."

"You what?" asked Jane with a puzzled look, but she didn't get a response. Gabriela reached down into the wastebasket and pulled out the business card she had dropped in there earlier. She pinned it to an empty spot on the corkboard in front of her, jumped out of her chair, and hurried toward the sliding doors that burst open to reveal *a gurney being rolled in by two ambulance attendants. The intermittent flashing red light from the ambulance bounced off the ceiling.*

The business card contrasted the corkboard, with its red, green, and blue lettering and single handwritten line.

Remember to smell the gingerbread.

Eve Discovered

Science Fiction

Cari Jehlik

*Prompt: Your adoptive mother tells you, while on her deathbed, that
you were born on a different planet. You have always suspected you
were different because of the one thing that separates you from the
rest of humankind.*

*A*PPREHENSION GRAPPLES AT MY chest. *No matter how many
times I do this, I never get used to it. Although, this way is
better than them dying alone and no one knowing about it
until weeks, months, or even years later.*

*I walk around a dumpy Bronx apartment building. Cars pass a
few blocks away, but there's not much traffic around here. The bright
sun and birds chirping at each other belie my purpose here. I know
she's in there and I know it's time. I check for people.*

No one is coming. It's time.

*I approach the front door. My reflection stares back at me from
the window. I've let my auburn hair grow out, and it hangs limply
down my shoulders. My eyes look even bigger, and my nose looks
even smaller in the warped glass. It still amazes me that nobody
knows.*

*I pull on the front door with the tips of my knobby fingers and
step inside the entrance. Various smells assault my nose—spices,*

cigarettes, and urine, among others I can't immediately identify —
and I cough. It takes a moment for me to regain myself. The urine
smell and the reason for my visit remind me of my mom, and tears
sting my eyes. Grief is weird like that. It's been almost fifteen years
and yet I still remember everything from her last day so vividly.

* * *

"IT'S TIME," MOM MUMBLED. "Tell her. No . . . more . . . time." Sweat
glistened on her skin. She'd been rambling on and off about this for
days now, but only when she occupied that space between asleep
and awake.

I didn't ask.

I didn't want to know.

Mom's raspy breathing and the perpetual urine stink of the
room grated on me, but I couldn't bear to pull myself away for even
a moment. I lived in terror of going to the bathroom and coming back
to find her dead. I wasn't sure how long I'd been watching. Her eyes
closed a while ago, and she almost looked peaceful. I supposed
morphine would do that to someone.

I opened my psychology book and tried to push away all the
thoughts racing in my head about my mom and her dying and me
being alone. I needed to read and learn this material.

"Eve?" she whispered. I peered over the top of my book, right
into her brown eyes, three shades darker than her brown skin.

"Yeah, Mom?" I snapped the book shut and set it on the floor,
leaning forward in the recliner. Hospice gave us the bed and
recommended the recliner for me since we had space in her massive
master bedroom. They said it would make my nights more
comfortable. They knew I'd be sleeping here more than I slept in my
own bed.

"I'm thirsty," she said, reaching her hand out to me. I pushed
the button that sat her up a bit and grabbed the plastic cup with the
bendy straw from the end table. Her lips looked dry, her skin taut

across her bones. She took three or four long pulls from the straw, closed her eyes, and leaned back. I set the cup back on the nightstand. She held her hand out to me and I grabbed it, her fingers long and smooth, mine long and knobby-knuckled. My nearly milky-white skin stood in stark contrast to the smooth dark chocolate of hers.

"Do you need anything, Mom?" I asked, resting my hand on her forehead. The final days loomed heavy ahead of us. The weight crushed me.

She shook her head. "There's something I need to tell you, though."

"What's that?"

"It's about your mother."

My chest tightened. "No, we don't need to go there. It's . . . it's okay. Really. You're my mom, not her."

"I know that, sweetie." Her lips peeled back into a strange smile, cracking her bottom lip, her teeth pronounced in her sunken face. She licked her lip, and I smeared some more Carmex on it. She rubbed her lips together before speaking again. "I know to you I'm your mother, and nothing else matters."

She took several breaths. I realized I was holding mine. I released it slowly through my nose. This anticipation wound me even tighter.

"I've always been honest that you were adopted. Our skin color couldn't make that more plain." She chuckled and rubbed my arm the way she always did whenever someone awkwardly asked if I was a foster kid—or some other weird question. Like a black mom and a white kid was the biggest anomaly in all creation.

"I know. Even mixed-race kids are darker than me." I laughed.

"Well." She coughed. I grabbed the cup, and she took another sip. "That's not all."

"Okay." Was my mother a drug addict? Found dead in the street? A celebrity?

Mom raised her eyes to the ceiling before she spoke. "Your mother wasn't of this world."

Cryptic. I squinted my eyes. "Okay," I repeated, not sure where she was going. "Not of what world? Ours? America? Was she an immigrant?"

Mom laughed again. A terrible idea. Soon laughing turned into coughing, and coughing turned to blood, and by the time the hospice nurse came and we got her calmed down and breathing normally again, nearly forty-five minutes had passed. She closed her eyes and fell asleep. The nurse left the room, closing the door behind her.

I collapsed into the recliner, trying to process what she'd said, picking at a bleach spot on my worn-out jeans. Could I still consider her lucid?

* * *

"EXCUSE ME, MA'AM," A deep voice says, interrupting my thoughts of the past. I jump and turn inside the entrance of this Bronx apartment. How long have I been standing here? The postal worker is here. My memory makes me miss my chance to get in undetected.

"I'm sorry," I say.

"Not a problem," he says. His thick mustache twitches as he shoves the master key into the lock and pulls open the rack of mailboxes. I glance over them. One box is packed. I know exactly whose that is. He works his way efficiently down the empty boxes and swears when he gets to that box.

"Is that fourteen's box?" I ask, years of practice making it easy to sound perfectly innocent.

"Yeah," he grumbles. "Hasn't picked up her mail for two weeks."

"I'm a friend," I say. "I was just going to visit her. I can take it with me if you like."

He looks at me suspiciously for a moment before his face softens and he nods. He pulls the wad of mail out of her box and dumps it into my arms. He goes back to filling boxes and doesn't look at me again.

I pull out my keys and find one that slips into the lock of the door. I hold my hand over the lock and the mechanism releases, unlocking the door. I pull the door open and slide the key out as the lock goes back into its place. I take one furtive glance back. He's still filling mailboxes, and I slip into the building. The door clicks behind me and I pull the stack of mail to my chest, taking slow, deep breaths. This building is a far cry from where I grew up, and even from where I live now, but so many things stay familiar.

I walk to the end of the hall, fourteen being the last one on the left. I knock.

"Anita?" I call out. "May I come in?" I close my eyes, listening. I don't hear anything. I run my hand down the edge of the door and the lock clicks open. I slowly turn the knob and push. The smell of rot pushes past me into the hallway. I pause for just a moment before slowly opening the door.

"Anita," I call again. "I'm here to help you."

Labored breathing greets me followed by a soft groan. I slide into the apartment and close the door behind me, relocking it. The bathroom is directly in front of me and the rest of the tiny apartment wraps around it like an L. It's overrun by stuff. A giant angel hangs on the bathroom door. My breath catches in my throat. Some things still surprise me when they remind me of Mom, even now.

* * *

MOM'S BREATHING TURNED SLOW and steady, still rattling in her chest. I rocked in the recliner, trying to process what she had told me, trying to determine whether or not she was still lucid.

Let's assume lucid for now. My mother wasn't of this world. Clearly she didn't mean an immigrant. Okay, so if not an immigrant, then what? Does she mean Earth? Is she an angel? Is that some euphemism for being dead now? Was my mother always dead?

I shook my head to clear out the increasingly ridiculous questions and picked up my book, opening to the page I'd been *trying to read before. Too many thoughts swirled around in my head, though, and this time I couldn't just push them away. I had to go, to move. I needed to walk. I slapped the book shut and stood.*

Glancing again at my mom, I hesitated.

"I'm going for a quick walk. Don't you die on me," I whispered as I planted a kiss on her forehead. What was left of her hair still smelled of fruity conditioner the nurse insisted we use. It drowned out the smell of the rest of the room for just a moment before I straightened again.

I wandered out of Mom's room and down the hallway of our two-bedroom apartment.

"I need to go for a walk," I informed the daytime hospice nurse, who was writing in her binder. Must be writing down what just happened.

"Sure, sweetie," she said, keeping her eyes on her binder. If anyone could sound more like a southern mother than this nurse, I'd eat my own arm. Sadie was her name, and I loved her. She was part of our family now, and she spent every day from eight to five in our apartment. The overnight person was always different, though, and they usually slept on the couch. I squeezed Sadie's shoulder as I walked past her and pulled my checkered Airwalks on. Opening the front door, I glanced back to Mom's room.

She better not die on me.

I walked to the elevator and pushed the button.

"Hey, Hector," I said as the door slid open. Hector was the overtalkative elevator man in our building. He always had a new story to tell us on the way down to the first floor.

"Eve," he said, nodding his head. He snapped his attention to the button panel. Weird. "Any news?"

"Nope. Mom's still hanging on." I clasped my hands behind my back and stared at the ceiling. "I just need to clear my head a bit."

"Of course. To the first floor? Or up to the top?"

"Down, please. I need to walk." I leaned against the back wall, chewing on my bottom lip.

"Of course." The door slid shut, and he pushed the button. He clasped his hands in front and faced the door. I'd just read something about how different people process death in one of my psychology books. Hector must be an avoidant person. Avoidant? Was that the term? No, it was — what was it?

The elevator dinged for the bottom floor. "Here you go."

"Thanks, Hector." I stepped out and through the lobby, shaking my head to clear the psychology talk in my brain.

"Any news, Eve?" Brian was today's doorman.

"Nope. Still hanging on. I need to clear my head." What was that term? Why can't I think of it?

"Okay. We'll be here when you get back."

I flashed Brian a smile as I passed through the doors. I turned right and started walking.

My mother isn't of this world. Not an immigrant. She's not an angel. That's just stupid. Maybe Mom means my mother is just special. She somehow stands out from this world. I tried to arrange each piece of the puzzle together, but no matter which way I turned the pieces, they didn't fit. I walked a two-block circuit trying to figure it out, but it was like trying to assemble a puzzle without the picture on the box. Nothing made sense. I wanted to keep walking, stopping at the corner, looking between crossing the street and turning back to our building half a block up this side of the street. I opened and closed my hands, then rubbed them against my shirt. I chewed on my lip. People passed by me, but I didn't look at any of them. Thoughts of Mom dying while I was gone turned me back to our building.

* * *

I STEP OVER PILES of magazines and garbage and clothes in the dimly lit apartment, holding my arms out for balance, following the labored breathing. I find her on the couch of her living room, surrounded by filth. It looks and smells like she hasn't left the couch for days. The curtains are drawn and the TV flickers, but it is silent.

"Anita," I say tenderly. "My name is Eve, and I'm here to help you."

Her eyes flicker to me, but nothing really registers. She'd probably die tonight or tomorrow anyway if I hadn't found her now. At least this way she doesn't die alone. Somebody knows and she won't rot for days or weeks before someone finally complains about the smell. If they would even notice it. The whole building is pungent. So unlike where I used to live.

* * *

WHEN I GOT BACK from my walk, trying to process Mom's cryptic message, Brian opened the door and smiled at me. I smiled back. I punched the button for the elevator and when Hector arrived, he smiled at me, too. I was thankful they didn't try small talk with me. My brain overflowed with questions about my mother and what Mom was trying to tell me. Hector dropped me off on my floor.

"There you go, Eve. Have a peaceful evening."

"Thanks." I smiled again at him and shuffled down the hall to our door. I turned the handle, noticing my knuckles. They were always knobbier than everyone else's. I thought of Hector's and Brian's hands, my mom's hands, their fingers smoothly tapering to the tips. I furrowed my forehead and pushed open the door. Sadie's voice drifted from Mom's room, and I rushed down the hall.

"Oh, there you are, sweetie." Sadie's voice was calm. "Your momma was askin' after you."

"Mom, I'm right here," I breathed, relieved to come back and have her still be alive.

Mom smiled at me. Sadie left the room, closing the door, and I set myself in the recliner. A chair scraped across the floor in the kitchen.

"Your mother," Mom said with a smile.

"I know. She wasn't of this world," I replied impatiently. Was this what Mom's sleep rambling was about?

"I'm sorry about the coughing fit."

"No problem, Mom." I smiled, trying to breathe through my own agitation. I hadn't wanted to know before, but now, I wanted to know nothing else.

"No more stalling. Your mother." She paused and pursed her lips, as though searching for the best way to deliver the news.

"Yeah?"

"Was an alien."

"What?" I leaned back in the chair. *Mom has officially lost her mind. I'm sure I read about the effects of morphine on the brain in my books. Craziness was probably in there.*

"I know. Not what you were expecting to hear. But it's true." She struggled to sit up more. I moved from the chair to her bed and stuffed a pillow behind her back. "I don't have all the time in the world to talk to you about this, so you're just going to have to listen, and you're going to have to choose what you believe."

"Okay."

"Eve, you aren't just a different kind of human." She paused.

I'd always known I was different from most people, but I'd never searched beyond the medical explanations. Rheumatoid arthritis. Alopecia. The symptomology fit well enough and Mom never seemed concerned.

Mom took a deep breath and continued. "You are not a human at all."

"I'm not a human," I repeated, stunned.

* * *

I KNEEL NEXT TO Anita, bracing myself to touch her, not knowing exactly what to expect. There's always pain. There's always a flash of memories. How much, though, is unpredictable. I grasp her hand, then take a deep breath and focus.

My entire body explodes with her pain and I struggle to catch my breath. Her memories flood into my mind. It's as though she's been waiting for me. Or, maybe just desperately waiting for death. Which I suppose could also be me.

When I catch up and my mind focuses again, I look over. Her eyes are locked onto mine.

"Are you an angel?" she whispers.

"I am if you need me to be," I whisper back and caress her face. The truth about me isn't important in this moment.

* * *

"I AM NOT A human," I said again. I couldn't decide if I liked the words or not.

Mom took a shaky breath. "You were born on Pegasus 2647B. That's Earth's classification, anyway. Your mom called it Torial."

Pegasus. That was familiar.

"But they've said there's no life on that planet." I remembered Mom obsessively watching the news coverage a few years ago about space anomalies in that area, but she'd always played it off as mere interest in science and outer space.

"That's because there isn't." She paused again. "Anymore."

"Anymore," I repeated.

"You were born there seventy-eight years ago."

"Wait, I'm seventy-eight?"

"You look good for your age." Mom winked. "Your mom fled Torial seventy-two years ago with you and a handful of others. You were all in a state of hypersleep—that's what she called it—and she said that in hypersleep, you don't age because your body essentially shuts down. You left there at six years old and arrived here at six years old even though you'd been in space for nearly sixty years, traveling here."

"Whoa. What?" I stood and wandered around the room, trying to absorb what Mom was telling me. The last thirteen years of my life have all been a lie. "This is impossible."

"Think about it, Eve," Mom urged. "Who ever heard of rheumatoid arthritis with no pain? Your people have knobby knuckles like that."

"Not arthritis," I said, rubbing them.

"And no hair on your body anywhere except the top of your head. Which, for what it's worth, I still wish you would grow out."

I ran my fingers through my short hair and stared at Mom's eyebrows. I rubbed the smooth skin on my face where my eyebrows should have been but weren't.

"Not alopecia."

"No," Mom said, shaking her head slowly. "Sure, I suppose it's sort of explainable medically, but again, very 'rare.'" Mom raised her hands just a few inches off the bed to use air quotes.

"So," I said slowly, licking my lips. "I'm an alien."

"Yes."

"And no one has noticed."

"You're close enough to human that it's okay. We live in New York City where people don't ask questions. Your facial features aren't as strange as you seem to think they are."

I pictured my own face—the flat forehead and eyes just a tiny bit too big and nose just a tiny bit too small.

Mom looked down at her hands. "A pediatrician we once saw wanted to do some DNA testing because of your not-quite-right symptoms, but I never consented because I already knew the truth. I knew if he got his hands on you, it would be the end of you living with me, of me being your mom. I couldn't do that to you!" Mom leaned forward, eyes bright. "You needed to have a mother, not become a circus freak or a science experiment. As far as anyone is concerned, you're almost twenty years old, and I'll soon be dead, anyway." She leaned back. "You can make up your own mind. You can decide what you want to do."

* * *

I PUSH OPEN THE only window in Anita's apartment to try to air out some of the fetid smell. I'll be in here for a little longer while I tie up some loose ends.

The first thing I do is try to find a semi-clean space to sit. A small stool holds a stack of magazines. I try to lift and set them on the floor, but they unceremoniously slide from my arms.

"Figures," I say. I sit on the stool and pull up my electronic sheet of funeral homes. I rotate through as many as I can based on the area. I find my Bronx list and call the next one in line. Of course, they're in no hurry to get here, but that's fine. I find a contact when I quickly filter through her friends.

I dial the number, which Anita conveniently has memorized.

"Hi, Rose?" I say. "Yes, my name is Eve, and I'm afraid I have some sad news for you."

Rose arrives thirty minutes after I call her and agrees to wait for the funeral home people to arrive. I give her my card and offer to help close out Anita's estate. Mom left me quite a bit of money when she died, but I still have to make a small living to keep it from running out. The small estates don't pay out much, but every so often, there's a decent-sized one that pays out. After all, how else is an alien supposed to get work?

* * *

MOM HAD KNOWN ALL these years that I was an alien and yet never said anything.

"Why did you wait to tell me?" I asked.

"Because I swore to your mother."

"Swore what?"

"That I would keep it from you as long as possible to keep you as safe as necessary."

"So you knew my mother?" My breath came fast, and my heart pounded. Wait, was it a heart? Do I have a heart?

"Knew is a strong word, dear." Mom smiled. "She was nearly dead when I found your shuttle. You were still in hypersleep. She made me promise, and she said you wouldn't remember anything until I told you, but the longer time it took, the safer you'd be."

"Safe from what?"

"Safe from humans. Safe from Orgallamans."

"Orgallamans," I whispered. Memories started filtering in as if the phrase had unlocked my mind. I could see my mother's face, the terror as she ran clutching me. The noise of the engines and shouting of the others in the shuttle. The vibration and pressure of lifting off. I remembered the muggy heat, the overgrown trees. Our remote village. The language.

Hold to me tightly, Eve. Don't let go. It wasn't English, but I knew the words.

Mom's voice broke through, bringing me back to our apartment from my memories.

"You'll have to decide what you want to do with this information, Eve, dear. If you want others to know, that is your choice to make."

My mind whirled as I tried to make sense of what she was saying and of the memories swirling around in my head. Memories of animals and plant life. My mother teaching me to cook. Singing songs. Walking along the path to . . . where? Torial? Is that like Krypton?

I clung to the memory of my mother holding me tight, her breath against my neck, feeling her muscles quiver.

* * *

I GIVE ROSE A quick hug, and she clutches me tightly for a moment, her breath hot on my neck. When she lets me go, I offer my condolences again and leave before the funeral home arrives. I feel the pull somewhere nearby. I wait for the name to drift to me. Thousands of people die in New York City every year. I'm trying to

235

make sure that fewer of them die alone, but I'm only one person and I can only work where others aren't. Of course, I have help that others don't and I've spent years honing my abilities. Still, I have to try to keep a low profile as much as I can. I've made it a habit of using other abilities to help people forget who exactly it was that helped them.

I approach another apartment building just three blocks away. This is it. Cookie's apartment. The names come to me when I get close. No locking outer doors in this building. I climb four flights of stairs and emerge in a darkened hallway. The unmistakable smell of drugs permeates the air. I walk down the hallway. I'm surprised by a red door. I have to check across the hall. The rest are gray. But not Cookie's door. Hers is red. I knock.

"Cookie?" I call out.

I try to calm my mind, but fear creeps in. I think of Mom to calm myself.

* * *

THE MEMORIES CONTINUED TO pour in, but nothing made sense. I blinked a few times, tried to focus on Mom lying in that hospital bed, struggling to process all this new information.

"What's in your mind, Eve?" Mom asked. I said the first thing that came to my mind.

"Do I have any superpowers, then? Am I like Superman?" Clearly, I'd seen too many movies.

"I don't know, my dear." Mom shrugged slowly. "I don't know, and I don't know how you'll find out. I'm sorry I can't be on this journey with you, to go with you and find answers." She closed her eyes and took a deep breath. Her voice quavered as she spoke again. "Tell your story, Eve. Write it all down. Don't let your people be forgotten."

I wanted to say something, but what? Generations of knowledge slowly seeped from deep recesses in my mind, flooding my consciousness and growing my awareness. I slowly reached out and grabbed Mom's hand. All the pain from her cancer flashed through my body. I gasped from the intensity of the physical pain and her emotional anguish. I could feel the toxicity of the medication, of the sick cells in her body, the fight against the invasion. My heart raced. I could do nothing to save her. Even if I'd known sooner, I couldn't have done anything. But how did I know this? This new knowledge conflicted with my human worldview. I now had a worldsview, but I didn't know what to do with it.

Mom coughed, jarring me out of my thoughts. Suddenly, I knew there was one thing I could do for her, and I was determined to do it.

* * *

COOKIE LAY ON THE bare floor of the near-empty apartment, sweating. Her matted hair lay in a puddle of vomit.

I close the door behind me and lock it.

"Cookie?" I say gently. I approach and her arms jerk out to the side, her wide eyes following me before they roll back in her head and she begins shaking. I have to close my eyes for just a moment. It's hard to do this, but I have to. I've been given life first by my birth mother, then by my adoptive mother. Mom said I could choose what I do with it and this is what I choose.

I open my eyes again. Cookie is still convulsing. I can sense her pounding heartbeat. Had I arrived an hour ago, I could have saved her life. I'm not in the business of saving lives, though. There are plenty of people around who do that. I'm in the business of helping the forgotten and marginalized not die alone.

I kneel and take Cookie's hand. I focus and breathe, preparing for what comes next. I do the same thing every time, the same thing I did for Mom.

* * *

THE ONE THING *I could do for Mom. Something I couldn't have done ten minutes ago. I glanced at the closed door, then leaned forward to Mom.*

"Are you ready to go?" I asked.

"Go where?" Mom replied, one eyebrow raised, trying to catch her breath after her coughing fit.

"To go home? To stop suffering?" My voice caught on the last syllable and I had to stifle a sob. I couldn't bring myself to say to die.

She stared at me for a moment before slowly nodding, understanding dawning across her face. I took a deep breath and focused. She laid back and squeezed my hand. Silently, I called to her soul and pulled it toward me. Ever so slowly, it detached from her body, lifting like a mist into the room. Her life raced through my mind. I saw her encounter with my mother. I saw myself. Her soul hovered in the room for just a moment. My insides wrenched as the presence faded away. Mom's eyes were closed. Her chest didn't move. She really was gone.

I clutched her hand and sobbed, burying my head into the blankets covering her soft belly. I shoved my other hand under her back and pulled her toward me, all at once desperately wanting her back and full of joy that all the pain she had experienced—that we had experienced—was gone.

A gentle hand pressed lightly on my shoulder. Sadie said something in a low voice, but I didn't hear the words. I couldn't explain exactly what I did, but I sent her out of her pain-filled body.

Mom would call this transition Heaven.

Me?

Yesterday I would have agreed.

Today, I'm not so sure.

* * *

I LEAVE COOKIE'S APARTMENT building. The sun hides behind some clouds that have appeared over the last hour and a half. The police have begun their investigation and I've helped them forget about me.

I feel both of my mothers whispering into my soul, reassuring me.

I've chosen the right path. Thousands of people who would have otherwise died alone instead died with someone holding their hand, helping them along. It's the best I can do as the last of the Ellessians of Torial. In wading through the memories, I learned that Ellessians can feel the presence of each other, no matter the distance separating us. I feel no one, so I honor my people and their memory the best I can. Most humans don't believe in life outside of Earth. Even if they did, this planet-bound civilization can do nothing about the Orgallamans. There is only me, and I choose to blend in here, writing down the Ellessians' story the best I can so that when I am also gone, someone else will know. We, like these humans I help, will not have died alone.

I feel another pull and turn left.

To learn more about this author, please visit:
https://carijehlik.com/

My Life in the End

Literary

Penny J. Johnson

Prompt: You are a pet cat. Write about your day.

WHEN THEY FIND ME in the morning, I could be dead. Or I will have pushed them over the edge. Just like the bottle shattered on the floor. Its night-blue ink seeps under my feet, intriguing me with its coolness. The metallic finger of the pen accuses me from its resting place on the edge of the ink puddle. Or is it prompting me to do what it no longer can?

I roll the pen's blue glass handle in and out of the ink, shifting blobs into the floor cracks. I lift my foot and lick a dark drip as it begins to fall.

Ack! Bleh! Ugh!

I shake my head as I shudder. Ink speckles the floor. Satisfaction rumbles in my throat, and I blink long and slow.

I take a step. As soon as I see my personal imprint pressed into the grain, I begin.

My First Life

MY EYES WERE THE first to open. So were my ears. My siblings wandered and stumbled around in the straw for days while I navigated our sleeping area. My mother slow-blinked her light-green eyes at me, letting me know she loved me enough to keep watching from a distance. But, I knew she was too busy with everyone else to worry about me. I stalked around the perimeter of our plywood crate, and I listened to the people. I cared less about what they said to us. It made little sense in those high-pitched voices. It was what they said when they thought I wasn't listening that I wanted to hear.

"You should have closed the door tighter," said the woman.

"I thought you'd closed it," said the man, sipping from an amber bottle and clinking it on the kitchen table.

"Well, obviously, one of us didn't," she countered, placing a coaster under the sweating bottle, "and now we have these little ones to deal with."

"Street corner marked 'Take two. They're small.'?"

"Don't be glib! You know who the father is."

"The big one?"

"Yes, 'the big one.' I didn't know they got that big! I love his white and gray hair. And those baby-blue eyes! But, I don't want people pounding on my door because their 'Take two. They're small.' turns into a giant like him!"

"Well, that might not happen. Sassy is average-sized."

"Maybe," mused the woman. "No, I think we should take them to . . ."

That was the last thing I heard as Mom pinched my neck and carried me — my legs dangling in the air like the woman's words — to my piled up, sleeping siblings.

Take us where?

My Second Life

WE WERE ALL WIDE awake now in "the observation room." Lots of legs with shoes came and went from this room with glass walls. Sometimes one of the yellow-vested people took me into "the interaction room." People with smaller shoes — my favorites had *flashing lights and dragging laces — rolled jingle balls for me to chase. Or they shook string attached to a stick in my face. I couldn't help myself. Compelled, I swatted the string and snagged it. I didn't mind that this activity stunted my true capabilities. I played along. The yellow-vested people said that it was the best way to find a home. I didn't know what "home" meant, but it seemed to be the only means of escape from this place.*

I discovered this truth as each of my siblings spent time in the interaction room, too. Then my brother or sister didn't return. Eventually, it was just me in the observation room.

Then they walked in — a lady and her son. He was older than the people with little shoes. I could tell from the smell of his leather jacket. But, a ball of hair flopped back and forth on top of his head, so I decided he was more young than old. I liked that better. He talked about me like I was a prize. I liked that, too.

"This is the kind you want, Mom."

I want that binder holding up your hair.

"I'm not sneezing at all," she said.

Not making someone sneeze will get me out of here? How did I accomplish that without trying?

A yellow-vested man said, "That's because he's long-haired."

"Really?" she said. "He's so sweet, too. Nothing like the ones I had around me as a kid."

"He's got an attitude, though," said the yellow-vested man.

How about I show you my attitude by untying your shoes with my teeth? But, I didn't. I kept batting around the string on the stick. I wanted this lady to like me.

Ultimately, the lady couldn't resist my sparkly blue eyes. Soon I was riding in a car with them. I had no idea where they were taking me. They said it was a place called "home."

My Third Life

"WHAT SHOULD WE NAME him?" said a loud voice. This boy wore white pants with wide legs that swished as he clumped across the

floor toward the boy who rescued me. A black belt was tied around the waist of his white top with arms that flapped like bird wings. When the boy who rescued me put me on the floor, I charged at the dangling belt and caught an end with my claws. I soft-bit the black-belt boy's hands as he tried to get me to let go.

Another boy leaned over the shoulders of the other two. He reached down and scooped me up. He kissed the tip of my nose, and I licked his lip. There was a special sweetness inside him. He swayed back and forth, and I went limp.

"How about Moggy?" said the lady. She rubbed the back of my ear.

"Moggy?" asked the boy who rescued me.

"It means 'cat,'" she said.

"How about Bob?" said a new voice. It came from a face with gray bristly hair. I reached up and tried to hook one of the black sticks connected to one of his black-rimmed glass eyes. He leaned back and swatted at my paw. But, not hard.

"Bob?"

"Sure."

"I think we can name him something a little more creative than Bob."

"I like Moggy," said the boy who rescued me. I named this guy "Dude" because that's what he called everyone, including Lady.

"Me too," said Buddy.

"Me three," said Tank.

"I'm calling him Bob."

I'm calling you Dumbass, I decided as he turned his gray bristly face and walked away.

Dude carried me upstairs. At first I only heard jingling and clicking sounds from behind one of the doors. Then came the sound that caused most of us in the observation room to arch our backs and hiss. First one voice then another echoed back and forth the way those fuzzy green balls they like bounce on concrete. I grunted.

Dogs.

I twitched the tip of my tail, listening to Lady explain to Dude how she would bring in each dog one at a time. I tried to sit still on my haunches with my front feet tight together. But, the fur on my back began to rise, and my tail started swishing from side to side. As the panting grew closer and louder from the hallway, I braced myself for the first glimpse of a pink slobbery tongue and a side-slitted, flaring black nose. One paw pressed a little less into the carpet in case I had to strike fast or dash under the bed if this canine lunged at me.

Instead, soft-brown eyes met my icy-blue ones. "Sit, Daisy," commanded Lady, holding a leash loop.

Daisy sat, leaning in and sniffing the air before pulling back. The thick fur on her neck fanned around her collar like a mane, and I wondered what it would feel like to knead it with my paws. She turned her yellow head until her nose touched Lady's knee and watched me with one of her deep brown eyes.

"Good girl," said Lady, and then she led Daisy back down the hallway.

A short time later, more panting—this time strained and wheezy—came from the hallway, and I prepared again for an attack. A low growl rumbled from the threshold as one rose up from my own throat.

"Sit, Boomer," commanded Lady, her knuckles slightly white as she gripped the leash.

Boomer, black and lean with flecks of gray on his chin and lips, sat. He pulled in his tongue and tipped his head.

"Good boy, Boomer," said Lady. Before guiding him away, she smiled over her shoulder. "Good boy, Moggy."

That first night, I tucked myself into Dude's right armpit and purred myself to sleep.

FOR THE NEXT FEW weeks, I batted toys hanging from lighted branches into a water bowl that I also drank from when no one was watching. Or I snuggled into the fluffy cover around the water bowl. One day, Lady took all the toys and lights off the tree. She scolded me with a smile every time I tried to run off with one of the toy's hooks between my teeth. But, she sighed when she discovered the holes in the plastic she pulled up around the tree. I stood in the door and watched as Dumbass shoved the tree through the opened front door and tossed it onto a snowbank. Before I could splay my claws, he scooped me up and swung his arms high. I mewed and flared my paws. If he threw me in the snow with the tree . . . but he laughed instead and took me back inside.

Dumbass!

NOT LONG AFTER THE lighted tree went outside, I crouched in the window and watched Dude drive away to a place they called "college." He took his armpit with him.

That's when I learned to sleep in different places.

I curled up to Lady's face at night and nuzzled her soft cheek. I stuck my nose inside her left nostril. She sneezed a lot in the morning, and her left eye swelled up. But, she didn't take me back to the glass rooms.

Some nights, I rested my face against Buddy's mouth to feel his warm breath or nestled into Tank's bulky arms. I smelled and licked the red bumps on their cheeks.

I spent my catnaps with the boys, too. If Buddy slammed doors or yelled at Lady, she said, "Take Moggy with you to your room." I let myself go limp in his arms. I laid my head next to his on the pillow. We slept for hours.

Lady kept telling Tank, "Pick up your room," but I'm glad he never did. I liked playing in Tank's room before naps. There was always something on his bed to do. I chewed the pink ball on the end of a yellow stick. Something they called "paper" crinkled when I stepped on it. My favorite thing was flattening myself over the smooth, cool paper of what they called "books."

"Moggy," Tank said. "I can't learn stoichiometry when you do that." He picked me up, rubbed his nose against mine, and set me next to him on the blanket. I slept next to him for hours, too.

By this time, I had also insinuated myself into the dogs' pack. Daisy tolerated me when I slept next to her on the couch. Boomer didn't mind if I curled up on his bed with him or chewed on his callused feet or licked inside his floppy ears. If their swift acceptance was any indication, I was certain I had assumed the alpha role.

But, Dumbass?

If I slept near Dumbass at all, it was because I wanted to cuddle with Lady, and Lady slept with Dumbass. She thought he was funny and sweet. I guess he had his good points. Although he didn't like it when I scratched the woodwork by the food closet, he gave me treats to make me stop. If I went to the sink, he turned it on. If I crouched by my ball toy, he flicked the ball around the track for me. He followed my backward-pointing ears wherever I led him. He was mine. But, he picked me up and teased me when I whined through my lips. He held on too long. He jokingly told me to turn off the faucet when I was done letting the water drip down my head into the drain. I still don't understand why that's funny. As if I can't turn off a faucet. I could if I wanted to do it. That doesn't mean I ever do it.

My Fourth Life

"I DON'T LIKE IT," said Lady one morning. "Something's wrong."

"You don't think it's from the Lyme disease?" asked Dumbass.

"No. He's kicking his front leg to the side. He's never done that before," she said. "Something's definitely wrong."

Lady was right. Boomer smelled different. I watched as he limped over to his water bowl.

I chirruped at Lady.

"Good morning, Moggy," she said.

I chirruped again and pointed my ears backward. Her chair scraped on the wood floor, and her bare feet slapped lightly behind me. As Boomer drank from his water bowl, I licked his forehead. Daisy came over, too, and drank from her bowl. I leaned my nose close to her forehead. But, I didn't lick her forehead. I stepped away instead.

Lady stared at me. She leaned over Boomer and placed her hand on his forehead. She gasped, pulled back her hand, and rubbed her fingers against her palm. She turned toward me again. I blinked long and slow. She reached down and touched Boomer's forehead again. She left it there longer than before, her head hanging lower and lower. She kissed the top of his head, rubbed one of his ears, laid her forehead against his, and sighed.

Boomer gave a low growl the next time I chewed his calloused feet. I curled up nearby. I waited. He spent more time on his bed. Whenever Lady kneeled to check on him, he placed his left leg on her hand. One day, he stopped short and whined while playing ball. He walked around the block one more time. Then, he got in the car with Lady.

He never came back.

After Boomer had been gone a few days, Dumbass held me too long again. This time, though, he turned on the faucets in his eyes. I tasted the streaks on his cheek. Ick. Salty. He rubbed his face against my fur and got me wet. I wriggled out of his arms and went off to clean myself.

Maybe you're just dumb, I decided.

Daisy and I slept on the couch, one of us on either end, for the rest of the week. Her eyebrows curved up more. Boomer had been her backup at the door when strangers rang the bell. She acted like she was the top dog. She might have thought she was tough because she had a birth-rank tattoo on the inside of her ear. But, I knew better. Inside, she was timid and uncertain. Something was happening to her, too. I could smell it.

My Fifth Life

"WHAT WERE YOU THINKING?"
    Surprisingly . . . wasn't.

"We talked about this."

"I'm pretty sure I said it was a bad idea."

I know it's a bad idea.

"How can you say this is a bad idea?" Lady shifted the gyrating yellow puppy in her arms.

She lifted him under his forelegs and set him on Dumbass's lap. My neck ached as it moved back and forth with the movement of the puppy's full-body wag. The puppy leaped at Dumbass's gray bristly cheeks, licked him, and then nibbled at his chin. "Ow. Okay. Okay. Stop now," said Dumbass, laughing. "What's his name?"

"I'll let you name this one," she said. When he started to speak, she held up her hand. "But, you can't name him Bob."

That's how Sonny joined our pack.

Figuring I needed to maintain my alpha role, I adopted a regimen designed to get young Sonny in line. When he was confined to his cage, I climbed onto its plastic top, peered over the edge, and batted at Sonny through the grated door. I knew he couldn't resist reacting when I rolled my tongue and chirruped as I sauntered by him. If he was lying outside his cage on his mat and gnawing on his peanut butter-flavored chewy bone, I lured him into a chase around the house. I leaped onto the table to get away. He showed his teeth, but he didn't bite me. I showed my claws, and I sometimes tapped him just to prove I could leave a mark. Daisy's eyebrows rose as she observed us from the corner of the couch, but she didn't interfere. At first I thought it was strange that she didn't engage in our daily tussles. Then I remembered.

Daisy revealed her secret a few days later. Her feet erupted with oozing pustules. I kneaded my paws along her spine as Lady felt for bumps on Daisy's back. I put a paw on her side the next day when Lady found more bumps on her ribs. The day after that, I curled up against the lump Lady discovered on her sternum. Pink spots multiplied on Daisy's lips. I heard Lady tell Dumbass about what the white-coated people said.

"It's lupus."

"Dogs get lupus?"

"I guess so. There are two kinds. This one attacks from the inside out."

"Meaning?"

"We have no idea how bad it is. But, it will get worse. She's breathing harder than she was yesterday."

"Can we give her meds?"

"Yes."

"Well, let's do that."

"Okay. But, it won't fix — "

"Let's just try it. For a little while."

"All right. For a little while."

Dude came home for his birthday that weekend. He picked up one of the medicine bottles and set it down with the others lined up on the counter. He looked over at where I sat next to Daisy. Her breathing was short and raspy.

"She can't go on like this," he said. Lady nodded.

Lady and Dumbass put Daisy in the car.

She didn't come back.

My Sixth Life

"WHAT IS THAT?"

"*Who* is that, you mean. This is Amber."

"Amber? Why 'Amber'?"

"See the color of her eyes?"

"Oh. Okay. But, she's as big as a pig!"

"She does need to lose some weight. But, she just had a litter of puppies."

"You didn't bring a litter of puppies home, did you?"

"Of course not, silly. All the puppies have homes. The breeder said that Amber liked cuddling on the couch with the family more than tending to her babies. So, they decided not to breed her again. She's absolutely sweet! And so good in the car. And — "

"We should call her Donut."

"We are not calling her that!"

"Well, we can't call her Amber. What if there's a little girl in the neighborhood named Amber?"

"Oh, and there would never be a guy in the neighborhood named Bob?"

They agreed on the name "Honey." Dumbass liked honey — which Lady found undigestible — and Lady liked that "Sonny" and "Honey" rhyme — which Dumbass thought was "funny" — and Dumbass didn't call Lady by "pet names" like honey, so that was that.

Honey was sweet to everyone and cuddled closer than Daisy ever had. But, her forehead crinkled when she heard whining. Her golden eyes stared at Sonny and me when we wrestled. If I nipped at her ankles or her saggy teats, she got up and waddled away. We existed together.

My Seventh Life

ONE OF MY FAVORITE spots to sleep was by the sliding glass door. The thing about dogs is that they go outside. They aren't smart enough to use the box like me. They had to step over me with their big floppy paws. Lady stood in the door and commanded them not to eat their poop. They aren't smart enough to bury their poop like I do. She told them not to eat other things, too, like acorns and buckthorn berries.

Sometimes Lady left the sliding door open a little too long. I casually stretched my toes over the threshold. Then I leaped. I was out!

She called to me. But, I was much smarter than the dogs. And I was smaller. I darted under the deck.

Then we played the fun game of "Where's Moggy?" First, I came out from under the steps. I dashed back under when she almost caught hold of my tail. Then I sauntered out on the other side where she couldn't see me and sniffed under one of the bushes for a while.

I scurried back under the deck when she got too close. Pretty soon I heard a *pop* and smelled the aroma of Ocean Blend cat food. She upgraded from tuna. The smell was quite tempting. But, I resisted. I crouched down and listened for real meat scampering in the dried leaves.

Suddenly, something black and bristly pushed me. It swept the leaves away. It lunged at me. Ah!

I ran out from under the deck into Tank's arms. I was foiled.

My Eighth Life

SOMETIMES HONEY AND SONNY slept on Dumbass and Lady's bed. Honey tucked her nose under Lady's chin, and Sonny curled into the back of Lady's knees. There was no room for me.

Dumbass said the boys should keep their doors closed. He didn't want me to get stuck in their rooms and not be able to get to my box.

So, nights belonged to me. I loved to lurk in the shadows. Once in a while, I would spring from spiderwebby corners to startle someone's bare feet tiptoeing across the moonlit wood floor. But, most nights started with clawing Dumbass's favorite chair, then scratching Lady's wooden lattice box where she stored her yarn. Mosquitoes flew through the holes I had poked in the window screens. I chased them, caught them, and ate them. Or I took the easier option by ripping the curtain sheers and picking out dead Asian ladybirds. I found twist ties, bottle caps, pieces of string. I flicked whatever I found into the air or slid across the wood floor to grab it. I absorbed the static surging through my body as I slid across the area rugs. Sometimes I even licked a light socket.

LADY AND THE DOGS came downstairs before everyone else most mornings. After she fed us and let the dogs out, she made her first cup of black stinky water. But then, she wrinkled her nose every time she opened my can of pureed salmon. She smiled and asked me if I *liked it as if my face pressed into her flowered custard bowl wasn't a clue. I guess she liked her black stinky water just as much because she pressed her face into her cup.*

One time, when I was done eating and dashing around the house in what she called my "crazy kitty mood," I peeked over the edge of the lighted box she called "her computer." The ink bottle and pen with the metallic finger and the blue glass handle were inside the computer. I jumped off the kitchen table, went to Lady's den, and hopped up onto her desk. Stacks of papers and books dropped onto the floor, but I ignored them and checked the top of the desk. There they were — the ink bottle and the metallic finger. How could they be in both places?

Just as I reached to touch the ink bottle with my paw, Lady found me and lifted me into her arms. She scolded me for making a mess of her piles. She put me down, and I swatted at the flapping papers as she restacked them. Then, she carried me back to her computer on the kitchen table. She sat down and pushed me onto her lap. Her finger swiped across the computer, and the ink bottle and metallic finger disappeared. Her fingers tapped the buttons with light under them. Then, the computer flashed white.

I leaned forward as she tapped the buttons again. Black marks turned into lines and filled the white. I didn't know what the black lines meant. But, when she stopped tapping and snuggled me closer, she told me her story. I did and didn't understand. How could the word home belong to so many places? Was it like the ink bottle and the metallic finger being on the desk and, at the same time, being inside the computer? There was something about "home" in Lady's voice, too. The more she told me, the more I leaned into her and purred.

My Ninth Life

ONE DAY, LADY PLACED me in the carrier. I spent time-outs there when I tried too many times to steal table scraps and when she took me to the white-coated people for a poke-and-prod. I mewed and mewed. While she drove, Lady talked louder and higher or ignored me.

Through the metal door of my carrier, I could see a large gray building with a big gray door. Lady had to pull hard to open it. The carrier swung back and forth as she approached a counter. Lady talked with the man behind the counter. I couldn't hear everything they said because dogs barked from somewhere else in the building. It sounded like the observation room.

But, it wasn't exactly the same as the observation room. A blue-shirted person removed my collar. I was placed in a room with a wire door. I squeezed myself between the litter box and a wooden sleeping box. My carrier was stacked with other carriers on a high shelf. The blue-shirted person put my ball toy, a bowl of my food, and a clean bowl of water in the room. She hung my treat bag with a sheet of paper on the outside of the door.

Lady wiggled her fingers between one of the holes in the wire door. "Bye, Moggy."

Then, she left.

Several times a day, the blue-shirted people talked to me. They petted me through the wire holes of the door. They slipped me treats. I got many treats because I blinked my blue eyes and sounded my best chirrup.

At night, the place filled with shadows. I sighed and scratched an itch between my ears on a protruding wire. The door shifted forward. I pulled back, then leaned in again. This time I heard a clink above my left ear. One more time just to be sure . . . yes, I saw the faint silhouette of thin wire connected to a metal pin. I reached up and snagged the wire with my claw. Slowly, I eased the pin from the bracket. I jumped back at the clang as the pin hit the wire door. I pushed my paw against the door. It opened.

I made a soft-padded landing on the concrete floor. A steel door at the end of the aisle was my next barrier to cross. I slunk toward it, guided by the sliver of light under the door. I raised myself up on my back legs, reaching for the handle. But, it wasn't a handle I could easily flip down. It was a knob. I stretched myself as high as I could. I couldn't reach it. I slumped back to the floor and arched my back to work out a kink. I made my way back to my room.

It was higher up than I thought, and my feet ached when I thought about how far I had jumped. The door of the room directly below mine was slightly ajar. I opened it a little more and squeezed my way inside.

In the morning, the blue-shirted person was frantic when she didn't see me in my room. She called and called. She ran into the lobby, and I heard scraping and sliding sounds. Her white shoes dashed back into the room and stopped in front of the lower room I had entered during the night. She turned and stood on her toes to check the stack of carriers before rechecking my room to make sure she hadn't missed seeing me the first time. I yawned and appeared from my hiding place on the lower level. She gasped, scooped me up, and snuggled me. I found this oddly comforting and annoying at the same time. She placed me back in the upper room. As she walked away, I leaned against the door. Yes! It still wiggled. I would just remove the pin again tonight, and . . .

But, she came back. She had a clip of some sort. I jumped back as she snapped it into place. When she left again, I tried pushing the door. It wouldn't budge. I was doomed.

Except they did keep giving me treats. I purred more. I got more. It was a beautiful game.

I don't know how many days or nights passed, but one morning I heard Lady's voice in the lobby. I felt strange. Was it relief? Or maybe it was something else because I couldn't stop purring. It was like smelling catnip. This was that feeling they call "love."

She picked me up. I gently pressed my claws into her shoulder. I suddenly didn't want her to let me go. Ever. She laughed and nuzzled my ear. She lifted the carrier, but I wasn't in it. I was draped over her shoulder as she walked out the door. She held me all the way home.

My Life in the End

BLUE INK HAS REPLACED my white fur-socks on my forelegs. My tongue tastes like my metal drinking bowl. I wonder if this dizziness is what Lady calls "writer's high."

I hear Lady's slow steps on the stairs. Sonny and Honey race past her and take turns skidding into the wall at the bottom. They are about to enter Lady's den when she gasps and yells, "Stop!" She commands the dogs into their cages before returning to me.

"Moggy?"

I give a choked chirrup, then blink long and slow. She is still blurry when I open my eyes.

She carries me to the kitchen sink. She turns on the faucet, and I flick my tongue under the steady water stream. When she starts rubbing something else blue into my paws and legs, I mew in protest. But, the water feels so good on my inky tongue, and the blue on my paws turns from dark blue to almost white. She whispers in my ear, and I relax against her pajama shirt.

Later, I hear her call the white-shirted people. I decide this is the end. This is when I won't come back.

I'm too depressed to meow when she places me in my carrier. I stay quiet in the car. But, I hear her muffled chatter the entire way.

We park, and I move with the sway of the carrier as she takes me inside. She sets down my carrier, and we wait.

I sleep. I dream as if I'm dangling from Mom's gentle grip again. I see myself licking Boomer's feverish head, curling against Daisy's shuddering chest, taunting Sonny into a chase, and touching Honey's nose with mine when she is fast asleep. I feel Dude's armpit, smell Buddy's sweet breath, and hear Tank turning the pages of his book. Dumbass holds me too long. But, I'm dreaming. There's no reason to complain.

Except I wonder where Lady is.

Then I hear her.

I suppose anyone who lives with a writer hears stories. Writers tell their best stories in their private moments. They share them with those they trust to keep their secrets. Those they know will never say a word.

Lady is no exception. She knows there are secrets in her story I can never tell. But, this story—the one she is murmuring in my ear while she rubs the spot Mom used to hold—is my favorite.

Because it's mine.

Later, I am curled up by the sliding door. I chatter at the squirrel sitting on the fence. But, then I look out at the green lawn through the glass dotted with doggy noseprints. I rotate my ears to hear the sounds of the house—protests about chores, spoons clanging on pans, sizzling meat they will let me taste when I jump on the table at dinner, Sonny's and Honey's gnawing on their peanut butter chewies. My throat rumbles, and I blink long and slow. As I listen to Lady schedule the floor-sanding company for next week, I think about what Lady whispered in my ear before the white-coated people told her that nontoxic ink isn't life-threatening.

She told me that I have one life. With them. In this place they . . . we . . . call "home."

To learn more about this author, please visit:
https://pennyspagesonline.com/

Varsity Dreams

Literary

J. C. O'Neil

Prompt: Opportunities wait for no one, but there's always a second chance. You only have to work hard to get it.

"WELCOME BACK, AND IF *you're just joining us, Lakeview Hawks lead the visiting Riverside High Giants 1–0 going into the top of the seventh. If Hawks pitcher Jonah 'Ace' Scott can get these three outs he will start the season holding the school record for no-hitters. And we're ready to go as batter Brady Mercer steps into the batter's box . . ."*

Jonah kept the ball hidden in his glove as he lifted his arms above his head, keeping his eyes locked on the location of Tyler's mitt behind the plate. He drew his front knee to his chest and twisted his body back. He briefly took a breath of the cool, crisp March air before he kicked forward, stretching his body toward the batter, letting the ball fly out of his grip in a downward motion.

Jonah grinned at the batter as the loud smack of the ball hitting the leather of Tyler's mitt could be heard, and a small cloud of dust formed less than a second before the umpire could shout, "Stee-rike one."

Tyler shook off his hand before tossing the ball back to Jonah. "That's it, Ace. Keep it up."

Jonah walked back to the rubber on the mound after snatching the ball out of the air. He took a moment to look around the stands. His girlfriend, Kelly, was jumping up and down next to the home bleachers, leading the cheers. Scattered in the fans, Jonah noted a couple of men with clipboards; that could only mean the colleges he'd been in contact with were watching. A breeze picked up, sending a wave of dirt and the scent of hotdogs and hot pretzels across the infield.

Jonah threw another pitch. He watched from the mound, pointing toward the ball with his glove as the ball popped straight up and the batter ran toward first base. Jonah shouted over the crowd noises, "Don't you let that fall, Tyler."

Tossing his face mask to the side, Tyler jumped up and stood in front of the plate as he shielded his eyes from the sun with his mitt. Jonah shouted over the home crowd's eruption as Tyler captured the ball in his mitt. "That's my boy! Two more."

Jonah set as the next batter stepped in the box. The smirk on the batter's face made Jonah want to wipe it off with three strikes right by him. The two boys held eye contact for a second or two before Jonah whipped the ball to the plate then watched it sail down the third-base line.

"Foul ball!"

Jonah breathed a sigh of relief as he reached up to grab the new ball Tyler tossed him. "All right, just a long strike," he said to himself as he kicked the dirt at the rubber on the mound. "Let's get him inside."

Jonah stared down the batter, daring him to swing at the next pitch. His palms started to sweat as he tightened his grip on the ball's stitches. He aimed for the inside corner of the plate, looked at the ground for less than a second, then fired the pitch. There was a thud and the crowd silenced. The batter fell to the ground and grabbed at his lower back. The crowd applauded as the boy got to his feet and jogged to first base. Tyler called time and trotted to the mound.

"Ace, it's just one pitch. You got this," Tyler said as he put his hand on Jonah's shoulder.

Jonah took off his cap and ran his hand through his hair. "He had me timed, man. He had me. Fucking knew it, too. The idiot winked at me."

"Settle down. You've got a new batter. You got this," Tyler said before he turned around and headed back to his position behind the plate.

Jonah picked up the rosin bag and tossed it a few times in his pitching hand. As he paced a few moments he said, "I got this."

The batter stepped in the box and took a few swings as Jonah turned to his team and said, "Let's get two. Let's do this."

Jonah looked over his shoulder at the runner taking a couple steps away from first base. He made a quick movement off the mound and threw the ball to the first baseman, who laid a tag on the runner a second too late.

"You're not setting foot on second," Jonah said to the smiling runner who took a smaller lead.

Jonah threw his pitch as the batter squared up and connected for a bunt down the first-base line. Jonah broke for first base as the first baseman sprinted toward the ball. The runner going to second stumbled, and Jonah shouted, "Go for two—two!"

Jonah reached his glove up to catch the ball that came from second base as his foot touched the bag. He cradled the ball in the leather basket just before the batter ran through first base. Giving a shout fueled by pure adrenaline, Jonah raised his fist with a quick pump as the umpire yelled, "You're out!"

"Oh my, what a game this was. Hawks open their season with the tenth no-hitter of Jonah 'Ace' Scott's high school career, and the way he pitched tonight, I wouldn't be surprised if he doesn't add another two or three to the school record by the end of what is looking to be a season headed to the state championship."

After the obligatory handshaking, Coach released the team by telling them, "Go celebrate. Have fun. Enjoy the weekend. I'll see you *guys Monday. Don't be late or everyone runs laps. Now get out of here."*

Jonah and Tyler grabbed their bags and slung them over their shoulders. Tyler gave Jonah a small push as they headed toward their cars. Jonah crouched down and pulled his fists up, giving Tyler a fake jab.

"Dude, you were throwing some major heat out there today," Tyler said as he dodged Jonah's fist.

Jonah wrapped his arm around Tyler's neck and pulled his head to his chest. He threw a few quick punches lightly into Tyler's gut before he let him go. "Wait until next game. I got a surprise that will get me that tuition covered for sure."

Tyler straightened his cap. "Who do you think was out there today in the stands?"

"I don't know. I think maybe Texas and Duke. They're the two I've been in contact with the most," Jonah said as they navigated through the maze of cars.

"Texas your number one?"

"Hell yeah. Longhorns, baby. Gotta follow that Roger Clemens path, man." Jonah looked up to see Kelly sitting on the hood of his car.

Kelly cupped her hands over her mouth and shouted, "Hey, hot stuff, got a girlfriend?"

"Yeah. There's this girl. It's kinda serious, but if you don't tell, I won't tell."

"See ya Monday, man." Tyler waved to Kelly and went off to his car.

Jonah dropped his bag and hopped on the hood of his car next to Kelly. He pressed his lips against hers. She pushed off him, slid off the car, and opened the passenger door. "You gonna drive me home or what?"

"You're such a tease," Jonah said before he scooted off the hood, picked his bag up, and got in the driver's seat. "You're lucky you're hot." Kelly clipped her seat belt and rolled her eyes. As Jonah turned the key in the ignition, he turned to her and said, "And that I love you."

As they backed out of the parking spot, Kelly tickled Jonah's thigh. "And you love it," she said after she licked her lips while winking at him.

* * *

JONAH PULLED INTO THE park and found a parking spot next to a pavilion. He got out and opened the door for Kelly to slide out. They sat on the hood and lay back, watching what was left of the clouds go by before the stars started to sprinkle the darkening sky. Kelly scooted closer to Jonah until her head pressed gently onto his shoulder. Jonah wrapped his arm around her and clasped her hand.

"So . . . there were some colleges in the stands?"

Jonah looked down into Kelly's hazel eyes, brushing her hair behind her ear. "There was at least two."

"Well, that's good, isn't it?"

"I mean, yeah."

"What's wrong?" Kelly said as Jonah turned his head toward the stars.

"It's just, I thought, if there was one looking at me, they'd talk to me."

"You were talking to them all last year."

"Not in person."

"If they weren't interested, they wouldn't have made time to send you literature on their schools."

"It's just, it's senior year. I need to know where I'm going to play next season."

Kelly lifted herself up and traced her finger down Jonah's jersey. "Maybe they just want to watch you play. I know I do." She kissed Jonah teasingly.

"Oh, do you?" Jonah said as he pulled Kelly by her waist on top of him and locked his lips on hers.

"So, how about Friday, after the game, we go celebrate?" Kelly said in between catching her breath and kissing him.

"What did you have in mind?"

"Oh, I don't know. It'll be a full moon. You can buy me roses, and I can sneak a bottle of my mom's wine," Kelly said, playing with the buttons of Jonah's uniform. "Maybe we can get a motel room."

"Consider it done." Jonah pushed Kelly onto her back and climbed on top of her.

Kelly wrapped her arms behind Jonah's neck. "Good," she said as Jonah's lips graced hers.

* * *

"... *AND HE'S HEADED HOME. Jonah Scott racing to the plate. Tyler Jones with the toss. The tag, and he's out. He is out trying to steal home. On a wild pitch from Jonah Scott, Robby Burns is out to end the game. Hawks win 4–3!*"

Jonah tossed his glove at the fence. Tyler picked it up and put it in Jonah's bag. As he plopped down on the bench, Jonah put his head in his hands. The team gathered their gear and patted Jonah on his back on their way to their rides, giving him some sort of words of encouragement like "Good game" or "Way to keep us in it."

"Hey, man. We won. What's got you so pissed off?" Tyler said as he sat beside him.

"I completely fucked up this game."

"Dude, you won. You pitched a good game."

"They were in the bleachers again tonight, and I had absolutely no control of the curve. I walked seven guys."

"Hey, it was the first time you used it in a game. And you won the game, allowed only one hit—yeah, sure, a three-run homer, but you still struck out eighteen."

"I let them see I have nothing besides the fastball. I'm going to have to settle for Pitt. I don't even want to go to Pitt. I want to pitch. Pitt won't get me to the majors. Texas or Duke will."

"Look, man. We just got to work on that curveball. And if you have to go to Pitt, then you go to Pitt."

Jonah lifted his head, sighed, and sprung up. He opened his bag and took out his glove. "Get your mitt."

"What?"

"Get your damn mitt out. I need to practice the curve."

"I didn't mean right this instant, I meant like Sunday or Monday."

"Look, I'm not blowing my shot of playing on a good D1 team. Now grab your mitt."

"Dude. Ace, don't you got to be somewhere?" Tyler hugged himself, grabbing at his jersey, exaggerating mocked moans.

"I don't care. I need to practice. Kelly can wait. Now pick up your damn mitt and get behind the fucking plate."

Sighing, Tyler grabbed his mitt. "Kelly is going to kill you, man."

Jonah grabbed a ball and jogged to the mound, motioning toward the backstop with his glove. "Just get behind the damn plate, Tyler."

Looking out at the parking lot, Tyler kicked at the air before he walked to his position and put his mitt up. "Your funeral."

Jonah threw the pitch, the movement on his curve catching the outside corner of the plate.

* * *

"YOU'RE STILL PRACTICING?" SAID Kelly, her legs crossed under the bench with her palms pressed into it, leaning forward. "Doesn't your arm hurt?"

Jonah hurled the pitch into Tyler's mitt. "I need to get control of this curveball."

"My knees hurt," Tyler said as he threw the ball back to Jonah.

"You need to rest, babe," Kelly said after hearing the smack of the ball in leather. "And I thought we were going to celebrate."

"Celebrate what?" Tyler tossed the ball back to Jonah.

"Mr. Big Shot over there and I were supposed to celebrate his record-breaking game the other day." Kelly's eyes widened while her smile flattened as she tilted her head, tapping her nails on the aluminum.

Jonah threw one more pitch and flung his arms up as he stepped off the mound. "Fine. You guys win."

"Thank God." Tyler jumped to his feet, hobbled to the bench, and gathered his gear. "Hey, I'll catch up with you guys tomorrow. Pizza at Iron Heads. Be there."

As Tyler raced off to his car, Kelly and Jonah made their way to the bleachers. "So, I guess I'm not getting my roses?"

Brushing the hair out of Kelly's face, Jonah took in the aroma of vanilla radiating from behind her ear before he gently placed his lips to hers. "I'm sorry. I didn't have time. I had a bad game an — "

Kelly pressed her finger to Jonah's lips. "I know. I saw the whole thing. That home run that put you guys behind sucked. I also saw you not allow another hit after and win the game. And I saw one of those college guys you two are raving about leave maybe ten minutes ago."

Jonah's eyes locked onto Kelly's as he softly grazed her knee.

"Now, I don't know about you" — Kelly smiled and brushed her hair back before taking Jonah's hat, placing it on her head backward — "but I think he liked something he saw today."

"You know, you always seem to find that way to cheer me up, Kel."

"Yeah?" Kelly said, walking her fingers up Jonah's thigh. "I know a few other ways that I can make your night."

"Maybe we should go," Jonah said as he gently squeezed Kelly's thigh before he gave her a kiss, "and open that bottle of wine."

* * *

JONAH SLID INTO THE booth and reached for a slice of steaming pizza. The cheese stretched from the rest of the pie as he navigated it to his mouth. "'Sup, Tyler," Jonah said, his mouth full.

"I see Kelly let you live." Tyler took a drink of his soda.

Sliding next to Jonah, Kelly ran her hands through Jonah's hair before signaling the waitress over to their table. "He's too cute to kill."

"Yeah?" Tyler took a breadstick and tore into it. "I don't see it."

"Hey!" Jonah picked cheese off his chin. "At least I got a girl."

Kelly rolled her eyes and shook her head. She looked up at the smiling waitress. "A water, please."

"Iced tea for me," Jonah said.

After the waitress brought their drinks, Kelly opened her purse, rummaging until she pulled out two envelopes. She waved them in Jonah's face. Before he could snatch them, Kelly pulled them back.

"What's that, Kel?" asked Tyler.

"Letters from colleges. My top two school choices."

Tyler reached for the paprika while he pushed the basket of breadsticks toward Kelly. "Where'd you apply to again?"

Jonah sipped his tea. "Duke and Pitt."

"Jeez. You two really do, do everything together, don't you?"

Jonah smirked as Kelly's face reddened.

"I can't help it that Pitt is close to home and they both have amazing medical programs," Kelly said as she pushed herself up, using the table for leverage.

Jonah patted her back before he gently tugged at the bottom of her shirt.

Tyler threw both hands up. "Chill, I was just joking."

Grabbing for the envelopes, Jonah said, "So, did you get in?"

Kelly snatched the letters out of Jonah's hand. "I don't know yet. I was waiting for you, babe."

"Why didn't you just open them with me last night then?"

Kelly smacked Jonah in the shoulder as he pulled back to avoid her hand. "We were a little . . . preoccupied, now weren't we, babe?"

"Hey, I'm trying to eat over here," Tyler said with a slice of pizza inches from his mouth.

"Sorry."

Jonah took Kelly's empty plate and dropped a slice on it before sliding it back to her. "You better have some before we devour this."

"I'm fine," Kelly said as she pushed her plate toward the center of the table. "It's too garlicky. I think it'll make me sick."

Tyler grabbed at her plate. "Cool, I'll eat it."

"Well, don't keep us waiting." Jonah waved his hand. "Are we going to Duke together? Or not?"

"Duke offer you a scholarship?" Tyler asked.

"No, but it'll be easier to choose them over Texas if Kelly will be there with me."

Kelly opened the first envelope. Her mouth moved quickly as she scanned the document. Her lips slowly rose into a smile as she read, "We look forward to seeing you on campus here at Duke this coming August." She quickly kissed Jonah before turning her attention to the second envelope.

"All right! We're going to be the hottest couple at Duke," Jonah said as he threw both his fists in the air before motioning to Tyler for a high five.

"I got into Pitt, too!"

"That's awesome, Kel," Tyler said. He turned to Jonah. "Hey, if Duke doesn't give you an offer, you two can rock it at Pitt."

Jonah kicked Tyler under the table.

"Babe, you got into Pitt, too? This is so exciting. Why didn't you tell me earlier?" Kelly knocked the pizza out of Jonah's hand as she grabbed his face, pulling him in for a kiss. She pushed off him and stood up. "I think I'm going to be sick. I'll be right back."

Once Kelly was out of hearing range, Jonah balled his hand into a fist and hit the seat. "What the hell, man!"

"I didn't know you didn't tell her," Tyler said. "Why didn't you tell her you got into Pitt, anyway?"

"Because I don't want to go to Pitt."

"Then why did you apply there?"

"Because, my parents and Kelly both thought I needed to have a closer school as a backup." Jonah reached into his pocket and pulled out his money. "I'll see you tomorrow, man."

* * *

"AND WITH THAT STRIKEOUT, Jonah Scott earns his third no-hitter of the season going into the back end of this stellar season. Hawks record 12–0 . . ."

Jonah high-fived Tyler as they made their way to the dugout.

"That's what I'm talking about!" Tyler tucked his face mask under his arm.

Jonah glanced into the stands; his smile vanished when Kelly wasn't anywhere to be seen. He shook his head and glanced up, his smile returning. He nudged Tyler in the arm and nodded toward the bench. "Look who's talking to Coach."

Coach turned and waved the boys in. "Great game, guys. I'll see you at practice tomorrow. Jonah, stick around. Meet me at my office."

Tyler gathered his equipment and tossed Jonah his water bottle. "Good luck, man. Don't get kicked off the team."

Jonah gave a small laugh as he put his glove in his bag and hoisted the bag onto his shoulders. He started toward the school. As he walked, he couldn't help but wonder where Kelly was. She had never missed a game before. Always there waiting to give him a congratulatory kiss. In fact, Kelly had been acting strange since she got her acceptance letter to Duke. Every time Jonah brought up Duke, she would shy away, change the subject. She couldn't seriously be considering Pitt, could she? It was always the plan that if they both got accepted to Duke, there'd be no debate. He would even pass over Texas, his dream school. No. No way Kelly was going to choose Pitt over Duke. She was probably just exhausted with her schoolwork.

Jonah sat in one of the chairs at Coach's desk. He spun the chair back and forth with his foot as he waited for him.

It wasn't long before the door burst open and Coach stepped in the small room followed by a man proudly sporting a Duke hat and polo. "Jonah, this is Mr. Atwood."

Mr. Atwood extended his hand. "Nice to finally meet you, Jonah. We've been in touch over the course of the year. I'm the head coach of Duke's baseball program."

Jonah jumped out of his seat and firmly grasped Mr. Atwood's hand, squeezing a bit too hard.

Mr. Atwood waved his hand toward the chairs and sat in the chair opposite Jonah at the desk. "I hope you don't mind, I've asked your coach to join us. Give you any counsel you may want without your parents being here. Or, if you prefer, we can reschedule this meeting."

"No, no," Jonah blurted out, not wanting to delay as he realized what was about to happen. "Now is fine."

"Good, good." Mr. Atwood adjusted his seat, pulling the chair closer to the desk, causing a loud screeching sound. "Let's cut to the chase. You seem to be a fine young gentleman. From what your coach has told me, you have tremendous leadership abilities. I can tell you're a hard worker; I sat and watched you work on that curveball after that second game. It's coming along nicely, by the way."

Jonah nodded, his feet locked under the desk so he couldn't push himself back. "Yes, sir. I've been working hard at perfecting it. I toss it about half the time in my bullpen sessions each week."

"It shows. You've certainly gained more control since that last game I saw. You got, what? Two, three no-hitters this season now? I'm sure it has a lot to do with it."

"Yes, sir. Three no-hitters." Jonah couldn't keep from smiling.

"Now, I know this is a big year for you. You probably have a list of twenty different schools you've been talking to."

"No, sir. Just two. You and the Longhorns."

"Just the two?" Mr. Atwood leaned back in the chair.

"I've really only considered Duke and Texas as the only two places I would play."

Mr. Atwood laughed and leaned forward. He looked over at Coach. "Kid knows what he wants." He turned back to face Jonah. "Here's the deal. I don't know what Texas has offered you, but what I am prepared to give you is a scholarship that would cover your first year's tuition costs."

Jonah sprung from his chair. Before he could get out a word of gratitude, Mr. Atwood continued, "Now settle down, son, I haven't finished yet."

"Yes, sir." Jonah lowered himself back in his chair.

Mr. Atwood reached into his bag and slid a package of Duke gear across the desk. "On the condition that you make the team, your performance on the field, and keep your academics a priority, we can talk about extending that scholarship to all four years you're with us. Now how does that sound?"

"That's wonderful, sir! I can't thank you enough."

"Take those home. Talk it over with your folks — "

Jonah grabbed the hat out of the package and pulled it down over his head. "I don't need to. I accept."

Coach stepped out of the corner and placed his hand on Jonah's shoulder. "I really suggest you wait, son. Talk it over with your parents, wait until you see what Texas offers you, if anything."

Jonah stood up and shook Mr. Atwood's hand. "I'm going to Duke."

"I'm glad to hear that. Keep a lookout in the mail. You'll be receiving your letter of intent for you to sign that guarantees your scholarship offer."

* * *

JONAH PICKED UP A rock and skipped it into the river. "I can't believe Kelly is avoiding me. Like, did I do something?"

"Yeah, you scared the fish away." Tyler reeled in his line before recasting it.

"No, seriously. It's been weeks." Jonah kicked the rocks on the bank then opened the cooler for a soda before sitting on it. "She hasn't answered my texts or calls. Hell, I even went to her house and she won't let me in."

"You gotta relax, man."

"Why? Why do I need to relax?" Jonah finished his soda, crushing the can in his fist. "My girlfriend is ignoring me."

"We still have a game to play. And we still have a state championship to win." Tyler stood up, pulling back on his rod as he started to reel in his catch. "Not everyone on the team got scholarships, man. This season is our last chance for glory. Besides, Kelly loves you, man. She's probably just really focused on finishing the school year, keeping her GPA up."

Jonah paced back and forth before he grabbed his rod and threw the line out. "You know what, you're right. I'm just getting in my own head."

* * *

"WE ARE SEEING HISTORY here today, folks. With just one more out to go, Jonah Scott is near perfect. I don't think there is any question if the Hawks will be going to state with a score of 17–0. What we're all looking to see is if Jonah Scott can get his first-ever perfect game. I mean, even Spartan fans are hoping to see something this special. And Dylan Brown steps to the plate. Boy oh boy, does Brown look determined to spoil this thing."

Jonah pulled off his rain-soaked hat and readjusted it, pulling his hair out of his face. As the rain softened, he looked past the drops slowly forming on the bill of his hat and focused on Tyler's mitt. "Just three more strikes. That's all. I got this." He looked to the bleachers. Kelly was still absent. "Where the hell is she?"

Jonah threw his pitch. The batter swung and missed as the bat made its way across the plate and up over his shoulder before the ball even hit Tyler's mitt. Jonah chuckled as the ball came back to him. "Oh, you want a fastball? Let's see you hit this."

"Ball!" the ump called after Jonah threw a fastball in the dirt, the batter stopping mid-swing.

Jonah used the rubber to kick the mud off the bottom of his cleats as the rain finally subsided. "Shit," he mumbled under his breath as his curveball got away from him, hitting the fence behind Tyler and the umpire.

Tyler called time and jogged to the mound. "What the hell, man. Rein it in."

"I want this out."

"Good. Then quit toying with him. Attack him." Tyler hurried back behind the plate.

Jonah looked around the stands again. Still no sign of Kelly. He reached back and let the ball fly. There was an echoing smack as the ball flew over the swinging bat and into the leather of Tyler's mitt.

Jonah smacked his glove with his hand before snatching the ball and digging his foot into the groove of the mound. He locked eyes with the batter, peering deep into his soul as he got set. "All right. Let's do this, Ace. Let's get that last strike and finish this."

"And there is strike three as that ball just caught the corner of the plate. What a way to cap Jonah 'Ace' Scott's senior season with a perfect game on top of his five no-hitters. I tell you what, folks, it's been a fun four years watching this kid play. I don't remember when the Hawks have ever had a kid pitch this dominantly, and I don't think we will see another for many years. We'll see you next week when our Hawks compete for their first state championship in twenty years!"

Coach gathered the boys around the dugout. "Congratulations, boys. It's been a hell of a season. But it's not over yet. Tonight, go celebrate. Have fun. Don't do anything stupid. But enjoy yourselves. You've earned it. Monday, we get serious again. We have a championship to win."

Jonah packed his gear in his bag and pulled out his phone and smiled. The screen lit up with a text message from Kelly. "Meet up at the park after the game."

Tyler patted Jonah on the back. "Hell of a game, man. Can't believe I caught a perfect game."

Jonah zipped his bag and hoisted it over his shoulder. "Catch one? I fucking pitched it. I did all the work."

"Whoa, man. I'm not taking anything away from you. So, we're headed to Iron Heads. You coming?" Tyler packed his mitt and face mask.

"Nah. I've got somewhere better to be."

Tyler lifted his bag. "All right. But if you and Kelly want to join us, we'll be at Bobby's farm later for a bonfire."

Jonah started walking to the cars with Tyler. "How'd you know?"

"Dude, Ace. She's your girl, and the only person you'd ditch us for."

* * *

JONAH PULLED UP NEXT to Kelly's car as the sun was setting. Kelly was sitting on the swings waiting for him. He couldn't help but smile, watching her rocking back and forth. He reached over to the passenger seat and grabbed the roses before he stepped out of his car.

"Hey, lady on the swing." Jonah waved with a big grin reaching from ear to ear. "Have you seen a hot girl by the name of Kelly? She's supposed to be meeting me here."

Kelly flashed him a smile as he made his way over to her and sat on the swing beside hers. Jonah handed her the roses and leaned in for a kiss. She gave him a peck on the lips and said, "Thanks for the roses, babe. You didn't have to."

Jonah was confused by her lack of affection but quickly shook it off. "You missed a good game. Hell, it was the best game I've ever pitched."

"I'm sorry, I had a lot on my mind."

"What's wrong?"

"Nothing's wrong." She pulled the chain around her neck out of her shirt and looked at the ring attached to it before turning her attention to Jonah. "You guys won?"

"Obviously." Jonah looked at Kelly, worried. She had been distant these past couple of weeks, and now that they were talking, something seemed off.

"Oh?" Kelly took her eyes away from Jonah and focused them on her feet, drawing circles in the mulch.

"Yeah!" Jonah said as he pumped the swing in excitement. "We're going to state. And we're going to dominate. I'm on fire right now, and nothing's going to slow me down."

"That's nice, Jonah."

Jonah stopped swinging and turned to look at Kelly. "Babe, what's wrong? You're acting really weird. I thought you'd be excited."

"No, Jonah. I'm excited. Really I am."

"Then what's bothering you?" Jonah twisted his swing to look at Kelly head-on. He placed his hands on her knees to keep his swing steady.

Kelly took a deep breath and looked up at the sky. The cool spring breeze gently blew her hair in her face as a cloud opened up, and the moon and stars were becoming more visible. She opened her mouth and hesitated before she said, "Jonah, I know you're set on going to Duke, but would Pitt really be that bad?"

Jonah let his hands fall from Kelly's knees. "What are you saying, Kel?"

"They both have top medical programs. I can become a doctor there, and you can become a physical therapist. We're closer to home.

And it's like half the cost. It just makes more sense to go to Pitt." She grabbed his hands.

"But we've talked about going to Duke. It's been our number one choice together when we sent out applications. It's the best chance I have at going pro."

"I don't care about you going pro. I care about you being with me. And I've made up my mind about this. I'm going to Pitt."

"Is this why you've been distant?"

"Jonah, please."

"No. Don't 'Jonah, please' me. Kel, we should have talked about this. Why did you wait so long to ruin our plans?"

"Because, Jonah." Kelly jumped up and stood in front of him. "Because I didn't want to ruin your season. To tell you that I'm pregnant, and going to Pitt will allow me to actually still go to school with my parents able to help me."

Jonah opened and closed his mouth a few times before he could find the words. "Preg . . . pregnant?"

Kelly nodded, tears starting to swell along her lashes. She let the roses fall from her hands to the mulch as she tried to hide her face in her hands. "I'm sorry, Jonah. Please don't hate me."

Jonah just sat there blinking as he shifted his focus to a tree. He tried to wrap his mind around what he'd just heard. After a few moments he finally said, "How could this happen? I thought you were on the pill."

"And I thought you were able to control yourself and pull out."

"Don't blame this on me, Kelly."

"I'm not, Jonah. I'm just as much at fault for not making you cover it."

Jonah stood up and started to pace, mumbling incoherently under his breath. He stopped and ran his fingers through his hair. "What are we going to do about it?"

"What do you mean 'what are we going to do about it?'"

"I mean, do we need your parents' signature to get an abortion?"

"An abortion? Jonah. I'm not getting an abortion. I want to keep it."

"Keep it? You know how much responsibility a baby is? How much work they are? What do your parents think? You can't have a baby."

"The hell I can't! I want to keep it, Jonah. That's why I'm going to Pitt. My mom and dad will help us — help me. I'm having this baby whether you want it or not. And if you want to leave or have nothing to do with us, that's fine." Kelly reached for Jonah's hands. "If you want to go off to Duke and be a huge baseball star and forget about us, that's fine, too. I'll manage. I'd love for you to stay, be with us. That's why I'm hoping you'll go to Pitt with me. But I love you too much to ask you to give up your dream."

Kelly waited, her hands still on Jonah's. Jonah let her hands drop and ran his fingers through his hair as he walked toward his car. He picked up a rock and threw it into the open field. He picked up another and another. "Fine. Ruin your life, Kel. Keep it. Give up on your dreams and have a baby." He felt his heart drop the moment he said it, willing himself to take it back, but he couldn't.

Jonah jumped as Kelly stormed toward him, tears leaking down her cheek, her hand raised. "Don't ever accuse our baby" — she slapped him across the face — "of ruining my life, Jonah. We made the decision to fuck. Not just me. You don't want it? Then leave."

Kelly turned to her car and opened the door. She grabbed at the ring around her neck and chucked it in the wooded area behind the car. Before Jonah could take her hand, she slammed the door shut and threw the car in reverse. He watched as she sped down the street blowing every stop sign until her taillights were out of sight.

* * *

JONAH PULLED HIS PHONE out and turned on the flashlight. He got on his hands and knees and searched through the mud and leaves for his class ring. How could he have been such an ass toward Kelly? He *loved her. He just wanted the best for her. That's why he was so adamant on her going to Duke with him. No. That's not true. He wanted what was best for him. And for him, the best thing was to go to Duke. He knew he had what it took to make it big, and he knew Pitt wasn't going to get him drafted. But he could find another job in baseball. More importantly, Pitt would keep him close to Kelly and his unborn child.*

Jonah used the palm of his hand to hit himself in the head a few times. "Stupid, stupid. Why am I such a dumbass? So what, I miss a season of college ball if I go to Pitt over Duke. What's more important, Jonah? Baseball, or Kelly?"

Out of the corner of his eye, Jonah caught the reflection of the light from his phone beaming off his class ring, which lay next to a log. He reached and picked it up by the chain and put it in his pocket before he opened the contacts in his phone.

* * *

JONAH DIGS HIS FOOT into the groove and looks around the field. He pulls his glove to his chest and starts his windup. Letting the ball fly down the center of the plate, he gives a small smile as the batter swings and misses. The batter slams his bat on the plate before hoisting it above his shoulder, ready for the next pitch.

"Keep your eye on the ball, son. Keep those eyes open while you swing," Jonah says to his fourteen-year-old son, Ryder.

"Just throw the ball, Dad," Ryder says as he leans on his back leg. "And don't go easy on me."

Ryder swings as the ball flies into the cage behind him. "Were you really going to be a major leaguer, Dad?"

Jonah removes his glove, lifts the bottle of water by his feet, and takes a sip while Ryder takes a few practice swings. "Yeah. It's true."

"What happened?"

"I was given a scholarship to Duke, which would have been a great platform to be scouted by the big teams."

"I thought you and Mom went to the same schools."

"We did."

"But Mom went to Pitt."

"She did."

"What happened? Why didn't you go to Duke?"

Jonah seals the bottle of water and lets it drop to the ground as he puts his glove back on. Ryder steps up to the plate. "Sometimes, there are more important things, son."

"Like what?"

Jonah looks around the ball field. In the parking lot, he sees Kelly putting their newborn in the stroller while their three-year-old daughter jumps out of her car seat in the SUV. He smiles and turns back to his son. "Coaching you, for one. Another is being here to help you and your sisters reach your dreams. And taking my Hawks to — and finally winning — the state championship. Now, I'm throwing harder than any kid you will face this season. If you can hit me, you'll hit any of them. Keep your eye on the ball."

Ryder swings and connects with the ball dead center. Jonah quickly turns around to watch the first homer he's ever been happy to give up sail over the center field fence.

To learn more about this author, please visit:
https://www.facebook.com/jconeilauthor/

Gotta Have Rhythm

Romance

Colin D. Palmer

Prompt: You did everything right, but you're still the villain.

*T*HERE CAN BE RHYTHM but no rhyme. They don't always go together.

Berek and Ursula knew this adage, but they made the most of their time anyway. A unique moment of shared interest drew them together, and both were mature and quick-thinking enough to understand it was their only mutual connection.

At first, anyway.

Berek saw her first, or so he believed. Above the cacophony assaulting their ears from the heavy metal beat, the soaring guitar solo, thumping bass, and splash and crash of cymbals, he spied her in the mosh pit, the slashing lights from the stage highlighting her presence.

This was before mosh pits were even known as mosh pits — the heavy-metal crowd used proximity to the stage to unleash themselves to massive harmonic pounding and were probably the first to do so.

In quieter venues, less rowdy crowds just swayed to a rhythm. Loud, heavy music demanded more, and Ursula was delivering, surrendering to the moment as she absorbed and redistributed what the music induced.

Near the rear of the auditorium, Berek ceased singing and waving his arm when he saw her. Even the music seemed to mute itself. The lights kept flashing onto her face, and even though the strobes were probably doing the same to hundreds in the writhing throng, she was the only person visible to him.

The song abruptly ended in a blinding crescendo of pyrotechnics, lights, and music — and she was gone. Less than twenty seconds and gone in a literal flash. Standing where he was, there was no hope, but it didn't stop Berek from trying. He peered through the haze and half-blindness, trying to ink his vision to solidness.

Those at the back began to move through the exits to evade the mad rush for public transport, or maybe they hadn't really enjoyed the concert in the first place. Others grouped and moved around Berek, jostling and carrying him, forcing him to retreat with them. His eyes remained glued to the front of the auditorium as howls of "encore, encore" rose from the pumped-up crowd closer to the stage.

A shrill reverb — that electronic annoyance signifying the removal of a live cable from speakers — effectively announced there would be no encore. An even heavier groan of disappointment resounded, with a few overlaying "boos" as accompaniment.

Positioned at the back for a quick exit, Berek found himself resisting the pushing crowd. Usually one of the first out the door, he began to shove back, then in the increasing awareness of futility, understood his impetuous attempts were ridiculous — not because it was futile but because those nearest the stage, and indeed, all of the audience in the lower tiers, would leave via different exits.

He turned quickly and went with the crowd instead, shouldering and pushing to gain leeway and free space to accelerate his escape.

Reaching the fresh air, the inside of his head still pounded from the musical assault. Crowds piled into queued buses with auditorium staff waving and yelling to "start at the front, fill the front bus first, don't push, be patient." The buzz from the concert continued to envelop the departing audience, and they acted with boisterous enthusiasm.

The mingling, surging crowd directed his momentum toward a further bus, and Berek fought his way sideways and free. Fortunate happenstance got him into the shadow of one of the yelling staff, the moving crowd flowing around them like some boulder in a gurgling creek.

There she was. The girl from the mosh pit. No mistaking her above-average height, the flame-colored hair, the green oversized T-shirt. Borrowed from her husband, boyfriend, an ex? he wondered.

They provided instant identity, but the moment she looked in his direction, he let loose a voluminous sigh loud enough for even the crowd controller to offer a glance and ask if he was okay.

"Fine . . . now," he answered without looking away from the tall green-shirted redhead peering directly at him.

She was still ten yards away, which was closer than the forty yards or so in the auditorium. But confirmation was there — the eyes, a glaring demon of emerald green that sent sparks flying in whichever direction they shone. Right now, they were zeroed in on Berek, just like he swore they had been when she was dancing crazily in the mosh pit. Those eyes — the first thing to gain his attention. He watched her approach, his head turned down and away to make his observation less obvious, something he'd perfected over the years.

Her enthusiasm had waned, but excitement still glowed across her face, especially in those eyes. Despite his downturned head, she must have known he was looking because she pursed her lips and lowered her own head, eyes now peeking through the sweat-soaked tangerine fringe of hair.

She appeared alone, even though part of a mass movement. There was no hand-holding or guiding hand on her elbow or back that he could see. The crowd around gave her room, as her dominant presence marked her majesty. At least that's how Berek saw it. Her apparent awareness of that presence, conscious or not, meant she used it nobly. Her cut-off denim shorts flashed that insidious fashion trend of exposed inner pockets, her long slim legs comfortably gliding her along toward him. He didn't move his head, just allowed his eyes to appraise her.

Two yards. Two more steps. He took a deep breath — Here goes nothing — leaned in and stepped out beside her. Her head was still down but she turned a little toward him, green eyes sparkling, a smile displaying an even row of dazzling white teeth.

"You're a brave little man," she teased.

"I'm taller than you," Berek countered, surprised at his instant temerity.

"I'm taller than you," she mimicked in a little girl's voice with an accompanying giggle. He swayed away, detouring from the tone of her comment. She rolled her eyes in a "why me?" way and ordered, "Sit with me on the bus." Berek immediately moved back into her presence and she delivered a knowing, cheeky smile.

He looked at her eyes. He didn't look anywhere else, and Berek could see she was assessing him and, he hoped, accurately concluding he was one of the quiet ones. Always at the back, always quiet unless drawn out, always ready to walk away if there was a risk of getting hurt. "Beware the quiet ones," her mother had probably told her. They observed everything. They saw everything. They remembered every tiny nuance. And they were damn hard work.

They merged tighter with the surrounding crowd to board the bus and, as if she'd read his mind, she asked, "So, are you hard work?"

The ensuing conversation was the best he ever had. In the hours that followed, nothing stole his gaze from her eyes, not the other concert goers nor passengers on the bus, the ferry across the river nor the other groups in the little all-night café sipping cappuccinos and sharing apple pie. Nothing was as captivating. Only embarrassment halted his concentration.

She mocked surprise when he timidly asked if she'd seen him at the concert.

"How was I supposed to do that? There were thousands there!"

"I saw you," he answered.

"Sure. Outside in the lights maybe."

"No. Inside during the concert."

She shook her head. "I was near the stage. Where were you?"

"On the upper tier, near the back. I . . . I thought you looked at me."

"Is that why you waited? Oh my God! Because a girl a hundred yards away might have looked at you in a crowded, dark room full of flashing lights and smoke machines?"

"It was only about fifty yards, and . . . and . . . oh, it doesn't matter."

"You're the self-admitted gray man, Berek. How is anybody supposed to see you?"

"It . . . it doesn't matter. I just thought you looked at me, that's all."

She tucked one long finger under his chin and lifted his drooping head. "I did," she teased, a smile playing across her lips.

"Hey? Did what?" The impact of her words made him miss their first physical contact.

"See you, silly." She kept smiling. "I'm just teasing you, Berek. You better get used to it if you wanna hang out with me," she ended seriously.

"Hang out? With you?" He must have looked the epitome of incredulous, because she laughed.

"Stop repeating everything I say. Yes. You. Me. Hanging out together. That okay with you?" she asked as her emerald eyes flashed again.

He gulped and felt his Adam's apple bob as she leaned across the table and placed a petite hand on top of his. This time, he acknowledged the physical connection, imprinting a memory that he would fantasize and embellish forever. There was a spark at that contact, nothing that made either of them jump, but enough for her to embrace and Berek to fondly remember in his oh-so-logical mind.

"What, what's your name?" he managed to eke out.

She laughed again and peeked at her teal-colored, silicone children's watch. "Four hours we've just had together, and finally he gets down to the nitty-gritty!" She finished laughing and watched him seriously studying her. His eyes, a deep brown — almost black — stayed attached to hers, never wandering, even when a few young late-night clubbers in short sequined dresses promenaded past them. She held his gaze and leaned closer across the table. "Ursula," she whispered and was rewarded with his smile.

Still smiling, he let his eyes travel down to her hand on top of his, turned his hand over, and grasped hers. He shook it gently. His smile, he knew, erased years from his true age. He saw the effect it had on her, but before she could offer the comment he could see about to burst from her lips, he spoke his mind.

"It's very nice to meet you, Ursula," he mouthed, tasting the sound of her name on his tongue. "I'm Berek."

"I know." She smiled back.

"How, what . . . ?"

"You told me on the bus, silly. It's one of the first questions I asked. It's what normal people do, you know."

"Oh." He grinned. "Sorry. I . . . I forgot."

Their first night turned into an entire night, then an entire day, then a whole weekend. Work on Monday morning was the first interruption. Not for Berek, who worked from home, but for Ursula who had to go. For the first time as far as he could recall from the past two days, she dragged a phone from a tiny little rucksack. She winked at him as she told whoever was on the other end that she'd be late.

She came back after work, bringing Chinese food and a few bottles of beer. Apart from the dreaded work, she never left him again.

Berek displayed a focus of love and attention nonexistent outside of a Disney film. He never ordered her to do anything, discussed anything he thought was worthy of attention, big and little things that sometimes new relationships ignored.

He was an introvert. She was an extrovert. They melded perfectly.

She introduced many things he had never considered. Reef snorkeling, bungee jumping, hiking, camping.

"You sure you've never done this before?" she asked on one of their camping trips.

"Never. Well, never like this anyway. It's so peaceful out here, and I get to share it with you." His smile reflected in the campfire light as he swept an arm around the encroaching forest.

She slapped playfully at his swinging arm. "Ha! You didn't say that when we went bungee jumping. You screamed like a little girl!" She broke into a loud laughing fit.

Berek let her settle before answering. "I'm more than happy to do the snorkeling thing again. That was amazing. And I'll climb any mountain with you. But, yes, if you don't mind, I'll pass on repeating the bungee jumping."

"Okay, buster. I understand. You'll go anywhere with me except hang off a giant elastic band."

"Of course. I want to be with you."

Her friends were confused at first. They had no idea what Ursula saw in him. Her parents loved him from the start. "Such a gentleman," her mother told her in the kitchen, "but are you sure? He's nothing like the other boys you used to bring home." Ursula gave her mom a hug and convinced her that she'd never been surer of anything before in her whole life. "Well, you are thirty now, dear. It's about time for you to settle down." The typical parental hint and scarcely veiled nod of agreement. "Your father said Berek is a very interesting man." The final seal of approval, and a first as well.

Berek had no family — "all gone now" being the explanation — and Ursula didn't seem to need more information. He knew people *at the local supermarket and a few of the nearby restaurants and cafés. They all spoke casually and warmly to him, but Ursula understood that she was his only actual friend.*

He was shocked when he learned her occupation.

"I'm a stock procurement manager at the local hardware franchise," she told him.

"A what?" he asked.

"I locate and order goods for the stores." She shrugged. "Why you so surprised?"

"I don't know. I just figured you'd be in retail or something. You have the personality for it."

"You saying I'm dumb?"

"No, not in the least!" His shock turned to horror. "You're the cleverest dumb person I've ever met, if that was the case." He smiled, then laughed as she smacked his shoulder and laughed, too.

"Really, Berek . . . and you . . . you are the dumbest smart person I ever met." They laughed.

"I can't argue with that," he said once the laughter died down.

They spent almost a whole year together before she asked about his job.

"Anyway, what do you do on that computer all day?" She nodded to his large office.

"I was wondering when you'd get around to asking."

"We've been busy." She laughed. "So? What? Money market? No, you don't look, or act, like any kind of broker. Um, trader of the arts, antiquities, something like that? Oh, no." She glanced around his large apartment. "There's no evidence of that here either. I don't know. What do you do? Just tell me, Berek, don't tease!"

"I'm not teasing. You are! Well, anyway, seeing as you finally asked, what I am . . . is a ghostwriter."

She responded with the exact same words he produced when she'd told him her job. "A what?"

"A ghostwriter. I write things for other people, and they pay me to do it."

She chuckled, more a nervous kind of laugh, not her usual roar. Berek learned her less- outrageous laughs meant she was either confused or simply laughing out of courtesy. He believed it was confusion this time. He started to explain more but she jumped in first.

"Like, you mean stories, or in-depth articles about the latest vacuum cleaner trends—like that?"

Her serious look—so rare—made him laugh, too. She always made him smile.

"Not far from the truth, actually. I started off many years ago writing articles . . . like reviews . . . for magazines, newspapers, and journals. Things like that. And yes, there were a few about vacuum cleaners, believe it or not. But, that was a long time ago. Now I just write novels, biographies, memoirs. Books."

"You mean for other people?" She looked aghast. "Somebody pays you to write a book, and they put their own name on it?" She eyed him incredulously. "Why?"

Berek took a sip of water and gently placed the glass onto the coffee table before answering. "In some cases, because they can't write it themselves. They have the story but not the ability to put it down on paper. In other cases, it's because they don't have the time."

Ursula flipped her head back in disbelief. "And your name never appears anywhere. These . . . these people just claim it as theirs?"

"Yes, exactly. Because I insist on it."

"You do?" She tilted her head to one side as she spoke, a habit Berek adored.

"Yes." He smiled and reached for the glass again. After a short sip, he went on. "I have a reputation for confidentiality and I will never breach it. Besides, every work has a secrecy agreement within the contract, so even if I wanted to, legally I can't talk about it."

"How come?" She tilted her head the other way this time and Berek's smile broadened.

"Because that's the way it is. It's also the way I prefer it."

"The gray man. Ghostwriter," she said almost to herself. Suddenly, her adorable eyes widened, and she stared directly at him. "Any, you know, famous authors?"

"Yes." He laughed. "There have been a few, but I can't tell you who."

"Yeah, yeah, secrecy, confidentiality, blah-blah-blah," she said and poked her tongue out at him before snuggling back into the sofa.

"Even for you, darling, I can't tell. But most of them are just mom-and-pop kind of deals. You know, the memoir of some experience, or even their whole life. There's been quite a few of them . . . war survivors, victims of diseases, major injuries, abuse, family trauma . . . things like that."

"Oh, yeah. I get it. Hey! Maybe you can write a story for me?" She bounced up and down on the sofa, waiting for his answer.

He laughed. He never tired of her youthful exuberance. "Yes, sure. What do you want me to write about?"

"Us."

"Eh?"

"Us. We'll both write it. The Ursula and Berek story." A veil dropped across his face, his eyes unfocused and far away, looking straight through her. "Oh, hun. You all right?" Ursula leaned forward, peering intently at him.

It lasted only a moment, his eyes flashing in and out of focus while his whole face drooped at the same time. If Ursula had been looking elsewhere, she wouldn't have seen a thing. He gave a little head shake and smiled at her as if nothing happened.

"Yes, I'm fine." His voice was steady, as was his gaze. "But we've only been together a year. What do we write about?" It happened so quickly, and Berek didn't appear to notice his own hesitation.

"We can write about all the things from before. I can tell you all about my married sister who lives in Canada, school . . . you know, everything right up to where and how we met." She giggled.

"Then we can add volumes to it later, you know, sequels. Maybe Netflix will pick it up!" She threw back her head and laughed.

He repeated his episode, even faster this time, then joined her laughter before replying. "Yes, okay, if you really want to. But after work though. The paid stuff comes first."

"You better believe it, buddy, and I'll be looking for your professional guidance, too, Mr. Ghostwriter."

They began the next day. Ursula sat on the sofa, her laptop propped up on the coffee table. When she turned her head sideways, she could look over her shoulder and see Berek slapping away at the desktop computer in the office. He seemed to zone out when he was writing, and she had never seen him at his computer before, which was strange. People were constantly checking e-mails or the new craze of social networking. Berek appeared oblivious to all those things. He didn't even own a cell phone. Who didn't own a cell phone these days? Even her mom and dad had little Nokias.

For weeks, they punched away at their respective computers. They took weekends off, went into the mountains—their go-to retreat from work, family, and city life. But after work on weekdays, they kept at it. Many times, Ursula burst into laughter at some ditty she recalled from the past, and once there were tears when she remembered the death of a much-loved pet. Berek just kept pounding the keyboard, off wherever his mind took him.

About five weeks later, he sighed. The roll of the castors reached Ursula as he pushed the chair away from the desk, and she looked back over her shoulder.

"Don't tell me you're finished?" She smiled.

"Yes," was all he said, with a gloomy look.

"I . . . I'm nearly done. Maybe another few nights anyway."

"I can wait," he added flatly. He seemed to shake himself, more like a full-body shiver, then he smiled. "Have I told you how much I love your eyes?"

"Many times, buster, many times." She smiled back at him. "Now stop interrupting. I'm working here."

He brought her favorite tea, then sat and watched as she worked. She didn't appear to find his unspoken attention a distraction at all. In fact, it seemed his calm presence helped her focus. At ten o'clock — her self-appointed finish time — she lowered the lid of the laptop and yawned. She looked at him watching her, got up, stretched, and walked over and plonked herself on his lap, draping her arms around his neck.

"I'm writing about you and me at the moment," she told him.

He reached and placed a gentle finger against her lips. "Shh, not now. Finish first. Then we'll read it together."

She yawned again. "Okay, but no laughing at my bad spelling and grammar, understood?"

"Yes, ma'am." He gave a little salute. "Go on. Shower. Then off to bed with you."

She lifted one arm off his shoulder and saluted him back. "Yes, sir! Um . . . maybe, sir . . . would like to . . . you know . . . wash my back?" She winked.

Two evenings later, Ursula pushed back into the sofa and released a heavy sigh. Berek was sitting in his now-accustomed place, the armchair opposite from where he watched her work. He leaned forward and put his forearms on his thighs.

She gasped. "It's like . . . wow, I did it!"

"It's always the same when you finish a story. A relief, joy, disbelief, shock even. Every time."

"Every time, you say?"

"Yes. Every time."

"I don't know how you do it, buster. I'm not sure I'd want to do that again."

"Let's go out. It's still only eight o'clock. We can do dinner and toast our joint literary success." He smiled.

"You don't want to read it now?" Ursula was surprised. She had kept going for over five weeks thinking she was doing it just so she could read what Berek wrote. As she went on pulling out long-forgotten memories, she found it cathartic and began to enjoy the

endeavor, hard work as it was. But always, always, there was whatever Berek had written to keep her motivated. She was dying to read it. She knew how her story ended, and her deepest hope was that his finale would shine with a similar desire.

"I do." He smiled warmly, encouragingly. "But, I want it on paper. It's too difficult to read off the computer. Do you think they'll let you print it out at work?"

"Yeah, yeah, I know what you mean. Um, sure. It's only about thirty-something pages, so it won't take long to print. How many pages is yours?"

Berek averted his eyes before answering.

"Oh, a few more than that — than yours. But remember, I'm a professional writer." He smiled, and thankfully his eyes returned to hers.

She jumped up. "Dinner. Wine. Toasts! What's your preference, hun?"

"Thai. Yes, I think I'd like something spicy. Okay?"

"You and me, hun, you and me. But when we get back, I want a bit more of that back-scrubbing in the shower you do so good." She laughed.

"You're on." Berek laughed along with her.

The next night, they sat together on the sofa. A sheaf of paper sat on the coffee table in front of them.

"Forty-one pages actually." Ursula beamed at him. "Where's yours?"

"Yours first," he answered.

Before she arrived home from work, he had put together chips and crackers, dips and cheeses, olives, gherkins, a small selection of cold meats, and opened her favorite bottle of wine. He poured a glass now.

"Help yourself," Berek said and picked up her story.

He read of her childhood, laughed with her when they shared a funny account, hugged her when her cat got run over, laughed again at the surprise revelation of being a Bay City Roller, an enthusiastic fan of that tartan-kilted boy-band from the mid-1970s. He was reflective when he read about her older sister marrying then leaving the country, her sadness, her constant missing of their once-tight sibling union. He read about old boyfriends, new boyfriends, boys from the wrong side of town, bad boys who were never welcomed back to her family home. Her music tastes were eclectic — Bay City Rollers to Black Sabbath — no need to say more.

There was surprise that she used to draw and illustrate little stories like a comic, but she hadn't done it in years. She even added a caricature of him in the margin as an example of her work.

"You did this today?" He showed her the page.

"Yes. You like it?"

"Better than the mirror, that's for sure." They laughed.

He read on — the first meeting, seeing this dark, mysterious stranger at a gig standing at the back of the room, watching her.

"You really think I fit the bill of dark, mysterious stranger?"

"Yes. You are, Berek. To me, that is."

She really only outlined their year together, pointing out the fun trips they had, the smooth communication, his caring and sharing and just how much she adored him because of those things.

Then came her bombshell of a finale. She loved him. She really loved him, and she knew he loved her even more, if that was possible. So why hadn't he asked her to marry him? She wanted his babies. She wanted the rest of her life to be with Berek. She wanted to be happy, forever.

He closed the folder holding her loose pages, her story, her past, her hopes, her dreams. He didn't look at her for quite a long, drawn-out moment. It could have been just seconds, but to Ursula, it must have felt like hours. Then he did look. The depth of his sadness was almost heartbreaking, was heartbreaking, and Ursula began to cry.

Berek folded her in his arms straightaway, cradled her as she wept. Her sobbing subsided quickly. She wasn't a crier normally, and she let self-control grab her.

"Am I that bad?" Tears created halation in her eyes.

He smiled warmly and hugged her closer. "No. No, a thousand times no."

"Then why? Why won't you ask me?"

"I was going to. But best you read my story first."

"Okay," her little-girl voice whispered.

He gave her another hug, kissed the top of her head, and stood up.

"I love you, too, Ursula. From that first moment I saw you." He walked away into his office.

She would have heard his shuffling around the desk, a drawer being opened and closed, his soft footsteps padding back. She looked up as he rounded the sofa. Lying across his forearms appeared to be an encyclopedia.

"Berek!" Ursula almost yelled.

"It's 1,213 pages." He grinned. "But it is double-spaced." His face went to that faraway focus she'd seen several times now. "Best you read just the beginning and then decide if you want to read the rest," he advised. Ursula did not hear the heavy seriousness of his tone.

He offered her the bundle of pages, held together in a large four-ring binder. Ursula almost laughed at the relief that it wasn't printed back to back. On the front, she was looking at the page sideways, landscape, but she could still read it because there were only two words. She looked up at Berek, who smiled and nodded for her to go on. She turned it around and began to read. On that first page, centered perfectly, were the words:

For Ursula

She looked at him again as he sat down in the armchair. He nodded once more, and she turned the page. Her eyes almost immediately flashed back to Berek's. Again, he only nodded.

- 1 -

Ursula, as you read this, know one thing. You give me rhythm.

That's all there was on the first page. She turned to the next, satisfied that it was full of text, and started to read.

- 2 -

Where to begin? Let us begin at the beginning, for is it not the most logical place to start anything? The beginning is this.

I was born in 1759. My name is Berek Josel, but on the day of my birth, it was Dow Baer Joselewicz. My birthplace was a small city named Kretinga in what is now Poland. What occurred during the next forty-four years is of little consequence now. You see, I died in a battle, the great Battle of Koch in the year 1804.

I died. But was born again.

Ursula read of wars and revolutions, death and constant rebirths. She read about the son of Berek, the only child Berek fathered throughout his many lives, who escaped and took his family to England where he became a successful novelist of his time. Ursula was not surprised.

She was surprised that she was only just over the hundred-page mark. So many lifetimes and she was still reading about the nineteenth century. A thousand more pages to go and well over a hundred more years. But where was she? Where did she fit into this story? She half closed the magnum opus and looked to Berek. Her biggest surprise was the lack of doubt. So far, she believed every word.

"But . . . but what? How?" She cocked her head over to one shoulder.

He didn't acknowledge the cuteness this time, wasn't even aware of it, in fact, concentrating instead on the apparent lack of disbelief. He saw only questions in Ursula's face, bursting forth from every pore. Questions, questions, so many questions, and so far, after more than 250 years and umpteen lives, not one solid, viable answer. He shrugged, as solemn and heavy a shrug as he'd ever delivered in all of his lives.

"I don't know. I wish I did." For a single, tiny moment, the thought crossed his mind, *There goes the best thing I ever had.* Ursula, as usual, surprised him.

"And what about us?"

"You want to know where you and I come in?" Berek smiled as he asked. Ursula didn't trust herself to speak. She nodded meekly. "Page 1,211."

She gaped. "You write over 1,200 pages and only give us two?"

He didn't wonder why she didn't ask anything about what she'd read. He didn't waste time considering whether she believed or not anymore. She would, or she wouldn't. It was Ursula, and there was nothing more to think about.

"Three. Three pages. One year over three pages is a pretty good result, mathematically speaking." He grinned. "Work it out for yourself since you're the numbers specialist. Or, maybe, just read it?" He raised his eyebrows, inviting action or more questions.

She began thumbing through, sure it was fiction but not caring because it was believable even if implausible. She thumped the tome over and flicked back a few fingers' worth of pages, releasing a couple to flutter back until she saw the page number.

- 1,211 -

It was like seeing an angel. Never have I experienced such a moment before, such an epiphany that life for over two centuries was merely to prepare me for this moment. It was just a glance, but oh, such wonder it did bring to my heart. I am a man, and men are such brutal, realistic brutes, so to feel what I did then made me as the child I was two centuries before. For the very first time, I was in love. Real love.

Whomever first anointed that love at first sight is some mythical beast did not witness that first touch of eyes between Ursula and me. That person was probably a man.

A green more lovely than any grassy mountain, a glimmering pair of eyes that I believed could see straight through me. They did so, they did just that, and she was as aware of me as I of her, even though distance and surrounds were not our friend. Did she love me as I loved her, immediately? I doubt it, for such are these times, things like that remain ensconced in books of romance and fairy tales only. And dreams. Certainly mine.

We did not dither; we fell into each other like two opposing magnets, drawn inexorably to what is good and true. Never once have I doubted that force.

Her name is Ursula, and with all that is within me to express, it superimposes into three simple words. I love you.

She read on, heart warming to every word. He summarized every meeting with friends, family, but used more detail in the time they spent together, in the apartment, on a short trip away, even at cafés, restaurants, shopping, and walks in the park. She turned the page.

More and more she read until arriving at the final paragraph, and she saw he was addressing her directly in the first person. She glanced quickly at him sitting there confidently and flicked her eyes back down to the paragraph.

Ursula. I have all confidence in you, and complete confidence in us. You have shown me a different way of life. I have trod a road with you the like I have never before envisaged and each and every day brings you, and that breath of fresh air you exude onto all blessed to be in your presence. Your presence is everything that I never knew existed and now is simply everything to me. I love you, Ursula, and I always will.

She quickly turned the page, the final page. Just like the cover, there were only two words. Centered, directly in the middle. Two words that leaped off the page like a 3-D hologram. She burst into tears, wiping blindly at the page so she didn't smudge those two words.

MARRY ME?

To learn more about this author, please visit: https://www.facebook.com/darktimesinlove/

What Dwells in REM

Fantasy

E. R. Smo

Prompt: Beware the shadows.

*P*APERS LAY SCATTERED AROUND the living room of the small apartment, torn from their original binding. Each held a quick sketch, whether it be a person, an object, or scenery. To most people without the talent, the doodles would be impressive, perhaps even creative. But to Ryan, none of them were right.

Lately, he'd been copying what he'd seen elsewhere, his own creativity blocked. Slumped on the couch, he could think of nothing else, even with his girlfriend sitting next to him gently rubbing his back with one hand, the other holding a gift.

"So, you're in a rut. It happens. Don't worry so much about it. It'll all come to you when you least expect it," Emma said, staring at him from behind a few strands of auburn hair.

"Yeah, because you know all about being an artist, right?" Ryan asked, rolling his eyes.

Emma's hand stopped, retreating to grip the box with both hands. "Well, here. Happy birthday," she said with a forced smile.

When she offered the gift, he took it and half-heartedly tore off the red-and-gold-patterned wrapping paper. Ryan appreciated her consideration but couldn't express it. The idea of a relationship had become less appealing over the past several months. He removed the lid. A pencil lay inside: black instead of yellow, illegible writing etched into the side, and perfectly sharpened. As if he didn't have about fifty pencils lying around somewhere.

"The person at the shop said the writing means 'This tool will solve all of your problems.' So I figured, why not? Maybe it'll help you get out of your funk," Emma said, eagerly glancing between Ryan and the pencil.

"What, like some sort of therapist pencil or something? Uh, yeah. Thanks." He closed the box and set it beside him on the couch, not even glancing her way. This was like buying her a bobby pin for her birthday.

Emma huffed. "You could at least show a little bit of appreciation. I bought it to help you, you know."

"You bought an artist a pencil for his birthday. It's a little . . . thoughtless . . . don't you think?" Keeping his eyes elsewhere, he tossed the wrapping paper at her. The pencil itself didn't matter too much. Each time he spoke, he mentally kicked himself for his attitude. Though not enough to apologize.

"What the hell is wrong with you?" Emma stood, fists clenched at her sides, then paused. Her face softened for a second as if internally she'd answered her own question. "I love you, or at least the you that you used to be. But for the past several months you've been taking your frustrations out on me. Do you really think so little of me?" She released an exacerbated sigh. "I can't deal with this anymore. Sorry for trying to help." Without glancing back, she left the apartment, slamming the door behind her.

Ryan grunted, hunched over, and covered his face with his hands. Upsetting her gave him no pleasure, but in the long-term, this was probably best. Six months ago, he may have been naïve enough to believe in true, happy relationships. But, not anymore. He'd seen the truth himself, and it wasn't worth trying.

For the remainder of the day and evening, he stayed glued to the couch, occasionally grabbing his sketchbook and drawing something on a blank page before ripping it out in frustration, each sheet fluttering to the floor. Today had been a repeat of the last six months and put a halt to adding anything worthwhile to his art portfolio. On occasion, he came up with what he thought to be an original idea, yet he couldn't transfer it accurately from his head to paper. He felt as though he'd actually eaten a pencil from the taste of eraser rubber and the smell of wood after chewing on his tool throughout the day.

Checking the time on the cable box, bed sounded like a good idea. Nearly midnight, he needed to get some manner of sleep. He began to push himself off the couch but stopped as his left hand rested on the box with Emma's gift inside.

"Solve all my problems, huh? Stupid." Even so, it came from Emma. Though he'd been fighting with the idea of ending the relationship for his own protection, that didn't make her any less special. Grabbing it and his sketchbook, he entered his room, tossed them on the bed, and began his nightly routine: changing into pajamas and brushing his teeth.

He picked them up again when he finished and sat on his comforter. One more sketch before he turned in.

After mulling it over for a minute, he took the black pencil and touched it to paper. If nothing else the pencil did seem to feel a bit more natural than some of his others. The lines came easier, and the grip was comfortable. After two minutes of sketching and the occasional erasing, he examined his work: a simple, undetailed sketch depicting a samurai sword. He took another look. As easy as such a thing should've been to draw, his shading wasn't quite right, and the overall appearance seemed boring and traditional. Staring, he attempted to figure out a way to make it more unique, but nothing came to mind that wasn't cheesy or childish. He simply couldn't focus on it with so many combating thoughts about his relationship with Emma flooding his mind. Groaning, he placed the sketchbook and pencil on the nightstand, turned off his light, then curled up in bed and closed his eyes.

Standing among swirly black smoke that coated the ground, Ryan stared in awe at the void. No, not smoke. The deep darkness and the way it reflected light, it was more like ink, or some combination of the two. Aside from the ink, which reached no higher than his ankles, gray filled the rest of existence. He couldn't call it cloudy — more like someone took a gray sheet of paper, colored the ground black, then stopped. Glancing down at himself, he'd intended to make sure he was normal but then realized that he held a sword in his hand. Examining the blade, the hilt, and the guard, there could be no doubt. He held the same sword he'd drawn before bed, including faint remnants of the lines he'd erased as if he held a physical manifestation of his drawing in his hand. Running his index finger over the sharp edge of the blade, he yelped and quickly pulled it back. Droplets of blood fell from the fresh cut in his skin.

"What is going on?" he asked aloud. He'd never been in a dream and known it. He sucked on the cut and began to walk, though he had no destination. Perhaps one didn't exist here.

After several steps, the black ink ahead of him rose and twisted around itself, forming a vague, humanoid figure. He stopped, heart thumping in his chest.

The shadow took long strides toward him, and Ryan brandished his lazily sketched sword with both hands.

"Hey, don't move!" He swung the blade from side to side, hoping it would keep the figure at bay. It didn't. "What is this place? And what are you?" The shadow remained silent as it drew closer. When close enough to strike, Ryan slashed through its head, which reformed instantly.

Before he could bring the sword back for another swing, the figure wrapped its fingers around Ryan's throat and squeezed. He could hardly breathe. Any attempt to grab at the hand or arm left his own brushing through it as if it weren't there. Small gasps escaped as he tried to fill his lungs. The figure reared its other hand back, then thrust its hand toward Ryan's face.

Ryan shot up to a sitting position in his bed, coated in sweat. He coughed between gasps, desperate to fill his lungs with air again. A dream. One hell of a dream, but a dream nonetheless. His inner child took over, and he slid his upper body over the edge of the bed and peeked underneath. Nothing. Of course, nothing.

"Jeez! Get ahold of yourself," he muttered. His hand balled into a fist. A sharp pain resonated from his index finger. Slowly uncurling his fingers, he glanced down and noticed the cut on his index finger. Was that his mind playing tricks on him? No, this was real. How? He glanced at the clock. If he mulled it over much longer he'd be late for work. He pushed himself out of bed to start his routine: shower, eat breakfast, brush his teeth, put a Band-Aid on his finger, and head to work, all the while attempting to mentally solve this puzzle.

Even at his day job, while pulling up customer auto insurance information on the computer, and occasionally being yelled at, the dream was foremost on his mind. If it wasn't for the cut on his finger, he could have pushed the experience away by now. Maybe Emma could give some insight on . . . No. He had to stop relying on her, or risk ending up like his mother. What she thought was love turned out to be an illusion. Why would the same not be true for Emma and him?

* * *

ONCE WORK ENDED, HE headed home and put his favorite frozen pizza in the oven. Cheap, but delicious. He ate dinner then went to his bedroom, propped his pillows against the wall behind his bed, and tried to relax. Before reaching for any of his tools, he grabbed his phone and placed a call.

"Hi Ry-ry. How's your day going?"

That nickname. She still had to call him that. "Hi, Mom. It's whatever. Just a workday. How are things?"

"The usual."

"Are you feeling okay? How's the recovery going?" If he didn't specifically ask, she wouldn't bring it up herself. Stubborn woman.

"I keep telling you it's going fine. I'm still doing light exercises and no problems. Stop worrying so much."

"Of course I'm going to worry. You should have let me move back home to help you."

"Ryan." His mother sighed. "It's been six months. If I've managed on my own this long, I'll be fine for the foreseeable future. Besides, I'm almost back to normal. You have your own life, and I'm fine. You can visit any time, but I can handle myself."

She wasn't wrong. If that weren't true, she'd be the dead one instead of his dad. Picturing him made his body tense. He'd never been a particularly violent man, and his parents always seemed happy, but Ryan supposed he never could truly know someone . . . or trust someone. All it took was one instance of anger reaching the boiling point, and his mother found herself with a knife in her gut. An act returned in kind. Receiving the news his mother was in the hospital in critical condition, and the reason why, had consumed his mind ever since. It caused him to question the idea of love—who one could trust. Anytime he attempted to create a work of art, these concerns whispered to him from the back of his mind, sabotaging any focus he could muster. "I will visit you soon. Maybe spend a weekend."

"I look forward to it. How's Emma? She needs to come, too."

"She . . . We're sort of . . . maybe or maybe not together anymore. I don't know."

"What? Why? What happened?" his mother asked, though it sounded more like an order to tell her.

"I don't want to talk about it. We're just having issues." That was putting it mildly. "Anyway, I'll let you know when I can come visit. I'll make sure it's soon. Love you."

"Okay, then. I love you, too."

He hung up and sighed, reaching for the black pencil and sketchbook. After several minutes of stretching his mind in all different directions, inspiration struck. This would be no mere sketch. Over the course of several hours, he ignored the dull pain of the pencil against his cut and drew a landscape view that showed a single street of a medieval town. Straw roofs, sturdy wooden studs lining the exteriors of each building, wooden signs above the doors identifying each business. Once he finished the initial drawing, he went over it all again with a thin felt-tip pen so it didn't look so sketchy. He then erased any remaining pencil marks. Ryan smiled at the final product. Though not quite up to par with his older work, it was certainly an improvement over what he'd created the last several months. He'd have to enjoy it more tomorrow. Already he'd stayed up too late—nearly midnight again—though thankfully he had the day off tomorrow.

Placing the sketchbook and pen aside, his eyes fell to his phone. Emma hadn't texted him all day, likely still upset. Whatever. She had no reason to be upset. She'd overreacted. Simple as that. Turning off the light, he curled up under his comforter and closed his eyes, allowing his head to sink into the pillow. Expecting him to get excited over some voodoo pencil for his birthday? Yeah, she overreacted.

Similar to the previous night, Ryan found himself standing ankle-deep in gaseous ink. The gray sky looked almost grainy, like a sheet of paper if he looked closely enough. Yet this time, he did not stand in a void. Hand-drawn buildings surrounded him as well as a variety of odds and ends: barrels, crates, and vendor stands. Like the sword from last night's dream, he stood within his own drawing.

"This is too weird. Again?" He gazed around, somewhat in awe of standing in the middle of his work, receiving a new perspective he could never have otherwise experienced. Crouching, he ran his hand over a barrel. Despite it consisting of black lines, he could feel the vertical ridges as if it were made of wood. Perhaps because his mind knew what it should be? Also peculiar, since he hadn't colored this drawing, he'd assumed everything would be transparent. Instead, while everything outside the black lines held the same gray color as the sky, the items and structures had solid exteriors.

Standing upright, he slowly wandered through the short street, this medieval town only being as large as what he could fit on paper. He rolled his eyes when he saw occasional pencil marks he'd failed to erase, or at least completely. Between this and the sword, he clearly needed to be more vigilant with that. Six months ago he never would have been so sloppy.

"I guess this is actually pretty cool. So long as I don't . . ." Ryan paused. On the far side of the road, the shadowy figure from the previous night appeared again. "Crap," he mumbled, stepping backward.

As the figure approached, Ryan turned and ran. When he glanced behind him, the figure had already closed half the distance between them. He made a sharp right, slipping through the gap between two buildings. If only he'd drawn more space between them. Back pressed against the wall, he panted, more out of fear than lack of breath.

His eyes fell to the cut on his index finger, and he remembered his lack of breath when he woke from the last dream. Allowing that creature to get its hands on him couldn't be an option. Slowly, he slid along the wall until he reached the corner then peered around. No sign of it. Ryan inched along the adjacent wall, careful to keep his breathing as quiet as possible. It didn't help. The dark figure's hand grasped the back of his head and forced him to the ground face-first. Thrashing, he managed to roll onto his back and stared up at the shadowy silhouette between the dark, almost fluid fingers that gripped his face. It lowered its head to rest inches from his own. The shadows shifted and twisted, starting to form a face.

For the second morning in a row, Ryan shot awake, panting, shirt soaked in sweat. He ran his fingers gently over his face, swearing he could still feel the grip of that thing. This was getting ridiculous. Having completely skipped the groggy phase of waking up, Ryan grabbed his phone and dialed Emma's number.

"Hi, Ryan," Emma said, her voice soft yet hopeful.

"Where did you get that pencil?" Ryan asked, standing from the bed.

"Um, there was an antique shop downtown, next to that ice cream shop on Fourth Street. Why the sudden interest?"

"I'm pretty sure you bought me a cursed pencil. I've been having weird dreams since I started using it."

Her huff traveled through the phone. "Don't blame me for some weird dreams. It was supposed to help you, you know."

"Well, it's likely going to kill me instead." Ryan paced around his room.

"Don't you dare accuse me of being out to get you. Jerk!" The call ended.

Ryan released a loud grunt and chucked his phone onto his pillow. He didn't know if his bubbling rage was directed at Emma or himself. After several deep breaths to compose himself, he glanced at the black pencil on his bedside stand. He reached for it and ran his finger over the engraving. "Solve all my problems, my ass."

After showering and eating, Ryan left the apartment. The ice cream shop was close enough to walk to and not waste money on public transit, although close still meant a thirty-minute walk. When he arrived, he stood out front. A barbershop sat to the right. She certainly didn't buy it there. To the left was the antique shop Emma mentioned. It didn't look different from any other shop, though the interior could use more lighting.

Wasting no time, he walked in and approached the counter an elderly woman tended. She had so many lines on her face, she could've been considered an antique herself.

"Excuse me. My girlfriend bought some black pencil in a black box from this shop. Is there anything you can tell me about it?"

The woman's eyes had been on him since he entered, a soft smile on her face. "Oh? A black pencil . . . Yes, I remember that," she said in a slow, raspy voice. "Let's see. That was purchased recently from a collector of antique art tools, who obtained it about . . ." Her eyes fell to the counter, finger tapping on the wood as if trying to remember. "Oh." She raised her eyes to Ryan again. "I believe he said he obtained it about thirty years ago. The man said it was carved out of an old voodoo wood golem from somewhere in West Africa, quite illegally actually. But don't worry, you won't be arrested for it nowadays." She chuckled. "I bought it from that man rather cheap. He seemed quite eager to be rid of it."

Ryan's brow quirked. "That's a hell of a history for a pencil."

The woman chuckled again. "If I had to guess, the original creator likely thought carving it from a voodoo golem would give it some sort of mystic power. But that is only a guess."

"Is there any way to stop what it does?"

She tilted her head slightly. "I'm sorry. I don't know what you're referring to exactly. I know nothing more than what I've already told you."

Ryan closed his eyes and sighed. "Okay. Thanks." Leaving the shop, he started back home. The other day he'd never have believed such words. Today, the information sounded as true as his own name.

* * *

RYAN LAY ON HIS bed, unsure of what to do. He couldn't exactly look up voodoo pencil and see what came up. At least he had the day off from work, giving him the chance to think about his current predicament. It had to do with that pencil, he just knew it. He considered breaking it, but what if the dreams continued with no way to stop them? That night he attempted to draw a pair of pistols to see what happened when an average number two pencil was used. Hardly a true artistic tool, but it didn't get more common than that. Anything more elaborate, and he'd be unlikely to figure out how to use them, as he'd never fired a gun in his life. Before the first line could be drawn, the yellow pencil morphed into the voodoo pencil, *like a dissolve video transition. "Fantastic. So much for not using the creepy pencil," he muttered.*

He fell asleep and found himself once more in a void, no hand-drawn scenery to hide behind. When the figure appeared, Ryan wasted no time firing his pistols. They worked as intended and fired bullets, but each flew through the approaching figure and did no harm. Frustrated, he threw the guns and ran.

He didn't get far. The creature grabbed and yanked what it could of his short, black hair with one hand and choked him with the other. Kicking, punching, trying to pull away—nothing he did helped. His vision blurred and muscles grew weak. Right before he would have fallen to his knees, he awoke.

He felt the back of his head and his hand came back with some loose hair. Not enough to leave a bald spot, but enough that it couldn't be seen as normal. It seemed weapons wouldn't do him much good. Maybe something else.

In his dream the following night, he stood on the beach he'd drawn before falling asleep, though the waves didn't move. At least he thought to color it this time. If he failed and died, he might as well be somewhere pretty. Once again, the figure appeared. As it approached, it stepped on a plate hidden under the sand. The plate sprung, walls bursting forth and trapping it in a solid steel box.

"Ha! That's what you get!" Ryan kicked the wall then pressed his face against it to allow his voice to reach his enemy. "What do you say now? Ready to talk yet?"

Its hand phased through the wall and grasped Ryan's throat. The rest of its body followed. Ryan growled and punched at its head, though as always, his fists hit nothing solid. Its face began to take shape again. Nose, lips, eyes—though it didn't finish before he woke up again.

Weapons didn't work; neither did traps. He couldn't hide, either. What else could there be? Unfortunately, he had to think it over while at work. His performance suffered: he stared off into space, not hearing what customers said over the phone. But, he didn't care. The dreams left him exhausted; even his coworkers commented on how terrible he looked. This had to end. Four nights of dealing with that creature were too much.

By the time he returned home, he had another idea. Perhaps he could outnumber the creature. So he got to work, drawing an army of soldiers with various weapons: broadswords, axes, polearms. Even if the weapons didn't help, the individuals should still be solid. Perhaps they could pile onto it and keep it trapped. Having a large group of living beings — for lack of a better term — might work better than a solid wall.

No scenery this time. Ryan stood among a group of twenty soldiers clad in armor and ready for battle. As expected, his shadowy nemesis appeared.

"Charge!" Ryan shouted, and they obeyed his command.

As they ran, one soldier caught his eye before being hidden by others. He was sure he'd only drawn male soldiers donning helmets, yet he saw a head of long, wavy auburn hair among their ranks. They struck with their weapons, but like the ones he'd used, these phased through the creature and did nothing to stop its advance. It seemed the creature only had eyes for Ryan, completely ignoring the hand-drawn army.

Soldiers tried to grab it with their bare hands, yet once again they failed. But it did give Ryan an idea.

"Keep at it! Swipe away at its body until there is nothing left," he shouted.

They did just that, using their arms to slash through the gaseous shadow, continuing to dissipate its body before it could reform. Ryan released a sigh of relief when no trace of it could be found. Finally, he allowed his body to relax. The soldiers cheered in a group of manly voices, accented by one feminine.

Before they knew it, the figure reappeared amid their ranks. One by one, it crushed their heads and ripped holes in their bodies, completely bypassing their armor. Though they were only colorless drawn people and no gore or blood could be seen, it was no less horrifying to watch.

The last of the soldiers was no soldier at all. It was a woman in shorts and a T-shirt. She backed away, frightened, shivering.

Ryan stared with wide eyes, no longer breathing. Had he drawn her without noticing? Her facial features were more pronounced. The style of her hair, the shape of her body—there could be no mistake. Emma.

She turned to run, but it grabbed the back of her shirt. She reached out for Ryan, tears streaming down her face. Her frown and wide eyes showed the poor woman was terrified beyond belief. The creature grabbed her hair and pulled back hard. The other hand pulled her wrists behind her back, and its foot kicked at the back of her legs to get her onto her knees.

Real or fake, he couldn't stand to see Emma like that. Did she feel this way in the real world when dealing with him? Did he frighten her, upset her this much in both reality and in this dream world? Before his mind registered the actions of his body, he ran toward them. He reared his fist back, then thrust it at the creature's head. Somehow his strike connected, sending it falling hard to the ground. Ryan glanced at Emma. She stared back like a frightened child. As the creature tried to stand, Ryan leaped at it, tackling it to the ground. He straddled its hips, punching at its face, releasing all his frustration over his inability to do anything before now.

Another punch. Another. He went for it again but paused. The creature, with its face fully formed, stared back. Its features were pronounced now.

Ryan's own face stared back.

The rest of his body took shape, wearing the same white T-shirt and blue pajama pants as Ryan. It grinned.

"Look at you, acting like a good guy. Why do you care? Who needs her, right?" Its voice sounded like his own, with a slight high-pitched echo trailing behind each word.

"Shut up!" Ryan shouted, punching across its jaw. It groaned.

"You don't want to get rid of me. I keep you safe. Without me, you'd just trust anyone who says they love us without a second thought. You saw how that worked out for Mom. With a knife through the gut by the man she shared vows with." It reached up and gripped Ryan's hair tight. "I'll make sure you don't make that same mistake."

Ryan turned, staring at the frightened image of Emma, who stared back. Emma, a mistake? One day he could be in the same situation that befell his mother. Or perhaps not. Would it be worth the loneliness for the remainder of his life to avoid such an outcome that had a minuscule chance of becoming reality?

His teeth clenched, and his fist tightened. "Not worth it. I'm done being afraid of a problem that doesn't exist. And I'm done breaking her heart because of my own cowardice." Staring down at his shadowy self and with a loud cry, he thrust his fist into its head.

From top to bottom, its body began to dissolve, the remnants like shredded paper floating into the air then disappearing completely. Ryan exhaled heavily then stood. Emma did the same and ran toward him, arms open. Before he could grab her, Ryan woke up.

The white ceiling of his bedroom consumed his view for several minutes as he lay unmoving. He felt lighter somehow. When he finally found the will to move, he sat up and stared at the black pencil on the bedside stand, and his phone next to it. Retrieving his phone, he selected Emma's number. To his surprise, she answered.

"What?" she asked angrily.

Instead of returning the harsh emotion, he spoke in a softer voice than he remembered using in a long time. "Hey. Can we talk?"

To learn more about this author, please visit:
https://www.facebook.com/E.R.SmoAuthor

Tempus Fugit

Suspense

Tyronica Smith

Prompt: You are lost.
and
Prompt: Dreams last longer when you . . .

*D*EAR READER,
  I confess, I do not know what you'll make of the things you see here. For all you know, this is just the disjointed ramblings of a crazy woman . . . or the unfortunate glimpses of reality from a person with a gift. I'll need you to be the judge. You'll read these things and will not believe them. You will think this is all some story created for your entertainment. You found these writings among others and you will believe this all to be a work of fiction, that I am a work of fiction — but I assure you, I am very real. Characters don't go about asserting themselves in reality, do they? I don't think so either. Never read of one that questioned their existence or that of their readers for that matter. And if anything I speak of here matters to both of us . . . it will be what you perceive.

  I am going to lay out for you the events that happened over the course of my week and, well, I need your help. I battle with truth every day. Not in the way that others do — I fight with the validity of things . . . the realness of people. So there are some rules you will need to understand.

First, once our minds make up what we'll see, that image remains. Those fleeting figments of our imagination — our dreams — are much the same. Nothing is set in stone in the wake of a summer night. Be careful what you wish for or your dreams will take flight.

Second, dreams last longer when you don't realize you're dreaming, but the moment you do and realization sets in, you find yourself back in Kansas with a knot the size of Texas on your forehead and an ache that won't quit. At least Dorothy was able to find her way home in the midst of her chaos and consternation. Whereas I struggle, even now, to know the difference. We'll press on. Those two rules boil down to this: our minds are our own worst enemies.

Got it? Understand these things as best as you can. We'll start from here.

I used to wonder why we always associated dreams with nightfall when they very well happen during the waking day. I'm not talking about daydreams. I mean full-on lucid visions that disrupt our lives from time to time. Maybe I'm thinking of hallucinations . . . which would make sense given my mental state as of late.

Bear with me, dear Reader — all is not as it appears.

My mama always used to say, "Ain't nothing in the dark that wasn't there in the light." She got that saying from Grandma Flora. I didn't believe either one of them, so I would lie in bed with the nightstand lamp or flashlight on. To calm my fears, beneath my covers I would rattle off a series of prayers in the merciful God's ear like I did last night. I'd find out for a fact that my dear mother was wrong.

I was just coming out of a dark place where all manner of monsters and demons lurked in the shadowy spaces of my mind. I'm finding the darkness lingers in ways I can no longer imagine; there simply is no need to stretch my brain for such. Our imaginations *either work with us or against us—and that is a truth. I landed in a place where everything around me seemed so surreal. This was real. Darkness is a hell all its own, and what roams there is the stuff of nightmares, but nothing can prepare you for the mind game that is reality.*

When I finally came out of the nether of mental illness, I realized I was lost. I couldn't help but think I was on the path of Alice being led away from all that was sane. That the things I'd gone through were just figments of my imagination and fragments of a broken mind. "No such thing as demons, personal or otherwise," Mama would say. "Just the ornery things that people did and the bad decisions they made." She'd reiterate over and over to calm my fears that no such things ever existed. "The monsters that roam about the earth are the ones we've created—no one is born that way." Makes sense doesn't it? How could you argue with that? More importantly, how could I know they were real when she never prepared me and dispelled all my doubts with her reasoning? What chance did I have against them? A snowball's chance in hell still left room for hope where I had none. I was told to abandon it along with anything else at the gate as if I were invited, when it was more like being thrust in without warning.

* * *

IT WAS AROUND THREE O'CLOCK *in the morning, what they call the witching hour, when my new tattoo began to itch. Dear Reader, please understand this was no ordinary itch. This was a beneath-the-skin irritation that just wouldn't let up no matter how hard I scratched or what moisturizer I used. It was around 5 a.m. that same morning when I realized something had changed.*

Let me explain.

A week ago, I decided to commemorate a very important time in my life with a tattoo. I'd been scoping it out for weeks. The tat was of an open pocket watch set among a bouquet of red roses. The time on the pocket watch was 10:10. The precise time my whole world changed and became a bit sadder than it already was.

As I sat in the chair and tried to remain still while the artist etched the image into my skin, my vision did that thing again. Where I saw images overlaid on reality, causing me confusion. I sat tight-lipped as my mind and eyes contrived to deceive me. I knew full well what was happening. I was hallucinating. One of the fun parts of being schizophrenic is losing yourself in the world your mind creates at inopportune times. I didn't understand it. I'd been on medicine and in therapy for four years when that happened. It was the middle of the day and I hadn't been stressed out or anything. It just happened.

There she was, narrowing her brown eyes at me in the indignation of my refusal to acknowledge her presence aloud. I'd never seen her so angry. The last time I saw her, she was full of peace and strength, not a lick of regret or resentment in her. But that day, she looked highly pissed to see me in that chair getting a tattoo. I knew what was real then. I knew there was no way I could be seeing her like that, but yet and still, there she stood with her hands on her hips, tapping her foot away on the checkered floor of the parlor.

I closed my eyes and hummed a tune to myself and the artist laughed at me, probably believing me to be deflecting the pain he was causing elsewhere—when in reality, I felt very little physical pain at all. However, my heart wrenched in my chest. I listened as the artist sat his instrument down and asked that I give him a second. I nodded my approval.

"Not now . . . not here! Get a grip, girl," I said under my breath, trying my best to calm and rid myself of what I was seeing. Then she spoke.

"Here is as good a place as any." I slid down in my chair as my heart leaped at her words. "I have something to tell you and you are going to listen."

Feeling compelled to respond to the apparition before me, I mumbled under my breath, "Yes, ma'am," so as not to look strange to the other artists and clients in the shop.

"If you won't see me here — I'll see you there." My heart all but stopped beating in my chest. I think maybe it skipped beats. What did she mean she would see me there? I was too afraid to ask and just shook my head no.

I opened my eyes to see her cross her arms over her chest, still tapping that foot of hers in those house shoes that made an audible rapping against the floor. Rick, the artist, was on his way back and walked right through her — whereupon she disappeared back into the nether. I remarked to myself how strong the hallucinations were getting. There was no way it should have been that real.

Listen . . . I question my sanity on a daily basis and answer in the same breath most days that everything is fine. But that day gave me reason to think otherwise. Grandma always said, "Nothing haunts us more than the things we don't say." Or was it the actions we refuse to take out of fear of failure? I remember her saying both on separate occasions. She said they seem to revolve around us — piercing our minds with the woulda, shoulda, couldas that escaped us and left us behind haunted and stuck.

When the tattoo artist finished, I stood up from the chair and took a good stretch. Much to my surprise, it was raining. I wondered how I would fare in the elements with my new ink. Would the thin plastic cover over the tattoo be enough? I had not thought of wearing a jacket nor had I paid any attention to the weather forecast before I left. It had been so hot that day, I'd decided on a tank top for easier access to my arm and to remain cool in the heat.

A sickly image of it melting from my arm and dripping to the ground, forming puddles of colorful molten flesh, filled my mind as I gently rubbed at the reddening site. My arm was sore but not in terrible pain. I shook the gross thoughts away as best I could and tried to pay attention to the artist. He gave me a list of instructions on how to care for the tattoo during its healing process; all I had to *do was stick to the program and everything would be fine. I paid the man and left his shop.*

I briskly walked home, the whispers of people's voices circling me — so much so that I kept looking back to see who may have been following. There was no one. Just me on the sidewalk in the rain, nearly running with no umbrella. Having shaken away the voices, ghostly images began to appear in my vision of things that couldn't possibly be there. Faceless people, giant spiders crawling up the sides of buildings, and the bats . . . my god, the bats. I looked down on the sidewalk and mistook a pigeon scavenging for food as one of them. My heart thumped wildly in my chest as I tried to focus on the real things in front of me. The lamppost was real. The sidewalk was not lava but concrete. The man walking slowly on the other side of the street with a cigarette hanging from his lips beneath his umbrella was questionable . . . and I was real, too. I had an ache in my arm to prove it. Pain is the realest thing there is.

Here was another incident etched into my belt. I broke into a run with the feeling that I was being watched too closely or hunted. But I realized there was nothing chasing me out into the street. A car swerved to miss me on the wet pavement then slid to a complete stop and nearly hit a delivery truck parked on the side of the road. That snapped everything back to reality for me. Despite the gray stormy day, all was clear and bright in my eyes. I was soaked to my soul in the middle of the street with my eyes clenched shut, until the man got out of his car to see if I was all right.

"What possessed you to run out in the street like that, gal?" he asked, and for a minute I heard my grandmother's voice asking the same thing. I was quickly tossed back into a memory of running after a ball that rolled into the street and being reprimanded for doing such. Much like this older gentleman was doing. "Pay attention!" he said in my grandmother's voice. "Do you hear me?" This time they spoke together. "Wake up!" I snapped back to the present, clutching my purse to my chest. I stared into the stranger's green eyes and nodded my head as a weak "okay" left my lips. He walked me over

to the sidewalk where I crumpled like the wet thing I was. I stayed there for a moment too long. People slowed down to look at me, but none stopped to help. I pulled myself upward and leaned against the red brick of a pizzeria, its pleasant scent reminding me that all I'd had was water. Drinking it, soaked in it—and soon, bathing in it.

Having been "cleansed" by the elements, I felt a bit heavier than when I left the tattoo parlor. The day was quickly going downhill. A shower was needed. Twice I was splashed by cars hitting puddles at high speeds. I know the kind of devil that leaps inside people when they see a pedestrian in the rain. Far too often he wins, leaving us poor souls drenched due to their wayward proclivities.

During my shower was the first time I noticed it. The tingling in my arm just beneath the skin of my tattoo. Just a tingle—like menthol rubbed heavily across the skin. I gently lathered the soap over the tattoo as instructed, rinsed, and finished with the rest of my body. As I stepped out of the shower, patting my body dry, I saw the redness on my arm. I was confident that it was due to the tattoo being fresh and thought nothing more of it. I applied my usual moisturizer to my skin and a healing ointment I bought at the local pharmacy.

I ordered food from the little Italian restaurant on the corner and they delivered, but after the day's events, my appetite was shot. I lay down on the couch with my bowl of chicken fettuccine and willed myself to eat. After a couple of bites, I rested the bowl on the coffee table then lay back staring at the rain falling on the other side of the window behind the sofa. I hadn't bothered to turn on the television; I just wanted to hear the rain. When I looked at the dark screen where nothing played, I saw her. She was standing to the side of me, arms outstretched in a gesture for me to come to her. I looked at the dead air between me and the small kitchen of my apartment where she stood in the reflection of the television screen. No one was there.

I closed my eyes tightly and whispered to myself, "No, no, no . . . This can't be." When I opened my eyes, she didn't speak this time. Instead she lifted a finger to her lips and patted the air with the other hand — in a gesture for me to calm down — then dropped her arms to her sides and turned to walk away. I stood and walked to the kitchen cabinet where I kept my medications. I dropped an anxiety med and a sleeping pill into the palm of my hand and threw them to the back of my throat, then chased them with water. I wanted it to stop. I would've taken another pill for the hallucinations, but the bottle said one at bedtime. I plopped back down on the sofa and rubbed the soreness around my new tat. I hadn't noticed how sore it was until then.

That was last week.

Last night was a different story. I'm not sure if I was awake, hallucinating, or dreaming. She was there again. Repeating words I didn't know or understand the meaning of. In one breath she was stating, "Tempus fugit," and in another, "Tempus neminem manet." She was stern about the second grouping of words. I know next to nothing about what sounded like Latin to me so I wrote it all down as best I could. I didn't even recognize my own handwriting. I remember grandma having a scrawl similar to what I'd written. The thought of her acting through me made my head hurt.

I took my phone and began to search for the words. *Tempus fugit* means "time flies." *Tempus neminem manet* means "time waits for no one." I didn't know why she chose to pass that on from the afterlife. I couldn't quite wrap my mind around it all. As I thought back to that day in the tattoo parlor, my ink not only began to itch but burn as well. It had been irritated from me scratching it off and on, rubbing at it incessantly, and applying the wrong stuff to it to get the itch to calm.

I was floored when I looked at it in the mirror.

The hands on the clock had moved.

I visibly shook all over. I know for a fact that the pocket watch read 10:10. I looked at it before I left the parlor that day. Looking at it in the mirror made me question my sanity once more. The hands read 12:00 and it was midnight. There was redness all over the tattoo site and a deep purple beneath the hands of the watch. I tried to make sense of it all with my feeble mind. I must have stood looking in the mirror for an hour, washing the tattoo over and over thinking the watch hands would go back to their original setting. That didn't work.

Then I had the bright idea that I was still dreaming. So I did a little more than pinch myself—I inflicted a bit of pain. Something sure to wake me up. I rushed toward the living room to the sewing kit I kept beneath one of the side tables and extracted a large sewing needle. I made sure its tip was sharp. I didn't prick my finger. I dragged the sharp point over the tender part of my wrist and watched as blood blossomed to the surface of my skin. It hurt but not more than receiving the tattoo did.

Something was happening beneath my skin. I wasn't sure what it was. I wiped away the blood and prepared to pull the sleeve down. I stopped mid-roll and stared at where I'd dragged the needle across my skin, and sore as it was, there was something else going on. There was a pushing sensation in my arm from the inside. It looked as though my veins were reordering themselves beneath the surface. I peered closer. They weren't veins at all but roots or vines pushing themselves forward and wrapping around my wrist. I squeezed my eyes closed and whispered to myself, "Not there, not there, not there," but it was there.

I reached over to feel them with my free hand, and the vines shot up toward my face, knocking me off the couch and onto the floor. The veins found the floor and started to dig in, leaving me unable to move or get up from my squatting position. I pulled and pulled then hit the vines with my fist, but nothing worked. I let out a scream in an effort to put all my force behind my pulling. There was a loud snap and the vines loosened, releasing me and tossing me on my back. I stood to defend myself against the vines that had grown as tall as I was, swiping and kicking and ducking the shoots that shot out at me. I backed up to a wall rather hard and knocked a mirror down. It shattered on the floor, leaving jagged edges of glass everywhere near the door. I thought to pick up one of the shards and use it as a weapon. No sooner had I had that brilliant idea, the piece of mirror sliced right through my hand, causing me to drop it where I stood. I saw them coming for my throat and flailed my arms against them to keep them from latching on. I continued to kick and scream and shout until I found myself backed into a corner.

The hands on my tattooed watch were moving slowly toward the hour. I gripped my shoulder with my free hand to ease the hurt. My body shook at the pain. With each tick toward the hour, the pain pulsed beneath my skin. The hands kept moving while my eyes were on it and that couldn't be.

I took drastic action to stop everything, slapping myself several times until redness formed across my cheeks with a palm print. Nothing worked. I conceived a plan that would stop it all . . . I hadn't caused enough pain before. I needed more pain, a bigger, more vibrant sensation to wake me up. Something that would bring me right out of the carnival of terror and pain I was trapped in. With my bloodied hand, I picked up another shard of mirror and dragged it over the same wound I'd inflicted with the needle, widening the thin line into a gash in my flesh. I screamed out, and there was silence. As if they were phantoms of my imagination and nothing more, they vanished into thin air. All of it.

There were no more vines or roots shooting out of my arm, they weren't there threatening to choke me, and no more noise of them swarming around me. There was no broken mirror, no blood. Just me backed into a corner of my apartment, sweating up a storm and out of breath from what felt and appeared to be real. I opened my clenched fist to see that my acrylic nails had left little crescent-shaped cuts in the palm of my hand. I looked at my tattoo and saw that the hands of the pocket watch were a blur smeared over with blood from my flailing. My mouth dropped open when I looked at my arm. There was no thin line made by a needle, but a nice-sized cut from where something sharp split my skin open. Out of breath, I looked all around to find the source of the harm I'd caused and spotted the flat blade wedged beneath the corner of the wall, firmly planted on the floor. I shook my head quickly and closed my eyes to try to gain some semblance of sanity. I leaned my sweating face against the wall and took deep breaths before heaving myself upward, and found myself face-to-face with an unbroken mirror. Tears of fear for my safety and sorrow for the breaking of my mind ran warm down my cheeks. I'd been fighting an invisible force.

I walked out of the living room sorely defeated. I crossed the hall to go into the bathroom to wash the blood away from my hand and face, then my arm and my tattoo. The clock still read 12:00. I rushed to my bedroom in search of the business card Rick slipped me with his phone number circled, should I need anything more of him. I thought, at that moment, I required something more. It never dawned on me that my eyes may have deceived me in the parlor. Thinking one thing and seeing another causes us to see only what we want to see. I called on him, uncaring of the time of night that it was. That did not matter to me.

I crumpled to my knees in the bedroom at the foot of the bed as lightheadedness overtook me. I was not going to faint; this was too important. I took several breaths and grabbed the nearest article of clothing next to me and put it on. In a hushed whisper I recited the number while pushing the buttons on my cell phone. I waited while the phone rang, trying my hardest to think as clearly as possible. He answered. He didn't sound as if he'd been asleep.

"Hey, Rick, this is Danielle Gwynn. You gave me your card after doing some ink for me last week. I was wondering if you had a minute to talk."

"Sure. Sun's not up yet. I got time. Shoot," he said, to my surprise.

"Well, I don't know if you remember or not, but the tattoo you did was of a pocket watch . . ."

"In roses? Yeah, I remember you. What seems to be the problem?"

"How do you know there's a problem?"

"No one calls me at midnight just to shoot the shit. What's wrong, Danielle?"

"My tattoo . . . the time on it . . ." Hesitant to continue, I wrapped the phone's charger cord around my finger.

"Yeah, I took a picture of it — let me look in my phone." I could hear him humming to himself, the same tune that I hummed when I saw Grandma Flora in his shop. Was he mocking me? "Got it! The time on your tattoo says 10:10. Wasn't that what you wanted? That's what you told me you wanted."

"That is what I wanted, but . . . the tat now . . . it has . . . I mean . . . it says twelve o'clock."

"Bullshit. I have proof right here."

"Well I have proof too, Rick, and it's my fucking arm!" I said, screaming my indignation into the phone. I shook and fumbled the phone, nearly dropping it to the floor and releasing the power cord.

"Calm down . . . Did you go to someone else and do it? Were you drunk or something?" Rick fell silent, either waiting for my reply or thinking deeply about what I'd told him. I could hear audible clicks through the phone. Was he texting while talking to me?

"No! It's been tingling and itching and burning ever since, and now the hands have moved to midnight. If you don't believe me, I can show you!" A rush of anger quickly overtook me. He wasn't taking me or this situation seriously. I calmed myself in order to carry on the conversation.

"Welp, you sure better in order for me to believe this," he said in half a chuckle.

"Where do you live?"

"No, sweetheart, how about I come to you?" Rick sounded amused — as if this were all some game.

"How about we meet halfway? I can catch an Uber to a bar . . ."

"No, I'll come to you. It's too late for you to be traipsing about in the night. Besides, this weather isn't fit for an impromptu rendezvous."

"What about you? Isn't it dangerous for you, too?"

"Nope, can't be afraid of the big bad wolf if you are one." He laughed into the phone. I could hear his smile. It put me at ease.

"Fine. 58 Harlequin Road. Apartment 4B. Buzz me when you get here, and I'll let you up." I could hear more clicking in the phone.

"I'll be there!"

* * *

HE ARRIVED ABOUT TWENTY minutes after I hung up. Later I found out he lived near my place, a few blocks away, and he said my apartment was easy to find. I could hardly wait for him to get there. I'd worn a path in the carpet of my apartment from my pacing around the coffee table and trying to avoid seeing the faceless person and Grandma in the television screen. I turned it on but turned the volume way down. I didn't need the extra noise. My head was loud enough. He came bearing gifts—a vintage wine that he swore he didn't steal from his mother's cabinet when he went to visit her last month. Who am I to judge?

Rick looked around for what I assumed was a boyfriend. He said he hadn't thought that I might have someone with me until he got there. I would have called him anyway, boyfriend or not. This was much too important to me. I showed him in and motioned him to the sofa where I had taken up residence since last week. My apartment was a mess, but Rick didn't seem to mind. The rain was just starting up again. Only this time, there was no storm, just mild thunder and a shower.

Being a courteous hostess, I asked him if he'd like a drink. He nodded his quick agreement as he sat his umbrella in the rack near the door. While I removed two wine glasses from the shelf in the kitchen, Rick took out his phone and scrolled through the images to find the picture of my arm. He found it. He walked over to me and held the phone up to meet my gaze. I swallowed a hard lump in my throat and nearly dropped the glasses. Rick removed them from my hand and, to my surprise, he poured the wine. I did not protest. My week had been filled with me doing things out of character; inviting a complete stranger in for a drink was one of them.

The brief bout of trepidation I had was quickly consumed by the desire to drink and calm my nerves. I sat in the crook of the couch next to Rick. We sipped and made small talk to get over the initial feelings of "stranger discomfort" until we were both at ease.

My head began to hurt, and I didn't know if it was from the wine or the moment causing me discomfort. Rick moved down the sofa to sit right next to me. My right arm throbbed in pain, and the redness from the dried blood was nearly visible through the long sleeve of my white T-shirt. He asked if he could see my arm. I could have patted myself on the back for choosing to put on a camisole beneath the shirt. I switched on a lamp for more light before removing my shirt to show him the tattoo. Rick's jaw dropped.

"What did you do to it?" he said, appalled by what he saw.

"Nothing. I—"

"It's so swollen, and the skin looks like it's about to break." His eyes trailed down to the rest of my arm. "How . . . What did you do to yourself?"

"All I did was scratch and rub it. It's been irritated for a while. Is it infected?"

"Well . . . no. But it shouldn't look like that." His eyes trained downward, pointedly at my wrist. "What about that?"

"Forget all of that—do you see what I was saying about the hands on the clock?" My eyes were desperate, imploring him to see it, too.

Rick sat still a moment. He looked me dead in the eye, then back at my arm, then to his phone. It must have all been a bit too much because he lifted his glass to his lips and didn't put it down until the wine was gone.

"That says twelve," he choked out while using the back of his hand to cover his mouth. "I didn't put twelve on your arm." He poured himself another drink then stood to pace the living room. "How in the hell . . ."

"I don't know. I've been seeing things and hearing things . . . That day in your shop, I saw my grandmother."

"Your grandmother was a customer?"

"No, she's dead. There's no way that should have happened, but it did. She told me she wanted to talk to me and did — in a dream. She told me time flies and time waits for no one, but she said it in Latin. I don't . . . Am I dreaming? Are you real? You seem to be the only thing that's different from last time."

"Last time? What last time? Honey, look at me. I'm as real as you are!"

"Maybe I'm not real," I said, feeling myself slip off into the darkness.

"Snap out of it! What's the matter with you? There's something seriously wrong with this moment."

"I know, and it's threatening to take me with it. God, why can't I wake up?"

"Listen to me, calm down. I'll prove that you are real and that I am real. Okay?"

"How are you going to do that?"

Rick kneeled in front of me and gently rubbed my forearms in his soft, warm hands. I could feel warmth. Just as I could feel the cold of the rain the other day. Just as I could feel the vines moving beneath my skin earlier. He leaned in and kissed me on the cheek, then on the forehead, then on the nose. He leaned back to look at me then kissed me full on the lips. When he was done, he planted another kiss on my forehead.

"You felt that, didn't you?" he whispered in my ear. "It's not always about pain. Sometimes the pleasurable things can bring us out, too."

I looked at him and narrowed my eyes. "What are you doing?"

"I'm trying to show you that you are real and that I am real."

"Why would you kiss me if . . . if this weren't a dream?"

"Why would I circle my number on that card? Why did I charge you half price on that tattoo? Why did I come here instead of being a deadbeat and making you come out in the rain? Why? Why? Why? Because I like you, Danielle," he said, throwing his hands up at his sides.

"What?"

"Remember the first time you came into my shop, scoping out tattoos? Do you remember? I saw you come in and look through the books, look in the magazines, and then at the photo albums, then I would watch you walk out. You did that for a few weeks like you were working your way up to it, and I never said a word."

"That was real?"

"Yes!"

Nervously, I giggled a bit under my breath. Something snapped on the inside. Some sort of cloud seemed to be lifting from my heart and my eyes. I could see him clearer now. I felt a little better. To get me to feel more things other than pain, he tickled me, and I laughed. There was a time when I didn't laugh at all when I was tickled. Some spell seemed to be broken. I could feel my heart thumping in my chest for something not concerning fear.

I looked at Rick and smiled. I lifted my hands to his face and rubbed his cheek, half expecting his face to fall apart in my hands. He leaned into my hand. I closed my eyes, and behind my eyelids was the face of my grandma smiling and clapping. She said, "Wake up now. I have to go."

When I opened my eyes, Rick was saying the same thing. "Wake up now. I have to go."

I hadn't realized I'd fallen asleep. I was lying in his lap while he shimmied out from under me. He stood up and raced toward the bathroom. It was early morning, still dark out. My head hurt and my mouth was dry. We had nearly finished the bottle of wine sitting on the coffee table. There was just enough for two more glasses. I walked to the kitchen with the bottle and glasses in hand. I placed the bottle of white in the fridge and the glasses in the sink. I walked back to the sofa and sat down and before too long I'd fallen back to sleep.

"*Tempus fugit*" played itself over and over in my dreams with various people saying it, some I knew and some I didn't. A scene unfolded of me sitting on the couch in the arms of a stranger whose face I could see. Rick. More unfolded — there on the side table of the couch sat a pocket watch whose hands were spinning out of control. I looked away from it — the spinning made me a bit dizzy. Then I heard what sounded like the bells of a grandfather clock striking the hour. I looked back to the pocket watch and it read 10:10. A sinking feeling hit the pit of my stomach as I looked around the room. She was there — in a hospital bed, hooked up to machines with wires and tubes coming and going from various places. She motioned for me to come to her. I walked over slowly on uneasy legs.

"Chile," she said in that whisper of a voice, "be it not as it may but what it will be." I didn't understand. She repeated herself this time with vigor and light in her eyes I hadn't seen in months. "Be it not as it may — do not believe the things you see, but what it will be — but trust the things to come." I could hear it in her voice. This was some sort of warning . . . or was it a blessing? I was unsure. A long mechanical beep went off from one of the machines, and just like that, the light died from her eyes. There she lay, lifeless, disappearing from existence and from view. Her voice lingered on from where she was. "Live. Live. Live!" I snapped awake.

I stood up to search the apartment. I checked the bathroom, the hallway, and my bedroom. I looked out into the hallway of my building. Nothing. No one. Just me and my apartment empty of the remnants of a visitor. Tears filled my eyes and an itch overtook my arm. I scratched at it until I pulled my fingers back bloodied from breaking the skin. I rushed to the bathroom to wash away the blood and get the itching to stop. When I looked at my arm in the mirror, the hands were back at 10:10. A fire burned beneath my skin where the hands moved back into place. I returned to the living room, where I found my shirt lying on the floor in front of the sofa where I left it. I went into the bedroom to find another shirt. I put it on, then grabbed my keys and purse and bolted out the door.

I all but ran to the tattoo parlor. When I got to the door of the building, I could see that one of the windows was covered in a dark cloth and the inside was dark. No one had been there to open up. I waited outside on the sidewalk where I found a bench and sat still until someone came to open the shop. A young guy with hair longer than his arms walked to the door with a set of keys and opened the door. I rushed in behind him.

"Hey! My name's Danielle. Danielle Gwynn. I was here last week getting a tattoo. This guy Rick . . ." The young man paused in his steps. "He did my tat . . . too . . ." I trailed off. The look on his face, I could have bought him for a penny. The color drained from his skin, leaving me with a pale young man fighting to make sense of what I was saying.

"You said Rick?"

"Yeah, Rick. He was here a week ago, and I saw him last night."

"Miss . . . Danielle? That's impossible." Shifting his attention back to the door, he fumbled with its lock.

"Why is that impossible? I'm telling you I saw him here; he did this tattoo." I rolled up my sleeve to show him the mess I'd made of it and explained that he did the work and that he wasn't the one who messed it up, but I was.

"Look, lady . . . Rick . . . he's no longer among the living. So, sure, he may have done that tattoo, but you couldn't have seen him here or anywhere for that matter. At least not in the last twenty-four hours."

"What do you mean, no longer among the living?"

"He's dead."

"That can't be!" Grandma's words swam in my ears, and I whispered them as I heard them — be it not as it may but what it will be.

I felt like a large weight had been dumped back onto my shoulders as my knees buckled, sending me to the floor of the shop. The young guy rushed to my side and helped me up into a chair. He offered me a bottle of water and a clean, cool towel to put on the back of my neck to abate the dizziness threatening to take me into the dark.

"Yeah. He was struck by a car on his way out someplace. His roommate said he got a call late at night and went out to meet someone. On the way to wherever, he was hit by a car that jumped the sidewalk. Busted him up really bad—he passed away late last night. We all got the call. Our store owner blacked out the window last night when he got word. I'm just here because I left something I needed."

"God help me. I'm losing my mind."

"Were you a friend of his?"

"Yeah . . . no . . . not exactly."

He looked at me with something akin to pity and compassion then offered up a few words of wisdom while I shook in the chair.

"Grief does strange things to people, man." His eyes level with mine, he continued. "I've read on the internet, those people who really have it bad see their loved ones everywhere before they are able to let go. I've never experienced it myself, but I hear it doesn't get any easier. You just have to solidify yourself in the knowledge that they are better off where they are now."

He said a mouthful. How could I not have known that? I prepared to leave the shop, uncertain of what to make of the past few hours and the night's events. Was it all some elaborate game being played? I had no clue, and there was no way for me to get to the bottom of it. Before I left, I asked a question.

"What time did he perish?"

"Midnight."

I passed out. There on the black-and-white checkered floor. It seemed to twist into a cyclone with a black hole at its center swirling beneath me. I succumbed to the darkness and let it engulf me, and it swallowed me whole. There in the darkness was the faceless person looking down on me—waiting for me to join him in the nether. The bats flying around us, and the long shadows of what I could only imagine were his minions. Was this hell? Had I died, too? If so, where were Grandma and that bright light everyone carried on about? Where were the angels and God? I didn't know what was happening—I could feel myself spiral down into an even deeper darkness, a place totally devoid of light, and then there was the voice.

I stirred from my silence and unconsciousness as my eyes fluttered open. A voice that sounded so calm and assuring, yet behind it another voice cackled. "I have you now." My breath hitched in my throat. A crew of emergency workers rushed around me and placed me on a gurney. I was wheeled to the ambulance and whisked away to Northeast Hospital. There, my tattoo—which had become infected from my incessant scratching—was taken care of, and the knot on my head was tended to. I was also given fluids to cure the dehydration and a round of my regular psych meds to keep the darkness at bay, but between you and me, I don't think they're working.

I look out the eighth-floor window and see the lightning striking in the distance and faces in the clouds, some friendly and others gruesome. The floor tiles here seem to shift colors and sing when I set foot on them, and the television has spoken my name twice now. I would have forgotten my own name if it hadn't been for the weatherman speaking it to me to get my attention to relay a message from Grandma Flora.

"Tempus neminem manet," he said with a wide smile on his face.

He almost looks like Tom Cruise. They say we have a twin elsewhere in the world, and there's Tom's doing the evening weather report and pestering me with Latin. Time has not waited for me. It has bulldozed over my life and left me in shambles. Everything I once questioned is now valid and the unquestionable invalid. I don't trust my eyes or my mind or my ears to lead me to the truth anymore. What is truth? A thing we've made up to be right at any given time? I don't know.

Several hours of me trying to explain what was happening and a psych consult later—I'm here in my hospital bed, writing this to you. My handwriting is rushed, and thoughts are broken as I try to make an account of all that has happened inside of one of those cardboard composition notebooks with black-and-white splotches all over it. I detail my past events and current nightmare so that you'll try to understand what is happening here.

The darkness has settled over me once more. I can feel it penetrating my mind, like those vines, looking for ways to wrap its fronds around my entire life. The walls of this room have melted away into a soundless black void. The inhabitants of the room have all fallen to dust, leaving nothing behind; I am all that remains. Here in this present darkness is Rick and Grandma and one other whose face I can't see, looking down on me, scratching their head . . . I think. Is it you? Are you here, too? The faceless one who has stuck through it all with me this entire time? I think I'd like it very much if you were.

Beneath the bandages on my arm, there is a pain and an itch I can do nothing about; my nails have been removed. My restraints are just long enough to reach this notebook with one hand. I can hear them ticking now, and I believe the hands of time are moving again . . . maybe . . . in regard to you. Yes, I see clearer now. It is you! I've asked the voices that have begun to speak if they can hear and see you as well. They assure me that no one is there, but you and I know better.

So here we are, dear Reader, and I leave it to you to tell me the truth. Are you a figment of my imagination or should I believe in you?

To learn more about this author, please visit:
https://bloggishone.wordpress.com/

Follow the Light

Paranormal

Kerry A Waight

Prompt: You are lost.

I WANDERED THROUGH THE DUSTY *house, sure I had the right place. The broken windows served no purpose except to catch the tattered curtains as they fluttered in the breeze. Peeling wallpaper revealed lead paint that was also losing its grip on the walls. The rotting wood on the once-magnificent staircase told of abandonment and neglect. Floorboards creaked in protest with every step I took, disturbing the shadows I saw from the corner of my eye — just as I had dreamed it.*

That was how it always happened. I would dream of the place I needed to go to — and I always found it. Not for the first time in my life, I wished I knew more about my ability. It was too vague: dream a place, then go off to save a soul. This place, however, was a little overwhelming. There was more than one soul here, and I wasn't sure whom I was supposed to be helping.

To complicate matters, the dead looked like the living to me. For numerous reasons, they walked among us, blending into our existence. But I felt their presence. They spoke to me. And if they were ready to go but didn't know how, they needed me.

I felt a presence now, drawing me upstairs, compelling me, requiring me to ascend the disintegrating staircase. Running my fingers along the railing, I wondered if I would, in fact, get up there — and down — without joining the land of the dead myself. The banister moved as I gripped it for safety, which was not reassuring. I felt the bottom step bend but not break as I stepped on it. But I knew I had to do it.

From necessity, I began the ascent slowly, treading as gently as possible on the edges close to the wall. Less noise and stair movement that way. No point rushing. I didn't care how long it took to get up there as long as I reached the soul in need of help.

I arrived at the top of the stairs and saw it — the door I needed to go through. In contrast to the darkness of the remainder of the house, an ethereal light was escaping through the gap underneath. I slowly turned the rusted doorknob and found that it moved with surprising ease. I expected it to be locked or so badly corroded it would not turn. I nudged the door open. It, too, moved without difficulty.

The light flooding the room blinded me. I brought my hand up to cover my eyes. The brilliance toned down to a bearable level as if the light itself were sensitive to my thoughts and feelings.

When my eyesight adjusted, I saw a young boy sitting on the floor. A pure white light with a halo of colors shone from somewhere over his right shoulder. I couldn't always see it — only when necessary for me to complete the task by pointing out to a lost soul where they needed to look. And it filled me with overwhelming peace, wonder, and love every time.

The boy's knees were pulled up to his chest with his arms wrapped around them. When I walked in, he raised his head. The red rims around his eyes showed me that he had been crying. My heart broke at seeing such a young child so confused about what they needed to do in order to cross over.

"You're lost, aren't you?" I asked gently, kneeling so I wasn't towering over him. The boy didn't speak, just nodded. Tears started to well up in his eyes.

The steady presence of the light caused me to think this one might be easy. "Can you see that beautiful light right next to you?" This time, the boy shook his head. I frowned, wrinkling my forehead. *Why can I see it and he can't?*

"Do you know why you're here?" Again, the boy shook his head. *Is this the reason he can't see the light? Because he's truly lost?*

"What's the last thing you remember? Did you get hurt? Were you sick?"

I had learned that if I could get a soul to remember their death, they often knew what to do to go into the light. The boy shook his head one more time before again burying his face between his knees. His body trembled as he resumed crying. I nearly began to cry myself; I never got used to the fact that the souls often reacted physically the way they would in life.

Taking a deep breath, I stood up. He was too distraught. I'd have to figure this out on my own . . . starting with why he was here in this house. There was more to this than met the eye. It was clear from the condition of the house that no one had lived here for a long time, and his clothing was the latest fashion—for a ten-year-old.

I slowly canvassed my surroundings. There must have been some clue here about this poor lost boy. The room was large but sparsely furnished. There was a dilapidated wardrobe, a rusty old bed with threadbare sheets and a blanket, and a desk and chair in the far corner.

I wondered if he had died here. Part of me desperately hoped not; if he had, it was most likely a lonely and horrific death. But if I can find his body, I might be able to help him remember and pass over.

Systematically, I worked my way around the room, looking for any possible clue. My eyes lingered on the wardrobe first. *Tackle the scariest one first, Magda. Tackle the scariest one first.* I often talked to myself when I needed to do something that I wasn't sure of. It made me feel like I wasn't alone. All too often, someone's eternal rest relied on me finding courage. Before I could lose my nerve, I grabbed the handle of the wardrobe and yanked it open, shutting my eyes tightly as I heard a heavy object roll out. Oh, no! Please, no! I could feel tears welling behind my eyelids as I squeezed them tighter. Then I remembered why I was there. I would have to see what it was if I was to help this little soul.

Holding my breath, I cautiously opened my eyes. A tattered canvas bag lay at my feet. The handle was broken and the color so faded in places that the red was now pink. I bent down to open it, checking behind me first to make sure I had an escape route if necessary. As the rusted zipper grudgingly gave way, I breathed out in relief: an old Game Boy, a stuffed teddy with a missing ear, and a collection of clothes that had seen better days. I picked up the teddy, hugging it to my chest. Maybe it was his. Maybe it would help me work out what I needed to do.

"Is this yours, honey?" I hoped the bear would spark his memory.

Without lifting his head fully from his knees, he nodded.

I held it out to him, but his nod quickly turned into a refusal as he shook his head and buried his face into his knees again.

My face fell along with my hope. "Can I hold him?" I really was at a loss on how to proceed with this sweet child.

He looked back up at me, and I caught a barely perceptible nod. He at least seemed to trust me with his teddy, so maybe I was making some kind of headway.

My next option was under the bed. So many children loved hiding under beds. And so many hid there for fear for their lives. I lay on the dusty floor and looked under the bed, which sagged in the middle with broken springs poking through the mattress. I saw nothing but dust and cobwebs. Thankfully, he wasn't there. The dust from the ragged sheets made me sneeze, and my head collided with the floor. I heard a giggle behind me and, despite my pain, I smiled. Maybe he was starting to feel more relaxed with me. I fought the impulse to interact with him about my sore head; the last thing I wanted to do was scare him. It was the first time he had reacted to anything without my prompting.

Dragging myself back to my feet and rubbing my head, I sighed. There was nowhere else in the room where a body could be hidden. Now I was looking for clues alone. All that was left for me to explore was the desk. I moved toward it, crossing the trail of the light and feeling its warmth penetrate my living soul, reinforcing my need to help him find peace within the light. The desk was my final hope for at least a clue. I was running out of options.

The desk had only two things on it: a notebook and a beautiful fountain pen. Carefully, I opened the book—it was a diary, with entries recorded in exquisite handwriting. I glanced back at the boy. He sat in the same position but now looked at me with hope in his eyes.

"Is this yours?" I asked, picking up the diary and showing it to him. He shook his head. "Do you know who it belongs to?" This time, he lifted his head and nodded enthusiastically. Relief washed over me. "Can I read it?" The boy smiled and nodded again. I smiled back and reopened it to the first page.

Nobody understands him or me, so I have taken him away. I have to make sure that I am not caught—if they find us, we won't be able to stay together anymore. I have to stay strong for Nathan's sake.

My smile widened. I was sure I had found something important.

"Are you Nathan?"

The boy stood up, nodding with gusto and a grin. He clapped his hands together, jumping up and down, clearly excited that I was working it out.

I clapped, too, hoping it would increase the trust he seemed to be gaining in me, and went back to reading.

My boy is the light of my life. I see his smiling face, his joy in life's simple pleasures like ice cream and sunshine . . .

I wiped away an escaped tear. It was sad that the world had lost such a beautiful soul. Spellbound, I turned the page and continued reading.

Disability is not a word that fits my Nathan. He has more abilities than anyone will ever know. He doesn't need to say anything to let me know his inner thoughts. He makes everyone smile. He understands nature. He knows when I need one of his special cuddles.

I looked at Nathan, who had gradually moved closer. I could see the depth of soul in his eyes — that same depth his mother wrote so eloquently about. He looked at me and gently touched my arm. I could feel the trust in his fingertips; the gentle pressure told me he was confident he was safe with me.

The more I read, the more I was convinced Nathan's mother was scared for herself and her son. She wholeheartedly believed Nathan would be taken from her if she stayed in the community.

Nathan's father wants Nathan for himself. I can't let that happen to my beautiful boy. That man has given my child nothing but grief. He may be his "father," but he is certainly not his "dad." It's me and Nathan — simple as that.

The entry went on to explain how she brought him to this abandoned house to keep him with her. I skimmed through a few more pages. She talked about their life here and their struggles. How his happiness and safety was worth far more than her own comfort. But the last page of the diary alarmed me.

I really don't feel well but I can't go to the hospital. They will find us, and I will lose Nathan forever. I just have to hope that I get through whatever this is. I need to look after him!

It was at that moment I realized the truth. I had made all the wrong assumptions. Reaching out, I touched Nathan's shoulder — and the warmth beneath my fingers confirmed that Nathan was still very much alive. Nathan couldn't see the light because Nathan wasn't dead. I turned, looking directly into his knowing eyes. "Do you know where your mummy is?"

Nathan hung his head and turned to face the bed. My breath caught in my throat—how had I not noticed the lump? Hesitating, I approached the eerily still form, hesitating again before lifting the covers. Dead people presented no problem for me as long as it was their souls, not their physical bodies. I had already confronted the "body" possibility earlier and I had been spared finding one. I knew it would be different this time. But, if I was to help Nathan, I had to lift those covers.

Cautiously, I peeled back the fraying blanket, revealing the pale, gaunt corpse of a thin young woman with wispy blonde hair just like Nathan's. She had not been dead long—rigor mortis had set in, but not decomposition. I turned toward Nathan and saw the soul of the deceased woman standing behind him. She and Nathan had the same gentle, knowing eyes. She looked relieved to have my attention.

"I'm here for you, aren't I?" I asked as gently as I could. This must be so hard for her, I reasoned.

She shook her head, then looked at Nathan, the love pouring from her to him. "No, you're here for him. He needs to be taken to my mother's so he has someone to look after him. If you hadn't come, he wouldn't have known what to do. He would've starved to death. I couldn't leave him here on his own."

Then, and only then, did I realize why I was here. Her love for Nathan had drawn me to this house to save him. If ever I doubted the power of a mother's love, I certainly had no doubts now. Looking at her, I could see love and pain in her eyes. Love had brought me here, and the pain of leaving him alone was keeping her here.

"Can you see the light?" I had to encourage her to pass over. It was no good for either of them for her to remain here.

"Yes—I've seen it since I passed last night. But I couldn't go. Not until you came. Please don't let them take him to his dad. Nathan's father is violent and tried to take him from me just to be spiteful. He doesn't really want him. Nathan will be neglected and *injured if he goes with his father. Please help us."* Her anxiety was palpable.

"I promise you I'll do whatever I can." Not that I know what I can do. I've never had to save the living before. *"Where can I take him? I don't know how to find your mum."* Why can I not dial up a dream when I need information?

"You can take him to the local police. They have a record of what his father is like. I stayed local, knowing my ex would expect me to run far away. Now, I'm so glad I did that."

"Can Nathan see you?" Saying goodbye to his mother might help him. I could see Nathan looking over his shoulder in the direction I was looking and talking. This must be so confusing for him. I'm talking to thin air.

"No. It would scare him to see me. But he knows I am here for him." She touched Nathan's head lovingly. *"Goodbye, little man. Always remember that I love you."*

Nathan brought his hand up to his head, feeling for his mother's. His eyes told of love and loss.

I looked at the two of them, mother and son, trying to find the right words to say. It didn't feel right to help only one half of this family; what if his mother needed help, too? All I'd ever done with this ability was help the dead, so at the very least I should try to do that here. It was a starting point, anyway.

"I don't think Nathan will leave while you're here. He feels your love and he won't want to leave you. I know it's hard—I don't know what else to say to you. I don't even know your name."

She smiled, first at Nathan, then at me.

"Lisa. My name is Lisa."

I took a deep breath. *"Are you ready, Lisa? You aren't leaving him, really. You are moving on so that he can move on. He will always feel your love and light. And you can visit him anytime."* I glanced down at him still grasping above his head, trying to reach his mother. *"Nathan is a beautiful boy. You have raised him well."*

My heart was breaking for this young woman who, essentially, gave her life for her son's safety.

When I looked back up, my eyes locked with Lisa's. It was a surreal feeling — a departed soul addressing my soul.

"I trust you. More importantly, he trusts you. Look after my baby. And thank you."

I took Nathan's hand as his mother walked into the brightness of the next life.

Nathan seemed to know she was gone. He shed a single tear as I took his hand and patiently led him down the stairs, outside of the old house, and into the sunshine. He stopped at the unhinged gate, put his head back, and closed his eyes, seeming to soak in the light. The moment didn't last long. A honking horn in the distance destroyed the mood.

Nathan looked at me in alarm. I looked back at his little face: so scared, so sad, and yet so trusting. What would have happened if I hadn't been led to him and his mother? I quickly pushed the thought from my mind. I was too emotionally drained to deal with those dark possibilities. Instead, I concentrated on Nathan.

"It's going to be okay, sweetie. I know you're sad about your mummy. But it'll be okay. I'm so glad I found you — you aren't lost anymore."

To learn more about this author, please visit:
https://storiesofthen.blog/

Writing Prompts

Each week in Authors' Tale, a member presents a new writing prompt to the group. These are the weekly prompts from September 2017 to September 2018.

1: *You can call it luck, but I know it's magic.*

2: *Opportunities wait for no one, but there's always a second chance. You only have to work hard to get it.*

3: *It's unfortunate to be good at something that's not good at all.*

4: *A road trip gone wrong.*

5: *You hear a knock at the window and find a bird, a metal bird, waiting there. It has a message for you.*

6: *There was a secret place in the basement where they used to have rendezvous. The door could be unlocked only after saying the code word. Will the place remain a secret?*

7: *You are a pet cat. Write about your day.*

8: *The most romantic night of my life.*

9: *The year is 2038. The first astronauts have safely landed on Mars. Their first mission is to explore a cave that couldn't be explored using the automated rovers in previous years. They discover a human skeleton in the cave with four words written on the wall.*

10: *A rose, an open bottle of wine, and a full moon.*

11: *You wake up in the morning and look out your window. You see dinosaurs, a T-Rex with a moose in its mouth, farm animals, and a cowboy.*

12: *And then the murders began.*

13: *A character finds a talisman that gives him/her extraordinary* luck. But, the universe must have balance, so other people have to pay for that "luck."

14: *Your adoptive mother tells you, while on her deathbed, that you were born on a different planet. You have always suspected you were different because of the one thing that separates you from the rest of humankind.*

15: *Often people remark, "If only these walls could talk, the stories they would tell!" What stories do you think the walls would tell?*

16: *You open a journal to discover an old storyline you never fleshed out. The dust parts from the fibers like water off a duck's back, and the whispers of the many lost voices speak to you. You close your eyes and listen. When you open them, you're at the beginning of your unfinished idea, exactly where you had put your main character.*

17: *Stars are falling faster than a smile after a broken heart.*

18: *You are lost.*

19: *A mysterious stranger hands you a business card.*

20: *I survived the cold.*

21: *As quietly as possible, she lifted the sleeping infant from the crib and crept down the staircase.*

22: *I can give you everything you ever wanted.*

23: *All the things she said.*

24: *What if you knew you'd be the last person to ever speak to someone?*

25: *Write about the voice mail you don't remember leaving yourself.*

26: *"I'm going to pretend I didn't see that."*

27: *You never think that you'll be that person. Until you are.*

28: *"Despite the rumors, I'm only human."*

29: *Beware the shadows.*

30: *The pharmaceutical industry invents a pill that eliminates your need for sleep without negative side effects.*

31: *A woman falls in love with a man on the internet. She flies to meet him. He doesn't show. He leaves her a note at the hotel lobby.*

32: *Take me through your typical day in colors.*

33: *The light was hauntingly surreal.*

34: *Your character travels to a faraway place. Is it a dream come true?*

35: *"I loved it."*

36: *In your rush to get off one flight and catch the next one, you grab the wrong carry-on. You don't discover this until later, and one item in there changes your life.*

37: *He'd always hoped he could . . .*

38: *You open a fortune cookie that says, "Don't look behind you."*

39: *The day I lost my wings.*

40: *Dreams last longer when you . . .*

41: *What if memory lane was a real place? Imagine you were walking down the lane. Which stops would you take again? And what is at the end.*

42: *You buy a pair of pants from a thrift shop and notice when you get home there is a piece of paper in the pocket with an address and a future date and time on it.*

43: *Pick a word. One with multiple meanings works best. Write a story that focuses on that word without mentioning the word by name.*

44: *You volunteer to be the first human to test time travel, only going an hour forward in time. When you step out of the travel pod all humans are gone.*

45: *There are two kinds of people in the world.*

46: *You encounter a seer. They offer to peer into your future.*

47: *The most important person in your life tells you the meaning of your life in a dream. When you wake up, you write it down but can't figure out what it means.*

48: *You did everything right, but you're still the villain.*

49: *Write about the first odd thing that comes to mind when you think of the word ink.*

50: *You win a live duck at a local fair. At home, you find out the duck can talk.*

Authors' Tale

Write and surprise others, but keep learning and surprise yourself.

https://authorstale.wordpress.com
https://facebook.com/groups/authorstale

CPSIA information can be obtained
at www.ICGtesting.com
Printed in the USA
BVHW031108080419
544913BV00003B/159/P